MIDDLE SCHOOL AND OTHER DISASTERS

Weirdest Weekend Ever!

BY WANDA COVEN
ILLUSTRATED BY ANNA ABRAMSKAYA

Simon Spotlight
New York London Toronto Sydney New Delhi

This book is a work of fiction. Any references to historical events, real people, or real places are used fictitiously. Other names, characters, places, and events are products of the author's imagination, and any resemblance to actual events or places or persons, living or dead, is entirely coincidental.

SIMON SPOTLIGHT
An imprint of Simon & Schuster Children's Publishing Division
1230 Avenue of the Americas, New York, New York 10020
First Simon Spotlight edition August 2024
Copyright © 2024 by Simon & Schuster, LLC
All rights reserved, including the right of reproduction in whole or in part in any form.
SIMON SPOTLIGHT and colophon are registered trademarks of Simon & Schuster, LLC.
Simon & Schuster: Celebrating 100 Years of Publishing in 2024
For information about special discounts for bulk purchases, please contact Simon & Schuster Special Sales at 1-866-506-1949 or business@simonandschuster.com. The Simon & Schuster Speakers Bureau can bring authors to your live event. For more information or to book an event contact the Simon & Schuster Speakers Bureau at 1-866-248-3049 or visit our website at www.simonspeakers.com.
Text by Alison Inches
Series designed by Chani Yammer, based on the Heidi Heckelbeck series designed by Aviva Shur
Cover designed by Laura Roode
Illustrated by Anna Abramskaya, inspired by the original character designs of Priscilla Burris from the Heidi Heckelbeck chapter book series
The illustrations for this book were rendered with digital ink and a bunch of love.
The text of this book was set in Minou.
Manufactured in the United States of America 0525 BVG
10 9 8 7 6 5 4 3 2 1
This book has been cataloged by the Library of Congress.
ISBN 978-1-6659-4924-8
ISBN 978-1-6659-4925-5 (ebook)

To my readers:
You are magical.
Love,
Wanda

TWO-FACED WITCH?

Okay, I have to read Lucy's letter just ONE more time.

I've already read it, like, TEN times, but I can't resist reading it again.

I'm giddy with excitement because, *newsflash*! This weekend is Friends and Family Weekend at Broomsfield Academy!

And do you know what?

Woo-hoo!

I study every detail of Lulu's cutest stationery *ever*.

It has a pink-and-white polka dot border. Then in the lower left-hand corner there's an adorable purse with a pink daisy latch and a yellow loop handle. Leaning against the purse is a pair of strappy, platform sandals with a daisy on top of the front straps over the toes.

So fun!

Oh, and Lucy's name is engraved in pink at the top.

One word: *love*.

As I read Lucy's letter, I can actually *hear* her voice ring through the words.

Lucy Lancaster

Hey, Heideeeeeee!
I can't believe I get to see you this weekend!

In PERSON! ☺

Somebody please pinch me.

Eeee! I can't wait!

I already picked out all my outfits, and my bag is packed. I can't wait to meet your friends—not to mention your old crush and your new crush. They all sound amazing!

And what about Melanie? I CAN wait to see HER.

Lol!

I know you've said she's changed, so I'll try to keep an open mind. It's hard to forget how snooty she was in elementary school.

The WORST! And now she's your BROOMMATE.

I mean, it's still hard to believe.

I'm literally crossing off each day on my kitten calendar. Only a few days to go! 😺

And don't forget, you HAVE to give me a private tour of your school. I want to be able to picture you in all the places you go when we're apart.

See you soon.
Your bestie 4-ever
and ever!

LULU LUCY

I fold the letter and put it on top of my dresser. I'll probably read it again before I go to sleep tonight, and then I'll place it in the memory box with all the other letters I've received from Lucy so far this school year.

I can't believe how long it's been since we said goodbye to each other in my **driveway**, and then I got into the car and rode off to start living at Broomsfield Academy.

Lucy and I have never been apart this long before.

Will she look different to me?

Will I look different to her?

Eek!

Will our friendship be exactly the same? Or will it have changed?

So many questions!

And what about my family?

I'm so excited about Lucy coming, but I also can't wait to see my parents and brother. I'm sure Henry will be the same annoying but lovable little brother he always has been. And it'll be great to have Mom and Dad here, **but having Lucy is the ultimate icing on the cake.**

We'll stay up all night talking—or at least until we get so tired that we start talking gibberish.

We'll talk about my new—*sort of*—crush, Nick. I say "sort of" because I'm trying *not* to go too gaga over him like I did with my first crush, Hunter. That crush kind of got out of hand.

One word: *understatement.*

But I have a confession!

There is one topic I'm *always* nervous about when it comes to Lucy.

You see, she *still* doesn't know I'm a witch.

Can you imagine hiding *half* your identity from your best friend?

This is the *worst* thing about being a witch.

Sometimes I feel like a lying, two-faced friend. I positively hate keeping my secret from Lucy.

When I give her a tour of the school, I can't even show her the best parts, like the cool **secret passageways** to the fabulous School of Magic.

Ugh.

And I can't tell her how I cast a spell to make my teacher's dog talk, or how I gave myself Rapunzel hair when I goofed up a spell.

She would crack up SO hard if she knew!

Sometimes I wish Lucy had never forgotten that I'm a witch, after the whole Perfectus Malus incident back when we were in elementary school. But it's good that she did. The rules are rules after all. Now that I'm studying magic at Broomsfield Academy, it seems harder than ever to keep this secret from her.

What if I weigh the pros and cons of telling Lucy I'm a witch?

Who knows—it might make me feel better.

Here it goes:

Pros of Spilling My Secret	Cons of Spilling My Secret
- I'll be honest and open.	- I can never take my secret back.
- Lucy will know the real me.	- She'll be mad at me for keeping this secret for so long.
- I can share all my witch stories.	- It might make her feel weird and left out this weekend.

This exercise reminds me of the time my mom went to traffic school for a speeding ticket. She had to relearn all the rules of the road and why we have them. She said it was really helpful.

Sometimes I need to review the rules of the witching world. As my mom and Aunt Trudy have always told me, being a witch is a privilege. And witches *have* to protect their identities. There really are no loopholes.

So there you have it. I *have* to keep my secret.

But this realization still gives me a little ember of sadness.

Right after I make the decision to continue to keep my secret, a sudden gust of wind blows through my open window.

Flutter! Flap! WHACK!

Lucy's letter flies off my dresser, and the picture of Lucy and Bruce falls face down.

Weird, I think.

I pick up the letter and set the picture upright. I also take a long look at my friends' faces.

I've kept this secret from them for as long as I've known them. And what they don't know can't hurt them.

Right?

So don't worry, Heidi, I reassure myself. *This weekend will be a total blast. I mean, what could POSSIBLY go wrong . . . ?*

Okay, please don't answer that.

QUEEN HEIDI

Clang! Clang-clang-a-lang!

That's the dinner bell. Yup, they still use an old-fashioned dinner bell here at Broomsfield Academy, and it makes my stomach growl every time.

Before I head to the cafeteria, I first do a quick beauty check. I zip to the bathroom and help myself to Melanie's super-red blush.

Don't worry.

She's totally cool with me borrowing her makeup.

She actually *encourages* it, because according to Melanie, I'm **seriously** *ordinary.*

As if!

Maybe I'm not as EXTRA as Melanie, but I know that I'm a seriously special person.

I dab red blush across the tops of my cheeks with my finger, like Melanie taught me.

She is, *in fact*, a genuine beauty queen, and her beauty tricks are amazing—even if I don't like to admit it to her face.

And I never would've thought fire-engine-red blush would look good on **anyone**, except maybe a clown, **but it DOES.**

It makes you look like you've been out in the sun—sun-kissed, you could say.

I magically twist my hair into a bun. I've gotten really good at this.

My hair practically does itself!

To top everything off, I smear on some pink lip gloss, or as I like to call it, bubble-gum slime.

I dash to the Barn, where the cafeteria is, and slip in the side door.

There's Nick, my sort-of crush.

He's reading something on the bulletin board and doesn't see me—*yet.*

Melanie's flirting tips flick through my mind.

No hair flip since I have my hair up in a bun, and big eyes are definitely not my thing. I tried big eyes on Hunter, and he mistook me for the big, bad wolf, as in: *My, what BIG EYES you have!*

It was mortifying.

So, I go with a compliment instead.

"Hey, Four Square king," I say casually.

Nick looks at me and flashes his braces, which happen to be on every single tooth.

His smile is so dreamy.

He has his dark hair swept back from his *adorable* widow's peak. His hairstyle looks effortless and *sooo* good. His brown eyes sparkle.

One word: *adorable*.

"Excuse me?" Nick says dramatically. "What do you mean, Four Square queen? **You totally knocked me off the Four Square throne yesterday!**"

Actually this is true. I *did* get Nick out, which was a first for me. I'm definitely getting better at Four Square.

I put my hands up and give a smirk, like, *Yeah, I know I rock.*

"It feels good to be royalty," I tell him.

Nick laughs and shoulder-bumps me as we walk toward the cafeteria.

The arrow on my inner crush-o-meter just went off the charts.

"Well, don't get *too* comfortable, Heidi, because I'm coming for your crown!" he teases.

We both laugh, and I have to say, it's **pretty hard not to rush this crush.**

"So will your family be here this weekend?" I ask.

Nick holds the cafeteria door open for me. "My parents and my best friend, Max, are coming. I'm **really excited!**"

I playfully swat Nick's arm with the back of my hand.

"That's great! My family and my best friend are coming too. Her name is Lucy, and **she is my absolute favorite person in the whole world.**"

Nick smiles. "Hey, I have an idea. Maybe we can all hang out together! Me and Max and you and Lucy."

Whoa, did Nick just say we should all hang out together?

I'm IN!

"That would be a blast," I say. I try not to sound too eager as my heart thumps loudly with sheer happiness.

Eeeeee!

Nick waves to some friends at his table, which unfortunately is not *my* table. One of these days we'll be assigned to the *same* table.

Fingers crossed!

"Catch you later, Queen Heidi!" he shouts as he waves goodbye.

I pretend to adjust my crown. "Later, King Nicholas!"

And I'm pretty sure there's a halo of hearts circling around my head right now, and my feet are floating off the ground.

But I still have to eat, so I head for the main food station. It's Make-Your-Own-Grain-or-Noodle-Bowl night. **Yum!**

I load up a bowl with rice noodles, grilled chicken, shredded carrots, and sliced mini cucumbers. Then I drizzle peanut sauce and put roasted peanuts on top. I grab a water and zoom to my table.

As soon as I sit down, my two besties at Broomsfield Academy, Sunny and Annabelle, give me an intense look.

"**We saw you talking to** *Niiiiiick*," they say, singing his name.

I blush, laugh, and cringe—all at the same time.

"You will never believe what just happened! Nick said his best friend, Max, is coming for Friends and Family Weekend, and he asked if Lucy and I want to hang out with them!"

Sunny and Annabelle look at each other excitedly.

"Wow, Heidi, you're acting so calm about it," Annabelle remarks, and then smiles. **"Well, calm for *you*."**

I laugh out loud, because on the inside **I feel like there are a thousand butterflies in my stomach,** but I roll with it.

"It's the *new-and-improved Heidi*, that's all," I joke.

Sunny gives me a friendly kick under the table. "Well, he must *really* like you!"

Annabelle puts her arm around me and Sunny. "Of course he likes her. *Everyone* likes Heidi!"

Well, not EVERYONE! I think. But then I realize that Annabelle is onto something. I've never had as many friends as I do at Broomsfield Academy.

"That makes me feel—dare I say—*popular?*" I venture.

Sunny and Annabelle share a glance.

"Heidi, you're, like, one of the most popular girls in our class," Sunny says.

I am?

A sudden surge of terror washes over me. Being popular sounds like *a lot* of responsibility. I mean, what if someone gets *mad* at me?

"If you say so," I respond. "Because as far as I'm concerned, I'm just silly old me—now and forever!"

CHARMED BRACELETS

"Today we're going to talk about something of *vital* importance." That's how Mrs. Kettledrum starts our special spells and potions class the next afternoon. We're having an extra class to prepare for Friends and Family Weekend. We all look around the room at each other, wondering what could possibly be so very important.

"Class, does anyone know what an *aura* is?" Mrs. Kettledrum asks.

We stare blankly at our teacher. **Nobody knows.**

"An aura is the energy that comes from a person,"

Mrs. Kettledrum explains. "It's a feeling you get from somebody—a sense of who they are. **It's the energy that makes up your personal self."**

Sunny's hand goes straight up. "Is it the same as the *vibe* you get from somebody?"

Mrs. Kettledrum nods.

"Yes, it can definitely be a vibe, but a vibe can also be the *mood* of a situation, too, like a relaxing vibe at the beach or a fun vibe at a dance."

Then Mrs. Kettledrum calls on me.

Eek!

"Heidi, can you tell us what kind of aura your friend Sunny has?"

Well, *that's easy!* I look at Sunny, who's sitting next to me. She tries not to laugh as I describe her aura.

"Sunny is just what her name says. She's upbeat, positive, fun, smart, kind, and easygoing. From the moment I was lucky enough to meet her, I knew we were going to be friends."

Mrs. Kettledrum smiles, so I know she likes my answer. "Very good, Heidi. That's a great description of Sunny's aura."

Then she asks Sunny the same question about me.

Sunny studies me, and I have to try to hold a straight face too, but I can't. **We collapse into giggles.**

Then Sunny pulls it together so she can answer the question. "Heidi is daring, goofy, super-fun, bold, hilarious, headstrong, smart, loyal, and *reckless*. When I met Heidi for the first time, I knew we'd get along. **I just felt like myself around her.**"

We both burst out laughing, because it's all true—**even the reckless part.**

I remember the moment we met on the beach—way before we ever came to Broomsfield Academy. **We hit it off instantly.**

Mrs. Kettledrum's dog, **Momo, barks her approval.** Momo has a very friendly aura.

Mrs. Kettledrum claps her hands in approval. **"Well done, both of you! What other kind of auras have any of you felt? Have you ever noticed the energy change when somebody walks into the room?"**

Hunter raises his hand. "I remember one time when I came home from school and my dad seemed super-sad. I didn't know why, but then he told me that my grandfather had passed away. **But before he said anything, I could *feel* his sadness."**

Mrs. Kettledrum tips her head to one side. "I'm sorry, Hunter. That must've been hard for both of you. And, of course, that energy you felt was certainly from the sadness your father was feeling. Thank you so much for sharing."

Isabelle raises her hand. "I can feel my grandmother's kindness the same way I can feel warmth coming from a radiator."

Mrs. Kettledrum's face lights up. "Another wonderful example of an aura, Isabelle! Each one of us is broadcasting like a radio station without even knowing it.

"Now imagine when all those different auras arrive on Friends and Family Weekend, and *then* imagine mixing those different auras with all the magical energy at this school. What do you think could happen?"

We give our teacher more blank stares.

We have *no* idea what could happen.

Mrs. Kettledrum explains. "When *non-magical* students and guests and all their auras— **which contain emotions and energy—** get mixed with the auras of *magical* students, faculty, and parents, sometimes, for lack of a better expression, **wires can get crossed. It can create chaos.** It can be too much energy and emotion, **and things can even become *dangerous*.**"

The whole class gasps. Then everyone starts talking and whispering at once.

The last thing we need on Friends and Family Weekend is chaos! I think.

I have been looking forward to this weekend so much, but all of a sudden I feel unsettled.

Eek.

Mrs. Kettledrum claps her hands, and the classroom grows quiet. She smiles at us, and I instantly feel reassured. "Rest your minds, everyone. I only wanted you to know all this so you'll understand why this next part is so important.

"The witches and wizards at Broomsfield Academy have developed a magical way to handle this situation."

Mrs. Kettledrum pulls the lid off a plastic tub and pulls out a sparkly bracelet.

The bracelet shimmers as if it is covered with hundreds of tiny diamonds.

A collective "*Oooooooooooh*" circles around the classroom.

Mrs. Kettledrum digs into the tub again and loops more bracelets onto her fingers. Then she passes them out. Everyone gets at least six.

A string of sparkly gems spells out BROOMSFIELD ACADEMY on each bracelet. The rest of the bracelet is all sparkles.

"Class, please pull out your wands."

Wands? We get to use wands today?

I love *anything* that involves wands and magic.

Obviously.

I open my backpack and pull out my wand. Mine has a purple gemstone on the handle and is absolutely bewitching. Did I mention how much fun it is to be a witch?

"So, what does everyone think of the new visitor bracelets?" Mrs. Kettledrum asks.

We all hoot and holler because **we *love* the bracelets!**

"Would you say they're *irresistible*?" Mrs. Kettledrum asks.

"**YES!**" we shout.

Mrs. Kettledrum smiles. "Good. **We want them to be so attractive** that our visitors and guests won't want to take them off. These bracelets will keep the emotions and energy this weekend at a manageable level.

"And there's one more very important requirement. One that all students at Broomsfield Academy must adhere to, whether they are students in the School of Magic or not. Everyone *must* make sure their guests wear their bracelets at *all* times.

"**Without the bracelets, there could be trouble.** And your guests will want to keep them on not only because they look so fun but because visitors will also need the bracelets to get into events, meals, and dormitories. And then when the weekend is over, **they can keep the bracelets as a souvenir.**

"Is this clear?"

We all nod vigorously.

Mrs. Kettledrum picks up her wand. "Then let's get started! You, class, are going to put the *charm* in these charm bracelets."

The class cheers, especially *me*!

I know that my family and Lucy are going to love wearing theirs. I only wish I could get one. The bracelets are just so much fun.

"You will perform the spell at your desks. I'll write the spell on the board. Then you'll hold your wand over *one* bracelet at a time and chant the spell. When a ring of light is released from the bracelet, that means the spell has been cast properly. Please repeat for each bracelet."

Mrs. Kettledrum picks up a marker and writes the spell on the board. Excitement wells up inside me.

This is so cool! I think.

How lucky am I to be a student at the School of Magic?

Answer: *the luckiest!*

Our teacher steps away from the board, and we read over the spell.

TAKE THIS BRACELET OF SPARKLE AND SHIMMER.
FILL IT WITH MAGIC TO MAKE IT
GLISTEN AND GLIMMER.
PROTECT THE WEARER FROM A CLASH OF EMOTION.
AND STILL ALL AURAS FROM ANY COMMOTION.
PEACE AND JOY WILL RULE THE DAY.
AND YOU CAN ENJOY YOUR BROOMSFIELD STAY!
SHAZOO! SHAZING! SHAZAY!

"Remember, charm *one* bracelet at a time. And follow the spell *exactly*, or you may run into problems," Mrs. Kettledrum warns. "Is everyone clear on what to do?"

Everyone's clear—or at least I think so.

"I'll be right here if you need any help," says Mrs. Kettledrum. "Okay, students. Raise your wands."

We all raise our wands.

"Begin," she commands.

I hold my wand over my first bracelet and chant the spell. All around the room I can hear the murmurs of my classmates as they chant too. Light glows around the bracelet.

Then a ring of light separates from the bracelet and floats away.

Eeee! I did it!

One down, **many to go.**

Turns out, not everyone finds this assignment as easy as I do. I hear clatters, pings, and groans. I stop what I'm doing and watch my classmates.

One of Hunter's bracelets launches off his desk like a rocket. *Zooop!* It loops around a light and dangles overhead.

One word: *oopsies.*

Another bracelet flings across the room like a rubber band and lands on Mrs. Kettledrum's desk.

Thwack!

Then another bracelet ricochets off the whiteboard and lands on Momo's head.

Oof!

Or, I should say, "Woof!"

A few glowing halos float from bracelets, so some kids are getting it. *But why are so many kids having trouble?* I wonder.

It's so easy. Could I really be becoming that great a witch?

Soon all my bracelets are charmed. And it looks like everyone is getting the hang of it.

There are glowing rings all over the room. They eventually wink out, like soap bubbles.

Since I'm the first one done, I call Momo to my desk for a love session. Momo wags her tail and trots over to me happily. Momo and I have been close ever since I performed that spell that made her talk.

Buds for life!

Mrs. Kettledrum hands out purple velvet pouches to protect the bracelets until they are given to the guests at arrival.

I'm about to run out the door when Mrs. Kettledrum waggles a finger at me to stay after class. I hurry to her desk.

"Heidi, your skills as a witch are coming along nicely," she tells me. "I can see you've been practicing your meditation."

I smile at the praise and sling my backpack over one shoulder. "It's getting easier each time."

Mrs. Kettledrum looks pleased. "I also want to mention something that might happen this weekend," she says. "Don't worry if you find your mind-reading skills aren't as strong as they usually are. As I mentioned in class, there will be so much more energy on campus, and it may be harder than normal to get a read on what your friends and family are thinking."

I nod. Being able to read minds is my gift as a witch, but I'm still learning. I can't hear everyone's thoughts all the time. It's spotty. Like, I'll catch a moment of what someone is thinking, and then I won't hear anything else. Or if I concentrate on someone very hard, I can sometimes hear their thoughts. And maybe that's a good thing for now, because I don't want to hear everyone's thoughts all the time!

The person that I'm most in tune with is Sunny. We think it's because I've known her a long time and we're such close friends.

"Thanks for letting me know, Mrs. Kettledrum," I reply. "I'm so excited to see my family and best friend, I doubt I'll even notice."

Mrs. Kettledrum pats me on the shoulder. "It will be a memorable weekend."

BROOMMATE BONDING!

"Heidi, I have something to tell you," I hear a familiar voice say as I wave goodbye to Mrs. Kettledrum.

Melanie is waiting for me as I exit Mrs. Kettledrum's class.

"What?" I ask. You never know what's going to come out of Melanie's mouth, so I hold my breath.

"I got to class early, and I heard Mrs. Kettledrum talking on the phone. There are going to be reporters here covering Friends and Family Weekend. I guess it's a really big deal," she whispers.

This should be interesting, I think as we walk back to our dorm together. As we enter our room, I notice that Melanie's side is a complete disaster area. There are clothes, purses, and shoes *everywhere*. It looks like a clothes-and-accessories explosion.

"Melanie, what happened in here?" I ask.

Melanie looks around the room. "Oh, I kind of turned it into my designer lounge, and come to think of it, you're just in time."

I tilt my head to one side. "Just in time for *what*?"

Melanie runs to her pile of clothes and does a quick wardrobe change. She slips into a pink plaid skirt, a short gray sweater, and a pair of pink flats.

"It's runway time, Heidi.

"Will you pretty-please help me pick out my outfits for Friends and Family Weekend?"

I give Melanie a major eye roll.

"It's *just* Friends and Family Weekend. It's not a Hollywood premiere."

Melanie plants a hand firmly on one hip.

"That's where you're *oh-so-wrong*, Heidi. The Broomsfield Academy Friends and Family Weekend is the *Who's Who* of the magical world. You never know what powerful witches and wizards might show up or take your picture.

"And then there are the reporters who are coming. This could be my big break!"

It's true that families are coming from all over, and many of the students who attend the School of Magic also have magical family members, I think. Not to mention the reporters.

"Annabelle's family *is* coming all the way from London," I mention.

Melanie squeals as she picks up a pink purse and swings it in circles by the chain.

"*LONDON!* I would *love* to go to London. You see what I mean, Heidi? You never know what connections you might make."

She prances to the full-length mirror, spins around, and looks at me in the glass.

"I want to be *discovered*, Heidi.

"And who knows? Maybe somebody's mom or relative might be from Hollywood. I'll tell you one thing—*I'm* going to be prepared.

"Mark my words, Heidi Heckelbeck, one day my name will be in lights!"

Melanie struts back to me, like a girl on a mission.

"Okay, back to my fashion runway show— starring *me* and hopefully *you*!

"Seriously, Heidi, you are welcome to borrow anything of mine for your weekend wardrobe. Life is like an ongoing audition. We're always trying out for something, and you have to look sharp at all times."

"Okay, okay, I get it, Melanie. Go ahead, show me some of your outfits," I say as I sit down and get ready for the fashion show.

That's just the cue Melanie needs. She switches on some music—a fast-paced pop track. She zooms to her closet and grabs a chocolate-brown leather jacket and a pair of matching slouchy boots. Then she runs out our door and into the hallway. She cracks the door back open.

"You have to *announce* me," she instructs.

Is she kidding me?

Melanie is just TOO much sometimes. But I'm not gonna lie, I'm kind of into it. I grab her pink hairbrush for a microphone and hold it close to my mouth.

"And now for our *next* contestant—all the way from beautiful Brewster—the one and only; the star of stage, screen, *and* runway; the stunning Miss Melanie Maplethorpe!" I announce.

The door swings open, and Melanie strikes a pose. Then she sashays down the runway, also known as the middle of our room. She tilts her chin down and holds her shoulders back. Her sassy blond ponytail swishes from side to side. When she gets to the end of the runway, she whips off her leather jacket and swings it over her shoulder. Then she poses so I can see all sides of her outfit.

She definitely has this model thing down.

I add some hairbrush commentary. "Melanie is wearing her very own fashion line. Her pink plaid skirt is pleated, which gives it just the right amount of movement when she walks.

"On top she sports a short, fuzzy gray sweater and a leather jacket, along with matching slouchy brown boots. It's sophisticated and casual—a total showstopper!"

Melanie does a few more poses and sashays back out the door.

Now that we're not enemies anymore, I have to laugh when Melanie goes over the top.

Who knows? Maybe she *will* be a star one day.

Melanie smiles at me, and then she moves on to her fragrances.

Potions are Melanie's gift as a witch.

She selects a gold glitter-dusted bottle from the collection on top of her dresser. She pulls off the cap and lays a finger on the nozzle.

She turns to me. "You *have* to try my latest fall-to-winter fragrance, Heidi. It's called Cozy."

I hold up my wrist and Melanie spritzes. Tiny delicate droplets shower my skin. I rub my wrists together and sniff.

"It *does* smell cozy, Melanie," I tell her, and she smiles with satisfaction.

"It's my secret blend of jasmine and vanilla and just a little magic," she declares, spritzing herself. "It goes on like a snuggly sweater."

Then she gets a gleam in her eye. "And now it's time to work on *your* wardrobe, Heidi."

I groan.

But at the same time, I *would* like to look good with Lucy visiting—not to mention when the two of us hang out with Nick and his best friend, Max. The right outfit will give me a feeling of confidence.

Okay, sign me up for Melanie's wardrobe scheme.

"Go ahead, make me over," I say.

Melanie wastes no time. She rummages through both our closets and drawers. As snooty as Melanie can be sometimes, she's generous about sharing her stuff.

One word: *refreshing.*

Melanie lays out several outfits on her bed and hands me the first one. I run into the bathroom to try it on.

"**Ready!**" I shout.

Melanie cues up the music.

"Okay!" she calls. "Go out into the hall, and I'll introduce you. **And I'm not looking, I swear!**"

I slip out of the bathroom and dash out the room door.

Then Melanie announces me. "Our next top model is the girl next door. She's goofy, **quirky, and has absolutely no idea just how beautiful she really is.** Introducing our only redhead in the show, Ms. Heidi Heckelbeck!"

I open the door and grab the doorjamb dramatically, and then burst out laughing.

Melanie gives me a stern look.

"You have to take this *seriously*, Heidi," she scolds. "Pretend to be a *real* fashion model.

"Stand up straight, shoulders back, relax your arms, and make your hands look delicate and graceful. Got it?"

I attempt a supermodel stance, though I feel more like a super-awkward giraffe.

"Very good," Melanie praises. "Focus on something ahead of you and walk."

I stare at my dresser across the room and walk. Melanie critiques my every move.

"Loosen up!

"Be more fun!

"Bat your eyelashes!

"Don't swing your hips so much!"

I accidently kick one of Melanie's booties that she left on the runway, and giggle.

"Keep that groove walk going!" she instructs.

I strut toward the door.

"Strike a pose!" Melanie calls to me.

I lean into one hip and hold it. I do the same on the other side. Then I do a half turn and walk back down the runway and out the door.

Melanie claps.

"Well, done," she says. "You really pulled it together. And P.S., I *love* that outfit on you."

I can't wait to show Lucy. She won't believe it because I've never been this into my look before.

You know what? I could get used to having my own personal stylist!

And confession: Melanie has really grown on me.

After these weeks as broommates, we have learned how to have fun together. And with these outfits we're ready for a stylin' weekend.

Three words: *Bring it on!*

DECORATING DIVAS

Did I ever mention that I love party decorations? Well, I do.

And guess what? Jenna just asked *me* to help decorate the front of the school and the gym for the *BIG* weekend.

Jenna is the resident advisor, or RA for short, in my dorm.

I've enlisted Sunny, Annabelle, and Melanie to help decorate, better known as the Decorating Divas!

We follow Jenna to Crawford, the administration building. This is the first building our visitors will see when they arrive at Broomsfield Academy this weekend, so we have to make Crawford look AMAZING!

Boxes filled with fall-themed decorations—from balloons, pine cones, and colored leaves, to mini pumpkins, streamers, pinwheels, banners, hay bales, and straw-filled scarecrows—await us in front of the main entrance.

"The goal is to make the front entrance festive and welcoming," Jenna tells us. "Then you can decorate the gym and set the tables. Have fun. If you need me, I'll be on the soccer field setting up. Thanks so much for all your help!"

Then Jenna jogs off.

The upperclassmen always get to work on the carnival. It's a school tradition.

I can't wait to do that someday. But for now, I'll settle for decorating.

Time to bedazzle!

I look around. This is *a lot* of work, so maybe we can use magic discreetly...?

Technically we're not supposed to use magic outside of class or our homework, but there are four magical students who will be decorating, and there's a lot to get done.

Surely it won't hurt anything if we use a little magic to help hold up a decoration while we add some tape? But it wouldn't be right for all of us to use magic out in the open without permission.

As if he read my mind, Mr. Craftwood suddenly walks out the front doors. Mr. Craftwood is one of our magical teachers.

"Hello," he says to the four of us. "You are in charge of decorations, I see. Decorating this school is a big job."

He pauses and looks around. Then he lowers his voice to a whisper. "If you are very discreet, I do believe a touch of magic will not hurt in this case."

We all cheer. "Thank you, Mr. Craftwood!" Melanie squeals.

Mr. Craftwood nods. "Remember, just a touch, and don't get caught. We don't want non-magical students—or teachers—asking a lot of questions."

We all nod in agreement. We're so grateful to be able to use a little magic.

"We will be careful," I promise.

Mr. Craftwood smiles. "I'm sure you will. Carry on," he says, and heads on his way.

"Wow, that's great news," Sunny says. "What should we decorate first?"

"Let's come up with a design," Melanie suggests.

We all agree this is a great idea. We stand in front of the building and stare at it, like we're trying to make sense of a painting in a museum.

"How are we supposed to make a building like Crawford look festive and welcoming?" Annabelle asks.

Annabelle's right.

Crawford is an old stone building. It's spooky-looking, with a sinister gargoyle on either side of the main entrance. I haven't heard that it's haunted, but if there was a building that could be haunted, this would be it.

"Balloons," I answer. "*Lots* of balloons."

We laugh because **it would take a gazillion balloons to cheer up this building.**

"I say we do a beautiful arch of balloons over the front door," Melanie suggests. "It'll make it look more like a fun house than a haunted house."

Agreed.

"And the 'Welcome, Friends and Family' banner should go above the door," Sunny adds.

All we have to do now is blow up some balloons.

We quickly run into the building with all the balloons. We take them into the waiting room area and plunk down on the floor.

First we stretch the necks of the balloons so they'll inflate easily.

Then we blow until our cheeks puff out, like trumpet players.

"This is really HARD," Melanie says after a while.

"I feel dizzy," Annabelle adds.

"My ears hurt," says Sunny.

How are we going to blow up enough balloons for an arch, without passing out? I wonder.

It's hopeless!

I pinch the neck on one of my half-inflated balloons and pull. The air escapes and makes a high-pitched squeak.

PheeeeeeeeeeeeEEEEeeeeee!

Then everyone starts doing it. Our balloons hiss, howl, whistle, and meow. We let some of them fly around the room.

Fshhhhhhhh! Ffffffffffffft! Whisssssssst!

We laugh until our eyes water. When we *finally* pull ourselves together, we only have four balloons blown up.

At this rate the weekend will be *over* before we finish the arch.

That's when I make an executive decision.

"Mr. Craftwood told us we were allowed to use a touch of magic. I believe this is the time. All those in favor of using magic say 'AYE!'"

"AYYYYYYYYE!" we all shout.

We carry the box of decorations outside. Sunny and Annabelle stand guard. Melanie and I are in charge of magic. I'll do the balloons. Melanie will do the banner.

"The coast is clear," Sunny says—but not too loudly.

I quickly come up with an on-the-spot balloon spell.

On-the-spot and emergency spells are something I've been working on with Mrs. Kettledrum. I think I'm getting pretty good at them!

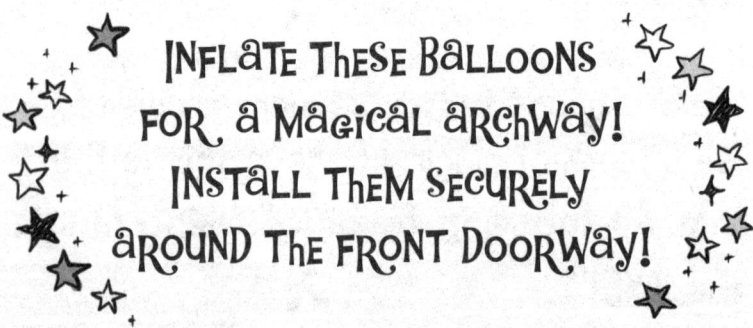

INFLATE THESE BALLOONS
FOR A MAGICAL ARCHWAY!
INSTALL THEM SECURELY
AROUND THE FRONT DOORWAY!

WHOOOOOSH!

The balloons inflate instantly and form themselves into a gorgeous arch—the color of fall leaves. The arch installs itself around the door. Melanie and I pretend to secure it—in case anyone's watching.

Melanie stands over the box with the WELCOME, FRIENDS AND FAMILY banner. She tries several spells, but the banner doesn't budge.

Melanie kicks the box.

"I can't do magic under pressure," she says. "*You* do it, Heidi."

"Happy to help," I say. After all, doing magic under pressure is what I'm best at, since I'm always making mistakes and having to find a way out of them. I focus on the banner and come up with another quick spell:

HANG THIS
FRIENDS AND FAMILY BANNER,
OVER THE DOOR,
IN A WELCOMING MANNER!

The banner rises from the box. I hold on to it. If anyone is watching, they'll think I'm just pulling the banner up and into place. It comes to rest above the front door and fastens itself to the building.

Melanie holds up her hand for a high five, and I slap it. "When it comes to spells, you're a pro, Heidi."

I smile. "We *all* have our strengths."

Next we secure the scarecrows—*without magic*—next to the steps. We also arrange fake pumpkins on the hay bales, and on the ground beside the scarecrows.

Then we stand back and admire our work.

"Totally welcoming!" Sunny declares.

It really is. *Eeee!*

Next stop for the Decorating Divas—the gym.

Someone has already set up round tables, chairs, and serving tables. We fluff the tablecloths—**and gab nonstop**—as we cover each table.

"So, who's coming from *your* family, Annabelle?" I ask.

Annabelle smooths a wrinkle from a tablecloth.

"My parents are coming, and my little brother, Charlie, who's six," she replies.

I grab another tablecloth. "Aww, I remember Henry when he was that age. **I'll bet your little brother is adorable.**"

Annabelle laughs. "I'm not sure the word 'adorable' describes Charlie **unless you think a wild beast is adorable.** He's definitely cute, but he's also **spoiled, bossy, outspoken, and moody. And . . . I can't wait to see him.**"

We all stop what we're doing and giggle.

"He sounds like a lovable nightmare," says Melanie.

Annabelle nods. "That's fair."

We laugh even more.

"My brother, Arjun, can't come this weekend, but my parents will be here!" Sunny says. "Who's coming from your family, Melanie?"

Melanie is working on pumpkin centerpieces. "My parents and my favorite living creature on the planet . . . my pug, Lola. I miss her SO much!"

Sunny, Annabelle, and I start on chair covers. Each chair gets a soft white slipcover with a pretty sash that ties in the back. It's amazing how you can make a regular chair look elegant.

"Sooooo . . . ," I say when I finish tying the last slipcover. "Now that the tables and chairs are done, let's decorate!"

We dig through more boxes of decorations.

"I'm going to magically cover the entire ceiling with helium balloons," Sunny says.

Sunny pulls out pearl-white, orange, and yellow balloons, along with ribbons.

And I know what I'm going to do, I think. "I'll decorate the walls with autumn leaves."

Annabelle picks up a garland of pine cones and mini pumpkins. "I'll hang these garlands."

Melanie holds up one of her flower arrangements inside a pumpkin vase. "I'll finish these centerpieces."

We each get to work. I magically cover the gym walls with colorful paper leaves. It **looks like peak foliage in the gym!**

"Your leaves look so beauty-*FALL*, Heidi," Sunny says, laughing at her own pun. Then she makes another. "I can't be-*LEAF* my eyes!"

I give Sunny a smirk. "Sunny," I say, "I didn't know you were so punny."

I look up at Sunny's balloons. They cover every inch of the ceiling. Pearl and gold ribbons dangle from each balloon.

Annabelle's garlands hang under each window. Then we sit down and help Melanie finish her centerpieces.

"Hello, girls," sings a voice from across the room. It's Mrs. Kettledrum. "We came to see how your decorations are coming. And they look absolutely gorgeous!"

Natalie Nguyen is with Mrs. Kettledrum. She smiles and waves to us, and then goes back to reading something on a clipboard she's holding. Natalie's an upperclassman, and she's a student in the School of Magic. She's also Jenna's best friend. I met her a few weeks ago when there was a school-wide contest to create a new Broomsfield Academy logo. Natalie was the winner!

"Mrs. Kettledrum, may I talk with you for a sec?" Natalie asks, still looking at the clipboard. She sounds kind of stressed.

"Yes, of course, Natalie." They step away from where we're sitting. **My ears go on high alert.** I watch Natalie and Mrs. Kettledrum from the corner of my eye. Natalie points to her clipboard.

"We have *way* more people coming this year than we did—*you know*—three years ago," she whispers. "And you remember how *that* weekend went."

Mrs. Kettledrum fumbles with her beaded necklace.

I look at Sunny. She heard it too. **I wonder what happened three years ago.**

I glance at Mrs. Kettledrum, and she catches me looking.

Ooops! I quickly look away.

"Well, there's absolutely nothing to be concerned about," Mrs. Kettledrum says loudly, **and I *know* she's saying it for our benefit.** She doesn't want me and my friends to worry about something that happened three years ago.

But it's too late.

I am officially worried.

And so is Sunny.

Mrs. Kettledrum and Natalie head for the door. They're still talking, but now I can't hear what they're saying.

Merg.

"Carry on, girls," Mrs. Kettledrum says over her shoulder. "Keep up the marvelous work!"

I motion for Sunny to follow me, and we meet at one of the boxes of decorations. We pretend to look for something.

"Whoa, what was *that* all about?" Sunny whispers.

I pick up a random pine cone.

"No clue," I whisper. "All I know is, **we *have* to find out what happened at Friends and Family Weekend three years ago.**"

Sunny glances over at Annabelle and Melanie. They're still working away.

"But how?" she asks.

I drop the pine cone. "Maybe we can find something in the library. **There's a whole section on school history.**"

Sunny nods.

"Hey! Sunny and I just remembered something we have to do at the library," I announce. "Meet you at dinner?"

Melanie and Annabelle don't even look up.

"Sounds good," Melanie says. "We got this."

Sunny and I bolt for the library.

We're officially on a mission to get to the bottom of what went wrong three years ago.

Why is it such a big secret?

One word: *intriguing.*

6

WITCH DETECTIVES

Sunny and I run across campus like nothing's going to stop us.

Our shoes thwap across the tile floors in the library. Everything sounds so loud in this quiet sanctuary.

A few people look up at us. I feel bad for making a ruckus in the library, but Sunny and I simply must learn the truth as quickly as possible.

We race to the circulation desk. Ms. Fernandez sees us coming. She and Ms. Egli run the library, **and they're *both* witches.**

We lean on the counter to catch our breath. **We sound like a couple of dogs panting.**

I can't help but notice that Ms. Fernandez has on the cutest library-book dress. The entire print has bookshelves with books standing, leaning, and stacked. You can even read some of the famous titles on the spines.

Ms. Fernandez tucks a lock of her shiny black hair behind her ear.

"Hi, Heidi. Hi, Sunny," she says. "How may I help you today?"

I launch right in with my burning question. "Hi, Ms. Fernandez. How long have you worked at Broomsfield Academy?"

Ms. Fernandez takes off her glasses.

"**Twenty years!**" Then she looks at us suspiciously, like, **why on earth would we need to know that?**

Sunny counters with another question. She sounds like a real detective. "So, would you say you were here *three* years ago?"

"I was indeed," Ms. Fernandez replies. "What are you two up to?"

We both lean in closer.

"Do you have any information about what happened three years ago on Friends and Family Weekend?" I ask.

Ms. Fernandez raises an eyebrow. "Why would you girls want to know about *that*?"

"Well, we overheard Mrs. Kettledrum and Natalie Nguyen mention something that happened at the Friends and Family Weekend three years ago," I begin, "but then they left the room and we didn't catch any details.

"Will you fill us in, Ms. Fernandez? We promise not to say anything."

Ms. Fernandez is quiet for a moment, like she is thinking of what to reveal, but then she begins to speak. "Well, I'm not sure I should be the one to tell you, **but I can't stop you from looking it up.** You can do a search on the history of Broomsfield Academy, Friends and Family Weekends," she tells us.

Sunny and I hurry to a computer cubby and pull up an extra chair. I type the info into the search bar. A bunch of Friends and Family Weekend headlines pop up. We scroll until we find an article from three years ago in the *Broomsfield Academy Gazette*.

YES! We dive right in.

THE BROOMSFIELD ACADEMY GAZETTE

Friends and Family Weekend Disaster!

By Student Reporter Penelope Broomsweeper

A harrowing incident has left the students and faculty of Broomsfield Academy scratching their heads. The story begins on the annual Friends and Family Weekend.

Each year parents, other family members, and friends come to visit the students for a weekend of fun activities. And this year began no differently. Trucks rolled in the day before with bouncy castles, slides, and obstacle courses. Carnival tents were set up on the soccer field with games, prizes, and cotton candy machines, and a petting zoo for the little ones. The campus was decorated inside and out, and everything was going as planned until . . . disaster struck.

On Saturday afternoon a huge storm moved in over the Broomsfield Academy campus. Meteorologists called it a sudden supercell thunderstorm. Forked lightning sizzled across the sky, damaging winds raged, and driving rain pounded students, faculty, and guests.

But the most astounding thing was that the storm was *only* on campus. Everywhere else in the town of Broomsfield, it was a beautiful autumn day. Some bystanders reported seeing witches on broomsticks soaring through the dark clouds. How's that for Broomsfield lore? While we know some townspeople are given to flights of fancy, this reporter cannot confirm that actual witches were sighted, but she can confirm that it was a chaotic scene for the entire student body and its guests. No one can explain what caused this violent storm, or why it hovered over the school and nowhere else.

Those I interviewed at the scene said that prior to the storm, tempers flared among those in attendance. What caused all this hostility? Like the storm that seemed to come out of nowhere, no one knows for sure. One can only wonder, could an angry crowd cause a massive storm to brew? Do angry emotions equal angry weather? The atmosphere was undeniably tempestuous, but meteorologists say science doesn't support this theory. Fortunately, everyone was able to get to safety. Including me, though I can't quite understand my sudden urge to return to my dorm.

By Saturday evening the storm had passed, and it seemed like everything was back to normal. Now it was all smiles and goodwill. The mess from the storm had been cleaned up, and it was as if there had never even been one. When questioned, students, faculty, friends, and families acted as if nothing had happened. It was almost like they didn't remember anything out of the ordinary. Peace had been restored. Visitors were given sparkly bracelets with the school's name as a parting gift.

One parent showed off her bracelet. "Normally jewelry isn't my thing, but I found this bracelet *irresistible*, so I put it on immediately. Well, the moment I put it on, I couldn't remember what on earth I had been so upset about the day before. It was as if all the negativity had magically disappeared!"

Other guests reported similar stories. It proves that there's nothing like a goody bag when you leave a party. It leaves everyone feeling *good*. And that's exactly the feeling visitors left with on that fateful weekend at Broomsfield Academy. The Friends and Family Weekend was a hit—with a record number of visitors at the event.

THE BROOMSFIELD ACADEMY GAZETTE

When I finish reading, I turn to Sunny. "Well, now we know why Natalie was so worried about having an even bigger turnout this year. With so many guests, something could go wrong again."

Before Sunny can respond, Ms. Fernandez comes to the cubby. "Did you get the scoop?" she asks.

"We did," I confirm.

Ms. Fernandez looks at us over the top of her glasses. "Good. There's nothing for you two to worry about. Just *make sure* your guests wear their visitor bracelets this weekend, and all will be well. We haven't had a problem in three years, and in that time my colleagues and I in the School of Magic have

added even more protections to make sure the Friends and Family Weekend goes smoothly."

Sunny and I thank her and head to the Barn for dinner.

"**We need to tell Annabelle everything,**" Sunny says as we walk across campus. "Let's have a dinner meeting in the Loft."

The Loft is a hidden place in the Barn that I discovered by accident. I showed it to Sunny and Annabelle, and the three of us meet there whenever we have something supersecret to discuss.

"Totally agree," I say.

We find Annabelle and take our food to go.

When we get to the vending machine, I *make extra sure* the hallway is clear.

Looking good.

I pull the secret lever, and the vending machine slides to one side. We clomp up the worn stairs. I love our secret hayloft, and I want to *keep* it a secret.

Sunny shares details from the article we read in the old *Broomsfield Academy Gazette*. **Weirdly Annabelle seems unfazed about this.**

"What happened three years ago is no big deal," she says. "The visitor bracelets have already solved that problem. And honestly, why would the school keep holding this event if they were *that* worried about it?"

I'm sort of surprised that Annabelle isn't the least bit concerned.

"So, you're not at all concerned?" I ask. "Even though Natalie told Mrs. Kettledrum, the crowd is going to be even bigger than it was three years ago?"

Annabelle shakes her head. "Nope! I'm not bothered at all. Why should I be? We have the best witches and wizards in the world at Broomsfield Academy. There's *zero* to worry about."

I look to Sunny for support, but she just shrugs. I guess she's lost all concern about this weekend.

"Annabelle's right, Heidi—the school has it covered," Sunny says. "It'll be the *best* weekend ever, you'll see. Try not to worry!"

I huff.

I'm glad that Sunny and Annabelle aren't stressed, but I'm not convinced. From now on I'll just keep my concerns to myself.

I feel like a washing machine midcycle.

One word: *agitated.*

MISS POPULAR!

But despite my concerns the day before, when I wake up the next morning, I can't help but feel one thing: super-duper extra totally EXCITED!

The BIG day is HERE!

Friends and Family Weekend starts *this* afternoon. I'm so amped up!

Today I finally get to see LuLu.

Woo-hoo!

I bounce happily all the way to breakfast. I walk past Jenna and Natalie, and as I grab a tray, Jenna gives me a friendly high five.

"Nice decorating job, Heidi," she praises.

And Natalie gives me two thumbs-up.

"Cute outfit, Heidi," she says.

I smile and thank them both. **I could get used to nothing but compliments to start my day!**

Then, some good news for my rumbling tummy. The line for French toast sticks is wide open.

That never happens.

I grab the tongs and tweeze some heavenly French toast sticks onto my plate. Then I fill a bowl with maple syrup for dipping.

Yum! I grab some orange slices and a glass of water. And I'm almost to my table when, of all things, I run into *Nick!*

"Hey, Heidi," he says brightly.

I'm *so* flustered, I unknowingly tip my tray, and my plate and water almost slide off the edge.

Oops!

I quickly tilt my tray back the other way, **and my plate and water almost slide off the *other* side!**

Finally I get everything back to center **and, luckily, not on Nick's shirt or crashing to the floor.**

It reminds me of that wooden maze game—the one where you have to keep the steel marble from falling into the holes. *Slant. Level. Tip. Straighten.*

"Nice save, Heidi!" Nick cheers.

I laugh nervously, afraid that if I laugh too hard, my tray will shake and I'll still manage to knock its contents to the floor. **My perfect morning would turn into a perfect mess!**

"What's going on, Nick?" I ask, trying to sound unfazed and enthusiastic. I glance at the omelet on his tray.

"Not much," he replies. "Just excited to see my family and Max. He's really excited to meet you. I never talk about girls, so when I mentioned you, he got really curious."

As soon as Nick says this, **he realizes that he's all but admitted he *likes* me,** and his cheeks flush pink.

And then my cheeks flush pink **because that's when I realize, it's true!**

Nick likes me!

The awkward silence is building, so I'd better say something fast.

"Well, I can't wait to meet Max," I say. "And my friend Lucy will be delighted to meet both of you."

Now we're just standing there not saying anything again. A girl behind us coughs because we're blocking the way.

"Um, catch you later, Nick," I say.

We smile goofily at each other, and then I skedaddle to my table.

My table is all witches and wizards this week. I can't wait to ask about everyone's family!

As soon as I set down my tray, Isabelle, who's sitting next to Hunter, leans forward. "Heidi, my parents are so excited to meet you. I told them all about you."

Wow! *Her parents want to meet me? But I'm not even royalty, like HER family is.*

I take this as a huge compliment. I recently found out Isabelle is secretly a princess in an ancient line of magical royalty. She doesn't want people to know in case they start treating her differently. So she begged me not to tell anybody.

It's been so difficult to keep such a huge secret, but I have. Isabelle has turned out to be a really special friend.

Before I can respond, Annabelle says the same thing. "My family can't wait to meet you either, Heidi."

Wow, I love all the unexpected attention! It feels amazing.

"How did I suddenly get to be Miss Popularity?" I ask.

Everyone at the table laughs.

"Because, Heidi, like we told you, you *are* popular," Sunny says.

Everyone nods in agreement.

But I shake my head, feeling self-conscious. "Oh pa-le-e-eaze! How on earth am I popular?"

Isabelle taps the side of her cheek with one finger.

"Hmmm, let's see, what makes Heidi so popular?" she asks the whole table. "Well, for one thing, she is friendly to everyone at school."

Hunter chimes in. "And she made Mrs. Kettledrum's dog, Momo, *TALK!*"

The whole table nods, **and the compliments keep coming.** Suddenly I imagine having my picture taken with everyone this weekend, like I'm some kind of glamorous celebrity.

But then I get a *reality check.* **Melanie stops by our table.**

"Oh, get *over* yourself, Heidi. You're still quirky Heidi Heckelbeck in *my* book." She laughs dramatically and walks off. **This has been Melanie's signature move since elementary school.**

But you know what? She's right. I am still quirky Heidi Heckelbeck, **and I'm also pretty popular!**

I smile at the friends at my table. "Thank you so much for all the kind words," I tell them. "I can't wait to meet all your families. **This is going to be such a fun weekend."**

After that, everyone starts chatting among themselves. I'm relieved the attention has moved off me. It gives me a moment to think about the weekend ahead.

As excited as I am, I wonder what Nick's friend Max will think of me.

What if Max tells Nick I'm not as cool and as interesting as he'd imagined? And then Nick will see me differently and he won't like me anymore.

And what if Isabelle's parents tell Isabelle I'm not the kind of girl a princess should hang out with?

See how my thoughts spiral?

The bottom line is, I just don't want to disappoint anyone this weekend. That's all.

And with that last thought, I push my breakfast tray away, because as I've been ruminating, I have also finished all my French toast sticks. All that's left is a pool of syrup that I swirl around with my fork.

This weekend is a WAY bigger deal than I thought it would be.

It feels like the pressure is on.

Somehow I'm going to have to step up my game.

INVISIBLE

My *first* outfit of the weekend is ON!

Twirl! I spin in front of Melanie in my green-and-white dress, and kick one of my legs up in the air to show off the cutest cowboy boots ever.

Actually they're *Melanie's* cowboy boots, **and so is the dress.** I have to ask for a pair of these boots for Christmas. They have a rainbow of crocheted flowers all over them.

One word: *stunning!*

Melanie looks up from her phone and nods approvingly.

Yes, her *PHONE.*

Believe it or not, **we got our phones *early* this Friday** so family and friends can contact us if they need to.

Melanie leaps up and shows off her jumpsuit, which looks so stylish. "And how do I look?"

Honestly, Melanie *always* looks amazing.

"Unreal," I affirm.

Then we do our hair, nails, and makeup with *magic*. I know we're not supposed to use magic outside of class, but let's be realistic. **Who's going to catch us in the privacy of our own room?**

I magically paint my nails green to match my dress. Then I add little white stars and crescent moon decals. Melanie does a pink version of the same thing. It's fun to twin with her on our nails.

Next I add a hint of blush and a touch of mascara—keeping it totally simple. My phone chimes and twinkles, like the wisp of a fairy's wand.

I glance at my screen and squeal, **"They're HERE!"**

Melanie squeals with me. "Same! My family and Lola are about ten minutes away."

We quickly finish getting ready. I smear some lip gloss onto my lips and spray some glitter dust onto my hair for a super-subtle shimmer.

I'm SO READY!

I grab my visitor bracelets. "See you at dinner, Melanie."

Melanie follows me to the door and spritzes me with her Cozy fragrance.

And I'm off.

I have to resist running all the way to Crawford, because I don't want to look like Hurricane Heidi by the time I get there.

Did I mention that every part of me is buzzing? I can't wait to see Lucy and my family!

Lucy spies me first and charges down the path toward me. I toss my beauty concerns to the wind and run toward her, too.

Obviously.

We grab each other by the arms and jump up and down—just like we used to do when we were seven.

"Hello, best friend in the whole world!" I scream, but not super-loud because I don't want to scare Lucy.

Lucy stops jumping and looks me up and down.

"Heidi, what are you wearing? You look so *chic*."

I strike a pose. "You like?"

Lucy folds her arms. "I *do* like. I just didn't expect you to be so dressed up. It makes me feel frumpy."

Lucy looks like herself.

She has on jeans and a light blue tee with ruffles around the edges of the sleeves and hem. Her brown curls are pushed back in a wide matching headband.

"And, Heidi, have you gotten taller?" she asks. We stand back-to-back.

I've always been a teeny bit taller than Lucy, but now it seems like I'm a full inch or two taller than her.

"Maybe I am a little bit taller," I say.

Lucy sighs. "I would love to be really tall," she says. "But both my parents are short, so I guess it's not going to happen."

"Don't worry. Tall or short, you could never look less than beautiful, LuLu," I tell her.

She smiles, and we hang our arms over each other's shoulders and walk toward my parents and Henry. Henry's spinning a fidget toy a mile a minute in one hand.

Speaking of growing, Henry looks a little taller. And, sadly, he doesn't run into my arms for a hug like he used to.

Has he gotten too cool for hugs?

Well, he's getting a hug from me whether he wants one or not.

Squoosh!

Then I run to Mom and Dad, and they embrace me at the same time.

"Heidi Kins, you look so lovely **and grown-up**," Dad says. Mom totally agrees.

I pull the pouch with the bracelets from my wrist.

"Look what I have for you," I say proudly, handing out the charmed bracelets to each member of the family and Lucy.

Lucy acts like I've given her a *real* diamond bracelet. She slips it on and holds out her wrist. The bracelet shimmers in the late-afternoon sun.

"It's so pretty, Heidi. I love it!"

The bracelets are definitely having the irresistible effect Mrs. Kettledrum hoped for. Even my little brother likes his.

Mom and Dad head inside to register. Henry, Lucy, and I hang out on the steps. So many families are arriving now.

"So do you like the decorations around the door?" I ask, pointing at them. "My friends and I put them up."

"They are really festive, Heidi," Lucy says. "But what are those ugly stone creatures near the entrance? They're so creepy!"

I guess the decorations didn't exactly hide the monstrous faces of the gargoyles.

"Those are just gargoyles," I tell her. "Old-fashioned carved figures."

Lucy stretches out her lower lip, like *Ew!* "Well, they look like they could come alive at any time and take flight!"

Henry's all over *this* idea. "Like in a horror movie!"

Lucy frowns at the word "horror." I try to put a positive spin on it.

"Gargoyles *aren't* evil," I explain. "They ward *off* evil."

My parents reappear from the building, all checked in.

"Can I give Lucy a quick school tour?" I ask. "We can catch up with you at the meet and greet later."

They're A-OK with my plan, so Lucy and I take off.

"First stop, Baileywick—that's my dorm," I tell her.

On the way, Lucy and I gab like we haven't seen each other in so long (because we haven't). She loves my dorm, which is old, but doesn't have any gargoyles.

I open the door to my room.

"Ta-da! This is my home away from home," I announce.

Lucy takes it all in.

"Well, that's definitely *Melanie's* side," she says, pointing to the fancy pink explosion opposite my tastefully decorated side of the room.

We both burst out laughing.

"So where will I sleep?" Lucy asks.

I point to two sleeping bags on top of my bed.

"I thought it would be fun for the two of us to sleep in sleeping bags on the floor the way we usually do when we have a sleepover," I say.

Lucy hugs me and says, "I love it!"

Then we walk all over campus. I point out the dorms and tell Lucy which of my new friends lives in each one. She loves Isabelle's dorm, which is a beautiful Victorian house.

I show her the lake, the fountain, the classrooms, the library—everything. Well, everything except the *coolest* parts of the school, which are the secret passageways to the School of Magic *and* the School of Magic itself.

One word: *frustrating.*

But there is *one* cool thing I can show her.

"Come on, Lucy. You're going to love this!" I say as we approach the Barn.

Lucy follows me to the side door, and we walk down the hall to the vending machine.

"I admit it's a well-stocked vending machine," Lucy says, "but I'm not sure why it's so special."

I wiggle my eyebrows. "Watch this."

I make sure the coast is clear. Then I lean against the wall, reach my arm behind the vending machine, and pull the secret lever. The vending machine slides to one side and reveals the secret stairwell to the Loft.

Lucy gasps as I head toward the stairs.

"Come on," I say.

Lucy follows me up the steps to the Loft, and I show her around.

"This was a part of the original barn, from all the way back in the 1800s," I announce. I also tell her the story of how I discovered the Loft when I was hiding from Hunter. I hop onto a prickly bale of hay.

"This is also where Sunny, Annabelle, and I have all our private convos," I continue. "As far as I know, we're the only students who know about it."

Lucy sits down next to me. "This is beyond cool, Heidi. I can't believe you never told me about this in one of your letters."

Honestly, I can't believe it either.

I usually tell Lucy *everything*.

I guess there were just so many other things to tell her that I never mentioned the Loft. Luckily, she's not mad about it. We have a good talk instead.

"So, how's everything back in Brewster?" I ask.

Lucy picks a piece of straw from the hay bale. "Well, I've made a few new friends since starting middle school, but no one like *you*, Heidi.

"Of course, Bruce and I are still buds, but it's different. You left a *humongous* hole in our lives when you left. I miss you more than you'll ever know. And I've tried to be strong, but I'm not gonna lie, it's been really hard."

Ouch.

Being left behind is **way worse** than leaving.

I'm having the adventure of my life, and she's navigating middle school without her best friend.

Two words: *That stinks.*

I put my arm around Lucy to comfort her. "I miss you so much, LuLu. Maybe we can convince Melanie to move home and then you can take her place."

We both laugh.

"Don't worry," Lucy says. "I'm slowly getting used to it, and besides, I'm so happy to be here at this moment. We might not be in school together anymore, but we'll always be close, **you know what I mean?**"

I squeeze Lucy's arm because I do. "I'm so happy you're here."

Then I let out a *huge* snort—yes, like a pig—to snap us back to our silly selves.

And it works. We giggle as we hop off the hay bales and hurry to the meet and greet.

The school band is playing, and the cheerleaders are getting everyone into a great mood. A surge of excitement washes over me.

I can't wait to introduce Lucy to everyone!

Mrs. Kettledrum climbs the steps to a platform that is wrapped in tinsel and foil. It looks like a parade float. She taps the microphone, preparing to give her welcome announcements.

"Welcome to this year's Broomsfield Academy Friends and Family Weekend! Please help yourselves to refreshments and appetizers, followed by a barbecue dinner and make-your-own s'mores. There are tables inside and outside the grand tent. The dinner bell will sound shortly.

"And one more thing. If you are a visitor and don't have a visitor bracelet, please get one. These bracelets are your ticket to everything this weekend, and you *must* wear them at *all* times! Students wearing staff T-shirts will be happy to give you one.

"Thank you. Now enjoy getting to know one another!"

It's time to get our mingle on!

I scan the crowd and see Annabelle waving me over.

"Come on, Lucy," I say, grabbing her hand. "I want you to meet my friends!"

We run over to Annabelle's family. Annabelle takes my hand and introduces us. "Mom, Dad, this is my friend Heidi and her friend Lucy, who is visiting today, just like you."

Annabelle's parents both look very friendly, with big smiles on their faces. Annabelle's dad is wearing a suit and tie, and Annabelle's mom is wearing a beautiful blue dress that matches her blue eyes. A cute little boy is hiding behind Annabelle's mom. He must be Charlie.

"Hello, Mr. and Mrs. Williams," I say. I turn to Annabelle. "I see you got your blue eyes from your mom."

"Hello, Heidi, we've heard so much about you," Mrs. Williams says. She turns and smiles at Lucy. "And it's nice to meet you, too, Lucy," she says.

Lucy smiles and says hello.

Mr. Williams looks behind Mrs. Williams and laughs. "Charlie, what's going on?" he asks. He turns back to us. "It's not like him to be shy," he adds.

"I also have a little brother," I tell him. "He can be shy sometimes, especially around new people."

After introducing us to her parents, Annabelle grabs my arm and pulls me aside to tell me something privately. "Heidi, you're *not* going to believe this," she begins.

I look back at Lucy. She's standing there all by herself.

Eek!

"What?" I say, hoping I can get back to Lucy in a moment.

Annabelle nods toward her little brother, who just knocked over a folding chair—on purpose. "Charlie found out that *I'm a witch* on the way over from England."

I wonder why Annabelle's so upset about this.

"He was bound to find out sooner or later," I tell her.

Annabelle wrings her hands. "Yeah, but I was hoping it would be later. You don't know Charlie. He has a big mouth and can't keep a secret."

I look over at Charlie and back at Annabelle.

"Just tell him why it's important to keep this info quiet," I say. "And, Annabelle, even if he *did* say something, I doubt anyone would believe him. We know that witches are real because we are witches, but people who aren't? They think magic is all just pretend."

Annabelle sighs. "Maybe you're right, but still . . ."

Charlie tips over another folding chair. Annabelle runs over to her little brother. I follow and signal for Lucy to come too.

"Stop it, Charlie!" Annabelle says firmly.

Charlie folds his arms. "Why should I? It's FUN!"

Annabelle shakes her finger at her brother. "Because it's *bad* manners."

Charlie sticks his freckled nose in the air. He clearly doesn't care what his sister says.

Then Annabelle introduces me to him. "Charlie, say hello to Heidi, one of my best friends at Broomsfield."

Charlie turns to me.

"Hi, best friend *never*!" Then he squinches his face at me. "So, are *you* one too?" he asks.

Uh-oh, I think. *I just reassured her, but I see why Annabelle is worried.*

And that's when I notice that Charlie doesn't have on a visitor bracelet. He needs one and *fast.*

"Hey, Charlie, let's get you a visitor bracelet," I say in my cheeriest voice.

Charlie wrinkles his nose. "I don't want some *stupid* bracelet!"

I put my hand to my chest and pretend to act shocked.

"But, Charlie, those bracelets are like *pirate* treasure." This gets his attention. "And besides, if you *don't* wear one, you won't be able to get cotton candy *or* make s'mores. You won't even be able to jump in the bouncy houses without a visitor bracelet."

I've successfully convinced Charlie he needs a bracelet. But wow, Annabelle sure wasn't kidding when she said Charlie could be a little terror.

"Come on," I say to him, and point to Jenna, who is one of the people handing out bracelets.

Annabelle looks at me and mouths, *Thank you!*

"Be right back," I tell Lucy and Annabelle.

I track down Jenna, and she gives Charlie a bracelet.

Charlie and I hurry back to Annabelle and Lucy. I feel bad having taken more time away from Lucy, but I couldn't risk Charlie asking me more questions about **being a witch** in front of her either. *Eeek!*

I link arms with Lucy and take her to meet Sunny's family. Sunny runs toward us. I wave to her parents, who I remember from when I first met Sunny all those years ago on the beach.

"You must be Lucy," Sunny says enthusiastically. "I'm so glad to finally meet you! Heidi talks about you *all* the time. I'm *so* glad she's at Broomsfield. I don't know what I'd do without her. She's my absolute best friend in the whole school."

Then Sunny turns and throws her arms around me to emphasize her point.

Oh no! A *look* just washed over Lucy's face.

She steps back, like she's a little stunned. And I kind of don't blame her.

Everyone keeps calling me their best friend, which is nice, but it must make my 100 percent bestest friend in the world feel completely weird.

"Great to meet you, Sunny," Lucy says, trying to cover her shock. "We sure miss Heidi in Brewster."

"I would miss Heidi too," Sunny says, latching on to my hand and pulling me closer so she can whisper something into my ear. "Have you seen Melanie prancing around campus? She's spritzing people with her Cozy scent. And I only know what it's called because she's giving everyone a detailed description." Sunny scrunches up her nose. "She's basically using Friends and Family Weekend to promote herself."

I glance at Lucy. She looks *so* left out!

Ugh! I would never leave her out on purpose. But I can't help it if she doesn't know about Melanie's magical potions.

No excuse, I tell myself. *You have to keep Lucy in the scoop loop!*

Sunny shakes her head, thinking about Melanie as I pull her back toward Lucy. And at that very moment I see Melanie making her way over to us. She's waving to anyone who catches her eye, like she's a famous movie star or something.

"That's just Melanie being Melanie," I say to Sunny, and then look at Lucy. "Wasn't she always a bit showy even in Brewster?" I nudge Lucy with my elbow. I want her to know that she is a part of this conversation.

"Oh," is all she says at first. Lucy seems a little surprised by my nudge, but she smiles when she notices that she's being invited into the conversation. "Yeah, Melanie will always be Melanie, I guess."

And no sooner does she say this than Melanie prances up to us. Her pug, Lola, is at her heels. Luckily, she didn't hear us blabbing on about her. *Phew!*

"Well, well," Melanie says. "If it isn't Lucy Lancaster." She gives poor Lucy the once-over. "I'm so glad you're here, because Heidi and I can give you a makeover. Is that still the style in Brewster?"

I have been a victim of Melanie's digs for years, and *believe me*, I know what it feels like. *Horrible!*

But Lucy holds her own. She gives it right back to Melanie, the way she always used to do.

"Well, well. If it isn't Melanie Maplethorpe," Lucy says with all the confidence in the world. "I can see *you* haven't changed."

Melanie loves Lucy's reaction. She likes someone who can stick up for themself. Melanie opens her arms wide and offers Lucy a hug.

"You know, *I'm only joking,* Lucy," she protests. "But, if you're up for it, we would be happy to glam you up. I mean, just look at Heidi! Doesn't she look great? She's come a long way since our Brewster days."

I look at Lucy for her reaction. I'm pretty sure what I see is shock. Ugh. To make matters worse, Melanie hangs on to me, like we're the bestest friends in the universe. And let's be clear. Melanie and I are still just *friends in progress.*

With Melanie it's always **three words:** *Proceed with caution!*

"May I borrow Heidi for a moment?" Melanie asks.

Sunny and Lucy look at each other like, *What is going on?* Then Melanie drags me aside and Lola follows.

"Have you seen any reporters yet?" Melanie asks.

I am so annoyed! "That's what you dragged me away to ask?" I say.

Melanie looks shocked. "Heidi, you know how much time I spent on my look. I don't want it to go to waste."

I sigh. "Melanie, I haven't seen the reporters. If I do, I will let you know. Now if you will excuse me, I have to get back to my best friends."

As we walk back to Sunny and Lucy, the dinner bell rings. And Lucy's not smiling.

She's annoyed, I can tell. Melanie sees it too. She tries to smooth things over.

"Sorry I had to steal Heidi from you, Lucy. I had a totally burning question.

"So, has Heidi told you how *close* we've become this year? I mean, who would've ever believed it? Well, I have to run. Toodles!" Then she bounds off with Lola, but not before spritzing us with her perfume.

We all wave our hands in the air to push away Melanie's misty ambush. At first I really liked this scent, but now Melanie is just overdoing it.

I turn to my best friend, who must officially hate me. "Sorry about all these distractions, Lucy. For the rest of the weekend, I promise to stick by your side."

Lucy seems to shake it off, but I'm pretty sure she feels like she just landed on an alien planet.

I really need to be a better friend.

"Let's go grab some dinner and eat with my family," I chirp as happily as I can.

Lucy perks up a little. "That sounds good. I'm pretty hungry."

We hop into the barbecue line, **and guess who gets in line behind us?**

Nick and Max!

I wonder if they picked this line because we're in it.

I hope so!

One thing Nick forgot to tell me is that his friend has red hair, like me.

"Hi, Heidi," says Nick. "This is Max, my best friend."

It looks like Nick dressed extra nice for the weekend, because he's wearing a supersoft cream-colored sweater with navy blue trim that I don't think I've ever seen on him before. He's paired it with casual khaki pants and crisp white sneakers. Okay, so he's adorable *and* stylish.

One word: *swoon.*

I can feel myself turning bright red.

"Hi, Nick. Hi, Max," I manage to blurt out. "This is Lucy." Lucy nudges me, which I'm pretty sure means she approves of Nick—or maybe she approves of Max. . . . Or both?

Then Lucy asks Nick and Max how long they've been best friends, and I can't help but feel relieved. *She's finally feeling comfortable at Broomsfield,* I think.

Nick starts telling us a cute story about how he and Max met. Max had just gotten a new puppy, and it had run away. He was searching his neighborhood with his dad and couldn't stop crying. Nick saw them and offered to help them search. Together they found Max's puppy, and they've been best friends ever since.

It is such an adorable story.

"It's funny that we both have best friends who are redheads," Lucy says to Nick, and we all laugh.

But then, for some reason, Nick starts going on and on about me, like everyone else has today.

Normally this would make me feel great, but this time it makes me feel weird, because I know it must make Lucy feel weird.

And that's a lot of weird!

"Did you know Heidi is one of the most popular people at Broomsfield? Everybody *loves* her, and this week she's become queen of the Four Square court. She's so awesome at everything," Nick gushes.

I laugh loudly because I want to make light of it. But instead this calls more attention to me.

Gack.

"Well, *for everyone's information*, I am *not* awesome at everything," I say. "I'm actually a total bust at *most* things. Lucy knows since she's been with me forever."

And just to add to all the *weird* going on, Lucy steps out in front of me to speak directly to Nick. "I was Heidi's best friend way before she ever even thought about coming to Broomsfield Academy. And I'm still her bestest friend."

Nick doesn't have a chance to say anything more because we're next in line.

We build our hamburgers and grab some fries and drinks. I give a big smile to Nick, hoping what Lucy said wasn't as awkward for him as it was for me.

It sort of felt like Lucy was trying to remind everyone, including me, of the fact that we go way back.

Nick and Max return my smile, so I guess everything is fine.

Phew!

Lucy waves goodbye to them, and we say see ya to the boys until later.

When we finally get to the tent, I'm ready to relax and be ourselves.

"Wow, Lucy, it must feel so weird to be dropped into the middle of my new world. I hope it's not too much and we can spend more time alone together," I tell her. I'd rather just be open about things and enjoy our weekend together.

Lucy quietly nibbles one of her fries. I can tell things are *off* with us. But *how* off?

"Well, it's definitely different," she finally says. "Your friends are all really nice. I just kind of feel like an outsider, you know, like I'm invisible."

I can barely swallow my drink. *Invisible?*

Lucy and I have been waiting for this weekend for so long. I need her to feel great, not feel invisible. I need to fix this, but how?

I wish Lucy would just tell me exactly how she wants this weekend to go. *Wait . . . maybe she's thinking it!*

Could I read Lucy's mind?

It's worth a try, I think. I try to concentrate on Lucy and block out all the noise around me.

Om . . .

But nothing.

I try to concentrate even harder, **if that's even possible.**

Nothing.

Mrs. Kettledrum did say my mind reading would be a little funky this weekend, but I thought I'd at least be able to tune into the thoughts of my bestest friend in the whole world. **I guess things are a lot more off between us than I realized.**

But I can fix it!

"It'll get better, LuLu. *I promise.*" But there's a little part of me that's worried that I can't *keep* this promise.

Oh merg!

I never knew it would be so hard to mix an old friend with new friends. Lucy has this look on her face like she doesn't even know me anymore.

Have I really changed that much since the last time I saw her?
I hope not.

I hear a rumble in the distance.

Thunder.

Oh no!

Mrs. Kettledrum told us the weather this weekend was going to be beautiful.

What if the visitor bracelets aren't working?

What if everything goes bonkers like it did three years ago?

I spy Mrs. Kettledrum under the tent. She sees me, and I can hear her thoughts loud and clear.

Two words: *Thank GOODNESS!*

There's nothing to worry about, Heidi. Just some thunder in the distance.

I sure hope Mrs. Kettledrum is right, because I feel so uneasy about *everything* right now, especially about my friendship with Lucy.

A GHOSTLY GAME

As the evening goes on, it starts getting colder. My parents, Henry, Lucy, and I are clearing our table when I suddenly realize it's *freezing*. The temperature dropped, and it's still thundering in the distance.

Most families have left for the evening, but not us. A few die-hard families have stayed outside. Lucy and I pull up chairs around one of the portable campfire stoves. I cocoon myself in a blanket because my cute outfit has left me shivering from the cold.

Lucy and Henry lean over the fire and toast marshmallows. Mom and Dad skewer more marshmallows.

"We haven't done this in years," Mom says.

I *really* want another s'more, **but I want to be warm even more.** I hug the blanket tighter around myself. The good news is, I'm way less stressed than I was before dinner.

It's so fun to be out here with just Lucy and my family. It feels normal, cozy, and safe— **that is, until I see something really weird. . . .**

What IS that? I wonder as the something floats through the air and heads right for our campfire.

Oh my gosh! It's a flying saucer?

I sit up and am about to shriek, *UFO!* when I realize it's only a paper plate. But this isn't your ordinary plate blowing around in the wind. This plate seems to be moving purposefully, like it's remote-controlled or something.

Wait, I think there's something *on* the plate. *Hold up, Heidi!* I think. *Who ever heard of a remote-controlled paper plate?* Then it hits me. *This has to be MAGIC!*

Duh!

I try to inconspicuously walk toward the magic floating plate and catch it. And I'm pretty impressed by how easy it was, almost like it was coming right for me. I walk back to our campfire, holding the plate.

"Wow, Heidi, where'd you get the s'more?" Lucy asks.

I look at the s'more on my plate. It has a swirly *H* for "Heidi" written in chocolate on top.

"Oh, just a classmate," I say, trying to sound casual.

Meanwhile my heart is pounding. *Who could have sent me this. And why?*

Henry wipes marshmallow from his face with the back of his hand. *Ew.* "But I wanted to make you one," he says.

I bundle back up in my blanket and sit on my chair. "I'd love that, Henry," I say.

Lucy didn't see the floating plate. *What a relief!* It would have been awkward trying to explain how the s'more magically floated over to me.

I glance at the families sitting nearby, looking for anyone who could have sent this plate my way. But it's no use. The only magical students I see are Isabelle and Hunter. Their families are sitting together around another campfire.

But Hunter and Isabelle wouldn't use magic in front of all these people like that. **No way.**

I set the magical s'more on the ground beside me, because **there's no way I'm eating *that* one.**

While the embers glow, my family catches me up on what's been going on in Brewster. It makes me wish Aunt Trudy had been able to come this weekend, but she had a trunk show for her perfume business. My aunt is a witch, like my mom and me, and she's also a Broomsfield alum, also like Mom.

Then I give everyone some highlights of what my life is like at Broomsfield.

I can't share *the magical stuff* with Lucy here, so I'll have to wait until Thanksgiving to tell my family about what I've been learning in the School of Magic.

I hug Mom, Dad, and Henry before they head to their room. There is a building on campus with a room for every family visiting, and they'll be staying there tonight.

But Lucy is sleeping over in my room!

Lucy and I walk back to my dorm, still wrapped in our blankets.

"Dinner was really fun," Lucy says.

I sigh with relief. Part of me wants to apologize for all the attention on me earlier, but I don't want to bring it up again. I just want to have fun with Lucy!

"I had fun too, Lulu," I say. **"And tonight we get to have a sleepover, just like old times!"**

We bump each other as we walk along. The campus is quiet and peaceful **until we hear a great flap of powerful wings.**

Thwap! Thwap! Thwap!

A shadow passes over us. Lucy and I look up, but whatever it is, it's already gone. Lucy grabs on to me, and her blanket falls to the sidewalk.

"Hei-i-i-deee! **What was *tha-a-a-at?*"** she whispers. Her voice is panicked, but it's like she doesn't want to talk loudly **in case whatever it was hears her.**

Of course, I have absolutely no idea what just flew overhead, but I take a wild guess.

"It was probably, um, an owl," I say. I don't actually believe this, as it sounded bigger and heavier than an owl, but I also don't want to scare Lucy any further.

"Come on. Let's get back to my dorm," I say. We throw our blankets over our arms and make a run for it.

When we get to my room, Melanie is already in her pajamas. She unrolled the two sleeping bags and placed them neatly next to each other on the floor. The room is tidy.

Melanie can actually be a thoughtful human being sometimes, **and it still shocks me.**

"Hey, you two," Melanie says cheerfully.

"Wow, Melanie, thanks for setting up our sleeping bags," I say.

Melanie shrugs. "It was purely selfish. I didn't know when you'd be back, and I didn't want you to wake me up, giggling and setting things up after I was already in bed."

Lucy unzips her suitcase. "Where's Lola?" she asks Melanie.

Melanie sticks out her lower lip. "Mrs. Kettledrum says no dogs in the dorm—**even though she lets Momo live here.**"

Lucy fishes around in her suitcase for her pajamas. She pulls out navy-and-white plaid bottoms, and a white top with interconnecting red hearts on the front.

I have the exact same pajamas.

We bought them together last year. I want us to match tonight, so I search through my dresser to find the same pajamas.

After we get changed, Melanie has words for us.

"Matching pajamas is *so* dorky," she whines. I bet she's just jealous because she doesn't also have a pair.

Lucy and I strike a silly pose.

"Okay, I guess they're dorky *and* cute," Melanie says. Then her eyes get wide. "Heyyy, do you two want to tell ghost stories tonight?"

I look out the window at the full moon, and I feel a chill when I think of the flapping wings we heard on the way back to the dorm. That was ghostly enough for me.

I look at Lucy. She is frowning.

"I don't *know* any ghost stories," I lie.

Of course I know *some* ghost stories, but I'm not in the mood to tell any, and from the look on her face, Lucy isn't either.

"Me either," Lucy quickly adds.

Melanie lies down on her bed on her stomach, and cups her chin in her hands.

"Okay, then let's play a ghostly game instead. Have you ever played Ghost Book?" she asks.

We shake our heads slowly because we're scared to find out.

"It's really fun, but first we have to turn off the lights and flick on some candles," Melanie says as she rolls off the bed, grabs three battery-operated tea lights, and sets them on the floor. Then she grabs a book from her desk and turns off the lights.

We gather around the flickering candles, making sure our blankets are close in case we need to hide.

Our faces glow in the candlelight. I'm not sure about this, but I guess we'll try it.

"Ready?" Melanie asks.

We squeal with fear.

Melanie holds up the book, which is called *History of Broomsfield Academy*.

"My parents bought this book for me at the school bookstore today," Melanie explains. "We can use it as the Ghost Book to play our game."

"All we have to do is ask the book questions, and it will give us answers. If the answers don't make sense, then you have to ask again. *I'll be the one in charge since I know all the rules.* Got it?"

Lucy and I nod—even though we have no idea what we're agreeing to.

"Lucy, you can go first since you're the guest," Melanie instructs. "Are you ready to play?"

Lucy bites her bottom lip. "Sure..."

Melanie sets the book in her lap. "First you have to shut your eyes."

Lucy looks to me for help.

"It's okay, Lucy. I promise I won't let anything bad happen to you," I assure her.

Lucy squeezes my arm and shuts her eyes. Melanie tells her the next step. "First you have to ask the Ghost Book if you may enter the game."

Lucy squeezes my arm even harder.

"Ghost Book, may I enter the game?" Lucy asks.

Then Melanie opens the book to a random page and places the book in Lucy's lap.

"Touch the page with your finger, Lucy," she says.

Lucy sticks out her pointer finger and lowers it onto the open page.

"Perfect. Open your eyes and read the words where your finger landed," Melanie directs. "Whatever the book says will come to pass. If the words don't make sense, then that means the book didn't let you into the game and you have to take another turn."

Lucy opens her eyes and looks where her finger landed. She pulls the book closer and reads the words out loud.

The gruesome stone gargoyles called Robin and Zee sit perched in front for all to see. These winged creatures are destined to be flying over Broomsfield, untethered and free!

Lucy yelps and drops the book to the floor. "Is that about those hideous gargoyles near the main entrance?"

Melanie and I look at each other like, *Holy moly!* Because that's *exactly* what the words are referring to.

One word: *super-freaky!*

"I think it might be," I manage to say.

Lucy covers her face with her hands. "I don't want to play this game anymore!" she cries.

Then she leaps to her feet, runs into the bathroom, and slams the door. I'm about to go after her when I hear a bloodcurdling scream come from within the bathroom.

Melanie flicks on the light, and I race to the bathroom and yank open the door.

"Lucy, are you OKAY?" I ask.

Lucy stands frozen in front of the mirror, with her hand over her mouth. I look to see what she's staring at.

There, written in toothpaste on the mirror, are the words:

BEWARE THE GARGOYLES!

OH MY GOSH! I slap *my* hand over my mouth too!

"*Mel-a-nieee!*" I shout. "You have to come see this!"

Melanie walks in, reads the mirror, and screams. Lucy and Melanie both latch on to me like koala bears.

This has to be a practical joke, right?

"Did you write this to scare us, Melanie?" I ask her.

Melanie shakes her head, and I actually believe her because her eyes are bulging with fear.

"It's THE BOOK," Melanie says seriously.

We run back into the bedroom, shrieking, and then all three of us jump into my bed and bury ourselves under the covers, like somehow this will protect us **from gargoyles.**

"I told you I didn't like those creepy stone creatures," Lucy says.

We thrash around under the blankets—desperately trying to keep every inch of our bodies hidden.

No sooner do we begin to collect our wits than we hear piercing shrieks echo inside and outside the dorm.

Swoosh!

We throw off the covers and jump to our feet.

It sounds like some kind of a prehistoric bird, maybe a pterodactyl . . . or **maybe more like GARGOYLES!**

Lucy, Melanie, and I scream at the top of our lungs. But, weirdly, the shrieking echo sound continues, and I think I may know what it is. . . . I creep to the door and peek into the hall. Kids are filing downstairs.

I breathe a huge sigh of relief.

"It's just a fire alarm, you two. We have to leave the building." Okay, *why* did the school pick Friends and Family Weekend to have a practice fire drill?

Lucy and I wrap ourselves back up in our blankets, and Melanie puts on a white spa robe. We hurry down the hall, arm in arm, all wondering the same thing.

Is the building on fire?

And did the gargoyles start it?

We're the last ones out of the building, except for Mrs. Kettledrum. She does a final sweep to make sure everyone's accounted for.

We sit on the steps and wait for the fire inspector to check the building. It takes *forever*!

We've kind of forgotten about the whole gargoyle thing—that is, until we hear the sound of those heavy flapping wings again.

The same ones Lucy and I heard on the way back to the dorm!

This time *two* shadows fly overhead and disappear into the night. Lucy and Melanie cling to me again, like somehow *I'M* going to save them.

"Heidi, I don't like this," Lucy whispers. She looks like she's about to cry. "I want to go *home*."

Okay, those are the *last* five words I want to hear from Lucy this weekend, but can I blame her? Everything has been pretty weird so far today, and definitely not how I wanted things to go either.

It's time to reassure Lucy.

"It'll be okay, Lucy. You'll see. We are going to have so much fun tomorrow at the carnival," I tell her.

But do I believe myself? I'm not really sure *anything* will be okay right now.

"Hey, did you see that?" shouts some kid from our dorm. "Something with *huge* wings just flew overhead!"

Mrs. Kettledrum claps her hands.

"It's nothing to worry about," she says. "Just some friendly neighborhood owls. Everyone, back to your rooms."

I try to catch Mrs. Kettledrum's eye to find out what's *really* going on, but she's too busy trying to figure out why the fire alarm went off. We all trudge back up the stairs to our rooms.

I'm pretty sure those shadows *weren't* owls. But could they really have been gargoyles?

At this late hour I can't exactly go check to see if the stone gargoyles are still sitting on their perches outside Crawford, so the best I can do is put the thought out of my head.

When we get back to the room, I scrub the toothpaste off the bathroom mirror. I still wonder if Melanie wrote it, but Lucy and I were the last ones in the bathroom when we were putting on our pj's.

Not to mention, Melanie would **never** willingly stick her fingers into toothpaste— even to scare us.

Lucy, Melanie, and I lock the window and the door. We even put a chair under the doorknob to make it extra secure.

"Heidi, is it okay if we sleep in your bed together?" Lucy asks.

I pull back the covers. "On a night like tonight, *definitely.*"

We hop into my bed, and then Melanie grabs her pillow and pushes her bed as close to mine as possible.

"I don't want to sleep on the other side of the room. It's way too far away!"

We keep the bedside lamp on and talk for a little while. The talk lightens our moods. Melanie leans on one elbow and looks up at us.

"So, Lucy, did you know Heidi snores?" she announces out of nowhere.

Lucy giggles, which is good, because maybe she's feeling more relaxed. Well, I'm *not*, but *whatever.*

"Heidi has *always* snored," Lucy teases.

Okay, that's enough Heidi bashing for me. I pick up my pillow and bonk Lucy with it.

"Well, Melanie *talks* in her sleep," I say defensively.

Melanie and Lucy laugh. "I'm okay with that," Melanie says. "So long as I don't say anything *weird*."

She puts on her pink silk sleeping mask and flops onto her pillow. "Okay, you two, I've already lost way too much beauty sleep tonight.

"*Night, night!* And don't let the gargoyles bite."

Lucy and I squeal and hide under the covers.

"That's not funny, Melanie!" Lucy scolds.

Melanie doesn't answer, because when Melanie decides to go to sleep, she goes right to sleep.

Lucy and I talk quietly to each other a little while longer.

"Your friends are really nice, Heidi, and you're so popular," she tells me. "Is your friend Sunny really that happy all the time? Doesn't she ever get mad or upset?"

I look up at my glow-in-the-dark stars, which are barely glowing, because my light is still on.

Hmmm, does Sunny ever get upset? Well, she got a little jealous when Mrs. Kettledrum asked me to do private magic lessons.

And then she got a little annoyed when I wouldn't stop talking about my crush on Hunter.

"Sure, she gets upset once in a while just like anyone else, like if she's worried about a bad grade or something," I say. "But most of the time she's really upbeat—just like her name."

My light flickers, and Lucy instantly shrieks.

Melanie groans. "Will you two be quiet? I'm *trying* to sleep," she scolds.

"The lights just flickered," I explain to her.

Melanie rolls onto her side and puts in earplugs. I set my head back onto my pillow.

"It's okay, LuLu. This is a really old building. Sometimes the lights flicker."

And this is partly true. It *is* an old building. The lights have never flickered before, but best not to mention this to Lucy tonight.

I look over at my friend.

"LuLu . . . ?" I ask, but she's sound asleep.

Oh no, I'm the *last* one awake.

I finally muster the courage to switch off the light.

The room goes dark, and when my eyes adjust, I swear I see two gargoyles out the window flying across the moon.

I hope that was just my imagination.

Luckily, I'm so tired, I can't even stay awake to be scared about it. The good thing is, when you're asleep, you no longer know what lurks in the dark.

CARNIVAL FUN?

The thought of haunted gargoyles disappears like dew before the morning sunshine.

How can anyone think of gargoyles on a gorgeous day like today? The sun is shining, the birds are chirping, and Lucy is still here!

All I can say is, the magical bracelets *must* be working.

And even better, I get to put on outfit number two: a baby-doll top and jeans. And Melanie already has on an adorable crocheted top with her white jeans.

"You both look SO cute," Lucy says longingly. "My outfit has zero pizzazz."

Ding! Melanie leaps into action.

She runs straight to her closet and pulls out a navy-and-white striped polo sweater with a relaxed, cropped fit. Needless to say, it's adorable.

"This is all you'll need to jazz up your outfit, Lucy. It'll go great with your cargo jeans," she says.

Lucy takes the top gratefully. I can tell she's a little surprised. She's never seen this nicer side of Melanie.

So, of course, we all fuss in front of the mirror so that our looks are just right for what is sure to be a perfect day.

Then we head to the Barn for breakfast with our families. I have a light cereal breakfast, because my plan today is to pig out on funnel cake and snow cones at the carnival.

Clink! Clink! Clink! Mrs. Kettledrum taps the side of her juice glass to get everyone's attention. "Parents, friends, and students—welcome to Carnival Day!" she announces. "The carnival will open after breakfast and will run all day. For those of you who would prefer to do something else, please enjoy our hiking trails or take out a paddleboat on the lake. Parents who have signed up for conferences will meet in Emma Crawford, the main building, at your set time.

"Have a wonderful day, and don't hesitate to talk to our carnival staff. They are the same people who were helping yesterday. Let's all have some FUN!"

Chairs scrape the floors, dishes rattle, and silverware clangs as everyone begins to clear their tables and head to the carnival.

Lucy and I race to the playing fields, where the carnival is set up. I've been watching the carnival come together over the last few days, and I can say with all confidence that it is paradise.

I notice a woman and a man standing in the middle of the carnival. The woman is taking notes, and the man is taking photos.

Eeeeeeee! I point them out to Lucy.

"Those two must be the reporters we heard were coming," I tell her.

Lucy and I walk past them with big cheesy smiles on our faces, hoping we'll be photographed.

We run through the mega balloon archway and are greeted by a tall post with lots of signs that point in different directions: GAMES THIS WAY, ATTRACTIONS THAT WAY, FOOD AND DRINKS OVER THERE, RESTROOMS ON EITHER END.

Little red-and-white striped tents are lined up everywhere—each tent houses a game, an activity, or a refreshment.

There's so much to do.

There are even two climbing walls that reach to the sky. And then there's a petting zoo with goats, pigs, chickens, rabbits, and pony rides. **I officially declare I'm *not* too old to visit the petting zoo.** Even the whir of the bouncy houses fills me with excitement.

But the biggest and *best* attraction is the massive House of Horrors. **There's nothing more fun than a good fake scare.** It's the real ones that undo me. After last night, I am all for remembering that the fun house is just that . . . fun.

I turn to Lucy. **"I want to do everything!"**

Lucy gives me a big hug, and we start running!

The first booth we come to is the Temporary Tattoo Booth. **We stop because of course we *have* to get one.**

They have tattoos of anything you could be interested in: sports, cool designs, letters to write messages, and everything in between. **Trying to figure out what you want stamped on your body is a BIG decision.**

I'm trying to concentrate when Lucy starts tapping my arm like a woodpecker.

"Who's *that*?" she whispers.

Lucy's pointing at Hunter and Isabelle, **and I remember that she was never properly introduced to them yesterday. They're headed our way.**

"Oh, that's Hunter," I say. "The boy I used to have a *mad* crush on—remember? **I used to call him Hunter McCutie.**"

Lucy looks back at the tattoos, so she doesn't get caught staring. "**He's so cute**," she says. "I had no idea!"

I nod. "Yup. And if you like him, get in line. *All* the girls like him. And the girl by his side is Isabelle. They're kind of a *thing*."

Isabelle and Hunter catch up to us, and I introduce Lucy.

"So, are you getting tattoos?" Isabelle asks.

I slide a temporary tattoo from a hook. It says, GOOD VIBES ONLY. It's perfect, since those are the only types of vibes I want this weekend. "I'm getting *this* one," I proclaim.

Lucy unhooks a heart tattoo. It says, BE HAPPY.

"Those are so cute! I want one," Isabelle says, flicking through the tattoos.

She picks a flaming baseball for Hunter and a flaming soccer ball for herself, which are perfect because Hunter and Isabelle are both amazing athletes.

We take turns sitting on stools to get the tattoos applied to our arms. Two upperclassmen are in charge of the applications. **And P.S., our tattoos look so cool!**

Hunter and Isabelle head to the Strike 'Em Out baseball game, where you have to pitch a baseball into a hole in a wooden umpire's glove.

That game is not for me *or* Lucy.

Next!

Besides, I know what *I'd* rather do. I pitch my idea to Lucy.

"Want to do the House of Horrors?" I ask. "If we go early in the day, it won't be as crowded."

Lucy frowns. "Will it be super-scary?"

I shake my head. "No, it'll be *silly* scary."

Lucy's still hesitant. And, after last night, who wouldn't be? But she's a good sport and agrees to go.

We jog to the House of Horrors, and I have to say that I am impressed.

It's not some run-down tent full of jangly skeletons and ghosts made from old sheets. This is the *real* deal. It actually looks like a long, sprawling abandoned house with broken windows. One window has a black cat with glowing red eyes, and from another window a ghostly face peers out at us. We hop into line.

We stop talking when we realize we're up next. The door into the house says ENTER IF YOU DARE!

Lucy tugs my shirt.

"We'll be *fine*," I whisper.

We enter a cobwebbed hallway. The floors actually creak when we walk on them—or is it a recording? A hand reaches out of a crack in the wall and grabs at us. We both scream, because *duh*, who wouldn't?

Somehow we make it to the first room in the house without turning back.

A neon sign over the door sizzles like a bug zapper and glows with the words THE HAUNTED KITCHEN. A fun soundtrack—*not scary at all*—plays in the background. However, in other parts of the house, I can hear super-scary sound effects, like thumping, clanking, howling, moaning, and screaming.

Eek.

Outside the Haunted Kitchen stands a menu board. Lucy and I read it and giggle at the offerings.

Two skeletons wearing blue dresses, aprons, and white caps welcome us.

"Greetings," they say. "We're the *skull*-ery maids, and we'll assist you on your tour of the Haunted Kitchen."

The skull-ery maids have skeleton masks on, so we can't see their real faces. I know they are faculty working at the carnival, but it's fun to pretend they are real skeletons. Even their arms, hands, and legs look like they're made of bones.

"Honored guests," one of them says, "the headless chef requires you to wear blindfolds because his appearance is, well, *alarming*. The chef *does* have a head, but since its severed, he keeps it on a cake stand."

Then the skull-ery maids tie blindfolds around our heads and guide us into the Haunted Kitchen.

"The headless chef is ready to tell you about his latest creations," one of the maids says.

Lucy yelps, "Heidi, stay *close!*"

I reach out and try to find Lucy's hand, but I can't with this blindfold on.

"I'm right here," I call to her.

Our guides stop walking, but they hold on to us so we don't fall or crash into anything. It's so weird not knowing exactly where Lucy is.

"**Welcome to the Haunted Kitchen!**" booms a creepy, melodramatic voice. I can't help but think it sounds a little like Mr. Craftwood's, but I can't be sure. "**I'm your host, the headless chef!**"

The chef cackles. Even though I know it's fake, to scare us, he still sounds creepy.

"Come in, come in," the headless chef begs. "I want to tell you about some of the delicious ingredients I use in my dishes! Over here is one of my favorite delicacies. These tender morsels are freshly boiled pigs' hearts. *Mm-wah!* Exquisite!"

Oh yuck! Get me out of here, I think. But it's too late. My guide holds my arm by the elbow and moves my hand into a bowl of boiled pigs' hearts.

"*Eeeeew!*" I cry, not even trying to disguise my displeasure.

I know it's just pretend, but the "pigs' hearts" feel exactly what I would imagine them to feel like—spongy, moist, and 100 percent disgusting.

I know the moment Lucy touches the pigs' hearts, because she screams—a response I've heard a lot since she arrived.

We continue our blindfolded waltz around the kitchen and touch a medley of creepy delicacies, eyeballs, teeth, fingers, fingernails, toes, and, of course, brains.

Cre-e-e-e-e-eak!

An oven door just squeaked open.

"My dear guests, you're in luck," the headless chef announces. "A fresh batch of my world-famous witches' fingers has just come out of the oven. Would anyone like to sample one?"

Having not eaten much breakfast, I, for one, am *starving*.

"Me!" I volunteer.

The headless chef laughs, and I feel like I'm going to be more like a victim of his freaky baked goods than a taste tester.

And I'm not gonna lie, I am a wee bit nervous.

"What a brave girl you are, my dear," he says. "I beg of you, please open your mouth."

I reluctantly open my mouth.

I pray it's something tastier than a pig's boiled heart.

The witch's finger enters my mouth.

I wince and bite down. *Mmmm.* It actually tastes super-yummy, like a shortbread cookie.

"This witch's finger is *spook-tacular*," I declare.

The headless chef laughs hideously, yet again.

"Oh, I *knew* you'd like it. I use only the freshest witch fingers!"

"Gross!" Lucy says. And she totally refuses to try a witch's finger.

After we're done in the Haunted Kitchen, we get to take off our blindfolds, wash our hands, and see everything we've touched or eaten.

The first thing I notice is that the headless chef *is* actually headless.

I'm pretty sure his *real* head is hidden inside his chef's jacket, which is very clever.

And his so-called severed head is, indeed, sitting on a cake stand with a chef's hat on top.

We study the tray of cookies, which actually look like a stereotypical witches' fingers. They're green cookies drizzled with blood-red icing.

On the counters are several plastic cauldrons. Each cauldron holds one of the nasty ingredients we touched. The pigs' hearts are boiled tomatoes. The brains are cooked macaroni. The eyeballs are peeled grapes. The toes are sausages. The teeth are popcorn kernels.

It's amazing how the fake ingredients feel like the real things when you're playing along.

The guides usher us into the next room and bid us farewell. **We don't have to wear blindfolds anymore. Phew!**

As we make our way through the rest of the House of Horrors, **Lucy clings so tightly to me, I feel like I'm wearing her.** It also makes walking a challenge, but we gradually move from room to room.

Corpses pop out of coffins.

Ghouls burst through doors.

Moaning ghosts drag chains and follow us.

Eek!

It's all fun until we get to the graveyard at the very end. To enter we have to walk through a stone arch. But what's really *freaky* is that there is a gargoyle on either side of the arch.

At first I wonder if these are the gargoyles from outside Crawford, but then I realize they can't be. These gargoyles have fangs! And their eyes glow like molten lava.

Normally this wouldn't scare me, but after last night this feels like my worst nightmare come true. Lucy feels the same way—maybe worse, if that's possible.

"*Hei-i-i-deee*, let's get out of here," she whispers.

The fear in her voice is *real*.

I want to get out of here too, but for some reason I keep walking, and Lucy is still attached to me.

A ghostly soundtrack with moans, wails, and howling wind fills us with more dread. Spirits rise, like mist, from the tombstones.

That does it for Lucy. She screams and drags me toward the exit.

And that's when we hear that awful sound of flapping of wings, like the ones we heard last night.

"Lucy! Watch out!" I warn.

Lucy looks up. Then we both fall to our knees as two gargoyles swoop down after us.

Oh no!

We're going to be carried away by the gruesome gargoyles!

We cover our heads to protect ourselves, but it's pointless—we're DOOMED.

Lucy and I scramble to our feet and then sprint through the haunted house, screaming at the top of our lungs.

I honestly don't think I have ever run so fast in my life. . . .

We burst through the door and into the daylight. Then we crumple into a petrified heap on the ground.

We both look back at the haunted house to see if the gargoyles are coming. But there's no sign of them—not yet anyway. Because I'm never sure if we've seen the last of them.

"Well, I don't know *why* we were so scared," I say, trying to reassure myself that everything is okay. "Because everything in there was *fake*—you know, just a bunch of props and phony-baloney."

But you know what else is creepy? I think.

It was a gorgeous sunny day when we walked into the House of Horrors.

And now it's totally overcast.

Just like THAT!

I'm feeling stormy vibes on so many levels. . . .

WHICH WITCH?!

There's only one way to handle fear.

Eat funnel cake!

When each of us is holding a plate of deliciousness sprinkled with sugar, Lucy and I feel better.

As we munch our treats, we scope out less hair-raising carnival games. That's when we spy Sunny and Annabelle. I wave them down.

"Who wants to take silly pictures in the photo booth?" I ask.

Then Sunny gives me something she's never given me before. A scowl.

She literally scowls!

I look to Annabelle for help. Annabelle just shrugs.

"I'd love to get a photo with you," Annabelle says.

Sunny still says nothing. "What's the matter, Sunny?" I ask.

She huffs at me.

"What *isn't* the matter, Heidi?" she replies. "For openers, I sat on somebody's caramel apple and there's a huge stain on my pants!"

Sunny turns around so we can see the spot. There's just a little mark on her jeans.

"You can barely see it," I tell her. "And you definitely won't see it in pictures."

But Sunny isn't listening to me. I can tell.

For some reason she's studying our outfits, and her face has disapproval written all over it.

"Why are you two so dressed up?" she asks me and Lucy. "Are you going to Cinderella's ball or something?"

Lucy and I look at each other like, *What in the world?*

"We just, um, wanted to look *nice*," Lucy stammers. I know it's because she's so surprised by Sunny's snarky tone. Sunny picks up on the uncertainty in Lucy's voice.

"What are *you* so nervous about, Lucy?" Sunny snaps. "You don't even *go* to this school!"

Okay, that does it.

Now *I'm* mad.

Nobody speaks to Lucy *or* me like that.

I'm about to set Sunny straight, when she turns her back on me and storms off.

One word: *rude!*

Annabelle rushes to Lucy's side. "I'm so sorry, Lucy. I don't know what's gotten into Sunny. She's been a total grump-a-saurus *all* morning."

Lucy looks away. She really didn't like getting barked at by Sunny. Then she turns back and looks at me.

"Well, Heidi, I guess you were *wrong* about Sunny," she says. "You told me she rarely gets into a bad mood. Well, with the way she just acted, you should call her *Stormy*."

I plant my hand on my hip because I'm really worked up.

I'm frazzled from the House of Horrors.

I'm sick about Lucy not having a good time.

I'm furious at Sunny for acting out of line.

And I'm mad at Lucy for implying that I lied about Sunny's character.

"I *was* telling the truth, Lucy," I say. "This is the first time I've **EVER** seen Sunny act like this!"

Annabelle tries to calm us down. "Come on, you two. Don't let Sunny's bad mood ruin our day. She'll come around. **You'll see.** Why don't we go play a game?"

Lucy and I reluctantly follow Annabelle. None of us say a word until Annabelle spies her little brother, Charlie. He's with *my* little brother, Henry, and **Henry looks relieved to see us.**

"Hey, would you mind if I take off, Annabelle?" Henry asks. "I want to meet some of the older boys at the House of Horrors."

Annabelle puts an arm around her little brother, who has an empty cotton candy holder in his hand. Annabelle takes the paper cone from her brother and throws it away.

"No problem, Henry. Thanks for watching him!" she says.

Lucy and I toss the rest of our funnel cakes into the trash. After our encounter with Sunny, we've both lost our appetites.

"I want to play this *witch* game," Charlie demands as he leads us over to one of the booths.

I feel a little better when I check out the game. **It looks really fun.**

It's called Witch's Brew. A witch hovers over a smoking cauldron. **It's not a *real* witch. It's just another faculty member dressed up. And the smoke is just a fog machine.**

To play, you have to throw beanbag frogs and bats into the cauldron. The witch can block the beanbags with her broom. If you get three of a kind into the cauldron, you win a prize.

It's not as easy as it looks, because there are only three round openings in the cauldron, but there are stuffed-animal prizes, including a really cute panda.

"Sure," Annabelle says. "Let's play!"

We take turns throwing bats and frogs into the cauldron. Lucy really wants to win the panda. But like I said, it's harder than it looks, and none of us win anything.

This makes Charlie mad.

"This game is awful!" he cries. "I have a *better* game. Let's play Which Witch? I'll go *first*."

Then Charlie points his finger at his sister.

"You're a WITCH!" he yells.

Then Charlie turns around and points at me. "And *you're* a witch!"

And then he points at Sunny, who's standing at the booth across from us. "And she's a witch TOO!"

Then Charlie turns back around and points at Lucy. "But you're NOT a witch—are you?"

The color has completely drained from Annabelle's face.

"CHARLIE!" she shouts. "What on earth has gotten into you?"

Annabelle turns to Lucy and me. "I'm so sorry. Charlie's very into witches and wizards lately. Don't pay any attention to him."

Charlie's face turns red with rage. He balls his hands into fists and looks at Lucy.

"Don't listen to her, because she's LYING," he shouts. "My sister IS a witch!

"She has a treasure chest full of gems and crystals in her room, and she uses them for spells. **If you don't believe me, go see for yourself.**"

No sooner does Charlie finish his rant than thunder booms overhead.

I'm frozen with fear.

Angry Charlie runs off to find his mother.

Thank goodness!

And honestly I can't blame him for being mad. **He *was* telling the truth, but he also has to learn how to keep secrets.**

As I'm thinking all this, **suddenly the one thing I've always feared *happens*. Lucy asks me the million-dollar question. . . .**

"Heidi? Are you a . . . *witch*?"

Her face is as serious as I've ever seen it.

Annabelle, who's standing behind Lucy, shakes her head and waves her hands frantically.

And still, I hesitate.

How can I lie to my best friend's face?

Is it time to level with Lucy?

Help! I think I'm caving!

I look at Lucy's eyes, which are fiercely locked on mine, and then back at Annabelle, who is mouthing the words *Don't do it* over and over.

"Heidi, why are you hesitating? Is it true?" Lucy asks.

Then she turns around to see what I'm looking at. "And why are you looking at Annabelle?"

I take a huge breath. *No, I'm not ready for this moment.* I decide, then and there, to once again keep this secret to myself.

Phew! Maybe someday I'll tell Lucy, but today will *not* be the day.

"No, Lucy," I say. "Of course I'm not a witch! That's absolutely ridiculous! Charlie is just a little kid with a wild imagination. You know how kids like to make up stories . . . and we *were* playing a witch game after all."

Annabelle puts her hand over her heart and sighs. Lucy looks relieved.

"Well, I didn't *think* you'd keep something like that from me, Heidi, but Charlie did make me wonder," Lucy admits.

"Remember how I used to always say you're *magical*?" She laughs for thinking this might've actually been true. "And not to mention, the name of your school *is Brooms*field Academy, you know, like a witch's broom. I know that must sound a little far-fetched. . . ."

Annabelle and I double over with fake laughter. But I really *hate* all this lying. It makes me feel not-so-great.

"Well, I'd better go," Annabelle says. "I have to make sure somebody's watching Charlie."

So, Lucy and I are alone again, though Lucy might as well be by herself, because I'm all caught up in my own thoughts.

I mean, why is Sunny acting the opposite of herself?

And how come Charlie spilled the beans on the witches he knows?

And why are the clouds getting so much darker?

Is something going *really* wrong?

I guess there's only *one* thing to do.

Act normal.

"So, LuLu, you want to get pics of the two of us?" I ask.

Lucy likes this idea, so we head back to the photo booth. We dig around in the prop box. I put on a blond wig made of yarn. Lucy puts on giant glasses and a top hat. Then we both pile on feathered boas. I grab a little sign on a stick that says BFFS. Yup, that's us! We fling back the curtain and squish next to each other on the bench inside.

Poof!

The flash goes off. Lucy and I giggle and pose.

When the camera stops flashing, we tumble out of the photo booth, laughing and falling all over each other.

And guess who sees us as we're putting away our props?

Nick! Yes, *my* Nick, and his best friend, Max.

"What's going on?" Max asks. We're laughing too hard to answer, so he answers for us. "Well, Nick and I wanted to hang out with you, but clearly you should hang out with *your* friends, and we'll hang out with *ours.*"

And just like that, they walk off.

What was that about? I wonder. It seems like everyone's filters are off. And it's not just my friends. The grown-ups seem to be losing it too.

While Lucy and I are waiting for our pics to develop, I overhear Isabelle's mom blabbing to everyone how her daughter's a princess—the very thing Isabelle and her family want to keep secret.

And if that's not weird enough, my own mother has been telling everyone how I'm the *best* new student at Broomsfield. *Mom, I know you're proud of me, but what are you DOING?* I think.

Well, at least she didn't say I was the best *witch*, but still, it's mortifying. And it's also totally out of character for my mother.

"Heidi, look!" Lucy cries. "Melanie's dog is in a fight with another dog!"

Sure enough, Lola and Momo are in a brawl. And Melanie doesn't even seem to notice! Instead she walks up to me and hangs on my shoulder again.

"Heidi, I saw what just happened between you and Nick's friend Max, and I want you to know, I'm here for you," she says.

I try to shrug her off, but it's no use. Melanie wraps her arms around me and gives me a huge bear hug.

"I *really* am here for you, Heidi, because that's what best friends do!" she gushes on. "And by the way, have I ever told you, you're the coolest, most fashionable friend a girl could ever have? You're seriously my very best friend EVER."

And that's when thunder explodes across the sky.

Baboom!

BOOOM!

BOOOM!

BOOM!

I hear Lucy yell. But it's a different kind of yell from what I've been hearing all day. It's a happy kind of yell, like when you open up a birthday present and it's exactly what you wanted.

"Heidi! Look at me!" Lucy shouts.

I turn around and Lucy is . . . tall.

Why is this happening?
I think.

Then I remember Lucy saying, *I would love to be really tall, but both my parents are short, so I guess it's not going to happen.*

Could this have anything to do with all the magical and non-magical energy mixing today?

It must!

Lucy runs away from me, happily. She wants everyone to see the new tall Lucy.

She's laughing and waving her arms over her head like, *Look at me!*

As I watch her race away, I notice something sparkling on the ground.

It's a VISITOR'S BRACELET!

I gasp and pick it up. Is it Lucy's?

Is this the reason everything's going haywire? Surely all this can't have been caused by one bracelet. Or can it?

I want to run after Lucy, but for some reason I can't. That's because something strange is happening to *ME*.

I don't know why, but I suddenly feel like doing something reckless.

I can't seem to stop this feeling.

I fixate on Nick because I just overheard him say he was thirsty.

"Hey, Nick!" I shout. "Are you *really* thirsty?"

He looks puzzled, but nods, because he *is* thirsty.

"Okay, then watch THIS!" I take a deep breath and shout:

ROSES ARE RED, BUBBLE GUM IS PINK.
GIVE ME SOMETHING FOR NICK TO DRINK!

Sha-zing! A juice box magically appears in my hand.

I smile and toss it to Nick.

"Wow, Heidi! How did you *do* that?" he asks. He looks totally bewildered.

But before I can answer, Isabelle shows up out of nowhere and grabs me by the arm.

"Not another word out of you," she whispers. Then she turns to Nick and makes a joke of my magic.

"Just call her Heidi Houdini," Isabelle says. "My uncle taught her that trick. He's a magician. Would you please excuse us?"

Isabelle drags me away from the crowd.

"Heidi, are you okay?" she asks.

I rub my head.

The feeling of wanting to do something reckless has faded, and I feel more like my normal self.

"Whoa, I'm not sure what came over me. I kind of lost it back there," I tell her.

Isabelle grabs me by the shoulders and shakes me. "We can't keep giving in to these feelings! Something really weird has been going on. We have to hold it together, Heidi! It's like everyone's wires are getting crossed."

I gasp, because those are the exact words Mrs. Kettledrum used when she was teaching us about auras.

I wonder how many enchanted bracelets are missing.

"Isabelle, I'm totally fine," I say. "Now that I know what's going on, I can resist the urge to do magic if it comes again."

Isabelle gives me a hug. "Good. I have to go keep an eye on my mom. Let's meet up later."

Isabelle runs off. At the same time, a sudden gust of wind blows the long blond braids right out of the prop box. I watch the yarn wig swirl into the wind.

I worry that **things are about to get *really* hairy. . . .**

TAKE THE CAKE!

Lightning zigzags across the sky.

Thunder crackles and booms.

Help! I have to get inside!

But where's Lucy? And where's Mrs. Kettledrum?

I turn every which way, looking for my friend and my teacher.

Rain pelts my cheeks. Then it begins to pour, and every inch of me is drenched.

Students and visitors run every which way seeking cover from the rain.

I stop and look at the sky. **The clouds are so dark and low, it practically looks like night.**

And then I notice, not only is it pouring but **it's also raining stuffed animals.**

A tornado of prizes swirls around in the air.

Oh, and there's the stuffed panda Lucy wanted. I *have* to get it for her!

It's the least I can do.

As I chase the panda, other stuffed animals cartwheel past me like tumbleweeds. *I'm coming to get you, Mr. Panda Bear!* I think.

The panda flops onto the grass, and I lunge for it. I hug the panda close and run as fast as I can toward the Barn, ducking the flying debris.

Thunder rumbles. It sounds like a million bowling balls getting knocked down at the same time. And birds screech overhead.

Uh-oh! *Those are not birds,* I think. ***They're gargoyles!***

I cover my head with the panda and keep running.

When I near the Barn, I see parents and kids screaming and shouting as they run to the safety of the cafeteria.

There's a logjam of people at the entrance. People cover their heads with anything they can find—jackets, signs, their arms—to protect themselves.

I race to the back entrance. There's still no sign of Lucy *or* Mrs. Kettledrum.

And the gargoyles are right over my head!

But at this moment the gargoyles are the least of my worries. I leave them outside and blaze down the hall and into the cafeteria.

The first thing I see is Henry and Charlie laughing hysterically. I rush up to them. "Are you two okay?" I ask.

Charlie answers first. *"Oui, Heidi. Je vais bien!"* I do a double take. "Charlie . . . are you speaking FRENCH?" I ask.

Then I turn to Henry, who is still laughing. "Henry, SAY SOMETHING!" I demand.

"'Ello!" Henry says cheerfully. "Did you hear my mate's funny accent?" he asks. "Listen to him. I'm gobsmacked!"

Oh no! Henry has Charlie's British accent, and Charlie is speaking French!

Where is Mrs. Kettledrum? We need her help, and fast.

Everything is in chaos.

The next odd thing I see is Caleb Kim's little sister standing on a chair.

"Did you know my brother can turn food into anything he wants?" she tells the crowd.

Oh no! What is she DOING? I think. Caleb once did a spell in class where he turned a lemon into a banana. Now his sister is blabbing about his wizard skills to everyone.

Oh please, someone make her STO-O-O-O-O-OP!

But this time Caleb isn't turning one kind of food into another kind.

He's somehow made all the food in the cafeteria *come to life.*

And the food is on the move.

Loaves of bread launch from their trays and sail through the air, like squishy projectiles.

Bonk! Biff! Boof! Bam!

The loaves bash people in the head, the back, the stomach—you name it.

Boxes of cereal lift off from the cereal station. In midair the packages open all by themselves! They tip like teapots and shake cereal all over the crowd. It's showering cornflakes, raisins, and granola.

Lemon meringue pies slide from the dessert station and look for targets.

Splat! Sploof! Smack! Whap!

Whipped cream drips from the faces of students, parents—even faculty.

If this wasn't so frightening, it might actually be funny.

SMACK!

"Oh no! I've been HIT!" But not by a pie. It's a chicken nugget! It pings off the side of my head.

My hair is wet, greasy, and speckled with chicken nugget breading.

One word: *gross!*

Even worse, I finally spot Lucy.

She's in a corner of the cafeteria, posing like a model.

She's still seven feet tall and loving every minute of it.

I spot one of the reporters talking to her.

"I don't know how it happened," Lucy is saying.

"One minute I was short, and the next I'm **super-tall**." She giggles.

"I've heard of growth spurts, but I never dreamed it could be like this." She waves her hand over the reporter's head. "How tall are you? Five foot six, five foot seven? Look how much taller I am than you!"

Suddenly a bunch of kids are by the windows.

"Hey, look, it's SNOWING!" one yells.

Several of the students cheer. A few of them race outside to have a snowball fight.

"Henri! Regardez! Il neige!" Charlie says, pointing to the window. I don't speak French, but I'm pretty certain Charlie said it was snowing.

Henry looks out the window. "I say! Charlie, I do believe it's snowing," Henry answers.

Just as I'm trying to figure out what to do next, Melanie rushes over to me and takes my hand. "Heidi, come outside and make snow angels with me," she says.

I say the first thing that comes into my head.

"Melanie, WHY?"

Melanie laughs. "Because you're my BFF, silly! And that's the kind of thing best friends do together."

"Melanie, I'm kind of in the middle of something," I tell her. "Maybe later."

"Okay, buddy. But hurry up. It won't be nearly as much fun without you," Melanie says, and gives me a quick hug.

Then I spot one of my REAL BFFs, Sunny. But Sunny is still looking stormy.

"Sunny? Are you okay?" I ask.

Sunny glares at me.

"Do I LOOK okay?" she snarls. "I was just saying something fishy was going on, and then THIS happens."

Sunny has an entire fish stuck on her T-shirt.

I can't help it. I giggle.

"You think this is FUNNY?" Sunny yells.

"Sunny, come ON! You're not the only one who's a mess.

"Look, I have chicken-nugget breading in my hair. You say something's fishy and **you get smacked with a fish.**

"It's *a little* funny."

"**Not to ME it isn't,**" Sunny says, and stomps off.

Then, thankfully, I spy Mrs. Kettledrum on the other side of the cafeteria.

We're all saved!

At least I *hope* we're saved.

Mrs. Kettledrum has her hands in front of her face to block the onslaught of food. Her mouth is locked in the *Oh!* position.

I have to get to her.

I hold Lucy's panda in one hand and grab a food tray with the other. I hold the tray in front of me like a shield, and run toward Mrs. Kettledrum.

I deflect pink doughnuts, mashed potatoes, and a whole loaf of honey-wheat bread.

Squoosh! Pow! Splat!

"It's a losing battle!" a cafeteria worker shouts.

And it does seem hopeless, **but this is no time to give in!**

This is easy to say **until you're pursued by a bottle of ketchup—under its own power.**

Help!

The bottle squeezes itself and squirts ketchup all over the back of my head.

It drips down my neck.

Yuck!

But somehow I've made it to Mrs. Kettledrum.

She grabs me by the hand.

"I'm so glad to see you, Heidi," she says, pulling me along.

Cornflakes fall from her hair as we rush out of the cafeteria.

We run into the kitchen, until we're safe behind two doors.

Ahhhh, it's so quiet and peaceful in here.

Mrs. Kettledrum wipes the dew of concern—and soda—from her brow.

"Oh, Heidi, my worst fears for the weekend have come to pass," she says.

"We found several visitor bracelets in the House of Horrors kitchen.

"Guests lost their bracelets when they plunged their hands into the headless chef's slimy ingredients.

"And, without the bracelets, the magical and non-magical auras have created all this hullabaloo.

"The faculty and staff are restoring bracelets to all those who've lost them."

I knew this had something to do with the bracelets, I think.

I wonder just how many guests lost their bracelets.

It has to be more than several, considering what has happened.

"So how are we going to calm everyone down, Mrs. Kettledrum?" I ask. "**Things are completely out of control!**"

Mrs. Kettledrum pulls out her wand.

"Listen closely, Heidi. **I have a plan,**" she begins.

"First I'm going to go back out there and reverse Caleb's spells."

Mrs. Kettledrum runs into the cafeteria, and with a flick of her wrist, **all the food that was flying through the air flies back to where it came from.**

It's like Mrs. Kettledrum just hit the rewind button on all the food.

Phew!

"We'll go to the gym, **and I'll put an emergency forgetting spell** on all the cakes and refreshments," Mrs. Kettledrum continues as she returns to the kitchen.

"Once we have bracelets on all the guests again, we'll invite everyone into the gym.

"As soon as everyone partakes in the refreshments, **our guests and non-magical students and staff will forget about anything magical that has happened to them over the weekend.**

"The students and teachers in the School of Magic will keep their memories **so we can think of how to avoid another situation like this** at the next Broomsfield Academy Friends and Family Weekend.

"And then we'll tell everyone that due to bad weather, we'll have to cut the weekend's festivities short.

"If all goes well, all the guests will be out of here in just a few hours."

As much as I hate to see my parents, Henry, and Lucy leave, Mrs. Kettledrum's plan makes me feel better already.

Mrs. Kettledrum and I run to the gym. It looks completely untouched from the disaster that's happening everywhere else on campus. All the decorations that Melanie, Sunny, Annabelle, and I put up the other day are still in perfect condition. I'm about to ask her what I can do to help, when she raises her wand over the refreshments and chants a spell.

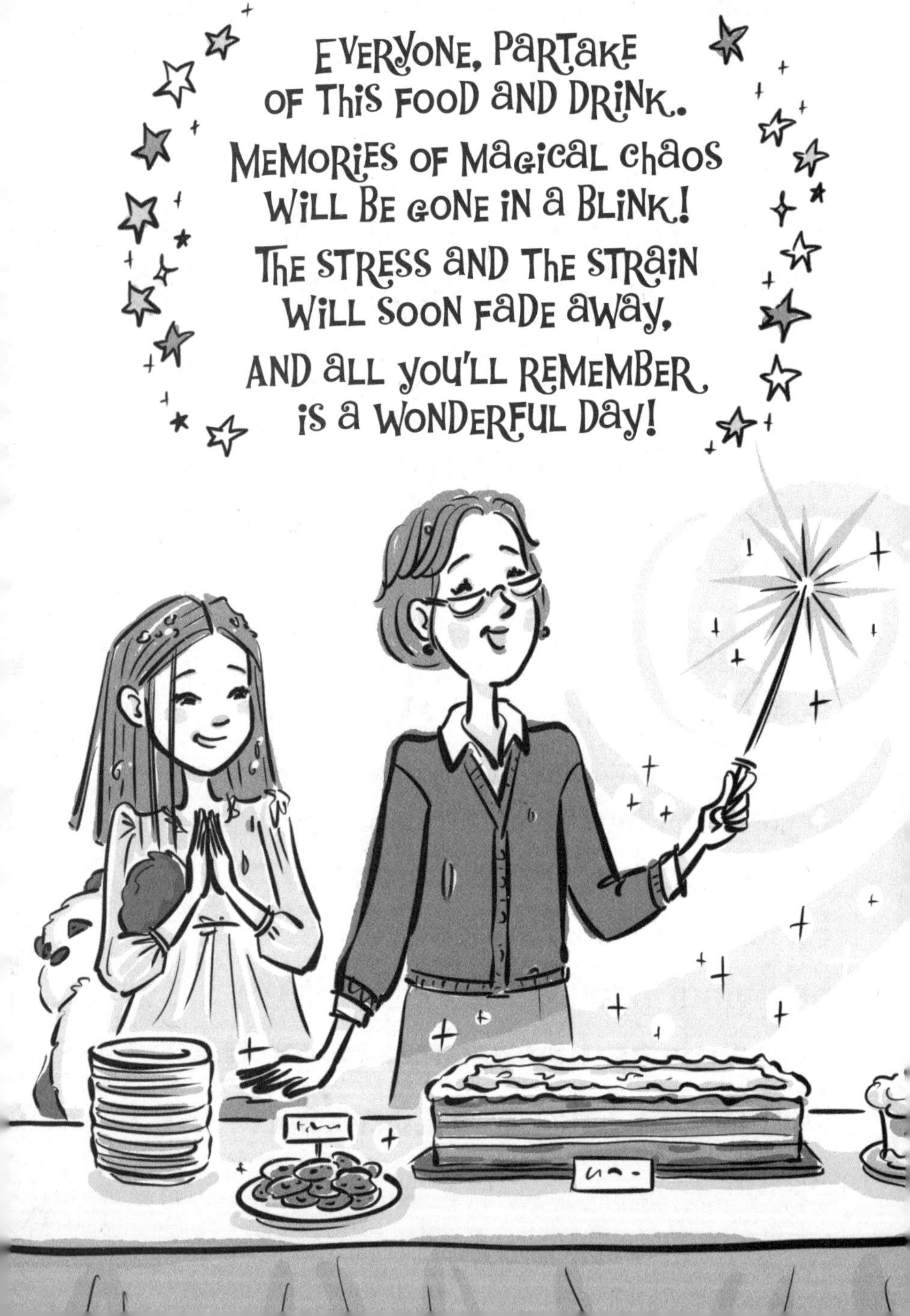

Poof!

Sparkles shower over both tables.

Mrs. Kettledrum and I sigh with relief.

"Well, that should do it, Heidi.

"Now I'm going to run back to the Barn and usher the guests into the gym. Your job will be to offer cake and drinks to everyone.

"Just make sure they eat or drink something. Even just a sip of water will relieve them of their memories of this afternoon."

Mrs. Kettledrum looks at my appearance.

I'm pretty sure I make the gargoyles look attractive.

"Let's tidy you up," she says.

Whoosh!

She waves her wand over me, and I suddenly feel showered, refreshed, and ready to go.

Even the stuffed panda looks like new.

Mrs. Kettledrum spruces herself up as well.

Did I mention how much I love magic?

Mrs. Kettledrum scurries from the gym.

I use a bit of magic to perfectly slice the cake and slide pieces onto plates.

I can't help but think about some of the out-of-this-world things that have gone on over the last two days.

This Friends and Family Weekend seems even wackier than the one three years ago.

The *Broomsfield Academy Gazette* article never said anything about **flying gargoyles or magical food fights.**

One word: *puzzling.*

Soon the students and guests begin to file into the gym. Everyone is still wet and bewildered, **but at least all the guests have on their bracelets.**

People line up for cake, and I pass out plates to keep up with the rush.

Mrs. Kettledrum switches on a microphone.

"Attention, everyone! This afternoon's forecast calls for more unstable weather," she announces. "We feel it's best to cut the weekend festivities short in order for everyone to travel home safely.

"Please help yourself to refreshments before we send you on your way. And thank you all again for coming!"

Everyone eagerly accepts the cake and refreshments.

I see my friends in line, and it's as if nothing ever happened.

They all look wonderful.

Their clothes are spotless, and everyone is clean and neat.

I can hear Sunny laughing.

Yay! Sunny is back to being Sunny!

I see the reporter and photographer eating big slices of cake.

Phew! We don't have to worry about anything out of the ordinary being reported about this weekend.

Even Lola and Momo are buddies again.

Then I see Nick and Max.

Uh-oh. I bite my lip and wish I could run away, **because I'm pretty certain Nick doesn't like me anymore.**

"Hey, Heidi," he says. "So bummed we didn't get to hang out today. I was really looking forward to that."

Max raises his water to me.

"I'm sorry too," he says. "You seem really cool, Heidi, and so does your friend Lucy."

Well, well! The food-and-drink spell is *definitely* working. Nobody seems to remember any of the chaos of today.

The photographer takes a photo of Mrs. Kettledrum and Momo. Then Mrs. Kettledrum and the reporter enjoy some cake and coffee. "Another **perfect Friends and Family Weekend at Broomsfield,**" I hear the reporter say.

Suddenly I realize, **what about Lucy?**

Where is she?

I hope she's not mad at me.

And *is* she still *tall?* I wonder.

"Hey, have either of you seen Lucy?" I ask Nick and Max.

Both boys shake their heads. But **all my worries are forgotten when I spot Lucy. She's sipping from an enchanted bottle of water** and finishing up a piece of cake.

She gets up to toss out her plate and starts walking toward me, and she's smiling.

She's my Lucy again!

My wonderful, beautiful, *short* friend!

One word: YAY!

"Oh, Heidi," she says, sounding like herself. "I had the *best* time at your school. I'm so sad we have to leave early, but maybe I can come again next year?"

Wha-a-a-a-a-t?

I almost fall over. Lucy actually WANTS to come back?

Wow, this is the best news ever! I grab a slice of cake and a cup of lemonade for myself.

"Yes! Let's go find a table to sit at—*alone*!" I say. This is the perfect time to give Lucy the panda I got her. "Lucy, do you mind bringing my cake with you? I have to grab something."

She nods and walks ahead.

While Lucy searches for a quiet corner of the room, I run back to the snack table where I hid her panda. As soon as I sit down, I give Lucy the panda **and spill my heart out to her.**

"LuLu, I want you to know that **nothing can *ever* come between us. We have a friendship like no other.** And even though I have new friends, I want you to know how special you are to me. **We have something none of my new friends will *ever* have, and that was our *whole* childhood together. Nobody can take that away from us.**

"Our friendship is built on the rock of all friendships!"

Lucy's face lights up.

"Oh, Heidi, I feel exactly the same way.

"I have to admit, when I first arrived yesterday, I was super-jealous of all your new friends—especially Melanie and Sunny, but I'm not jealous anymore.

"I know, in my heart, we're always going to be close no matter what. We are one hundred percent and always best friends forever!"

I hold up my pinky.

"Pinky promise to stay best friends?" I ask—just like we used to say when we were little.

Lucy links her pinky with mine. "Pinky promise."

Lucy goes over to get some lemonade. I'm sitting by myself happily eating cake when Isabelle and Hunter come walking toward me, looking embarrassed.

Hunter nudges Isabelle. "Go on," he says. "You go first."

Isabelle's face turns red. "I'm the one who sent over that s'more last night," she says.

I am stunned.

"You, Isabelle? WHY?" I ask.

"That was SO risky. Anyone who isn't magical could have seen the plate hovering. Then what would have happened?

"Why would you do that?"

"I don't know, Heidi," Isabelle replies. "It seemed like something awesome with magic that you would do, and I just thought it would be cool, I guess?

"I really don't understand why I did a lot of the things I did this weekend."

Hunter is still standing there, looking even more embarrassed as he confesses, "Also, we were the ones who magically wrote on your mirror with toothpaste."

I can't believe what I'm hearing.

"You two? That was so scary. So not cool. Are those the sort of pranks you two like to play on each other?"

Hunter shuffles his feet. "At the time we thought it would be funny to write something on your mirror. Just a silly prank."

"We're really sorry, Heidi," Isabelle says. "I hope you can forgive us."

Hunter has a baffled look on his face. "I honestly don't even know why we did it," he says. "I'm not a prankster. It's like something just came over me."

And then it hits me why Isabelle and Hunter acted so differently last night. *It was because of the magical energy in the air.*

Disaster was already brewing yesterday evening.

I let out a deep breath.

As I now know, when magic goes haywire, very strange things can happen. I smile at Hunter and Isabelle. "Let's put this behind us," I say. "You are forgiven."

Hunter lets out an even deeper breath.

"Thank you so much, Heidi."

"And it'll never happen again," adds Isabelle. "Since there has never been and never will be as weird a weekend as this one."

As Hunter and Isabelle walk away, Lucy returns. And right behind her are Charlie and Henry.

Henry snatches a piece of my cake with his fingers. "Henry, that's disgusting!" I say. I push the cake toward him. "You can have the rest of it."

"Gee, thanks! There are no more pieces up front," Henry says, and grabs my plate.

"Hey, Heidi, guess what? Charlie and I are good buddies now. I'm going to ask Mom and Dad if the next time they visit America, Charlie can stay at our house."

"I'm delighted," Charlie says. "And maybe Henry can come visit us in London sometime."

"That sounds great," I tell them. I'm just relieved that Charlie has stopped speaking French and Henry has lost his British accent.

I look up and spot Sunny and Annabelle waving at us from across the room. I motion for them to come over.

The minute they sit down, I can tell all is well with Sunny. Her aura is back to normal. She is her usual sunny self, smiling her beautiful smile at us.

"Hi, Heidi. Hi, Lucy," she says. "I'm so sorry I was so grumpy all day. I don't know why I was cranky. But I feel much better."

And of course Sunny *does* know why she was uncharacteristically cranky, but she keeps it hush in front of Lucy and throws me a wink.

She gives Lucy a hug. "I hope you come for another visit soon," she says. "I would love to hang out with you and get to know you better."

Lucy seems thrilled. "Same here," she says, beaming at Sunny.

I run through a quick checklist in my brain.

Is everything really back to normal? I think.

Charlie and Henry? Check.

Lucy? Check.

Sunny? Check.

The only one I'm not certain of is Melanie.

I quickly scan the room, but Melanie is nowhere to be found.

✧ ✧ ✧

My dad pulls the car around, and I help Lucy get her stuff from my room.

I say goodbye to my family.

Then Lucy and I have a huge hugfest.

"I had a great time, Heidi," she says. "But I still don't like those gargoyles. I don't know why, but I just don't."

I turn around and look at those statues. They seem to be staying put again.

Good, gargoyles!

"Me either," I say as Lucy climbs into the back seat with Henry. "See you at Thanksgiving!"

I watch them drive away, waving until I can't see the car anymore. Then I head back to my room.

I change into something comfy and sprawl across my bed. I think about all the out-of-this-world things that happened over the weekend.

As wacky as everything was, I'm sad it's over.

I miss Lucy already.

I wish I could tell her that for a little while **she was seven feet tall!**

I sigh.

Oh well.

Maybe someday, I think.

Just then Melanie flounces into the room.

I hold my breath for a minute.

Is she going to call me "buddy" again and hug me?

I shouldn't have worried.

She looks me up and down. "Well, Heidi, I guess now that everyone's gone, you're just going back to your old messy ways."

She shakes her head at me. "Look at that wrinkled shirt. And did you even comb your hair today? It looks like a mop on your head!"

I touch the top of my head and smile.

Melanie? Check, I think.

Everything and everyone are back to normal again.

I can only wonder what my next adventure at Broomsfield Academy will be!

DON'T MISS THE NEXT BOOK IN THE SERIES!

MIDDLE SCHOOL AND OTHER DISASTERS

Worst Wish Ever!

HERE'S A SNEAK PEEK!

THAT'S SHOW BIZ

Consider me old school when it comes to sending greeting cards.

I mean, seriously, does anyone other than me still send cards in the mail?

Well, I love to do it! And I found a cute one at the bookstore today. It has a bunch of turkeys driving in an old-fashioned station wagon. It's totally ridiculous and I think Lucy will love it.

I grab a pen with brown ink and fill the blank space inside.

Hey, Lulu!
How are YOU?! MISS you fiercely!

Guess what? I'll be home a week from TOMORROW for Thanksgiving! *Eeeee!*

Can you believe it? I'm SO excited to see you! And we have to have *at least* one sleepover while I'm home. We also have to do all the things we haven't gotten to do lately, like paint pottery, make new friendship bracelets, go shopping, and bake chocolate chip cookies!

Can you tell I'm a little excited? Well, I AM! And I'm begging you to reserve *all* your spare time for *me*!

No other friends allowed, except maybe Bruce ... oh, and Melanie really wants to hang with us too. But WE come first.

Okay, gotta go!
Gobble, gobble and all that jazz!
Heidi Kins

P.S. Love ya!
Hearts everywhere!

I seal my envelope and send it magically, of course, because it positively *has* to get there before I do!

Then I whiz out the door and down the steps of my dorm. The sun warms my back and the leaves crunch underfoot as I walk down the path to the Barn.

Even though I'm excited to go home for Thanksgiving, I'm a little sad to leave too. Every day at Broomsfield Academy has been really amazing so far, minus a few little missteps.

Okay, maybe some major flub-ups.

But, hey, I've gone a *whole* week without a single magical disaster. That's a record for me!

And I'm not mad about my mistakes either, because according to my aunt Trudy, *You should never fear failure,* for that's how you learn.

And I've learned *a ton*!

And hopefully, one day, all these lessons will pay off. But for now, I am happy learning magic right where I am.

I'm even a pro at staying calm through my magic mishaps—that's because I've been practicing my daily meditation. I even meditated before I wrote to Lucy today. I know that quiet thoughts equal better magic, and better magic means becoming a better witch— and possibly even a phenomenal witch!

Abracadabra to that!

As I walk along, I hear another person's voice inside my head.

I'm serious!

Hearing voices is a totally normal occurrence for me. Being able to read minds is my gift as a witch. And what's more, I *know* who this voice belongs to.

I stop and turn around to see if I'm right, and there she is, my favorite teacher, Mrs. Kettledrum! And she's walking my favorite dog, Momo, and just asked me to slow down for a chat. I happily oblige!

"Hi, Mrs. Kettledrum!" I sing. Then I drop to my knees and smoosh my face against Momo's. Momo wags her plump little Corgi body and licks my cheeks. One word: *slobberrific!*

We're total buds.

"I must say, Heidi, your mind-reading skills have really improved," Mrs. Kettledrum says.

"You heard me without seeing me—that's a first."

I hop back to my feet. Wow, she's *right*! I *did* read her mind without seeing her first. I really *must* be getting better at this!

That said, I'm still pretty much a beginner at mind reading, but I'll take the compliment.

"Thank you, Mrs. K! I'm getting better at my meditation too. I've been practicing every day and I feel more focused and peaceful in everything I do."

Mrs. Kettledrum smiles that warm, approving smile that feels as good as the sun on my face. This lovely feeling passes as my teacher's eyebrows suddenly jump, like she just remembered something.

"Heidi," she says in a more serious tone, "have

you been studying for my potions quiz and your magical wishes exam yet? Potions is tomorrow and your magical wishes exam is at the end of this week."

Her question puts me on the spot and I fiddle with one of the straps on my backpack. I know she wants me to do well in all my studies—not just in her spells and potions class. And even though Mrs. Kettledrum gives me private advanced magic lessons, she still questions my study habits.

"Um, not y-yet," I stammer. "But *don't worry*, I'm on it!" I say, sticking two thumbs up to reassure her.

Mrs. Kettledrum lifts her foot out of the dog leash, which Momo had looped around one of her legs. "I'm sure you'll do well, Heidi," she says. "Just use your time wisely! There are only so many minutes in a day!"

No offense to teachers, including beloved ones like Mrs. Kettledrum, but why do they always state the obvious? Of course I'm going to study.

Duh, duh, and double duh!

Oh well. I give Mrs. Kettledrum a courteous "Thank you" and an "Of course, I will." Then I bend down and pet Momo between the ears one more time and wave goodbye.

Yippy! It's lunchtime! I think to myself as I skip down the path. And this week, lunchtime means one wonderful, fantabulous thing.

I get to see my crush, Nick! *Woo!*

Nick Lee and I have been in a "flirtationship" for a few weeks. He's smart, funny, cuter-than-cute, and oh-so-sweet!

And to top it off, we're actually at the *SAME* cafeteria table this week. This is the first time we've ever been assigned to the same table.

One word: YES!!!

My stomach growls the moment I step into the cafeteria and breathe in that saucy, spicy smell, with a hint of baking bread.

My tray clatters as I set it on the counter. Today's choices are grilled chicken sandwiches with macaroni salad, and veggie burgers with sweet potato mash. I go for the veggie burger. The server nestles the veggie burger on a bun and slides it onto my plate. Another server slops sweet potato mash on the side. I pour myself some ice water and head to my table.

Sunny and Annabelle wave madly, like I'm some long-lost friend. This week they're at the table next to mine.

Oh geez, they're wiggling their eyebrows and making super-silly faces at me.

Aagh!

Why do they have to act SO goofy when Nick is around?

I guess since I'm crushing, they want to get in on the fun. I throw them a stern glance, like, *Act normal, you two!* **Nick doesn't need to see all this excessive silliness!**

Note to self: Educate besties on how to behave around my crush.

I finally dare to glance Nick's way, and clearly he's been looking at me on **my entire trip to the table.**

"Heyyyy, Heidi!" he croons, scooching over to make room for me at the table. He very quickly sizes up my lunch choice. "Are you a vegetarian?"

I laugh loudly. *Me? A vegetarian?* I think.

My family would love *that* one. I only ate buttered noodles, chicken nuggets, and absolutely **nothing** that resembled a veggie for my entire childhood. But for some reason—most likely nervousness—the word *yes* flies right out of my mouth. Oops, I'd better correct this!

"I mean NO!" I say a little too emphatically. "I'm *not* a vegetarian." Then I giggle awkwardly.

I have to pause to ponder something: *Will I ever be able to act like a NORMAL person around Nick?*

And then I think of another big oops! **I forgot to say hello to him!**

So much for being calmer in everything I do.

MERG!

I take a deep breath and start over. "Hey, Nick! Um, I'm not a vegetarian. I just like to try new things, so I thought I'd give this veggie burger a whirl."

Ugh! Did I just say *give this veggie burger A WHIRL?!* Who says that? That sounded like something Dad would say when he tries something new.

Two words: *Stone Age!*

"You're cool," Nick says, and blushes. "I mean, that's cool that you like to try new things."

I look at my plate for a sec. Well, at least *he* sounds as uncool as I do—and he also thinks I'm COOL.

That's a relief!

Then my thoughts are interrupted. I look up because I can tell someone is thinking about me. I'm getting more sensitive to other people's thoughts all the time.

And sure enough, my eyes lock on Melanie, who's sitting across the table from me. She's grins and points two fingers at her eyes and then back at me like, *I'm watching you and your BOYYYYfriend!*

She probably thinks Nick and I are awkward and pathetic, or maybe *I'm* the only one who thinks that, but either way, **who cares?!**

I shrug at Melanie, like it's no big deal—even though I'm a swarming mix of emotions, including **angst, self-doubt, and worry.** The usual suspects that come knocking when I have a crush.

I pick up my veggie burger, and I'm about to take a bite when my mind-reading gift kicks in again. This time, I can actually *hear* what Melanie is thinking, and her thoughts are coming in loud and clear.

You're totally blushing, Heidi! she says in my head.

I drop my veggie burger. *Splat!*

It lands on my plate and bursts apart. The patty looks suspiciously like the sole of an old shoe.

Ew.

At the same time, my hands fly to my cheeks because of what Melanie just said, I mean, *what she just thought*. And what's worse, Melanie is looking at me with wide suspicious eyes, like she's reading into my reaction.

That's when I suddenly realize that I've never told Melanie I can read minds—not to mention—that I'm getting better at it.

Oh no! I *should* probably clue her in, because now she thinks something's up.

There is so much happening.

Moment of meditation, Heidi! I take another deep breath and decide that I'll tell her later.

But my moment of peace only lasts a second,

because Nick just gently elbowed me in the ribs and it made me jump. I bang the table with my knees.

Bam!

"**Ow!**" I yell before I can stop myself.

"Oh, sorry, Heidi! I didn't mean to startle you!" Nick says.

I smile, like, *No problem*—even though I'm mortified for sounding like such a baby. Nick wrinkles his brow and points at my plate. "Don't you like your veggie burger?"

I pick up the patty with my fork and lay it back on the bun. Then I pop the top back on. Nick is watching my every move.

"Actually, I haven't tried it yet," I tell him. "It was too hot." And even though the burger looks less than appetizing, I take a big bite, because 1. I'm a good sport, and 2. I have an audience who knows that I *like to try new things*.

I squeeze my eyes shut and force myself to swallow. Then I gulp down half my water, which leaves me out of breath.

"It doesn't taste like a hamburger, that's for sure! It kind of tastes like . . . smushed peas and mushrooms!"

Nick—and everyone at the table—cracks up, even Melanie. She seems to have lost that *something-fishy's-going-on* look. Phew! And thankfully, the conversation goes back just to Nick and me.

"Well, this cafeteria usually has pretty decent food, but I admit the veggie burgers here aren't the best I've ever had," Nick says. "Not by a long shot. I've had some that were really good."

I nod. "I'll try them again sometime," I say. "Just not here!" Nick grins.

"So, what's your favorite food, Heidi?" Nick asks.

Oooh, that's a great question with such an easy answer, I think.

"Doughnuts!" I declare with conviction. Doughnuts are my best friend Lucy's favorite food too.

"*Mmmmm!*" Nick says, leaning back in his chair.

Two of the chair legs leave the floor. "Doughnuts are *my* favorite food too!" He holds up a hand and I slap it.

Wow. Another thing we have in common! It feels like we just cleared another hurdle in this relationship.

Eeee!

"And you know what, Heidi?" Nick asks. "My dad has a doughnut machine, and he makes fresh doughnuts all the time—any kind you can think of!

Glazed, powdered sugar, blueberry, s'mores, cream-filled, maple, birthday cake..."

My eyes grow larger with every flavor Nick names. "Wow, Nick, you are SO LUCKY!"

Clunk! Nick's chair legs come back to earth.

"I'll bring you some after Thanksgiving break," he promises. "You'll LOVE them!"

The only thing I'm loving more than doughnuts right now is Nick. I am so crushing on him!

Melanie sees it too, and out of the corner of my eye I see her wink at me, but I keep my focus on Nick.

"I'd love a box of doughnuts, Nick, but only

one condition—we have to share them," I say.

"Deal," Nick agrees, tossing his napkin onto his plate and pushing back his chair.

Nick stands and picks up his tray. I do too. Time to get to class. "So, what do you have next, Heidi? Maybe we can walk together?"

I almost drop my tray because Nick just asked to walk me to class! Another FIRST!!!

I'm about blurt out an overeager *YES* when I realize **I have history of magic next.**

Bzzzzzt! That game show buzzer sound goes off in my head, and suddenly I'm the unlucky contestant.

I'm sorry, Heidi! YES is the WRONG answer!

I scramble for how to respond. Nick isn't a student at the School of Magic, so I can't exactly tell him I have a magic class next, but I don't want him to think I don't want to walk with him either.

In the midst of my jumbled thoughts, the bell rings. And at the same time, Melanie pops in between Nick and me, like some kind of photobomber. She grins at Nick.

"She *can't*," Melanie says bluntly. "Heidi promised she'd walk back to our room with *me* first."
Then my broommate gives me a hard stare.
"*REMEMBER*, Heidi?"

What's Melanie up to NOW? I wonder, but I go along with her act and nod.

"Um, y-yeah," I stutter. "Sorry, Nick. I'd love to walk with you next time. But friend duty calls!"

Nick's face looks like what *any* guy's face

would look like when he gets caught up in some mysterious girl thing. **Confused.**

Melanie grabs me by the elbow and drags me away. "Talk to you later, Nick!" I call over my shoulder.

Melanie steers me to the dish-drop window and I set down my tray. She's still has a firm grip on my arm, so I can't even scrape my plate or separate the silverware.

Once we're outside, she finally lets go of my arm.

"Why do you look so shocked, Heidi?" Melanie asks. "I just *saved* you!"

ABOUT THE AUTHOR

Wanda Coven has always loved magic. When she was little, she used to make secret potions from smooshed shells and acorns. Then she would pretend to transport herself and her friends to enchanted places. Now she visits other worlds through writing. Wanda lives with her husband and son in Colorado Springs, Colorado. They have three cats: Hilda, Agnes, and Claw-dia.

ABOUT THE ILLUSTRATOR

Anna Abramskaya was born in Sevastopol, Ukraine. She graduated from Kharkiv State Academy of Design and Arts in 2006. Then she moved to the United States, where she's currently living in the beautiful city of Jacksonville, Florida. Anna has loved art since she was little and has tried different materials and techniques. The process of creation and seeing beauty in the simple things around her always brings her joy and the wish to share that feeling with everyone. Anna wants to believe that art can help bring more love into people's hearts. Find out more at AnnaAbramskaya.com.

ABOUT THE AUTHOR

Wanda Coven has always loved magic. When she was little, she used to make secret potions from smooshed shells and acorns. Then she would pretend to transport herself and her friends to enchanted places. Now she visits other worlds through writing. Wanda lives with her husband and son in Colorado Springs, Colorado. They have three cats: Hilda, Agnes, and Claw-dia.

ABOUT THE ILLUSTRATOR

Anna Abramskaya was born in Sevastopol, Ukraine. She graduated from Kharkiv State Academy of Design and Arts in 2006. Then she moved to the United States, where she's currently living in the beautiful city of Jacksonville, Florida. Anna has loved art since she was little and has tried different materials and techniques. The process of creation and seeing beauty in the simple things around her always brings her joy and the wish to share that feeling with everyone. Anna wants to believe that art can help bring more love into people's hearts. Find out more at AnnaAbramskaya.com.

Would you like to read another book about **Heidi Heckelbeck**? You don't need magic to find one! Look for more

books at your favorite store!

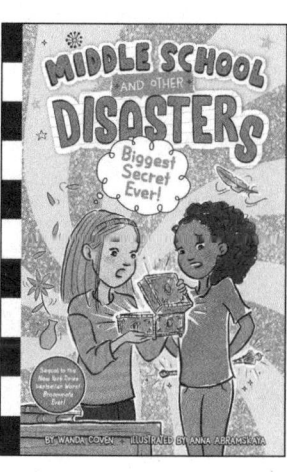

EBOOK EDITIONS ALSO AVAILABLE
PUBLISHED BY SIMON SPOTLIGHT
SIMONANDSCHUSTER.COM/KIDS

MIDDLE SCHOOL AND OTHER DISASTERS

Worst Wish Ever!

BY WANDA COVEN
ILLUSTRATED BY ANNA ABRAMSKAYA

Simon Spotlight

New York   Amsterdam/Antwerp   London   Toronto   Sydney   New Delhi

This book is a work of fiction. Any references to historical events, real people, or real places are used fictitiously. Other names, characters, places, and events are products of the author's imagination, and any resemblance to actual events or places or persons, living or dead, is entirely coincidental.

SIMON SPOTLIGHT
An imprint of Simon & Schuster Children's Publishing Division
1230 Avenue of the Americas, New York, New York 10020
First Simon Spotlight edition March 2025
© 2025 by Simon & Schuster, LLC
All rights reserved, including the right of reproduction in whole or in part in any form.
SIMON SPOTLIGHT and colophon are registered trademarks of Simon & Schuster, LLC.
For information about special discounts for bulk purchases, please contact Simon & Schuster Special Sales at 1-866-506-1949 or business@simonandschuster.com. The Simon & Schuster Speakers Bureau can bring authors to your live event. For more information or to book an event contact the Simon & Schuster Speakers Bureau at 1-866-248-3049 or visit our website at www.simonspeakers.com.
Text by Alison Inches
Series designed by Chani Yammer, based on the Heidi Heckelbeck series designed by Aviva Shur
Cover designed by Laura Roode
Illustrated by Anna Abramskaya, inspired by the original character designs of Priscilla Burris from the Heidi Heckelbeck chapter book series
The illustrations for this book were rendered with digital ink and a bunch of love.
The text of this book was set in Minou.
Manufactured in the United States of America 0625 BVG
10 9 8 7 6 5 4 3 2
CIP data for this book is available from the Library of Congress.
ISBN 9781665964142
ISBN 9781665964159 (ebook)

To my readers:
You are magical.
Love,
Wanda

THAT'S SHOWBIZ

Consider me old school when it comes to sending greeting cards.

I mean, seriously, **does anyone other than me still send cards in the mail?**

Well, I love to do it!

And I found a cute card at the bookstore today. It has a bunch of turkeys driving in an old-fashioned station wagon. It's totally ridiculous, **and I think Lucy will love it.**

I grab a pen with brown ink and fill the space inside.

Hey, Lulu!
How are YOU?! MISS you fiercely!

Guess what? I'll be home a week from TOMORROW for Thanksgiving!

Eeeee!

Can you believe it? I'm SO excited to see you!

And we have to have *at least* one sleepover while I'm home. We also have to do all the things we haven't gotten to do lately, like paint pottery, make new friendship bracelets, go shopping, and bake chocolate chip cookies!

Can you tell I'm a little excited? Well, I AM!

And I'm begging you to reserve *all* your spare time for *me*!

No other friends allowed, except maybe Bruce... oh, and Melanie really wants to hang with us too. But WE come first.

Okay, gotta go!
Gobble, gobble and all that jazz!
Heidi Kins

P.S. Love ya!
Hearts everywhere!

I seal my envelope and send it magically, of course, because it positively *has* to get there before I do!

Then I whiz out the door and down the steps of my dorm. The sun warms my back and the leaves crunch underfoot as I walk down the path to the Barn.

Even though I'm excited to go home for Thanksgiving, I'm a little sad to leave too. Every day at Broomsfield Academy has been really amazing so far, minus a few little missteps.

Okay, maybe some **major flub-ups.**

But hey, I've gone a *whole* week without a single magical disaster. That's a record for me!

And I'm not mad about my mistakes either, because according to my aunt Trudy, *You should never fear failure, for that's how you learn.*

And I've learned *a ton*!

Hopefully, one day, all these lessons will pay off. For now I am happy learning magic right where I am.

I'm pretty good at staying calm through my magic mishaps—that's because I've been practicing my daily meditation. I even meditated before I wrote to Lucy today.

I know that quiet thoughts equal better magic, and better magic means becoming a better witch—and possibly even a phenomenal witch!

Abracadabra to that!

As I walk along, I hear another person's voice inside my head. **I'm serious!**

Hearing voices is a totally normal occurrence for me. Being able to read minds is my gift as a witch. And what's more, I *know* who this voice belongs to.

I stop and turn around to see if I'm right, and there she is, **my favorite teacher, Mrs. Kettledrum!** She's walking my favorite dog, Momo, and in her thoughts she just asked me to slow down for a chat. I happily oblige!

"Hi, Mrs. Kettledrum!" I sing. Then I drop to my knees and smoosh my face against Momo's. Momo wags her plump little Corgi body and licks my cheeks.

One word: *slobberrific!*

We're total buds.

"I must say, Heidi, your mind-reading skills have really improved," Mrs. Kettledrum says. "You picked up on my thoughts and knew who I was without a problem. That's a first!"

I hop back to my feet. Wow, she's *right*! I *did* read her mind from far away *and* realized it was her without a hitch.

I really *must* be getting better at this!

That said, I'm still pretty much a beginner at mind reading, but I'll take the compliment!

"Thank you, Mrs. K! I'm getting better at my meditation, too. I've been practicing every day, and I feel more focused and peaceful in everything I do."

Mrs. Kettledrum smiles that warm, approving smile that feels as good as the sun on my face. This lovely feeling passes as my teacher's eyebrows suddenly **jump**, like she just remembered something.

"Heidi," she says in a more serious tone, "have you started studying for my potions quiz and your magical wishes exam yet? Potions is tomorrow and your magical wishes exam is at the end of this week."

Her question puts me on the spot, and I fiddle with one of the straps on my backpack. I know she wants me to do well in **all my studies, not just in her spells and potions class.** And even though Mrs. Kettledrum gives me private advanced magic lessons, she **still** questions my study habits.

"Um, not y-yet," I stammer. "But *don't worry—* I'm on it!" I say, sticking two thumbs up to reassure her.

Mrs. Kettledrum lifts her foot out of the dog leash, which Momo looped around one of her legs.

"I'm sure you'll do well, Heidi," she says. "Just use your time wisely! There are only so many minutes in a day!"

No offense to teachers, including beloved ones like Mrs. Kettledrum, but why do they always state the obvious? Of course I'm going to study.

Duh, duh, and double duh!

Oh well. I give Mrs. Kettledrum a courteous "Thank you" and an "Of course I will." Then I bend down and pet Momo between the ears one more time and wave goodbye.

Yippy! It's lunchtime! I think as I skip down the path. And this week lunchtime means one wonderful, fantabulous thing.

I get to see my crush, Nick!

Woo!

Nick Lee and I have been in a "flirtationship" for a few weeks. He's smart, funny, cuter-than-cute, and oh-so-sweet!

And to top it off, we're actually at the *SAME* cafeteria table this week. This is the first time we've ever been assigned to the same table.

One word: YES!!!

My stomach growls the moment I step into the cafeteria and breathe in that saucy, spicy smell, with a hint of baking bread.

My tray clatters as I set it on the counter. Today's choices are grilled chicken sandwiches with macaroni salad, and veggie burgers with sweet-potato mash. I go for the veggie burger. The server nestles the veggie burger onto a bun and slides it onto my plate. Another server slops sweet-potato mash onto the side. I pour myself some ice water and head to my table.

Sunny and Annabelle wave madly, like I'm some long-lost friend. This week they're at the table next to mine.

Oh geez, they're wiggling their eyebrows and making super-silly faces at me.

Aagh!

Why do they have to act SO goofy when Nick is around?

I guess since I'm crushing, they want to get in on the fun. I throw them a stern glance, like, *Act normal, you two!* Nick doesn't need to see all this excessive silliness!

Note to self: **Educate besties on how to behave around my crush.**

I finally dare to glance Nick's way, **and clearly he's been looking at me the entire time I've been walking toward him.**

"Heyyyy, Heidi!" he croons, scooching over to make room for me at the table. He very quickly sizes up my lunch choice. "Are you a vegetarian?"

I laugh loudly. *Me? A vegetarian?* I think.

My family would love *that* one. I only ate buttered noodles, chicken nuggets, and absolutely nothing that resembled a veggie for my entire childhood. But for some reason—most likely nervousness—the word "yes" flies right out of my mouth. Oops, I'd better correct this!

"I mean NO!" I say a little too emphatically. "I'm *not* a vegetarian." Then I giggle awkwardly. I have to pause to ponder something: Will I ever be able to act like a NORMAL person around Nick?

And then I think of another big oops! I forgot to say hello to him!

So much for being calmer in everything I do.

MERG!

I take a deep breath and start over. "Hey, Nick! Um, I'm not a vegetarian. I just like to try new things, so I thought I'd give this veggie burger a whirl."

Ugh! Did I just say "give this veggie burger A WHIRL"?! *Who says that?* *That sounded like something Dad would say when he tries something new.*

Two words: *Stone Age!*

"You're cool," Nick says, and blushes. "I mean, that's cool that you like to try new things."

I look at my plate for a sec. Well, at least *he* sounds as uncool as I do—and he also thinks I'm COOL.

That's a relief!

Then my thoughts are interrupted. I look up because I can tell someone is thinking about me. I'm getting more sensitive to other people's thoughts all the time.

And sure enough, my eyes lock on Melanie, who's sitting across the table from me.

She's grins and points two fingers at her eyes and then back at me like, *I'm watching you and your BOYYYYfriend!*

She probably thinks Nick and I are awkward and pathetic, or maybe *I'm* the only one who thinks that, but either way, **who cares?!**

I shrug at Melanie, like it's no big deal—even though **I'm a swarming mix of emotions,** including angst, **self-doubt, and worry.**

The usual suspects that come knocking when I have a crush.

I pick up my veggie burger, and I'm about to take a bite when my mind-reading gift kicks in again.

This time I can actually *hear* what Melanie is thinking, **and her thoughts are coming in loud and clear.**

You're totally blushing, Heidi! she says in my head.

I drop my veggie burger.

Splat!

It lands on my plate and bursts apart. The patty looks suspiciously like the sole of an old shoe.

Ew.

At the same time my hands fly to my cheeks because of what Melanie just said. I mean, *what she just thought.*

And what's worse, Melanie is looking at me with wide suspicious eyes, like she's reading into my reaction.

That's when I suddenly realize that I've never told Melanie that I can read minds, not to mention that I'm getting better at it.

Oh no! I *should* probably clue her in, because now she thinks something's up.

There is so much happening.

Moment of meditation, Heidi! I take another deep breath and decide that I'll tell her later.

But my moment of peace only lasts a second, because Nick just gently elbowed me in the ribs, and it made me jump. I bang the table with my knees.

Bam!

"Ow!" I yell before I can stop myself.

"Oh, sorry! I didn't mean to startle you!" Nick says. I smile, like, *No problem,* even though I'm mortified for sounding like such a baby.

Nick wrinkles his brow and points at my plate. "Don't you like your veggie burger?"

I pick up the patty with my fork and lay it back on the bun. Then I pop the top back on. Nick is watching my every move.

"Actually, I haven't tried it yet," I tell him. "It was too hot." And even though the burger looks less than appetizing, I take a big bite, because (1) I'm a good sport, and (2) I have an audience who knows that *I like to try new things.*

I squeeze my eyes shut, chew, and force myself to swallow. Then I gulp down half my water, which leaves me out of breath.

"It doesn't taste like a hamburger, that's for sure! It kind of tastes like . . . smushed peas and mushrooms!"

Nick, and everyone else at the table, cracks up, even Melanie. She seems to have lost that *Something fishy's going on* look. **Phew!** And thankfully, the conversation goes back just to Nick and me.

"Well, this cafeteria usually has pretty decent food, but I admit that the veggie burgers here aren't the best I've ever had," Nick says. "Not by a long shot. I've had some that were really good."

I nod. "I'll try them again sometime," I say. "Just not here!"

Nick grins. "So, what's your favorite food, Heidi?" he asks.

Oooh, that's a great question with such an easy answer, I think.

"Doughnuts!" I declare with conviction. Doughnuts are my best friend Lucy's favorite food too.

"*Mmmmm!*" Nick says, leaning back in his chair.

Two of the chair legs leave the floor. "Doughnuts are *my* favorite food too!" He holds up a hand, and I slap it.

Wow. Another thing we have in common! It feels like we just cleared another hurdle in this relationship.

Eeee!

"And you know what, Heidi?" Nick asks. "My dad has a doughnut machine, and he makes fresh doughnuts all the time—any kind you can think of! Glazed, powdered sugar, blueberry, s'mores, cream-filled, maple, birthday cake..."

My eyes grow larger with every flavor Nick names. "Wow, Nick, you are SO LUCKY!"

Clunk!

Nick's chair legs come back to earth.

"I'll bring you some after Thanksgiving break," he promises. "You'll LOVE them!"

The only thing I'm loving more than doughnuts right now **is Nick. I am so crushing on him!**

Melanie sees it too, and out of the corner of my eye I see her wink at me, but I keep my focus on Nick.

"I'd love a box of doughnuts, Nick, but on only one condition—**we have to share them,**" I say.

"Deal," Nick agrees, tossing his napkin onto his plate and pushing back his chair.

Nick stands and picks up his tray. I do too, because with that not-so-pleasant bite, I've completely lost my appetite and it's time to get to class. "So, what do you have next, Heidi? Maybe we can walk together?"

I almost drop my tray because Nick just asked to walk me to class!

Another FIRST!!!

I'm about to blurt out an overeager *YES* when I realize I have history of magic next.

Bzzzzzt! That game show buzzer sound goes off in my head, and suddenly I'm the unlucky contestant.

I'm sorry, Heidi! "YES" is the WRONG answer!

I scramble for a response. Nick isn't a student at the School of Magic, so I can't exactly tell him I have a magic class next, but I don't want him to think I don't want to walk with him either.

In the midst of my jumbled thoughts, the bell rings. And at the same time, Melanie pops in between Nick and me, **like some kind of photobomber.** She grins at Nick.

"She *can't*," Melanie says bluntly. "Heidi promised she'd walk back to our room with *me* first." Then my broommate gives me a hard stare. *"REMEMBER,* Heidi?"

What's Melanie up to NOW? I wonder, but I go along with her act and nod.

"Um, y-yeah," I stutter. "Sorry, Nick. I'd love to walk with you next time. But friend duty calls!"

Nick's face looks like what *any* guy's face would look like when he gets caught up in some mysterious girl thing. *Confused.*

Melanie grabs me by the elbow and drags me away. "Talk to you later, Nick!" I call over my shoulder.

Melanie steers me to the dish-drop window, and I set down my tray. She's still has a firm grip on my arm, so I can't even scrape my plate or separate the silverware.

Once we're outside, she finally lets go of my arm.

"Why do you look so shocked, Heidi?" Melanie asks. "I just *saved* you!"

I rub my arm where she was squeezing.

"Well, maybe this is a look of *pain* and not *shock*!" I counter. "And what do you need to get from our room anyway? We'll be late for history of magic."

Melanie waves me off. "Oh, that was just an excuse so you didn't have to think of something to say to Nick on the spot. And *you're welcome*!"

I sigh and then laugh. "Okay, thanks, Mel." Because that *was* pretty nice of her to save me.

"Anytime," she says. "And, on second thought, I *am* going to go to our room and grab a sweater. Save me a seat in class, Heidi!" And with that, Melanie flees for our dorm.

"I will!" I shout, shaking my head, because seriously, Melanie is a total conundrum sometimes.

Are we friends, or are we still rivals? I never really know.

I keep going, but I'm not alone for long. I hear friends calling my name.

"HEI-I-I-I-I-I-DEEE!" shout Sunny and Annabelle. I'm pretty sure everyone at the entire school can hear them.

My friends stampede to catch up with me.

"What happened with *NICK* at lunch?" Sunny says breathlessly. "You have to give us the love lowdown!"

What am I, *a twenty-four-hour news feed?* I wonder.

Well, I guess I don't mind when the news is good. And it's kind of fun to be the center of attention, too.

"We-e-elllll," I begin, trying to make my news sound as juicy as possible. "For one thing, Nick called me *COOL*."

This makes my friends both go, *"Oooh!!!"*

"And he also offered to walk me to class!"

Annabelle shoves me playfully. "No *waaaay*!"

I stick out my lower lip to emphasize the downside of the invitation. "But I couldn't walk with him because I have history of magic next!"

My friends waste no time making me feel better about it.

"I guess that's the only downside to being a witch with a crush on a non-magical boy," Sunny says. Then she stops in her tracks. "But Annabelle and I have some news that will really cheer you up!"

I stop and look at Sunny.

"What?!" I ask. My friends look so excited.

"Well, we just saw Natalie and Jenna putting up posters in the cafeteria," Annabelle says.

Sunny is jumping up and down. "There's going to be a TALENT SHOW *this* Saturday, and anyone can enter!"

This news makes my brain glitch and go:

Yay!

Really?

Oh no!

And **eek!**

All at the same time.

"A talent show?" I repeat. "You mean like dancing?" I say, wiggling my hips. "And singing?" I place my hand over my heart and sing, *"D-o-o-o-R-e-e-e-M-i-i-i!"*

Sunny and Annabelle practically fall over laughing, most likely because of my sheer *lack* of talent.

"YES!" Sunny affirms. "And it's not just about singing and dancing. It can be anything you want to showcase, like sculpting, painting, poetry, photography, creative writing, telling jokes—anything you're good at!"

Then Annabelle gives me one of her intense stare downs.

"But *NO* magic, Heidi!"

I sigh. "Funny you should mention that," I say. "I actually entered a talent show in elementary school. I used a spell that made me tap-dance like a pro! It was fun, but I'd never use magic in a talent show again."

Then I make a fake sad face. "But can't I even use fake magic, with a silk top hat and a white rabbit?" And even though I'm only joking, I'm kind of bummed, too, because magic is the *one* thing I'm good at.

Wouldn't it be so cool if I could make Momo speak in front of a non-magical audience? It would be *epic*.

"Well, I suppose you *could* do magician tricks, Heidi, if you know how," Sunny says. "I'm going to do an original painting, something bright and happy that will make everyone smile when they see it."

Annabelle and I grin because that is SO Sunny.

"If anyone can paint something like that, it would be YOU, Sunny," Annabelle agrees.

"And what about you, Annabelle?" I ask as we enter the library.

Annabelle looks off into space.

"Hmmm, I think maybe I'd like to sculpt something," she says dreamily.

Sunny and I look at each other in amazement.

"Have you ever sculpted anything before?" I ask.

Annabelle shakes her head. "No, not really, just a bowl and a pencil holder at summer camp. But I love to squish clay. It's very satisfying."

We slip behind the grandfather clock into the secret passageway that leads to the School of Magic.

"Well, that's adventurous of you," Sunny says as we pass all the witch and wizard alumni paintings.

I lift the iron latch on the arched door at the end of the hallway, and we enter the rotunda, which is a large round room with a domed ceiling, and also the center of the School of Magic.

"I'll catch you two later!" Annabelle says as she races off to her broomstick riding class with Mr. Craftwood.

Sunny and I wave goodbye to Annabelle and head to history of magic on the other side of the rotunda. My mind has begun to mull over the idea of entering the talent show. I'd love to be a part of it, but seriously, **what can I possibly do to dazzle an audience?**

I take a quick inventory of my talents. *Hmmm, let's see. . . . I can wiggle my ears, and I can raise either eyebrow separately. I can also blow a mean bubble gum bubble.*

Or better yet, I can make a super-loud whistle with an acorn cap. That might be a good one!

Then in one fell swoop, my inner critic shoots down all my ideas. *Sure, Heidi, these would be great talents if you were still in elementary school!*

It's true. These ideas don't do justice to the mature middle schooler I am today.

I have to come up with something!

What can I do besides magic?

Two words: *Stay tuned!*

THE WISHING WELL

Sunny and I slide into our chairs. Today our desks have been arranged in a semicircle around the wishing well. This medieval stone well has been here since before Broomsfield Academy was a school, **like more than a hundred years ago.** That's all I really know. One special thing about the well is that **it always has this golden glow coming from it.** It's pretty stunning.

As I admire the well, I wonder if we're finally going to learn more about it. I want to ask Sunny, but she's talking a mile a minute to Isabelle, who's sitting on the other side of her.

The rest of the class is buzzing with excitement too.

I decide to focus on our teacher, Ms. Charmsworth.

She's another one of my favorite teachers at Broomsfield Academy.

If there was such thing as a Quirky Witch Award, Ms. Charmsworth would win it hands down. Some people call her eccentric, but I think she's more like an enchanted fairy.

Her aura glows just like the wishing well.

One of my favorite things about her is her hair. It's a little longer than shoulder length, and she has bangs, but here's the best part—her hair is streaked in every color of the rainbow.

She also wears ribbons and bows in her hair when she pulls it back. **And her clothes are so cool!**

✧ 43 ✧

Everything she wears is made of fantastic fabrics—nothing you would ever find in a clothing store. She mixes silks, plaids, stripes, and swirls, and she loves buttons, sashes, and lacy collars.

She also wears bangle bracelets that jingle pleasantly when she writes on the whiteboard. To top it off, she almost always wears striped tights with her outfits.

I LOVE striped tights!

Three words: *witchy and stylish.* (If I do say so myself.) Anyway, I have my eye on Ms. Charmsworth because she's about to do something with the well.

Everyone else is chatting so nobody is watching her but me.

She raises her hands over the well and quietly chants a spell. I strain my ears to hear. The spell is only three simple words.

Well! Well! Well!

As soon as she's done, **the magical shield covering the opening of the well disappears.**

I probably wasn't supposed to hear the spell, but I, Heidi Helena Heckelbeck, **love to be in the know,** so I jot down the short spell in my notebook.

How can I be the best witch there ever was if I don't pay attention?

"Good afternoon, class!" Ms. Charmsworth says in her gentle, almost childlike voice, which is totally charming.

It's no wonder her name is Ms. Charmsworth. She could charm anyone!

"Today I have a special treat for you," she continues.

We all look at each other, like: *Oooh, what can it be?!*

She prances around the wishing well. The bangles on her wrists tinkle musically. "I know you've all been eagerly waiting to learn more about the School of Magic's enchanted wishing well."

We all murmur, *"Yes!"*

Our teacher smiles. "Well, I'm happy to say, *today* is the day!"

This time we erupt into claps and cheers.

"Now please listen carefully," Ms. Charmsworth goes on. "Because some of what I say today may be included on your magical wishes exam later this week."

We dutifully open our notebooks and get ready to take notes. *I probably got a head start*, I think as I underline the spell I just jotted down.

Ms. Charmsworth lays one hand on the edge of the wishing well.

"To begin, our beloved Broomsfield wishing well was here long before the School of Magic opened in the 1800s. Witches and wizards salvaged the well when they decided to build on this property.

"And as most of you know, this is by no means an ordinary wishing well. It is neither a decorative backyard wishing well nor a fountain wishing well as seen in a town square.

"Those kinds of wells are not really magical. They're just for fun, silly wishes, like wishing that your crush would like you," Ms. Charmsworth says.

Then Sunny nudges me. I nudge her back, keeping my eyes on the teacher.

"So, class, how do you make some other just-for-fun wishes?" Ms. Charmsworth asks.

Nobody waits to be called on. We just blurt stuff out one after another.

"Blowing out candles on a birthday cake!" someone shouts.

"Wishing on stars!"

"Breaking a wishbone!"

"Blowing dandelion fluff!"

This is where I decide to get in on the fun.

"Wishing on eyelashes!" I yell.

"Ladybugs!" shouts Melanie.

Ms. Charmsworth claps her hands and her bracelets jangle wildly. "That's very good, everyone! Those are all things for making just-for-fun wishes."

She walks back to the wishing well. "But here we have an authentic wishing well that can actually make your wishes *come true*! Wishes that defy the laws of science!"

Then her face becomes more serious and she shakes a finger at us. "But there are some things you must *never* wish for—no matter how much you desire them. Not even this wishing well will allow it.

"Can anyone name a forbidden wish?"

Sunny's hand flies up. "You can't wish for your pets to come back from the dead."

Ouch.

This comment makes my heart go out to Sunny, because her golden retriever, Alfie, passed away last summer, and it was really hard for her. He had been part of her family since Sunny was a baby.

Ms. Charmsworth nods her approval. "You're absolutely right, Sunny. You can't wish anything back from the dead. It's simply out of the realm of wishing possibility. Anything else?"

Hunter raises his hand. Hunter McCann was my first crush at Broomsfield. He's adorable and is head over heels for my friend Isabelle.

"You can't wish to be *all-powerful*," Hunter says.

Ms. Charmsworth gives Hunter a thumbs-up. "That's correct, Hunter! Wishing to be all-powerful is off-limits. No one could possibly contain that much power. It would be destructive to oneself and to others."

Melanie raises her hand and waves it back and forth. Ms. Charmsworth calls on her next. "You can't wish for people to fall in love," Melanie suggests.

We all burst out laughing, because this is classic Melanie!

Everyone remembers how she tried to make Hunter **fall in love with her** earlier this fall!

But then again, so did I.

I guess she's got a disaster she won't be able to live down either! I giggle out loud at what a failure *that* was for both of us.

Then Ms. Charmsworth does something silly. She hugs herself and turns around while she's doing it, like she's in love with herself, and we laugh even more.

"Melanie is spot on!" our teacher says. "You can't wish for people to fall in love with you or anyone else.

"And there are many other things you cannot wish for, like wishing something bad would happen to someone or meddling in other people's personal business.

"Wishes like that can be very harmful. In fact, even harmless wishes can become dangerous, but we'll learn more about that another day.

"For now I would like to show you how our magical wishing well works. Would anyone like to see the wishing well grant a wish?"

"**YES!**" we all shout.

Our teacher reaches into the pocket of her plaid dress and pulls out a quarter. She holds it up for all of us to see. "The wishing well will accept any coin currency, except for fake coins or poker chips." Then she flicks the quarter into the well and makes a wish.

"I WISH FOR MY CLASSROOM TO HAVE A BEAUTIFUL CHERRY TREE IN FULL BLOOM!"

Ms. Charmsworth says with glee.

POOF!

A cloud of pink smoke that looks like a vaporous puff of sparkling cotton-candy mushrooms flies from the wishing well.

When the smoke clears, a beautiful cherry tree in full bloom stands next to the well.

We all gasp at this amazing wish come true.

I'm breathing in its floral goodness.

Mmmm. The cherry blossoms are a wonderful blend of toasty almonds, honey, and fresh spring air.

"And this, class, is only a small example of the power contained in this wishing well. Would anyone like to see an even *greater* wish granted?"

We all squeal and shout, "*YES! YES! YES!*" as loud as we can. Ms. Charmsworth waits for us to quiet down. Then she tosses another coin into the well and makes a second wish.

"I WISH TO BE IN TWO PLACES AT ONCE!"

POOF!

Another pink sparkly cloud billows from the wishing well. I hold my breath until the cloud dissolves. But this time the wish is a total dud. Ms. Charmsworth and the wishing well look the same as they did *before* the wish.

"*Aaaaaaaaaaawwww!*" we all cry with disappointment. I'm sure my moan is the loudest.

But the funny thing is, Ms. Charmsworth doesn't look upset at all. In fact, she's grinning. Did we miss something?

"There's no need to look disappointed!" our teacher tells us. Then she points to something behind us.

We all turn around, and there, standing on the far side of the room, is a SECOND Ms. Charmsworth.

A perfect replica!

This is SO amazing that I literally fall off my chair. Sunny does too.

In fact, all my classmates are falling over.

This is *NEXT-LEVEL* magic.

Sunny and I pull ourselves back onto our seats. "Whooooaaa, this is unbelievable," I whisper to Sunny.

Sunny is completely speechless. I mean, totally silent with shock. But not me!

I want to know MORE. I raise my hand and wave it, as big as I can.

"Yes, Heidi?" answers Ms. Charmsworth.

I can barely stay in my seat. "May we take a closer look at the *second* Ms. Charmsworth?" I ask.

"Well, of course, Heidi," says Ms. Charmsworth.

Then the real Ms. Charmsworth walks to the back of the room and taps her doppelgänger (which is a fancy word for "double") on the shoulder.

"Would you please come with me?" says the real Ms. Charmsworth, holding out her hand. Her twin clasps our teacher's hand, and they slowly walk back to the wishing well. They're standing side by side in front of me, since I'm the one who asked the question.

I have to tune out the rest of the class, because they're all talking at once. Then I carefully examine the twin and compare her to our **real** teacher to see if I can spy any differences.

So far I notice that they both talk a little more slowly than usual. They walked more slowly too. Usually Ms. Charmsworth skips or scurries when she walks.

Another thing I detect is the lack of color in their faces. They both look pale. The real Ms. Charmsworth usually has rosy cheeks.

I raise my hand. "I have another question."

My teachers give me the go-ahead.

"Teacher Number Two," I question, "how do you feel? Do you think and feel like the *real* Ms. Charmsworth?"

The twin teachers look at each other and then speak at the same time. "We feel like the same person, Heidi, **because we *are* the same person.** We're just divided into two of us, but as two we're not as energetic in mind and body as when we were one. Does that make sense?"

I nod and note that **they're definitely talking a lot more slowly than normal.**

Melanie raises her hand.

"Yes, Melanie?" our twin teachers answer.

"**What if your double tried to take over your *real* body?**" Melanie asks. "**And if she did, what if she tried to take over the world?**"

A few people in the class laugh. Melanie's question **sounds like the plot from a sci-fi movie,** but secretly we all wonder if this could actually happen.

"Don't worry, Melanie," says the real Ms. Charmsworth in her slow drawl. "There's no chance of my double taking over my body, much less the world.

"For one thing, wishes don't last very long and eventually vanish. That means my twin will disappear because she's nothing more than a copy of the real me. She has no separate mind or power of her own. But if something ever went wrong, there is another way to reverse a wish."

Our teacher reaches into her pocket and pulls out a purple stone. She holds it up for all of us to see.

"This gemstone is called a Stone of Gratitude," she tells us. "Watch what it can do."

Ms. Charmsworth turns and faces her double. "Thank you for fulfilling my wish!" she says graciously. Then she touches her doppelgänger with the stone. And just like that, her twin vanishes from sight.

We all gasp.

"**SHE'S GONE!**" Sunny exclaims, sounding just like Dorothy in *The Wizard of Oz* when the Wicked Witch of the West melts into nothingness.

We all clap, because this is the best wish come true we've ever seen. Our teacher waits for us to calm down again.

"As I said, if you don't have a Stone of Gratitude to end your wish, **the wish will eventually vanish on its own.**" Ms. Charmsworth's voice sounds strong again.

Melanie asks another question. "**How long does a wish last?**"

Ms. Charmsworth smiles. "Very good question, Melanie.

"Most wishes last an hour, but occasionally a wish may only last a few minutes, and once in a great while, a wish may last for several days.

"We're not sure why this happens. The other witches and wizards and I have studied the magical properties of the wishing well for years, but we still have some unresolved inconsistencies. Maybe one day one of *you* will understand the mysteries of the wishing well more clearly."

Blink! The beautiful cherry tree winks out like a light bulb. Everyone gasps all over again. Then Ms. Charmsworth calls on Hunter, who's had his hand up for a while.

"So . . . if you *don't* understand all the magical powers of the wishing well, is it really safe for anyone to use?" he asks. "I mean, what if something did go wrong?"

Ms. Charmsworth clasps her hands together, sending her bracelets into another frenzy. "That is a very good question, Hunter, and the answer I'm going to share may well be on your exam."

We pick up our pens and get ready to write again.

"As you know, all magic comes with a certain amount of risk, and the same is true for the wishing well," Ms. Charmsworth begins. "As with a spell, **you have to be very careful how you choose and phrase your words.**

"One misplaced word **or using a word that is *close* to what you mean but not quite the *right* word can be hazardous—even disastrous**—to the outcome of your wish.

"This is why it's important to have a Stone of Gratitude. This stone can end a wish if something seems amiss **or if something really goes wrong,** as I mentioned before.

"But you bring up another important point, Hunter. And that is this: the wishing well is only safe to use under the supervision of an experienced witch or wizard. This well isn't for young, inexperienced magical students. It could cause great trouble or harm to someone who doesn't understand its powers.

"Is that clear to everyone?"

We nod and dutifully answer yes to this more serious side of making wishes.

Then I raise my hand, because I have two more burning questions.

"When will we each get our *own* Stone of Gratitude?" I ask. "And if and when we do get one, when can we start using the wishing well?" I know these questions are bold, but somebody has to ask! And besides, I *need* to know.

Ms. Charmsworth twists a lock of her rainbow hair. "Today was just a wishing-well show-and-tell," she begins.

I already feel a little pang of disappointment riffle through my body because it sounds like we're not going to get to use the well anytime soon, but I wait to hear the rest of what Ms. Charmsworth has to say.

"When I feel you're *ready* and *responsible* . . . ," our teacher goes on, emphasizing the words *"ready"* and *"responsible,"* "then you'll each receive a Stone of Gratitude and learn how to use the wishing well under strict supervision."

"PFFFFFFT," I sputter in rejection of what I've just heard, because I'm ready to use the wishing well right now.

Sunny kicks my foot, letting me know I made my disappointment a little too obvious. I'm not trying to be disrespectful, but sometimes it feels like we get treated like babies.

I mean, how much of a learning curve is there to using a wishing well?

Practically none.

When I glance up from my inner rant, Ms. Charmsworth is looking right at me, and she doesn't look pleased.

Oops, I'd better tone it down.

I smile politely, and my teacher continues. "The faculty at the School of Magic want to help you learn all the wonders of magic," says Ms. Charmsworth, "but remember, you're still *beginners*. In time you will be ready to use the wishing well, but in the meantime, study hard, and be the best magical students that you can be."

And with that, the bell rings. Wow, that class sure flew by!

"Keep studying for your exam!" Ms. Charmsworth reminds us as we gather our things to go.

I jet out of my seat and fling my backpack over one shoulder. "Come on, Sunny! Let's look inside the well before Ms. Charmsworth covers it."

Sunny follows me to the edge of the well. We hang our heads over the side. Melanie joins us too. Her blond ponytail flops upside down as she peers into the well with us.

"It kind of looks like any old wishing well," Melanie says. "Except for the golden glow of the water."

Ms. Charmsworth joins us. "Did you know that the wishing well is connected to a natural spring below it? The water goes deep into the earth. Over the years the wishing well has made the waters become powerful with magic. Our wishing well is a very sacred and extraordinary piece of our school's magical history."

Sunny, Melanie, and I stare at the water, and I'm pretty sure we're all thinking how lucky we are to be magical students at Broomfield Academy's School of Magic. It's really kind of amazing.

"Okay, girls! It's time to go!" Ms. Charmsworth says. "And be sure to study for the exam. You have only a few more days to prepare!"

As we head out of the classroom, I overhear Ms. Charmsworth chant the spell to seal the well. She uses the same words as she used to open it.

WELL! WELL! WELL!

Not one of my friends is paying any attention, but I am. I always pay attention because that's how a really good witch gets ahead.

Melanie hooks arms with Sunny and me. "Imagine all the things we could wish for with the

wishing well," she says dreamily. "You know what I would wish for? A trip to Paris so I could study more about fashion and perfumes.

"What would you two wish for?"

Sunny doesn't hesitate. "I would wish for world peace. How about you, Heidi?"

"If the wishes only last an hour, I'd wish for pizza, because then I could eat it before it disappears!" I say.

My friends laugh and shove me playfully.

"You think you're so clever, Heidi Heckelbeck!" Melanie says. But then she gives me a knowing look, because she's well aware that we both have our sights set on far greater wishes than just pizza.

MEGA TALENTED

Guess what?

I aced my potions quiz this morning! So did Melanie.

We studied together last night. Melanie is a potions expert. It's her gift as a witch, and not to brag—*okay, maybe a little*—but I'm pretty good at potions too.

One of the potions we got tested on was a shrinking and expanding potion. We had to bring something to class to shrink or expand.

I brought my Fair Isle sweater, which shrank in the dryer.

Who knew wool shrinks?

Well, it does.

A lot.

So I used my potion to expand my sweater back to its proper size.

Mrs. Kettledrum shouted, *"Bravo, Heidi!"* Which was embarrassing, but nice.

Oh, and Melanie shrank one of her fuzzy heart pillows and turned it into a backpack charm. **So cute!**

Anyway! As I walk back to my dorm, I see signs for the talent show everywhere. They say stuff like, YOU'VE GOT TALENT! And SHOW US YOUR STUFF!

It seems like everyone has an idea for the talent show—that is, except me.

I've been racking my brain *all* day to come up with an idea, and one thing I'm pretty good at is riding a unicycle. But I haven't done it in a while, and what if I accidentally ride off the stage?

Forget that one.

I can also use a pogo stick all day long, but who would want to watch *that*?

One word: **BOR-ing.**

Maybe I could use a Hula-Hoop to music. The only problem is, I can only swirl a few times before the hoop winds up around my ankles.

It would be a very short performance.

Or maybe I should try stand-up comedy? But what if nobody laughs at my jokes?

This is very frustrating.

Why does our school have to have a talent show anyway? All it does is emphasize my lack of talent.

Well, maybe I just won't enter, but that doesn't feel good either.

I'll have to give this more thought later.

Sunny and Anabelle are ahead of me on the path. Maybe if I focus on *their* talents, they won't focus on my lack of talents. I run to catch up.

"Hey, you two! How are your art projects going?" I ask them.

Anabelle lets out a long groan, which weirdly comforts me. "Mine's not going well at all," she says. "All I do is stare at my blob of clay and think, 'What are you supposed to be?' Then I'm like, 'Come out! Come out! Whatever you are!'"

Sunny and I laugh at the thought of Annabelle talking to her clay.

"Coming up with an idea for a painting has been harder than I thought too," Sunny says. "My go-to is always a sunrise or sunset, because it relates to my name, but I really want to paint something *original*, and so far I'm coming up empty."

I lean my shoulder into Sunny's. "Well, don't feel bad," I say understandingly. "I haven't even come up with an idea, let alone tried to execute it. I may not even enter the talent show."

My friends make pouty and *poor you* faces at me. Then Annabelle tries to make me feel better.

"Don't worry, Heidi. You'll think of something. You always do," she says as they turn off the path to their dorm. "Just don't do something that gets you in trouble!"

Both my friends think this last comment is hilarious and laugh like hyenas.

When I get to my dorm, I open the door to my room and walk right into a curtain of colorful wooden beads. They hang from the door frame in vertical strands.

The room is dark inside, except for our twinkly lights and Melanie's battery-operated candles, which are everywhere. I hear the sound of Melanie's acoustic guitar. She's sitting on a stool in front of the mirror. Her hair is down. She has on a peasant blouse, worn jeans, and cowboy boots. A circle of plastic daisies crowns her head.

Melanie stops playing. "Like the open-mic vibe?" she asks me.

The room actually looks pretty cool.

"Yeah, I love it," I tell her. "What are you doing?"

Melanie strums a chord on her guitar. "I just wrote a song for the talent show!"

Melanie has been taking guitar lessons since school started. She can play actual songs already. She holds her guitar pick, like she's getting ready to play.

"Want to hear my song?" she asks, looking at me hopefully.

To be honest, I kind of have mixed feelings about hearing her song. Is that bad? I mean, of course I really want to hear it because I'm genuinely happy for her.

But I also have a funny feeling it'll make me feel even more like a loser who doesn't have a talent.

All it will do is highlight the fact that I can't sing, play guitar—or apparently do anything else for that matter.

"Sure, let's hear it," I say, because I'm not about to be so totally self-absorbed as to say *no*.

Melanie's face lights up, and she sets one foot on the rung of the stool and plants the other on the floor. She concentrates on the neck of her guitar, trying to get her fingers in just the right spots. She looks up.

"Ready?"

I nod and she does an opening strum.

"This is a melody."

Strum.

"About a girl named, Melanie."

Strum. Strum.

"Have any of you heard of her?

"She's kind of a big deal."

I laugh out loud.

"When people first meet me, I know what they think.
They consider my style to be pink on the brink!
And, well, it's kind of true because I have..."

Then Melanie strums faster with pretty smooth chord changes.

"Pink pillows! Pink slippers! Pink outfits! Pink bedding!
And one day I'm sure I'll have a perfect pink
     wedding....
Unless, that is, I'm over it."

She looks at me a sec and then jumps into the chorus, strumming away.

"And I'm as perfect as perfect can be.
I have no flaws—at least ones you can see.
All I show off is the glamorous me.
Because I am Melanie! La dee dum dee!

". . . some people say I'm a little bit bossy.
I am.
And others think I'm snooty and saucy.
It's true.
So then why do you all want to be part of
         my posse?

"You know one day my name will be in lights.
That's the only place I've set my sights!
And I'll also have a fashion line.
And signature scents that smell divine.
Did I mention I'll be star of stage and screen?
And also a beautiful runway queen?
Yup, all in one lifetime! That's me!

"This is now my final verse.
You may be asking, 'Could it get any worse?'
Doubtful.

"'That Melanie sure seems full of herself.
Why doesn't she just get off of herself?'
Ouch.
Do you guys really think that?

"Everyone thinks I'm so self-assured.
But underneath I'm kind of a nerd.
And if you want me to really confess . . .
Inside my head I'm a total HOT MESS.
There, I said it.

"Because I'm the one and only Melanie.
I'm not as perfect as perfect can be.
I have a few flaws—they're easy to see.
But I'll still show off the glamorous me.
Because I am Melanie! La dee dum dee!"

Melanie does some final energized strums and looks at me to see what I think.

And, well, I'm blown away.

"That was amazing, Melanie! And hilarious! And I loved how you spoke the comments at the end of each verse. You're such a mega talent!"

Melanie sets down her guitar and gives me a humongous hug. "Wow, Heidi! Thanks! **That means a lot to me!**"

I slip out of the hug and lean back on my bed.

"You have a beautiful voice, Melanie," I tell her, because it's totally true.

Melanie twirls in front of me. "I love to sing, dance, and act! And I can't WAIT for the talent show. You know I *live* for the spotlight!"

She does a flying leap onto her bed, rolls over, and looks at me. "Are you going to enter the talent show, Heidi?"

I breathe in deeply through my nose. I guess that's the million-dollar question, huh.

"Well, I dunno," I say uncertainly. "Singing and dancing in front of people just isn't for me." Then, as I look up at Melanie, a sudden urge to be mischievous swoops over me. "But that's not to say that I can't bust a move in *private*!"

I hop off my bed and onto the floor. "Because, girl, I can do the *sprinkler!*" I put my left hand on my head and stick my right arm straight out. Then I jerk my right arm, like a sprinkler, and of course I add some sprinkler noises. *"Psst! Psst! Psst! Shhaaah! Shhaaah! Shhaaah!"*

Melanie hops off her bed and switches on some music, and we do the sprinkler together until we fall into a heap of laughter.

"By the way, and this is totally off topic, there's something I've been meaning to ask you ALL day," Melanie says.

I freeze, wondering what incriminating thing she has on me.

"What?" I say, trying to sound calm and casual.

Melanie pulls the crown of flowers from her head and sets it on the bed. "Well, remember yesterday at lunch when I was looking at you and you were totally blushing?"

I nod, and I'm pretty sure I know what's coming.

"Well, I was thinking, 'You're totally BLUSHING!'" Melanie goes on. "But then you reacted as if I'd said it out loud.

"It was as if you knew *exactly* what I was thinking."

Then she looks at me with her intense blue eyes. "Explain, Heidi."

Of course I remember the moment very well, and I also remember the look on Melanie's face when my hands flew to my cheeks. She was totally suspicious.

Well, now is probably a good time to tell her my secret.

I smile devilishly. "Okay, you totally busted me, Melanie!" I admit, and laugh a little nervously. "And honestly, I can't believe I haven't told you sooner. . . ."

Melanie's eyes grow wide.

"Told me WHAT, Heidi?!" she says,

practically bursting from the need to know. "I *knew* you had a secret! You have to tell me, or I'll go bonkers!"

I grab a pillow and hug it close. Why does it feel reckless to voice my secret to Melanie? But I *have* to tell her. It's only fair because I already know her gift as a witch. Potions.

"Okay, but promise not to tell anyone?" I ask.

Melanie places her hand over her heart.

But then I remember the **nightmare** that Melanie almost put Isabelle and me through when she learned Isabelle's secret.

Can I really trust her?

"Promise," she says.

I shut my eyes for a moment. *Okay, here goes. . . .*

"You're right. You didn't say, 'You're totally blushing!' out loud," I begin. "And you're also right, because I *did* hear you anyway. . . ."

Melanie stares at me in disbelief, so I say it plainly. "My special gift as a witch is that I can *read minds*. . . ."

Melanie pretends to faint onto her bed. Then she snaps back up.

"This is absolutely ASTOUNDING!" she exclaims.

"But why didn't you *tell* me sooner, Heidi?

"Have you been reading my mind the *entire* semester?!"

A grin like a fox.

"Pretty much," I confess.

Melanie covers her mouth with both hands. "But, Heidi, that's an invasion of privacy! My thoughts are my own personal business!"

Wow, Melanie seems genuinely terrified by my gift. I'd better tone it down.

"Don't worry, Mel. It's not like I can read your thoughts *all* the time—just once in a while.

"It's also something I'm learning to control because I don't want to hear everyone's thoughts. That would be way too much noise in my head," I say, trying to be reassuring. "But it also makes sense that I can read your thoughts, because the closer I get to someone, the easier it is to be in tune with their thinking."

Melanie huffs. "Well, I guess we *have* gotten to be better friends this year," she says, trying to hide a smile. "But you'd better not snoop around in my mind without asking."

I laugh, because it sounds ridiculous, but I totally get it too. I wouldn't want anyone to read *my* thoughts either!

"Don't worry, Melanie. Your private thoughts are yours and yours only.

"Well, *most of the time,*" I finish under my breath.

Melanie gives me a sideways glance.

"Yeah, right! They're mine until you *read* them!" Then she dares me. "Okay, what am I thinking *right now*?"

I've never been able to read someone's thoughts on demand.

"Honestly, Mel, I can't do on-command performances," I tell her.

She sighs with relief. **"Well, that's the best news I've heard all day!"** Then she picks up her guitar and sits back on her stool. "And by the way, that's a really cool gift, Heidi, and I'm so glad you shared it with me. **But from now on I'll try to think only good thoughts."**

I laugh.

"Good luck with THAT!" I say.

We both burst out laughing.

"I'm going to head to dinner and then study for our magical wishes exam. **Come with?"** I ask.

Melanie strums a chord. "Thanks, but I'm going to run through my song one more time, **but I'd love to study with you later."**

I throw on my black-and-white striped scarf and my jean jacket. "Cool. See you in a bit!"

I race through the beads in the doorway and on down the hall. As I step into the chilly autumn air, I feel warm with happiness. It felt really good to tell Melanie my secret, and I'm really glad we've become better friends. We've made a ton of progress.

One word: *yay.*

4

DOUBLE-BOOKED

It's dinnertime and I get to see Nick again!

I pick up my pace. I can't wait to sit next to him. This week *mealtime* is the best part of each day.

Woo!

I breeze into the cafeteria. It's not very busy yet—not even a line at the pasta-and-rice-bowl station. As I make my way to the food, I casually scan the room for Nick.

Ding! Ding! Ding!

I just spied him at the drink station!

Then I dial myself back. *Heidi, you have to cool your jets! You're acting way too eager! Just get your food like a normal student.* I force myself to slow down.

Okay, I can do this! Deep breaths!

I calmly reach for a tray, a napkin, and silverware. Then I gently scoop some brown rice into a bowl and glance over at Nick.

Oops, I lost my concentration for a sec.

Okay, back to the rice bowl. You'll see Nick soon enough.

I plop some grilled chicken, broccoli, and carrots on top of my rice, and drizzle teriyaki glaze on top.

Yum!

Then I walk calmly to the drink station, but unfortunately, when I get there, Nick has already left.

Drat. He must be at the table. *But don't you dare look, Heidi! He might catch you!*

That would look way too desperate!

I fill a glass with water, nice and easy, because I'm *so* together.

Hmmm, I wonder if it's weird that I have to concentrate on being composed. And that's when I hear his voice—right next to me.

"Hey, Heidi!" Nick says, sounding happy to see me.

Why does my heart pound extra hard when I'm close to him? I get so nervous around this boy!

Will I even be able to make it to our table without dropping something?

Come on, Heidi, just settle down and answer him!

Okay, okay!

"Hey, Nick! What's up?"

He's smiles his beautiful double-decker-braces smile at me.

"Not much!" he says. "I just wanted to let you know I saved you a seat next to me at our table."

Wow, Nick actually went out of his way to save me a seat **and admits it freely!**

That is *soooo* sweet.

"Thanks, Nick! That was really nice of you!" I say as we head toward the table.

*Eyes on your tray, Heidi. **Almost there!***

I set my tray on the table without a single mishap.

One word: **smooth.**

Nick checks out what's on my plate. **He always notices!**

"Hey, I got a teriyaki bowl too!" he says. "Only, mine's salmon instead of chicken."

My face lights up. This means Nick and I are *twinning*! Only, I'm not going to say this out loud, because that's too silly to say to a BOY, so I just laugh.

Then Nick pulls out two wrapped pairs of chopsticks from his back pocket.

"Do you know how to use chopsticks, Heidi?"

I giggle. "Um, poorly," I confess.

Nick laughs and hands me a pair. "I always bring chopsticks on pasta-and-rice-bowl nights," he says. "They're fun to use. Want me to show you an easy way to use them?"

I set down my fork, because I have a feeling I won't need it. "Sure!" I say, wondering if I can get the hang of chopsticks in one lesson. Guess I'll soon find out.

Nick shows me how to hold them properly, and surprisingly, it's not as hard as I thought. You just have to have the right teacher.

Nick pinches a piece of salmon with his chopsticks. "So, are you entering the talent show, Heidi?"

Oh no, not *this* again. "I'm, um, thinking about it," I say, trying not to chew too loudly. "Are you?"

Nick holds his chopsticks over his bowl. **He doesn't even attempt to eat while he's talking, which is probably a good idea.**

Note to self: *Stop eating when you talk. It's gross.*

"Definitely!" he says with enthusiasm. "I'm really into photography, so I'd like to enter some photos."

He sets his chopsticks on the side of his bowl. "Hey, Heidi, I was wondering. . . . If you're not busy Friday afternoon, maybe you could come with me while I take some nature photos . . . ?"

I pause to take in what he just said.

Did Nick just ask me to hang OUT?

For real?

One word: *swoon!*

"I'd love to come with you, Nick! But what do you need *me* for?"

Nick's face flushes.

Oops, maybe I shouldn't have said that.

Maybe he asked me not because he needs me to help but because he just wants my company.

I wonder if it sounded weirdly insulting.

Ugh, I am so not cool!

Nick is pretty good at disguising his embarrassment.

"Oh, come on, Heidi, of course, I *need* you. You have such a good eye for everything. . . . So would you help me find some cool stuff to photograph?"

I have to pause again to savor Nick's compliment. I'm pretty sure I'm floating above my chair.

Nick laughs. "Hey, earth to Heidi!" he says. "If you don't want to help me, that's okay. I just thought . . ."

Thunk!

I crash back to earth.

"No, no, no!" I jibber jabber. "Count me in! That sounds like a total blast."

Nick smiles and scratches the back of his head. He seems genuinely psyched, and a bit nervous, that I want to hang out with him on Friday.

Well, me too!

Then he looks up at me with those puppy-dog eyes.

"And, Heidi." He hesitates. "Would you possibly

consider posing for some of the pictures too?" he asks hopefully. "You absolutely don't have to if you don't feel comfortable. But sometimes nature photos look better with someone in them, especially someone like *you*."

I'm so flattered! Nick wants me to be *in* his pictures too!

Without question, **this is the boy of my dreams.**

I can't wait to tell Sunny and Anabelle—and maybe even Melanie.

What should I wear on Friday? I mean, photos are practically *forever*.

Then I suddenly realize that I haven't answered his question again.

"I'd love to!" I confirm.

Nick laughs.

He may not be a mind reader like me, but I'm sure he just read my thoughts since they're probably written all over my face: I am so excited!

"Want to meet in front of the main entrance of Crawford after classes on Friday?" Nick suggests.

Do I ever! I think.

"That sounds perfect," I tell him. "Can't wait!"

Nick grins. "Me too."

For dessert we get mint-chip ice cream cones—*my fave*—and eat them on the way back to our dorms.

We talk about places on campus to take pics until we get to his turnoff.

As soon as we say goodbye, I pick up my pace, because *Brrr!* the ice cream is making me shiver—or maybe I just have goose bumps from being with Nick.

Either way, I must not be paying any attention, and I practically crash into Ms. Charmsworth and Mrs. Kettledrum on the path.

"Whoa, Heidi!" Mrs. Kettledrum says.

I put on my brakes—*Eerrrr*!

I smile at my teachers, though I'm sure it's more of a cheesy grin, because I still have Nick on the brain.

"Let me guess," Ms. Charmsworth says. "You're rushing back to your dorm to study for your magical wishes exam that is three days away?" Her rainbow hair shines in the walkway lights.

"By the way, Heidi," Ms. Charmsworth goes on, "the exam will be held *after* classes on Friday, instead of during class time.

"I plan to announce this in class tomorrow, but since you're right here, I thought I'd let you know. It'll give everyone a whole extra period to study!"

I nod, but as I process this info, something about it doesn't sound right.

Then it hits me.

The exam is at the *same time* I promised Nick I'd hang out!

Oh nooooooo! Now I'm double-booked!

This can't be happening! Not when I have my first *real* date!

What am I supposed to do?

Mrs. Kettledrum must notice my horror-struck face because she sends me a mental message. *Heidi, why do you look concerned? You have nothing to worry about. I'm sure you'll do well on the test. Remember, you are a gifted witch-in-training!*

I give Mrs. Kettledrum an agreeable nod, like doing well on the test is the only thing I'm worried about, but of course my worries have nothing to do with the test and have everything to do with Nick. And just like that, all the joy I was feeling fizzles away.

One word: *discouraging.*

"Well, have a good night, Heidi!" my teachers say as they stroll on.

"You too!" I say halfheartedly. And little do they know, I feel like screaming *MERG!* at the top of my lungs.

I mean, what am I going to tell Nick? He's going to be so bummed.

I know *I am*!

Why does everything bad always happen to ME?!

DEEP DOO-DOO

Normally I'm thrilled to see Nick at mealtime. But not this morning.

I can't bear to tell him I have to—*aaack*—change our date.

The last thing I want is to let him down.

There's only one thing left to for me to do: talk to my besties. Fingers and toes crossed that they can help.

But first I have to make myself invisible in the cafeteria so Nick won't see me.

I hide behind random students as I wait for my waffle to cook.

Can you believe I'm actually hiding from my crush?

This is both tragic and necessary.

I grab a pear to go with my waffle and skip a drink. The weirdly good news is that I **don't see Nick anywhere,** so I'm free to hurry over to Sunny and Annabelle's table.

"*PSSSSST!*" I say to get their attention. They know full well that "Pssst" means I'm trying to convey secret info. I take one hand off my tray and point toward the hallway where our secret Loft is located. They both nod and pick up their trays.

Don't you love it when friends just *get it*?

I scurry out of the cafeteria and into the hallway.

As soon as Sunny and Annabelle get close, I trigger the lever on the back of the vending machine and it slides open. We all step through the secret entrance and into the old stairwell.

I slide the vending machine back into place and follow them up the stairs. Annabelle and I take a seat on a hay bale. Sunny sits on one of the old cow-milking stools. Then I start the meeting.

"By order of *your crushing friend,* aka *me,* I call this emergency meeting to order."

My friends set their breakfast trays on their laps and give me their attention.

"Okay, but this emergency meeting can't take too long," Sunny says. "I have to sketch some more ideas for my painting for the talent show. Painting something bright and cheerful is harder than I thought!"

"Same for me with my sculpture," Annabelle says. "It's tough work being an artist!"

"Don't worry. This won't take long," I tell them.

"What's going on, Heidi?" Annabelle asks.

I clasp my hands together in hopes that my problem soon will be solved. "My very dear friends," I begin, "I find myself in an impossible situation."

Sunny and Annabelle look at each other like, *Oh no, here it comes!*

And I understand where they're coming from. With me **it truly is *never a dull moment.***

"Impossible situation?" Sunny questions.

"Are you in trouble again, Heidi?" Annabelle asks.

I roll my eyes, because I know my friends are thinking the worst, like I accidentally turned some kid into a ball of dandelion fluff or something and may end up in jail.

"No," I confirm. "I'm **not**

in the usual kind of trouble. Instead I'm in a troubling situation."

And now to share my dilemma. "As you both know, Nick and I have been speaking a lot more lately."

I have my friends' *total* attention.

"And last night at dinner, Nick asked me to help him with his photography project for the talent show.

"He wants me to walk around campus— *just the two of us*—and find things to photograph.

"And by the way, one of the things he wants to photograph is *me*!"

"*Ooooooo!*" gush Sunny and Annabelle at the same time.

And I have to agree, that is some pretty amazing news.

"But here's the problem," I continue. "I bumped into Mrs. Kettledrum and Ms. Charmsworth after dinner last night, and Ms. Charmsworth told me she scheduled our *magical wishes* exam at the exact *same time* Nick wants to take photographs.

"Can you believe this? And as you can see, I'm in a major pickle."

My friends look genuinely sad for me, but they don't say anything at all.

We're talking, *zero*.

"Come on, you guys! Tell me! What am I supposed to do?"

"You're right, Heidi. Your situation totally stinks," Sunny admits. "But the answer is easy. You have to tell Nick the truth."

What?!

Tell him the truth!

Is that all you have to say?

I could've figured that out myself!

Ugh, why are my friends such goody-goodies?! Surely there's a better way to handle this than just telling him the truth!

I frown to show my displeasure.

"But if I tell him the truth, it might turn him off. Or he might think I don't like him!" I say. The last thing I want is for Nick to think I'm not interested in him."

Sunny and Annabelle look at each other like I'm completely off my rocker.

"So, you'd rather *skip* your exam?" Annabelle says. I can tell she thinks that's the worst idea ever.

I shake my head in frustration.

"Well, no! Obviously *NOT!*" I say. "I can't do that." At least my friends are beginning to understand how upset I am about this.

Sunny comes to my side and puts her arm around me. "Listen, Heidi, wouldn't you understand if Nick had to change plans with *you* for a good reason?"

I think about this for a second. It's a pretty good question, because of course I wouldn't mind. *I'd totally understand.*

I sniff a little and nod.

"Well, exactly," Sunny goes on. "And Nick will understand why you have to reschedule too. All you have to do is change the time. It's really no big deal!

"Then you can meet for your photography session— which, by the way, **sounds supercool**—and also take your exam!"

I look up and smile at Sunny. It sounds so simple and sensible when she says it.

"Thanks, Sunny. I knew you and Annabelle would make me feel better," I say, letting my frustration go.

"I kind of went into a brain spiral because I just couldn't imagine letting Nick down. But you're right. I would never be upset with Nick if he had to change plans, so why would he be upset with me?" I pick up my knife and fork, saw off a piece of cold waffle, and take a bite. "You guys are the bestest friends."

"Thanks," Sunny says. "Always happy to help!" Annabelle nods in agreement. Then we finish our breakfast, drop off our trays, and head to class.

I'll have to tell Nick at lunch. He'll be totally cool with it.

Right?

RIGHT.

Lunch rolls around all too quickly, and to be honest, I'm still nervous about telling Nick about the change in plans.

But the time has come. *Let's do it!*

I grab the seat next to Nick, and we have our usual **electrifying** hellos. Then I try to muster the courage to tell him the bad news, but as it turns out, it's going to take a lot more courage than I thought.

So I stall, of course. And for some reason it seems kind of funny that Nick has no idea what's on my mind.

But, of course, why would he?

He's just sitting there, innocently watching me dip the corner of my PB&J into my chicken noodle soup.

"I love that combo!" he says without a care in the world.

And the moment he says he loves that combo, I instantly want to shout, *Same-same!* But I can't be bubbly or free until I get this load off my mind.

I'd better just go for it.

"Um, Nick, may I ask you something?" I start.

Nick raises his eyebrows. "Sure, Heidi," he says with a hint of questioning in his voice. "What's up? Is everything okay?"

No, everything is not okay, I think. Then I unload my news.

"A little problem has come up," I manage to say. "And I just wondered if there was a way we could reschedule the photo shoot? Maybe we could do it an hour later on Friday?"

There, I did it!

I got it out!

No turning back!

But still, my heart races with **after-I-said-it angst.** Then I read Nick's face, and it's broadcasting one clear emotion: *disappointment.*

And just like that, my worst fear has come true. Nick is unhappy with me.

"Oh no, Heidi!" he cries. "Friday afternoon is the *only* time I have free, and if we go any later, I won't be able to print the photos in time for the talent show." Then Nick realizes he may have overreacted and backpedals in an attempt to mask his disappointment *and* to make me feel better. "But please don't worry about any of this, Heidi," he says. "Maybe we can hang out another time."

I drop what's left of my sandwich into my soup.

I'm *so* upset!

We were all set to hang out for the first time,

and now, because of me, it might never happen.

How can I possibly let a scheduling conflict **ruin everything?**

It was bad enough that we didn't get to hang out on Friends and Family Weekend when everything went bonkers, **but not now, too!**

That's when I make a decision, **right then and there.** Nick and I are going to hang out on Friday **no matter what!**

Nothing is going to wreck my dream afternoon with him— not even an exam!

I smile through my wacky reasoning.

"Never mind, Nick. I'll shuffle some things around in my schedule. I was just checking to see if the photo shoot could be part of the shuffle. . . . I really don't want to miss out on our afternoon together."

Nick grins, and seeing the smile come back onto his face makes me so happy.

Okay, we're back on track. *Yay!*

"This is great news, Heidi!" he says. "I mean, I suppose I could've done the photo shoot by myself if I had to, but the photos wouldn't be nearly as good, and it definitely wouldn't have been as fun without *you*! Okay, then we're all set for Friday afternoon, right?"

My brain knows very well that I shouldn't have suggested this idea in the first place, nor should I agree to it under any circumstances, because all it will do is create an impossible situation for me.

But I want to be with Nick on Friday more than anything else.

I agree without hesitation.

"RIGHT!" I say confidently, stomping out all sense of reason.

But no sooner do these words fly out of my mouth than I 100 percent regret what I've done, because I'm locked into a date with Nick *and* an exam at the exact same time.

Nice play, Heidi!

You're officially in a bind.

And all this makes me wonder: Is there something wrong with me? Because who knowingly double-books two important things?

Only *me*, of course.

Oh, merg it all!

A HAREBRAINED IDEA

Classes are over for the day. *Phew!* Now to think of how to hang out with Nick *and* take my test on Friday.

I take the long way back to my dorm so I can have some time to think.

Let the brainstorming begin!

Hmmm, what if I put Annabelle in a wig and have her take it?

No, Annabelle would never agree to it, and that would be cheating and that is very uncool.

NEXT! Ms. Charmsworth.

Okay, what if I ask Ms. Charmsworth if I can take the test early? I have a study hall Friday morning—maybe I could take it then. . . .

As I mull over this idea, I know exactly what my teacher would say. *If I do this for you, Heidi, I'll have to do it for everybody.*

Blah, blah, blah.

I've heard *that* one before.

Maybe I should just explain to Ms. Charmsworth how important being with Nick is to me.

Then I try to envision how *that* conversation would go.

Well, Ms. C, I have this **humongous crush on this boy,** and he asked me to do something at the same time as our magical wishes exam, so I was wondering if we could work something out.

Pa-leeeeeze?!

It's the ONLY time we can spend time together before Thanksgiving, and if it helps to know, we would be doing something for the talent show at the same time. Would it be okay for me to take a makeup exam at another time?

Okay, just talking it through in my head shows me **how ridiculous** this idea **sounds**, and it takes me right back to my teacher's first answer. *If I do this for you, Heidi, I'll have to do it for* everybody.

I'm at my door and out of ideas.

Melanie is sitting at her desk with her guitar. She's working on the lyrics to her song.

"Hey, Heidi! What line sounds better, 'fabulous me' or 'glamorous me'?"

I walk straight to my bed and flop onto my stomach.

"Glamorous," I mumble into my pillow.

Melanie puts down her guitar. "Eesh, girl! What's the matter with you? You look awful!"

I moan. "Thanks a lot," I say sarcastically. "That's good to know."

Melanie gets up and walks over to examine my condition more closely. "Sorry," she says, reeling it back in. "I didn't mean it that way. I just meant you don't seem like your usual upbeat self."

Wow, is the dark cloud over my head *that* obvious?

I lean on one elbow and prop my head in my hand. Then I spill my whole Nick saga to Melanie.

My broommate listens intently, and she isn't one bit snarky.

One word: *shocked.*

"Well, that's terrible, Heidi!" she says, sympathizing with my tale of woe. "I guess you're just going to have to cancel on Nick."

I flop onto my back. "But why, Melanie?! I thought *you* of all people would understand that I have to find a way to do BOTH things. Can you please help me figure out how I can see Nick *and* take my exam?"

Melanie's blue eyes are round with surprise.

"Are you kidding, Heidi?" she says a tad dramatically. "Don't get me wrong. I'm all for you seeing your crush, but missing an exam for a date?

"Seriously, Heidi, you *have* to take the test. I'm not sure how *even I* could get you out of that one."

I moan long and low. Even though I don't like it, I know she's right "It's true," I say, giving in. "There's no way I can miss the test. I guess I'll just have to bail on Nick.

"*Arrrrrrgh!*" I groan.

"Why is my life SO difficult sometimes?!"

Melanie sighs.

"I know," she says gently. "It's a total bummer."

We're both quiet for a moment. I stare at the glow-in-the-dark stickers on my ceiling.

"If only I could be in two places at the same time," I say wistfully.

Melanie nudges my leg. "I totally get it," she says. "It's a shame that—" Melanie suddenly stops midsentence. "Wait a minute. . . . What did you just say?!"

I sigh. "I said, if only I could be in two places . . ." Then I realize what Melanie is thinking, and I sit up faster than a released car seat.

"**AT THE SAME TIME!**" Melanie says, finishing my sentence. "Heidi, are *you* thinking what *I'm* thinking?"

"**THE WISHING WELL!**" we both say together.

I stop and think about this idea for a second, but there's no way I can justify it. "I don't think it's a good idea, Melanie. It's *way* too dangerous.

"What if the wish only lasts a couple of minutes and I get caught? Or worse, what if it lasts for hours and hours—or even for days! Without a Stone of Gratitude, I wouldn't be able to undo it."

Melanie shrugs. "Well, I'm not saying it's a perfect plan or anything, but Ms. Charmsworth *did* say the wishes *usually* last only an hour, which would be just enough time for you to take the test *and* hang out with Nick at the same time."

I try to imagine the whole thing, but I foresee another problem. "What happens once the wish is over? Where will I end up? Will I be in Ms. Charmsworth's classroom? Or will I be with Nick? Or worse, what if I'm with Nick and then *POOF*, I suddenly disappear?!"

Melanie laughs. "You're right! I didn't think about that. Maybe it's not such a good idea after all."

But it's too late. Melanie has planted a seed—*a very enticing seed*—and it has already sprouted and taken root in my brain.

It's even fair to say that it's taken over my whole mind. Think of it! I'd get to take my test *and* be with Nick!

A mad grin spreads across my face.

"I'll DO IT," I declare. "I'm going to wish to be in two places at the same time. I'll have the Heidi look-alike take my exam, and then the *real* me can hang out with Nick."

I look earnestly at Melanie for her reaction. She's biting her bottom lip uncertainly. "Are you *sure*, Heidi? It's a pretty risky plan."

The thing is, I'm past the thinking-about-risk-and-danger stage and running headlong into the *go-for-it* stage.

I try to make the whole caper sound simple. "All the Heidi look-alike has to do is answer some test questions—questions I could answer in my sleep. I mean, what's so hard about that?"

Melanie looks at me like I've grown a second head or something. "I can think of *plenty* of things, like what if the Heidi look-alike doesn't know *how* to take the test? What if *that* part of you is off with the *real* you, who'll be with Nick?!"

I wave Melanie off, because she's overthinking it. "Not to worry, Mel!

"The second Heidi is still *me*, and she'll know what to do because I know what to do.

"Remember how Ms. Charmsworth said her look-alike was still her—just in another body?

"Either way, I still want the *real* me to be with Nick, and I'll let the counterfeit take the test.

"The bottom line is, no matter what you say, it's too late to talk me out of it. I've already made up my mind."

And I know my train of thinking lacks some logic,

but I'm too far gone. There's no way to stop this train. It's already left the station.

"Okay, so you're *really* doing this?" Melanie questions.

I nod vigorously. "You bet I am!"

I'm pumped, and I'm not even the least bit worried, because I'm certain this plan will work.

I mean, what could possibly go wrong?

One word: *NOTHING!*

THE PLAN

Whoooosh!

That's the sound of how fast this week has flown!

And tomorrow's my BIG day with Nick. We're all ready.

Melanie and I have created a plan for our Wishing-Well Caper (that's what we're calling it), and we have to go over it one more time before bed.

Eeeee!

This is gonna be epic!

I'm on my way over to Sunny and Annabelle's to see their finished entries for the talent show. They promised me a private viewing.

When I get there, their art is covered with sheets. Two chairs face their masterpieces. Sunny shakes some dice to see who goes first. She has to beat Annabelle's four and a two.

The dice clatter across the floor. *Double sixes!* **Sunny wins.**

She leaps to her feet and gets into position beside her work.

Annabelle and I take our seats.

"Thank you for coming to our art show!" Sunny begins.

Then she grasps the sheet with her fingers. "And now, friends, the moment you've all been waiting for! My grand reveal!"

Annabelle and I clap as Sunny whisks the sheet from her painting.

"Ta-da!" she exclaims.

For me Sunny's painting is love at first sight.

She painted a rainbow over an ocean with a pod of dolphins leaping in the waves.

"Oh, Sunny, it's STUNNING!" I exclaim.

"And it's so YOU!" Annabelle adds.

Annabelle is absolutely right. The painting is Sunny through and through. It's completely joyful.

Our friend beams at our reaction.

"I chose this scene because the ocean is my happy place," Sunny explains.

I know exactly where Sunny's painting is referring to: Castle Spell Cove, a magical seaside town where we met when we were younger.

It's one of my favorite places too.

"Well, you definitely nailed it, Sunny," I tell her. And she really did. Her painting could win an award.

Then it's Annabelle's turn. Sunny takes a seat beside me, and Annabelle stands next to her work.

"As you all know, I was going to create something from clay," Annabelle begins. "But nothing was working, so I decided to do what I do *best*. I used crystals and metals to create a dazzling sculpture."

Wow, that makes much more sense for Annabelle than using clay, I think. That's because Annabelle's gift as a witch is healing and wellness.

She has a trunkful of gems and crystals that's positively drool worthy.

I can't wait to see her sculpture.

Here she goes!

Swoosh!

Annabelle swishes the sheet away from her artwork with the grace of a magician.

"Voila!"

Sunny and I squeal on cue.

Annabelle has created the most beautiful sculpture I've ever seen!

On a delicately hammered silver circle hangs a golden crescent moon. Five shimmering chains hang from the top of the circle, with two more twinkly chains hanging from the moon inside.

At the bottom of each chain is a dazzling crystal.

In the middle of each chain, she has fastened glistening gold and silver stars, creating a sparkly constellation.

One word: *bedazzling.*

We sit attentively as Annabelle explains the meaning of her sculpture.

"Each crystal has a special power," she tells us. "The Herkimer diamonds are a type of quartz and are supposed to calm the mind. The brassy yellow pyrite crystal is often called *fool's gold,* but it actually attracts wealth and good fortune. The blue calcite crystal brings relaxation and peacefulness. And the green amazonite brings truth, honor, and integrity to those in its presence."

"It's amazing!" Sunny says.

"And magical!" I exclaim. "Your sculpture should be displayed in an art museum. Both of your pieces should!" I sigh, because I can't believe my friends are so talented. It makes me realize, more than ever, how special they are too.

Annabelle does a little curtsy. Then she pulls up one of her mushroom stools and sits with us.

"How's Melanie's song coming along?" she asks.

I laugh. "Well, let's see," I say, feeling a surge of sarcasm. "She sings in front of the mirror. She sings in the shower. And she sings in bed.

"Let's put it this way, it's like having the radio on 24-7!"

My friends laugh.

"Seriously, is her song any good?" Sunny asks.

I nod. "Yeah, actually, it's *really* good—even after I've heard it five million times."

Then an idea for the talent show pops into my head. "And Melanie has even inspired me to *maybe* do a performance of my own!"

My friends applaud, like this is the best news they've ever heard.

"That's fantastic, Heidi!" Annabelle approves. "What are you going to do?"

I put my hands up and pull back, like I'm yanking on the reins of a horse.

"Whoa, go back, partners! I'm just saying I *might* sign up for the talent show.

"If I *do* sign up, it'll be a last-minute entry," I tell them. "And if I actually *go through with it*, I'll write a poem, since everyone liked my sense poem in English. The subject would probably be *time*, due to this whole scheduling nightmare with Nick."

Sunny claps her hands. "That a great idea, Heidi! You should totally do it."

Annabelle agrees, but then she asks me a *loaded* question. "So, what did Nick say when you told him you couldn't hang out on Friday?"

Weeeee-ooooow! A siren blares inside my head.

Danger! Alert! Alert!

This is the *last* question I want to answer.

If I tell them I plan to use the wishing well to solve my problem, I know Sunny and Anabelle will try to talk me out of it.

But I don't want to lie to my friends either.

I just want to wait until Friday is over, and then I can tell them how it all worked out perfectly.

For now I'd better get out of here. I jump to my feet, grab my backpack, and make up a quick excuse.

"Oh, I um ... Nick and I are working it out," I reassure my friends. Then I'm all **exit stage right.**

Sunny and Annabelle stand up as I beeline for the door.

"Well, hopefully you'll get another chance to hang out with him after Thanksgiving break," Annabelle says cheerfully.

"Yeah, hopefully!" I lie, squeezing the doorknob.

"Sorry, you two. I have to go work on my poem! Inspiration calls!" I back awkwardly out the door and salute my friends.

As I make my escape down the hallway, I shake my head.

A salute, Heidi? Really?

Sometimes you can be *mega* awkward.

Melanie is singing her heart out to the mirror when I walk through her drapery of beads and into the room. When she sees me, she hops off her stool and rests the neck of her guitar against her dresser.

"Heidi, I'm *so* glad you're back! We have to go over tomorrow's plan.

"It needs to be flawless, and I hate to say this, but I just found a BIG problem."

I throw my backpack onto my bed. "What's the big problem?"

Melanie hands me the plan and points to the middle of the page.

"We forgot something *really* important!" she says like we're doomed forever. She waits for me to read the part where our plan goes amiss. When I'm done, she looks at me intensely.

"Heidi, how are we going to get the well to *open*? You know it's sealed with magic, *right*?"

I hand the plan back to Melanie. "Well, I guess it's a good thing that I *know* the spell that unseals the well!"

Melanie shakes her head in total surprise. "And how do you happen to know *that*, Heidi?"

I smile slyly. "I may have overheard Ms. Charmsworth say it quietly before class the other day."

Melanie exhales dramatically. "Well, *that's* a relief! I thought we were going to have to scrap our whole Wishing-Well Caper!"

I scoff at the thought of scrapping the plan. "No way!" I say. "Now let's go over it one more time."

Melanie nods, and then she yawns. "Okay, but first let's get ready for bed."

Melanie's yawn makes me yawn too. "Yeah, good idea," I say.

We wash up, jump into our jammies, and hop into our beds. Melanie snatches the plan from her nightstand and goes over it step-by-step.

"We know that Ms. Charmsworth is going to her office during our fifteen-minute snack break to answer last-minute questions from students," Melanie begins. "The classroom will be empty, and that's when we'll execute our plan as follows.

"Step one: wait for everyone to empty the classroom and go on their snack break. Step two: magically unseal wishing well. Step three: toss coin into well. Step four: make wish. Step five: reseal wishing well. Step six: Melanie takes Look-alike Heidi to her seat for the test. Step seven: Original Heidi proceeds to photography date with Nick.

"Got it?"

I nod, reviewing each step in my mind.

"And don't forget a coin," Melanie reminds me. "That's really important. You should probably bring two, just in case."

Then my broommate gives me a funny look. "Heidi, are you okay?"

For some reason I'm shivering, but I know it's not because I'm cold or sick. "I think I'm shaking because the reality of what I'm about to do just hit me."

I sit up and take a sip from my water bottle. "I'm excited and nervous at the same time. It's like I can't wait to use this new form of magic, and I also can't wait to hang out with Nick.

"But if I'm being honest, it's also a little overwhelming. Are you confident our plan will work, Melanie?"

My broomie stretches her pink eye mask over her head and lets it rest on her forehead like silk sunglasses.

"Yeah, I'm totally confident it will work," she says. "But let's be real. I'm confident about *everything*."

It's true. Melanie is confident through and through, unlike me. I'm more like a mix of confidence, worry, and self-doubt.

"How do you do it? You know, stay confident *all* the time?" I ask, hoping she'll reveal her secret.

Melanie shrugs as she slides under her covers.

"There's no formula, Heidi," she explains. "You just have to *be* confident—you know, believe in yourself." She snaps her eye mask into place. "And in this case, you have to believe and trust the plan."

Trust the plan, I repeat to myself.

Then I roll onto my back and give myself a quick pep talk.

Remember, Heidi, this is a flawless plan, I tell myself.

You can succeed in being in two places at once.

If anyone can ace a test AND hang out with Nick, it's YOU.

You're an amazing witch, and you know it.

And you KNOW that you know it!

Okay, then why am I still so nervous?

One word: *merg.*

8

CAREFUL WHAT YOU WISH FOR!

If there's one thing that's true about me, it's that I never back down from a challenge, and this time is no different.

Ready or not, it's time to put the Wishing-Well Caper into motion.

Okay, this doesn't mean I'm not freaking out.

I am.

I'm just **not** *backing* out.

After the last bell, Melanie and I wait *forever* for the students to leave. Once the class is empty, we check the door to make sure the coast is clear. **We're wily witches on a magical mission!**

Whoosh! I run back to the wishing well.

The ancient wishing well glows with an alluring light. It seems to beckon me to make my wish.

Melanie stays by the classroom door and stands guard. "Heidi, hurry up!" she warns.

It's now or never, so *just go for it!*

I stand before the wishing well and grit my teeth.

Then I recite the spell to open it.

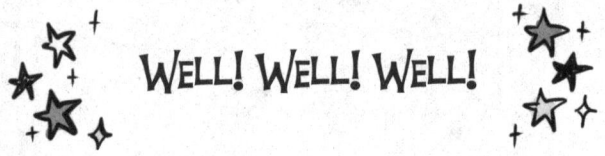
WELL! WELL! WELL!

I try not to say it too loudly, but still **the sound of my voice in the empty room is frighteningly loud.**

But no need to dwell on that because **the spell works. The well is open.**

I grab a coin from my pocket and toss it in, just like Ms. Charmsworth did in class on Monday. **Then I make my wish.**

"I WISH I COULD BE IN MORE THAN ONE PLACE!" I chant.

As soon as the words leave my mouth, I second-guess them.

Oh no, was that the wording Ms. Charmsworth used?

Or was it "in two places at the same time"?

Melanie and I should've gone over that more.

But it's too late, the wish is in motion.

POOF!

A swirl of smoke shoots from the well. Sparkles of excitement swirl inside me, too.

But when the smoke disappears, I'm still standing there all by myself.

I look behind me, but there's no Heidi look-alike there.

Uh-oh!

Maybe the wish didn't work!

That's when I hear Melanie gasp. "Heidi, look over HERE!"

I turn toward Melanie.

And there, standing beside her, is another ME!

I walk over and gape at this perfect likeness of myself. It's both fascinating and disturbing at the same time.

I study my look-alike from every angle.

Wow, *THAT'S* what I look like?

The only difference between me and my twin is that I'm wearing my hair down and she has her hair in a ponytail. Melanie taps me on the shoulder.

"This is *no time* to get stuck on yourself, Heidi," she whispers loudly. "One of you *has to go* before people come back for the test!"

She takes my Heidi look-alike by the hand and leads her to my desk so she can take my exam.

"Don't forget to reseal the well," Melanie hisses. I nod and quickly repeat the spell to close it up.

"Now *get going!*" Melanie urges frantically. "And remember, *Cinderella*, you only have ONE HOUR!"

Okay, that does it. I sprint from the classroom.

I'm on my way to see Nick.

Eeee! We're actually about to have some alone time together! And just think of it—I'll be magically taking my test at the same time.

One word: *brilliant.*

I'm partway to Crawford when I suddenly start to feel lightheaded.

Whoa, what's happening?

I slow down to see if that makes me feel any better, but it doesn't.

I rub my hands together because they feel kind of sweaty.

Don't worry, I reassure myself. *I'm **sure** it's just from running and the excitement of spending time with Nick.*

And there he is!

Nick is waiting for me at the bottom of the stairs in front of Crawford. He smiles and waves.

Wow, he's soooo CUTE.

Seeing Nick makes me feel better already! **Or does it?**

Something's still off, I think as I catch up to Nick.

"Hey, Heidi!" he says. "You look so *nice.* Are you ready for our photo shoot?"

His compliment makes me smile. It also makes me think about my outfit, which I kept simple but chic.

I have on a white long-sleeved waffle shirt with a chunky black-and-silver half-zip jacket, and my favorite jeans with embroidery on the pockets and hems. Oh yeah, and ankle booties.

"I'm SO ready!" I say, trying to sound energetic, but to be honest, I feel kind of woozy.

Weird.

"Great!" Nick says. "Let's head to the track. Maybe we'll find something worth photographing over there."

I try to respond, but this time I can barely get the words out.

"Worth . . . photographing," I repeat as I try to keep up with Nick.

Why is my brain so foggy?

And why am I suddenly sooo tired?

Come on, Heidi! Just rally!

I focus on the track. Natalie and Jenna are there with the rest of the varsity track team, stretching for a run. Natalie and Jenna are upperclassmen and best friends. Jenna also happens to be the resident advisor of my dorm.

The track team members all have on matching bright orange running shorts and white tops. The colors look great against the backdrop of grass and evergreens behind them.

I want to share this with Nick, but I can barely get out the words, so I tug Nick's arm and point.

"Look!" is all I can manage to say. Nick looks at where I'm pointing. He sees the team stretching in the sun.

"Oh yeah! That's a great shot, Heidi! See what I mean? **You have such a good eye!**" Nick says.

I cover my mouth and yawn. "Good eye," I repeat, followed by another huge yawn.

I think I may need to sit down for a sec. I wander over to a huge old tree, plunk down on the ground, and lean against the trunk. Nick runs over.

"Heidi, what's the matter?" he asks. "Are you okay? You don't look very well—I mean, you always look great, but you look kind of pale."

I smile weakly. "It's, um, nothing," I lie, because I'm seriously in a total fog. I don't know what's happening. "I just need to sit for a little bit. I'm really sorry, Nick."

Nick sits beside me. "Well, let me stay with you," he offers.

I wave him off. "No, no. I want you to get some photos of the track and maybe some of the Four Square court while I rest," I urge him. "I'll join you in a sec."

But Nick doesn't move.

"I'm *serious*, Nick. Please, I'll be fine," I tell him. Nick doesn't look convinced, but he decides to trust me and hops to his feet.

"Okay, I'll be right back!" he says. "Are you sure you're all right?"

"*Go*," I insist.

Nick walks away, and I'm kind of relieved, because I feel so weird.

Of all the times to feel crummy!

I try to relax and watch the runners on the track. I'm just about to start meditating to see if that helps, but then I suddenly see something.

Something I should definitely *not* be seeing.

Something absolutely terrifying.

My Heidi look-alike is on the track!

What is SHE doing here?

And if Heidi Number Two is HERE, then who's taking my exam?!

Then I notice something else.

THIS Heidi has her hair in a bun. The one taking the test had her hair in a ponytail.

Uh-oh.

Could there be *a third* Heidi?

But that's impossible! I only wished to be in TWO places at once, not three! Right?!

Either way, I can't let Nick see this other Heidi!

The only problem is that I'm so tired, I can barely stand up! On top of that, my brain is still stuck in Fogsville, USA.

Oh, help! Is there any way I could possibly have a fairy godmother? I look around desperately, but I see no sign of wispy winged help.

The universe has responded, and the answer is clear.

I, Heidi Heckelbeck, am doomed yet again.

CLASS CLOWN

When I made the wish to be in more than one place, I didn't know I would randomly swap points of view with my look-alike.

But I have.

And right now the *real* me is still sitting under the tree by the track.

So when I, *Heidi-under-the-Tree*, start to wonder about *Exam Heidi*, a shift in focus occurs.

Now I AM Exam Heidi.

Yup, I'm sitting in the classroom with Ms. Charmsworth and the rest of my class. And by the way, the exam is *not* going well. Every time I read a question, I have to reread it, and even then I can still barely comprehend it, let alone write an answer. That is so not like me. I always ace my School of Magic tests.

The only thing that's working in top form **is my sense of fear.**

I look over at Melanie and catch her eye. She smiles, because she has absolutely no clue what's happening.

I shake my head and point to the test to try to show her that **things are not going well.**

Melanie frowns as if to say, *Well, what am I supposed to do about it?*

And she's right. There's absolutely nothing Melanie can do about it. The only way out of this mess would be for me to confess to my teacher what I've done, **and, well, that's not going to happen.**

I stare at my test and try to remember the answers.

Argh! This is SO HARD!

I decide to randomly circle "true" and "false" around the page, **because it feels better to do something than do nothing at all.**

In the midst of all this, I get distracted by a weird sound. The noise sounds like a huge bubble popping.

POP!

There it goes again!

My classmates look up from their tests to see where the sound is coming from.

I'm so deep in the Land of Yuck, I don't really care what the sound is . . . that is, until someone taps me on the shoulder.

"Hey, Heidi," a voice says. "How's your test going?"

I look up and see something terrifying—more terrifying than my hair during my scary hair spell, way worse than the look on Hunter's face when he was under the isolation spell, and infinitely worse than flying gargoyles.

It's *ANOTHER ME.* Only *this* Heidi has curly hair.

And before I can scream, another Heidi in pigtails walks in through the classroom door.

"Hey, Heidi! Need some help on your test?" This makes three Heidis, including me, in this room.

One word: *monstrous.*

The entire class is shrieking with laughter.

Everyone's pointing fingers at me.

And me.

And ME!

Some kids are actually cheering.

"How are you doing this, Heidi?" Hunter asks. "Can you make another one of me, too? I could use some help on this test."

I ignore Hunter, because *both* Heidis are at my desk, one on either side of me.

Ms. Charmsworth throws her hands into the air. "Oh my goodness, Heidi! What have you done?"

I slump in my chair, partly because my teacher is disappointed in me, and partly because I feel so weary. I wish I had the strength to do something about this, but sadly, I don't.

Luckily, Melanie takes action.

She jumps from her seat, runs to the front of the classroom, and taps Ms. Charmsworth on the shoulder. Ms. Charmsworth doesn't even look at her.

"*Not now*, Melanie," she says as she madly searches through her purse. "I have a Heidi situation to deal with."

Ms. Charmsworth dumps the contents of her purse onto her desk and rifles through everything.

I hope she's searching for a Stone of Gratitude, I think. *Oh, please, please find one!*

If she doesn't find one, then the entire School of Magic faculty will probably have to round up all my doubles until the wish wears off.

I wonder if there are any more roaming around campus. But what if the faculty can't find them all?

Or what if it's one of those times when the wish lasts for days and days? *Then what?*

Oh no! This is terrifying!

I focus on Melanie to get my mind off these scary thoughts. She's still glued to our teacher's side.

"Ms. Charmsworth, I think I can help with the Heidi situation," I hear Melanie persist.

Ms. Charmsworth is madly rummaging through her desk drawers.

She'd *better* find that Stone of Gratitude.

She'd also better listen to Melanie!

Melanie tries again. "Ms. Charmsworth, Heidi made *a wish*, and now we need to find Nick Lee."

Ms. Charmsworth suddenly stops what she's doing and glares at Melanie. "What on earth do a wish, Nick Lee, and a bunch of Heidi clones have to do with each other?" she asks. "Nick is not even a student in the School of Magic!"

Okay, there it is!

My secret's out, I think.

And I'm in BIG trouble, for sure.

Melanie grabs Ms. Charmsworth's arm. "I know," Melanie says. "But Nick is with the *real* Heidi RIGHT NOW."

Ms. Charmsworth presses her hand against her heart. I'm pretty sure she just realized that a Heidi double is taking her test.

In her distress my teacher yanks opens her center desk drawer—the only drawer she hasn't opened—and grabs something from inside. Whatever it is, she shoves it into her pocket.

Oh, please, let it be a magic stone!

Ms. Charmsworth walks out from behind her desk and addresses the class.

Everyone is chatting up a storm about me and the other two Heidis in the classroom.

"Attention, class!" she says, clapping her hands. The room grows a little quieter. "I know everyone's very distracted, but I want you all to please continue with your exam.

"Has anyone finished at this time?"

Sunny's hand goes up.

Ms. Charmsworth beckons for her to come forward. Sunny quickly walks to the front of the room. "Sunny, I'm putting you in charge until I can get Ms. Fernandez to come over."

Then Ms. Charmsworth looks at the rest of the class. "Carry on, students! You may have extra time to complete your tests."

Then she zeroes in on me and the other two Heidis.

"All Heidis, please follow me, NOW!"

The class laughs hysterically as I pull myself out of my chair.

I still feel awful, but I have to listen to my teacher and keep going, because this could get me kicked out of Broomsfield—that is, if I even *survive* this ordeal.

As we leave the classroom, Sunny shouts, "Quiet, everyone!" But nobody can stop laughing—not even Sunny.

This is so humiliating. I've become the laughing stock of the School of Magic ... for yet another time!

Will I ever be able to face my classmates again?

One word: *doubtful.*

SEEING DOUBLE

As soon as we get out of the classroom, Ms. Charmsworth calls Ms. Fernandez (one of our school librarians) and explains everything.

Ms. Charmsworth slides her phone into her pocket and turns to Melanie.

"Do you know where Heidi and Nick were going?" Ms. Charmsworth asks.

And before Melanie has a chance to answer, the two fake Heidis butt in. I realize I'm a fake Heidi too, but I'm more in my right mind than they are—or at least I think I am.

"Oooh, Nick!" one of the Heidis sings. "Are we doing magic in front of Nick?"

I'm still *Exam Heidi*. These other two Heidis are duplicates of duplicates.

Melanie ignores the other me and explains to

Ms. Charmsworth how everything went down, from Nick inviting me to his photo shoot, to the time conflict with the test, and finally to the wish.

I grimace listening to it all.

"And that's when things began to spiral . . . ," Melanie says regretfully.

"But I have no idea where the real Heidi and Nick are. I just know they're somewhere on campus taking photos."

Ms. Charmsworth sighs as she thinks through the twisted logic that led to the appearance of a small basketball team of Heidis.

At the same time, we exit the School of Magic through a side door.

"Okay, everyone, follow me—*and quickly*," Ms. Charmsworth says.

We follow Ms. Charmsworth to the bottom of the stairs, and she herds us to one side of a stone staircase so no one can see us. "Let's see if we can spy Heidi and Nick from here."

We huddle between a boxwood hedge and the staircase and scan the campus for any sign of Nick and what was—*and is*—the original me.

I can also hear Ms. Charmsworth talking to herself.

"Honestly, in all my days at Broomsfield Academy, I've never been in a situation like this one," she mutters.

Her words make me cringe, but I can't blame her for being mad. Broomsfield Academy has probably never before had a witch who gets into as many sticky situations as I do.

Then Melanie elbows me.

"There they are!" she whispers loudly. "They're between the track and the Four Square court!"

Melanie is right.

Original me is trying to pull Nick away from the track.

Ms. Charmsworth suddenly begins to shake a finger in the direction we're looking.

"Oh dear!" she cries. "I see *another* Heidi on the track! Melanie, I want you to go grab that rogue Heidi before somebody sees her!"

Melanie keeps her eye on Track Star Heidi.

"Wow, Heidi, you should wear your hair in a bun more often," Melanie says. "It's a good look on you!"

How can Melanie think of hairstyles in the middle of a fiasco?

Ms. Charmsworth wonders the same thing. "Melanie! This is no time for style tips! *GO!*"

Melanie snaps to attention. "Oops, sorry, Ms. Charmsworth."

Our teacher shakes her head as Melanie runs off. Then she reaches into her pocket and pulls out the Stone of Gratitude.

I am glad to see that!

One by one, Ms. Charmsworth removes the Heidis with the Stone of Gratitude.

"Thank you for fulfilling this wish," she says once, and then again.

POP! POP! Two of the impostor Heidis vanish.

I'm next.

I shut my eyes. *POP!* And just like that I'm back in what should be my one and only body.

But this nightmare is *not* over! There are still two of me, and I have to get Nick away from Track Star Heidi.

I wish Melanie would hurry up and get that fake Heidi back to Ms. Charmsworth. I tug on Nick's arm, but it takes all the energy I have left.

Oof! Nick pulls his arm back.

"Heidi, what are you trying to get away from, anyway?" he asks.

Okay, this is a fair question, but not one I want to answer, so I think of another way to move Nick along. "Oh, I'm sorry, Nick. I just *really* want to get back to my dorm so I can lie down."

But my excuse is too late. Nick has just spied my twin walking across campus with Melanie.

He looks at me and then back at the copy of me.

"Heidi, do you see what I see?" Nick asks.

The only thing I can see is that I'm *finished*, as in *game over*.

Nick just saw the other Heidi!

This is really bad, and it zaps me of the last bit of strength I have.

I stagger to a bench and collapse.

"Nick, this is not what you think. . . ." And I'm done. I just don't have the oomph to give any further explanation.

Fortunately, Melanie, Track Star Heidi, and Ms. Charmsworth appear at our sides at just that moment.

Nick rubs his eyes in disbelief. "Heidi, what's going on?" he asks. "Since when do you have a twin?"

I have no words. I'm too tired to make anything up and way too out of it to be charming and witty.

Luckily, Ms. Charmsworth takes over. "Oh, Nick," my teacher says, hopefully coming to my rescue. "Heidi doesn't have a twin!"

Nick points at the second Heidi.

"Then, who's she?"

Ms. Charmsworth and Melanie look at each other.

Where is this going? I wonder.

"You know, Nick, Heidi did something today she was not supposed to," Ms. Charmsworth says.

Nick throws his hands into the air in frustration.

"And what does that have to do with anything?" he says. "I feel so confused."

Nick walks over to the bench, sits down beside me, and folds his arms tightly across his chest. "Will somebody *please* explain what's going on?"

Ms. Charmsworth shakes her head with concern. "Of course, Nick. You see, Heidi is a witch. In fact, there is a School of Magic hidden inside the halls of Broomsfield Academy."

I can't believe Ms. Charmsworth is revealing all this, but she continues.

Melanie looks as shocked as I am.

"Today, Heidi made a wish in an enchanted wishing well. She wanted to be in two places at once.

"Well, she got her wish and more."

But Nick doesn't buy it. His face twists in confusion.

And who can blame him? He just received news that anyone would doubt. Anyone who wasn't a witch or a wizard.

"I can't believe this," Nick shouts. "Heidi is a witch? There are actual witches and wizards in the world?

"Would someone please explain this?"

Ms. Charmsworth rushes to Nick's side.

"Oh, Nick. There's nothing else to explain," Ms. Charmsworth says. "Because you are going to get a forgetting spell and you won't remember any of this."

Nick turns to me. "Are you really a witch?"

I can't believe I'm about to admit the truth, but since he will forget any of this happened, I nod my head.

"Well, what if I don't want to forget this?" asks Nick. "Can you really make me forget any of this ever happened?"

Ms. Charmsworth smiles as nicely as possible. I can tell she feels bad for Nick, and I do, too!

It's all my fault that magic was exposed to a non-magical student—once again—and if we want to keep the School of Magic safe, we have no choice but to put a forgetting spell on Nick.

I feel even more sick than I did a few minutes ago.

And that's when Track Star Heidi says something that's hard to ignore.

"Nick is *CU-U-U-UTE!*"

Oh no! I really feel like I want to throw up!

How could Track Star Heidi do that?

I would *never* say something like that out loud.

Nick looks confused. His eyes dart back and forth between Track Star Heidi and me, and I can't tell if his cheeks are red because technically, I've just told him he's cute, or because all the blood has rushed to his head amidst all of this hocus pocus.

My head falls to the palm of my hand. *How could I let this happen?* I think.

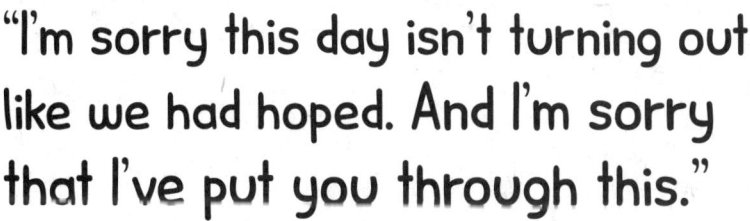

I turn and look sympathetically at Nick. "Don't worry, Nick. It will be okay, and all this confusion will be gone before you know it," I reassure him.

"I'm sorry this day isn't turning out like we had hoped. And I'm sorry that I've put you through this."

Nick runs his fingers through his hair and says nothing.

Then Ms. Charmsworth places her hand on Nick's shoulder and explains what will happen next.

"Please let Melanie walk you to the infirmary where our nurse will perform the forgetting spell," she says. "The nurse will take care of you, and you can also get some rest while you're there. When you wake up, everything will be all right."

Nick sighs and gets up from the bench.

"Okay, I'll go, but what about Heidi—the real Heidi, that is?"

"I'll be fine, Nick. Don't worry about me. This isn't my first magical disaster if you could believe it," I confess. I don't know why I'm admitting this to him, but since the cat is out of the bag, **why not?**

Nick just stands there, **stunned.**

I feel bad for him.

Is it always like this when a witch likes a non-magical person?

Why is my life so complicated?

"I'll take care of Heidi," Ms. Charmsworth says. "Melanie, go ahead and get Nick started on his way."

Melanie leads my bewildered crush down the path.

As soon as they're out of sight, Ms. Charmsworth whips out her phone. "I have to make two calls, Heidi. One to the infirmary and the other to Mrs. Kettledrum."

"Oh noooo...," I moan. "Why do you have to tell Mrs. Kettledrum? She'll be so disappointed in me!"

Ms. Charmsworth holds the phone to her ear and looks at me.

Her mouth is nothing but a thin straight line. "She's not the only one. You should have thought of that before, Heidi."

And I have no comeback.

My career as a **superstar witch** may be over before it even begins.

Two words: *I'm ruined!*

WISHFUL THINKING

Pop!

As soon as Ms. Charmsworth hangs up, she vanquishes Track Star Heidi with her Stone of Gratitude.

Now it's back to just me, the one and only Heidi.

And with just one of me, the brain fog begins to lift and my strength starts coming back too.

I don't feel 100 percent, but I feel

a bazillion times better than I did a minute ago.

As for my mental state of being, I feel like a total doofus. But I suppose that's normal after trying to pull off a stunt like being in two places at once.

Oh gosh!

Here comes Mrs. Kettledrum!

She's walking at superspeed. Her heels angrily smack the sidewalk with every step.

She didn't bring Momo either. That's a punishment in and of itself.

When Mrs. Kettledrum sees me, she begins to rub her forehead. I'm sure she's trying to ward off a headache—*a Heidi Headache.*

Ugh.

As soon as she gets to us, Ms. Charmsworth tells her everything.

"I don't understand how any of this could've happened!" Ms. Charmsworth says once she has gotten everything out into the open. "Heidi is one of my best students!"

Time-out.

You know what's weird?

It almost sounds as if Ms. Charmsworth feels partly responsible for what I've done.

No doubt I've made her regret showing our class the wishing well in the first place.

I certainly proved that I can't be trusted with it.

Mrs. Kettledrum, who's always calm and collected—even when things are completely out of control, nods calmly and sympathetically.

"Yes, Heidi is a very special student," she agrees. "I'd even go so far as to say an extraordinary one. She's smart and imaginative, but she's also impulsive and willful. And more often than not this gets her into trouble."

I sigh.

I wish she had left out the last two qualities she mentioned. I'd rather not hear about those.

One word: *oof.*

When we get to the classroom, my teachers ask me to take a seat. I sit down and face both of them.

The rest of the class is gone. They finished the test and left their papers on Ms. Charmsworth's desk. Mrs. Kettledrum and Ms. Charmsworth are standing in front of the wishing well, **the thing that got me into this mess in the first place.**

And then my trial begins.

"Heidi, we want to know *why* you used the wishing well without permission *and* without supervision?" Ms. Charmsworth begins. "Or why you used it *at all* when you knew it was forbidden.

"And we'd also like to know how you unsealed the wishing well without access to the spell?"

I squirm uncomfortably in my chair. I have a lot to own up to, and all these questions make me feel the weight of what I've done.

"*Well . . . ,*" I begin, unknowingly using the dreaded word "well" until I hear myself say it. "I, um, overheard you say the spell to open the wishing well before class began on Monday—so that's how I knew how to unseal it."

Ms. Charmsworth and Mrs. Kettledrum look at each other, like, *That will never happen again!*

Then they turn their eyes back on me.

I gather my courage and go on.

"I know it was *wrong* to use the wishing well without permission or supervision—or even at all. And for this I'm truly sorry.

"And this part may sound really silly. I feel silly even saying it now, but the reason I used the well was because I desperately needed to be in two places at the same time, and I thought it might work for me."

Ms. Charmsworth presses both hands against her cheeks. "Oh, Heidi! Were those the *exact* words you used to make your wish?"

I blink in surprise.

I wasn't expecting my teacher to ask me how I phrased my wish.

I was fully expecting to get yelled at. I look up at Ms. Charmsworth.

"I *think* those were the words I used?" I say uncertainly.

"Well, maybe it was more like, 'I wish I could be in more than one place.' It's hard to say since I was in kind of a rush at the time...."

Ms. Charmsworth and Mrs. Kettledrum sigh loudly, making me feel the full impact of my foolishness.

"Heidi, didn't you hear me say how careful you have to be with how you word your wishes?" Ms. Charmsworth asks, patting the wishing well with her hand. "This well is not a toy, and a rushed wish almost always ends in disaster.

"Student wishes must always be carefully planned and approved by a seasoned witch or wizard. You're very lucky something more dangerous didn't happen!"

Then it's Mrs. Kettledrum's turn.

"She's right, Heidi. You *also* exposed magic to a *non-magical student*," she reminds me.

"Thank goodness Ms. Charmsworth came up with a solution for poor Nick."

Then Mrs. Kettledrum stops and looks at Ms. Charmsworth. "I assume Nurse Robinson has already performed the forgetting spell. He has run into situations like this before, although we do try to keep them at a minimum."

"Nothing about today has been ideal," says Ms. Charmsworth, "but thank goodness for forgetting spells."

"Heidi, I hope you understand the gravity of this situation," Mrs. Kettledrum says. "Just imagine if this had taken place in the cafeteria or the library, with many more students watching?"

I shudder to think of it.

It was bad enough when my hair grew to Rapunzel length in the middle of the cafeteria one morning earlier this year. I can only imagine what a ruckus several Heidis would've caused.

My teachers look at me sternly.

"You are in serious trouble, Heidi," Mrs. Kettledrum affirms, as if I didn't know.

And as I await my punishment, the door to the classroom swings open.

Once I realize who it is, I'm not sure if I should be relieved or even more nervous than I already am.

Melanie comes barging in. "I object!" she says.

Mrs. Kettledrum and Ms. Charmsworth look at her, confused. "How can we help you, Melanie?" Mrs. Kettledrum asks.

"Um," Melanie's pace slows until it comes to a stop. And it looks like she's lost all the conviction she entered the room with. "May I please object?" Melanie asks in the meekest voice I've ever heard come out of her mouth.

I mean EVER.

"We're in the middle of a meeting, Melanie," Ms. Charmsworth says. "But what is it?"

Melanie walks toward us quietly. She looks timid, not a look I've seen on her either. She comes over and stands next to me.

"This is not *all* Heidi's fault," Melanie confesses. "I *helped* Heidi use the wishing well."

I can't believe this! Melanie, my former enemy, actually has *my* back!

Wow, that takes a lot of guts. A wave of warmth washes over me.

Even Ms. Charmsworth and Mrs. Kettledrum look surprised, *especially* Mrs. Kettledrum.

"How admirable of you to stick up for your friend, Melanie," Mrs. Kettledrum says. "And you're right. It *was* wrong to have helped Heidi to use the wishing well, but in the end it was Heidi's decision.

"We appreciate your stopping by, but first we need to finish our discussion with Heidi. We'll talk more with you later, Melanie. You can go."

Melanie squeezes my hand and then tiptoes quietly out of the room. The door clicks shut, and Mrs. Kettledrum smiles.

"Well, *that* was very thoughtful," she says. "I'm glad to see you two are getting along, though I'm less happy to learn you're now partners in crime." Mrs. Kettledrum looks straight across the top of her glasses at me, but at least the look of disappointment has faded a little.

Maybe I'll get a lighter sentence after all.

Two words: *wishful thinking.*

Mrs. Kettledrum says, "There *will* be a punishment for your behavior, Heidi, but first Ms. Charmsworth and I need to discuss it. We'll get back to you shortly. You may go too."

I stand up and head for the door. If I were a dog, my tail would definitely be between my legs.

I try to look on the bright side. At least they didn't mention anything about getting kicked out of school.

That's a relief.

And just getting away from this whole situation is a relief too, though I have a lot of explaining to do to my friends.

I wonder if Nick still likes me.

Phew, this has been a very long day.

I hurry to Honeysuckle, Sunny and Annabelle's dorm, and race up the stairs to their room. I still feel a little tired from the wishing-well spell, but my energy is improving.

When I get to their door, I stand in front of it quietly. I can hear them talking inside, so I know they're home.

Then I take a deep gulp of humility and knock on the door.

"Who is it?" Sunny asks.

"It's *me*," I answer.

Eek. I'm super-nervous.

"Come in!" my friends say.

I open the door and stand quietly in the door frame. My friends wait for me to spill.

"Well, um, I'm sure you guys are wondering what happened today." They both nod, and I can see the questioning looks in their eyes.

"Do tell!" Annabelle says.

"Yeah, I felt like I was seeing DOUBLE or something!" Sunny adds.

I walk all the way into the room. Sunny slides a mushroom stool over for me to sit on. They sit on the other two stuffed mushrooms. Then I tell them the whole story—from how Melanie and I came up with the wishing-well idea so I could be with Nick and also take my exam, to messing up the spell and creating a whole bunch of Heidis.

Then I brace myself for a lecture about always doing the right thing.

But instead my friends laugh.

Not in a mean way, but in a genuine *That's hilarious* way.

"Wait," Annabelle says, rewinding a bit.

"You're telling us that you and *Melanie* cooked up this whole plan?"

"Why didn't you tell us?" Sunny asks.

"I know. I should have told you," I admit. "But the plan just happened so fast! Melanie and I were sitting in our room, and one idea led to another.

I was going to tell you after everything was over, because I honestly thought the plan would go without a hitch . . . but then, of course, it didn't. . . .

"Honestly, I also thought if I told you beforehand, you might try to stop me. . . ."

Annabelle *UGHs* in disgust.

"Of course we would've tried to stop you, Heidi! And if we had, you wouldn't be in so much trouble."

Annabelle has a point, but it's a little late for that.

And for some reason Sunny starts laughing again.

"Well, one thing is for sure. All the Heidis were HILARIOUS!" she says. "I have to admit you have a lot of guts, Heidi.

"Everything you do is loaded with SHOCK value."

I'm not sure whether I should be proud or humiliated.

"What did all the kids in class think?" I ask.

My friends giggle.

"Oh, everyone loves you, Heidi," Sunny says. "You're bold, wacky, and totally wonderful."

I laugh with relief, because while this is somewhat unflattering, it's also spot-on.

Then Sunny gives me this look to end all looks. "What happened to poor Nick in all this?"

I frown. "Well, sadly, Nick got the worst of it," I tell them.

"He not only had to deal with the *real* me, who was **not** in good form, **but he also had to grapple with seeing a** *second* Heidi.

"Poor Nick was so confused, but then Ms. Charmsworth did something I never thought she'd do. She TOLD Nick that I'm a witch and all about

the School of Magic. I guess she could because she sent him to the infirmary for a forgetting spell."

Sunny and Annabelle both gasp. They can't believe that for a brief moment, Nick knew all about the School of Magic.

"Wow, what a day," Sunny says. "You need to be more careful though, Heidi, or you could really get in trouble."

"I know," I reply. "I've learned an important lesson today, and I'm not going to go rogue any more."

After that there is a wave of silence, and it reminds me that I *really* need to visit Nick, like, right now.

I get up to leave.

"Where are you off to?" Sunny asks.

I head for the door.

"I have to go see Nick," I say.

Sunny and Annabelle follow me to the door.

"It'll be fine," Annabelle says. "Just see what he remembers and don't give anything away."

I'm sure they're right. "Thanks. I'll see you later!"

I walk to the infirmary as fast as I can. The outside of the building is cool but creepy. The infirmary is in one of the oldest stone buildings on campus.

I ask a nurse for Nick's room, and he takes me there.

As soon as I walk into the room, Nick sits straight up on the cot he has been lying on.

"Heidi! HOW ARE YOU?" he asks with concern in his voice.

Totally embarrassed! I answer inside my head.

"I'm fine, Nick," I say out loud. "How about YOU?"

Nick shakes his head.

"I feel okay, but I don't remember what happened. I remember taking pictures with you and then all of a sudden I woke up in the infirmary. Did something happen?"

"We had a nice time, but then you started to feel sick so I encouraged you to go to the infirmary," I tell him. I know it's a lie, but it's the best thing I can think of on the spot and I don't want to have to explain to him that Ms. Charmsworth and Melanie were there since he doesn't seem to remember that part.

"And, by the way, I'm so sorry the photo shoot got messed up. I had been really looking forward to it."

Nick smiles, and I can tell he's not upset at all.

One word: *relief.*

"That's okay," he says. "I got some pretty good pictures, and I'll take a few more on the way back to my dorm.

"I think I can still get into the photo-developing room before it closes. I'm supposed to get out of here soon."

Then Nick's face lights up. "Did you decide to do anything for the talent show?"

I sit on the chair next to his bed. "Well, I've been thinking of writing a poem...."

Nick nods approvingly.

"A poem would be really cool and original," he says. "But the talent show is tomorrow night. Do you think you'll have time?"

I shrug.

"Who knows? But it's funny you mentioned time, because time would be the subject of my poem!"

Nick laughs. "You should do it, Heidi," he says encouragingly. "But I guess only *time* will tell!"

And this makes us both laugh.

IT'S ABOUT TIME

I stayed up super-late last night to write my poem.

Then this morning I had to practice reading it in the shower so I wouldn't wake up Melanie.

To be honest, I still don't know if I want to go through with it, but I kind of have to because I let Mrs. Kettledrum put my name in the talent show program.

Eek!

And it's almost showtime!

Melanie looks so cute in her dark-wash jeans and pink sequined sweater. **She spent hours hand-sewing the sequins on all by herself!**

I'm just going with my old signature look—a jean skirt, my black-and-white striped tights, sneakers, and a sage-green top.

The last thing I want to be thinking about onstage is my outfit.

I fold my poem and stuff it into the pocket of my jean skirt. Melanie grabs her guitar.

We fist-bump each other and head for the auditorium.

The lobby has been turned into a beautiful pop-up art gallery. Each artist has a panel to display his or her work.

The faculty also set up tables to show off three-dimensional art. Each piece is spotlighted with special lighting.

It looks like a *real* art gallery!

Tons of people are here too: students, faculty, and even some local families.

"Hey, Heidi, I need to drop off my guitar backstage before we check out the art," Melanie mentions. "Come with?"

I nod, and the two of us walk through the auditorium and to the backstage area. Melanie sets her guitar case on the floor. Then we hurry back to the art show to find Sunny and Annabelle. Their displays are next to each other.

People *ooh* and *aah* over Sunny's rainbow-and-dolphin painting and Annabelle's gemstone sculpture. Melanie and I rave too.

Then we move on to Isabelle's painting.

Melanie is super-impressed by this one. The painting is of a beautiful princess descending a spiral staircase inside a gleaming palace.

Everyone thinks the princess theme is just for fun, but I know Isabelle is a *real* princess.

If Melanie knew, she would absolutely flip.

And I know this is 100 percent true, because she totally did when she found out!

Thankfully, I created the right spell to make her forget. After all, Isabelle wants to keep her secret a secret, and my lips are sealed!

Isabelle taps me on the shoulder.

"Hey, Heidi," she whispers when Melanie isn't looking. "How do you like my painting?" She winks at me, and I wink right back. "Sometimes I still like to dream about dressing in gowns and tiaras."

I sigh dreamily. "Who doesn't?" I whisper back. "The only difference is, *you're the real thing!*"

Isabelle puts a finger to her lips, and we both giggle.

Melanie turns around.

"What's so funny?" Melanie asks.

Oops.

I give Melanie a friendly shove. "Oh, we were just talking about what a klutzy princess I would make."

All three of us giggle at the idea of me tripping down some palace stairs. What a royal mess *that* would be! Then I tug Melanie by the arm.

"Come on. Let's go check out Nick's photos!" I say. "See ya, Isabelle!"

Isabelle waves as we hurry over to Nick's exhibit.

As soon as Nick sees me, he opens his arms for a hug.

Wow, I can't believe he wants to give me a hug!

Nick squeezes me tight, and I'm pretty sure it's the best hug I've ever had!

I feel happy inside and out.

"Thanks for coming, Heidi!" Nick says. "You too, Melanie!"

Melanie pinches the back of my arm to acknowledge the hug that just happened. I glance at her and then quickly turn my attention back to Nick's photos.

They're so amazing—just like he is.

The first photo is black and white, and it's Nick's reflection on the lake. The ripples on the water's surface make his reflection look wavy. He calls it *Swirling Selfie*.

Pretty cool.

There's another one of Hunter McCann serving the ball in the Four Square court. The other players are in the ready position. It captures the action of the game, and Nick titled it *Four Square King*.

Perfect.

Another picture was taken at twilight—probably after Nick left the infirmary. It's a shot of Ms. Charmsworth and Mrs. Kettledrum walking down the stairs of Crawford.

Their figures look so mysterious in the shadows of the growing darkness, and what's weird is, my teachers look like

actual witches—or at least the way most people think of witches. Beside them the sinister gargoyles are eerily lighted by two spotlights.

One word: *chilling.*

The last image is positively cringeworthy. That's because it's a photo of *me* when I was under the spell of my wish.

But I love the composition. I'm sitting against that enormous tree trunk. The thick branch above me extends all the way to the edge of the picture, like a frame. It's called *Lean on Me.*

The title is not lost on me or Melanie.

"Wow," Melanie whispers. "He must *really like* you!"

I step on her toe because Nick is standing right next to us.

Then I shower Nick with praise.

"Your work is *amazing*," I tell him. "And so professional. You should try to get it into a real art gallery."

Nick blushes. "Thanks, Heidi. That means a lot to me, but I still have a ton to learn."

I don't get a chance to respond because Mrs. Kettledrum announces that it's time for the performers to get ready to go onstage.

Melanie grabs my arm. "Heidi, that's US!" she says. "Let's go!"

My stomach flips with performance anxiety. Melanie and I say goodbye to Nick. Then we head backstage.

Aaaaggh, this is getting *real*.

Since we're in the show, we get to watch the performances from the wings just offstage.

Performers are organized from first-year students to seniors, and Hunter McCann kicks off the program.

As soon as Mr. Craftwood announces his name, Hunter jogs onto the stage. He's wearing black track pants with a white stripe down the outside of each leg. He also has on white sneakers and a black-and-white T-shirt, not his typical look.

I wonder what he's going to do.

Then a steady driving beat with digital claps, snares, and drum loops begins to pulsate from the speakers onstage.

Hunter is hip-hop dancing!

Melanie and I look at each other in disbelief and then back at Hunter.

He glides, slides, and crisscrosses his legs high and then low and back again. His footwork is so precise and his arms move like blades. Sometimes his hands seem to strike invisible walls, and then he pulls them back.

Hunter has *all* the moves! Yay, Hunter!

After he's done, Hunter saunters offstage, whipping his sandy-blond hair to one side. Everyone is screaming and clapping for him.

One word: *heartthrob.*

I hold out my fist for Hunter, and he fist-bumps me. "Why didn't you tell us you danced hip-hop, Hunter? You're amazing!"

Hunter grins and waves the bottom of his T-shirt to cool himself off. "I wanted it to be a surprise!"

Oh, we're definitely surprised!

Melanie and I each give him a hug. Then Mr. Craftwood takes a stool onto the stage and announces the next act.

"And now an original song, performed by Melanie Maplethorpe!"

Melanie grabs the neck of her guitar and looks at us.

"That's ME!" she says. "Wish me luck, you two!"

Hunter and I wish Melanie luck, and I squeeze her hand.

"You've got this!" I tell her.

Melanie walks onto the stage with her usual confidence. Her sequined sweater sparkles in the spotlight. Everything about her says "superstar."

Melanie sits on her stool and adjusts the microphone.

And that's when I notice, something seems off.

Melanie looks at me pleadingly.

Uh-oh. My friend is not feeling as confident as she looks.

But I know what to do!

I smile, make a heart with my hands, and pump it in and out. Melanie must feel the love because she smiles back. Then she strums a chord.

"This is a song I wrote about *me*, and it's for all of *you*," Melanie says to the crowd.

The audience whistles and cheers. I can tell that Melanie is loving the attention!

She sings her song effortlessly, and everyone laughs at her wacky, wonderful words. Melanie finishes to thunderous applause and cheers. She slides off her stool, bows, and waves to her adoring fans.

As she walks back into the wings, I give my friend a victory hug.

"You were amazing!" I say with all my heart.

Melanie tosses her beautiful golden locks over one shoulder. "Yeah, I *was* pretty good, wasn't I?"

Confident Melanie is *back*.

"You were perfect!" I tell her. Melanie's face glows, like she just won her first Grammy Award.

And then, without any warning, it's suddenly— *GULP*—my turn.

"And our next act will be Heidi Heckelbeck. Heidi will read an original poem entitled 'It's About Time.'"

The audience claps, hoots, and hollers for *me*!

As I walk onto the stage, I pull my poem out of my pocket. It's wrinkled, so I smooth the paper against my leg.

Wow, the audience is super-quiet.

Eek!

I look at Melanie with the same dread she showed when she looked at me. **It's scary being up alone onstage with all eyes looking at you.**

Melanie gives me the same pulsing heart hand signal that I gave to her. I step toward the microphone.

Can I really go through with this?
I wonder.

My poem isn't funny like the one I did in English class earlier this year.

What if everyone expects it to be funny?

And then what if nobody likes it?

I look at the audience, and all eyes are on *me*. Then I see Mrs. Kettledrum. She smiles at me, and I can hear her thoughts loud and clear.

Just let your light shine, Heidi, she thinks. *It's not often we get to be in the spotlight. Just speak from the heart and enjoy yourself.*

I take a deep breath.

Oka-a-a-ay, here goes!

"'It's About Time' by Heidi Helena Heckelbeck."

I wait for the clapping to stop, and I begin.

It's About Time

Time is mysterious.
Sometimes it flies and is gone in a minute.
Sometimes it drags on for what seems like forever.
So when the days and months
Turn into a passing year, remember this:
You can't be in two places at once.
You can only live right where you are—
And that's in the here and now.

Sometimes when you're having fun,
You might want time to last longer,
And sometimes when you feel sad or lonely,
You want time to speed up.
But one thing's for sure.
You can't control time—that's just *wishful* thinking.
You can only control what you *do* with your time.

So spend time doing things you love.
Eat ice cream, watch movies, make friends!
Draw pictures, sing songs, laugh, play, and dance!
And most of all, treasure every single moment,
Because you can never get lost moments back.
So as the clock ticks on, ask yourself:
What will you do with *your* time?

I fold my paper in half, and everyone stares at me in silence, but it's not because they didn't like my poem. It seems like they're still thinking about it.

Then Sunny starts clapping and the whole audience joins in. Students whistle and cheer.

And you know what's really amazing? I see Ms. Charmsworth and Mrs. Kettledrum wiping tears from their eyes.

Wow, they must have really liked my poem!

I take a bow and race off the stage into Melanie's waiting arms.

"Listen, Melanie! They're *still* clapping!" I say.

Melanie pulls back and looks at me. "That's because you wrote an amazing poem, Heidi," she says. "And from now on I will never waste another moment."

I smile at my real-and-true friend. "I guess trying to be in two places at once has really taught me to appreciate the time I have too. . . ."

Melanie nods understandingly. "Me too," she says. "We both have great things to accomplish and no time to waste!"

On the way back to the dorm after the rest of the acts, Melanie and I wave good night to Sunny and Annabelle.

I already got to say goodbye to Nick in the auditorium as he was taking down his photos.

When we get to our room, Melanie heads straight for the shower. I flop onto my bed and find a note on my pillow.

It's from Ms. Charmsworth.

Dear Heidi,

   I was touched by your poem. It was so thoughtful and wise. It seems like you're learning your lesson about wisdom and patience. But you've always been a fast learner, haven't you?

   Here comes the hard part. Mrs. Kettledrum and I have decided on your punishment for using the wishing well without permission. The penalty is detention after classes each day for the next two weeks. In addition, we're not allowing you to take my exam over. I will, however, accept the grade the other Heidi handed in, and that will be your final grade on the exam.

   Remember, Heidi, it takes time to grow into the best witch you can be.

> More important than practicing magic is practicing wisdom and patience.
> Best wishes,
> Ms. Charmsworth
>
> P.S. Lucky for you, your Heidi look-alike managed to get a passing grade on the exam, but I know the real Heidi would've gotten 100 percent.

I hide the letter in one of my notebooks, because I don't want Melanie to see it.

I just want to leave this whole wishing well thing behind me.

I'm still bummed that I disappointed my two favorite teachers, **but I'm also so happy that they loved my poem.**

It makes me feel a little less bad about everything.

Like maybe I learned something from this mess and I'll have a lot of time to think about my actions in detention.

Thank goodness my Heidi look-alike passed the test.

One word: *lucky!*

On the other hand, I'm kind of annoyed because Ms. Charmsworth is right. The real Heidi would've aced that test!

Oh merg! I wish I . . .

Then I stop that thought before it goes one step further.

No more wishes, Heidi!

Uh-uh!

I'm going to work hard, have patience, be wise, and do the right thing.

Lesson learned!

Melanie crawls into bed and looks over at me. "Hey, are you excited to go home for Thanksgiving break?" she asks.

I rest my head on my own pillow. "So excited!"

Melanie sits straight up in her bed. "Promise me one thing. You'll let me help you pack for your trip home.

"You may be an amazing poet, but you still can't put a cool outfit together."

Now it's my turn to sit up in bed.

"Melanie, I'm just going home for the break! I'm going to see my family, Lucy, and Bruce! I don't need to dress up like a supermodel!"

"Heidi, you never know who you might run into just walking down the street! You must always keep up your appearance in case you are discovered!"

I lie back down and close my eyes.

I have to smile at Melanie and her dreams of being discovered someday.

"Okay, Melanie. You can help me pack," I tell her.

"Thank you," Melanie says. "And by the way? Speaking of Thanksgiving, I'm **really thankful we're friends and broommates.**"

"**Same here,**" I say as I get up to shower and change.

And you know what?

I really and truly mean it.

WHAT JUST HAPPENED?

I know two things that can make a classroom full of magical middle schoolers go completely bonkers.

The first day of spring and a teacher being late for class.

It's like a recipe for total madness.

My aunt Trudy calls it "double whammy."

That's what's happening right now in my potions class. Everyone has legit lost it—even me!

"Let's get some AIR in here!" I shout, thrusting open the windows and letting spring swirl into our classroom.

Ahhhhh.

The fresh breeze blows away months of dusty, closed-in winter air.

It also triggers some of the kids to shoot rubber bands and fly paper airplanes.

Snap! Swoosh! Doink!

Others hide behind chairs, laughing, dodging, and squealing.

Wow, it feels good to cut loose.

My friend, Hunter McCann, only adds to the wackiness. **He brought a prank sound machine to class.** He got it in a care package from his aunt.

He's pressing all the buttons, making one kooky sound after another—a blasting air horn, hideous laughter, squealing tires, shattering glass, and LOTS of really gross—*but funny*—bathroom noises.

We shriek with laughter.

Sophie Rodriguez laughs so hard, she falls off her chair.

Kabonk!

On the other side of the room, there are two kids hanging from the doorframe trying to see who can do more pull-ups.

As for my friends, Isabelle and Melanie, they're crumpling up notebook paper and shooting them into our teacher Mrs. Kettledrum's wastebasket.

This is when Mrs. Kettledrum walks into the classroom.

Nobody even notices her, except for the boys doing pull-ups on the doorframe, because they're blocking her way. Poor Mrs. Kettledrum does her best to get our attention.

"Class!

"Class!

"CLA-A-A-SS!"

Nobody hears her over the hubbub, though I'm vaguely aware of Mrs. K's dog, Momo, barking somewhere in a galaxy, light-years away. Soon our teacher has to resort to stronger means to get our attention.

BONG! BONG! BONG! BONG!

OMGosh! What is that *deafening* sound? It's like we're inside a big bell.

We clap our hands over our ears. Then the room falls silent except for the tickity-tick of a pencil falling onto the floor.

"*Well, that's MUCH better!*" Mrs. Kettledrum exclaims, shaking her head. "My goodness! I've never *seen* such a dreadful case of spring fever!"

Momo hops onto Mrs. K's chair and barks sharply to echo our teacher's dismay.

We quickly take our seats without a word. By now the whole class has already moved on to something else. Something much more interesting than spring fever.

Mrs. Kettledrum has not only arrived late. . . .

She's not alone.

There, standing beside our teacher, is a new girl.

I size her up in a millisecond.

She has straight chocolate-brown hair that falls halfway down her back and a thick curtain of bangs. Freckles smatter her perfectly upturned nose and cheeks.

Adorable.

Her eyes are a sparkling emerald green, outlined with dark feathery lashes. She's wearing a medium-wash denim skirt and a navy-and-oat-striped crocheted top.

My kind of outfit.

She's super-pretty *and* trendy—someone Melanie would **definitely** glom on to, which leads to my next question.

Who *IS* this girl?

What's she doing here?

Could she be Mrs. Kettledrum's niece? I doubt it. She's probably a visiting student.

Or maybe she's a new student starting today? Why would Broomsfield Academy bring in a new student so close to the end of the year?

I look around the room to see what my classmates are thinking. They look like they're wondering the same thing as me.

"Okay, now that everyone has settled down," Mrs. Kettledrum begins. "I want to first remind you that Friday is our field trip to the American Museum of Natural History."

We cheer our approval, though we hardly need reminding. We've been looking forward to this field trip for weeks.

What we *really* want to know is who is this mystery girl?

But Mrs. K tells us more about the class trip.

"This field trip has such special meaning for me," she says, pressing one hand to her heart.

"Each year I take my first-year magical students to this museum. It's so important to get out into the world and learn about a different kind of magic—the magic of science and the natural world. I know you're all going to love it! We'll depart for the museum after lunch on Friday."

Then our favorite teacher clasps her hands together and *finally* address the stranger standing beside her.

"Our field trip is also perfect timing for our new student!"

My heart skips a beat when she says *new student*. Wow, this girl IS starting now. . . .

Mrs. Kettledrum rests one hand gently on the new girl's shoulder.

"Attention, everyone!" our teacher says proudly. "I'm happy to introduce your new classmate, Jodi Thompson."

Jodi smiles and seems exceptionally comfortable with all of us staring at her.

It's like we're her adoring fans.

One word: *confident.*

Mrs. Kettledrum tells us a little bit about the new girl.

"Jodi has moved here all the way from Canada," our teacher tells us. "I'm proud to share that Jodi is also a *very* gifted witch, who was at the top of her magic classes at her former school. Please let's all give Jodi a warm welcome to Broomsfield Academy. . . ."

We clap courteously to make Jodi feel welcome.

I know this may sound weird, but the new girl already makes me feel a smidge uncomfortable.

I'm pretty sure it's because Mrs. Kettledrum called her a *very* gifted witch.

It triggered a feeling of jealousy inside me.

How ridiculous is that?

I push those thoughts away.

The funny thing is, no sooner do I *think* this, is when Jodi looks directly at me and smiles.

But it's not just any smile; it's a knowing smile.

I squirm in my chair.

Whoa, it's almost as if Jodi just read my mind!

Now that really *IS* ridiculous. There's no way Jodi can read my thoughts.

Right when I think *that*, Jodi smiles at me again and raises her eyebrow.

Wait, *did* she actually hear what I was thinking?

I'm so caught off guard, I gasp loudly. The sound draws attention, so I cough to cover it up. But I must have coughed too loudly, because Mrs. Kettledrum calls on me.

Eek!

"Is everything all right, Heidi?"

I quickly cover my mouth and pretend to clear my throat.

"Um, yes! I'm fine, Mrs. Kettledrum!" I say awkwardly. "Just had a little something caught in my throat." I grab my neck and clear my throat again to make my cover-up seem more believable.

Mrs. Kettledrum seems to buy it, but not Jodi. **She just openly smirked at me!**

I turn around to see if Jodi could possibly be looking at somebody else, **but there's** no mistaking it. **She's definitely smirking at me.**

Okay, what is going on right now?!

Suddenly everything seems strangely out of control.

I tap Melanie, who's sitting next to me, on the arm. She looks at me, like, *What?*

I give her a forceful look and nod slightly toward Jodi as if to say, *Do you notice anything weird about the new girl?*

Melanie shakes her head, totally clueless. She doesn't get what I'm trying to say or what's going on, at all.

I huff.

Well, whatever *IS* going on, it's not good.

Something's definitely off. I can feel it.

Why would I be getting totally

creepy vibes from this new girl? I don't even know her!

All I know is, she's a very gifted witch from Canada, who seems to be singling *me* out. What's the deal?

This is freaking me out.

Did she really just read my thoughts? Or was it my imagination?

One word: *chilling.*

USE YOUR NOODLE

Buzz of the new girl spreads across campus like wildfire. It's as if everyone wants to know her.

And I mean *everyone*!

It also appears that being *new* is the secret to popularity. All my classmates want to get to know Jodi, **but not me.**

It's **not** because she's suddenly more popular than I am. I'm keeping a side-eye view on this whole new-girl situation.

I have yet to tell anyone about the weird vibes I've been getting from Jodi, but I won't be able to keep this to myself forever. **At some point, I'll have to unload—or explode.**

By dinnertime, **I'm starving.** Feeling out of sorts has given me **a whopper of an appetite,** though it could be because **I only had three red licorice sticks for lunch.**

Oops!

I do have some good news! Jodi has *not* been assigned to my table.

Phew! At least I don't have to deal with her at mealtimes this week.

The other good news is that Hunter, Annabelle, and Sunny *are* at my table.

Yay!

But there's some bad news too. My crush, Nick, is at *Jodi's* table.

Argh!

She'd better not flirt with my crush.

Two words: *paws off!*

Thankfully, Jodi momentarily slips my mind when I realize its Pasta Night.

I *love* Pasta Night! It means we get to build our own pasta bowls.

Yum!

Melanie, Isabelle, Hunter, and I slide our trays in front of the pasta station.

"Look at all the **pasta-bilities!**" Hunter jokes.

Izzy shoves Hunter.

"Oh, *stooooop it!*" she exclaims at his noodle pun.

We all burst out laughing and Izzy keeps the fun going.

"Everyone, what type of noodle are you?" she asks.

Melanie narrows her eyebrows.

"What do you mean?"

Isabelle giggles.

"I mean, what's the pasta shape that best describes your personality."

Suddenly we look at the pasta choices with new interest. *Hmmm, if I were pasta, what would I be?* I wonder.

It takes me all of two seconds to figure out my choice. I'm definitely spiral pasta, **because as usual, my life is spiraling out of control.**

I decide to keep this to myself. Besides, Melanie goes first anyway.

"I'm *ANGEL hair* pasta," she says dramatically. "That's because of my halo of blond hair." Then she flips her blond ponytail with the back of her hand.

"Is that so?" Izzy comments with a dash of snark-asm. "Does *angelic* **really describe your character?**"

We all laugh—even Melanie, because she may *look* like an angel, **but she doesn't always *act* like one.**

Melanie shrugs and turns to Hunter. "So, what type of noodle are you, Prince Charming?"

Hunter elbows Melanie as he examines the dishes full of different kinds of pasta.

"Well, **my swag** is no secret," he jokes. "That **must** mean I'm *bow tie* pasta. Anyone who can wear a bow tie has to be fearless *and* confident, and well, that pretty much sums me up."

We roll our eyes and agree bow tie pasta definitely describes Hunter to a tee.

After that, Melanie takes it upon herself to dole out the rest of our noodle personalities—that's because she *loves* to be in charge.

No surprise there!

"Okay, if Isabelle and Hunter were a noodle *together,* then they'd have to be spaghetti, because spaghetti is the *romantic* pasta," Melanie says.

Then she explains how Lady and the Tramp, *aka Isabelle and Hunter,* would eat opposite ends of the same piece of spaghetti and wind up with *locked* lips.

"*Wooooooo!*" Melanie and I croon at the same time.

Isabelle's cheeks turn pink, but Hunter just laughs it off.

Then Melanie moves on to me.

Oh no, here we go. . . .

"Heidi, you're the spiral pasta, because

you're kooky, fun, and totally unpredictable."

I make a silly face, because she's totally right, but I still keep the part about me being a spiraling, out-of-control noodle-head to myself.

Instead, I decide to give Melanie *my take* on **her** noodle type.

"Well, Melanie, you may be angel hair pasta, but you're also *ravioli*, because you're so full of surprises!"

We all crack up and that's when we notice the kids behind us in line are getting annoyed and want us to hurry up.

We scoop some noodles into our bowls and top them with sauce and grated cheese before scurrying back to our assigned tables.

Yum!

When I get to my table, I plunk beside Sunny and Annabelle. They're already halfway through their meals. Before I dig in, I sneak a glance at Jodi's table, which is the next one over from ours.

Melanie and Nick are both talking to Jodi a mile a minute.

Ugh. I wish Nick wouldn't talk to Jodi. It makes me feel so *blah!*

Sunny nudges me, and I snap out of my thoughts. "Heidi, have you met the new girl?" she asks innocently—not knowing I've been stressing about the new girl *all* day.

"Her name is Jodi, and she's *sooo* nice," Sunny goes on. "She even offered to help me carry a bunch of sweatshirts to the lost and found in between classes. So sweet—right? She was also super-chatty and upbeat too—our kind of person."

Annabelle nods in total agreement. "Well, how *did* she act around you, Heidi?" Annabelle asks. "She was in your potions class-*right?* Did Mrs. Kettledrum have to slow down so Jodi could catch up?"

I shake my head. "Nope, exactly the opposite. Okay, I'm not one hundred percent sure," I whisper to them, "but I think Jodi may have read my mind in class today."

Sunny and Annabelle lean back in surprise. "Wow, that's SO cool!" Sunny exclaims.

Cool? I think. How could Sunny think this is cool? This is *NOT* cool.

It's *TERRIBLE.*

ABOUT THE AUTHOR

Wanda Coven has always loved magic. When she was little, she used to make secret potions from smooshed shells and acorns. Then she would pretend to transport herself and her friends to enchanted places. Now she visits other worlds through writing. Wanda lives with her husband and son in Colorado Springs, Colorado. They have three cats: Hilda, Agnes, and Claw-dia.

ABOUT THE ILLUSTRATOR

Anna Abramskaya was born in Sevastopol, Ukraine. She graduated from Kharkiv State Academy of Design and Arts in 2006. Then she moved to the United States, where she's currently living in the beautiful city of Jacksonville, Florida. Anna has loved art since she was little and has tried different materials and techniques. The process of creation and seeing beauty in the simple things around her always brings her joy and the wish to share that feeling with everyone. Anna wants to believe that art can help bring more love into people's hearts. Find out more at AnnaAbramskaya.com.

MIDDLE SCHOOL AND OTHER DISASTERS

Freakiest Trip Ever!

BY WANDA COVEN
ILLUSTRATED BY ANNA ABRAMSKAYA

Simon Spotlight
New York   Amsterdam/Antwerp   London
Toronto   Sydney/Melbourne   New Delhi

This book is a work of fiction. Any references to historical events, real people, or real places are used fictitiously. Other names, characters, places, and events are products of the author's imagination, and any resemblance to actual events or places or persons, living or dead, is entirely coincidental.

SIMON SPOTLIGHT
An imprint of Simon & Schuster Children's Publishing Division
1230 Avenue of the Americas, New York, New York 10020
For more than 100 years, Simon & Schuster has championed authors and the stories they create. By respecting the copyright of an author's intellectual property, you enable Simon & Schuster and the author to continue publishing exceptional books for years to come. We thank you for supporting the author's copyright by purchasing an authorized edition of this book.
No amount of this book may be reproduced or stored in any format, nor may it be uploaded to any website, database, language-learning model, or other repository, retrieval, or artificial intelligence system without express permission. All rights reserved. Inquiries may be directed to Simon & Schuster, 1230 Avenue of the Americas, New York, NY 10020 or permissions@simonandschuster.com.
First Simon Spotlight edition August 2025
© 2025 by Simon & Schuster, LLC
All rights reserved, including the right of reproduction in whole or in part in any form.
SIMON SPOTLIGHT and colophon are registered trademarks of Simon & Schuster, LLC.
For information about special discounts for bulk purchases, please contact Simon & Schuster Special Sales at 1-866-506-1949 or business@simonandschuster.com.
Simon & Schuster strongly believes in freedom of expression and stands against censorship in all its forms. For more information, visit BooksBelong.com.
Text by Alison Inches
Series designed by Chani Yammer, based on the Heidi Heckelbeck series designed by Aviva Shur
Cover designed by Laura Roode
Illustrated by Anna Abramskaya, inspired by the original character designs of Priscilla Burris from the Heidi Heckelbeck chapter book series
The illustrations for this book were rendered with digital ink and a bunch of love.
The text of this book was set in Minou.
Manufactured in the United States of America 0625 BVG
10 9 8 7 6 5 4 3 2 1
Library of Congress Control Number 2024043721
ISBN 9781665964166
ISBN 9781665964173 (ebook)

Would you like to read another book about **Heidi Heckelbeck**? You don't need magic to find one! Look for more

books at your favorite store!

EBOOK EDITIONS ALSO AVAILABLE
PUBLISHED BY SIMON SPOTLIGHT
SIMONANDSCHUSTER.COM/KIDS

ABOUT THE AUTHOR

Wanda Coven has always loved magic. When she was little, she used to make secret potions from smooshed shells and acorns. Then she would pretend to transport herself and her friends to enchanted places. Now she visits other worlds through writing. Wanda lives with her husband and son in Colorado Springs, Colorado. They have three cats: Hilda, Agnes, and Claw-dia.

ABOUT THE ILLUSTRATOR

Anna Abramskaya was born in Sevastopol, Ukraine. She graduated from Kharkiv State Academy of Design and Arts in 2006. Then she moved to the United States, where she's currently living in the beautiful city of Jacksonville, Florida. Anna has loved art since she was little and has tried different materials and techniques. The process of creation and seeing beauty in the simple things around her always brings her joy and the wish to share that feeling with everyone. Anna wants to believe that art can help bring more love into people's hearts. Find out more at AnnaAbramskaya.com.

MIDDLE SCHOOL AND OTHER DISASTERS

Freakiest Trip Ever!

BY WANDA COVEN
ILLUSTRATED BY ANNA ABRAMSKAYA

Simon Spotlight
New York Amsterdam/Antwerp London
Toronto Sydney/Melbourne New Delhi

This book is a work of fiction. Any references to historical events, real people, or real places are used fictitiously. Other names, characters, places, and events are products of the author's imagination, and any resemblance to actual events or places or persons, living or dead, is entirely coincidental.

SIMON SPOTLIGHT
An imprint of Simon & Schuster Children's Publishing Division
1230 Avenue of the Americas, New York, New York 10020
For more than 100 years, Simon & Schuster has championed authors and the stories they create. By respecting the copyright of an author's intellectual property, you enable Simon & Schuster and the author to continue publishing exceptional books for years to come. We thank you for supporting the author's copyright by purchasing an authorized edition of this book.
No amount of this book may be reproduced or stored in any format, nor may it be uploaded to any website, database, language-learning model, or other repository, retrieval, or artificial intelligence system without express permission. All rights reserved. Inquiries may be directed to Simon & Schuster, 1230 Avenue of the Americas, New York, NY 10020 or permissions@simonandschuster.com.
First Simon Spotlight edition August 2025
© 2025 by Simon & Schuster, LLC
All rights reserved, including the right of reproduction in whole or in part in any form.
SIMON SPOTLIGHT and colophon are registered trademarks of Simon & Schuster, LLC.
For information about special discounts for bulk purchases, please contact Simon & Schuster Special Sales at 1-866-506-1949 or business@simonandschuster.com.
Simon & Schuster strongly believes in freedom of expression and stands against censorship in all its forms. For more information, visit BooksBelong.com.
Text by Alison Inches
Series designed by Chani Yammer, based on the Heidi Heckelbeck series designed by Aviva Shur
Cover designed by Laura Roode
Illustrated by Anna Abramskaya, inspired by the original character designs of Priscilla Burris from the Heidi Heckelbeck chapter book series
The illustrations for this book were rendered with digital ink and a bunch of love.
The text of this book was set in Minou.
Manufactured in the United States of America 0625 BVG
10 9 8 7 6 5 4 3 2 1
Library of Congress Control Number 2024043721
ISBN 9781665964166
ISBN 9781665964173 (ebook)

To my readers:
You are magical.
Love,
Wanda

WHAT JUST HAPPENED?

I know two things that can make a classroom full of magical middle schoolers go completely bonkers.

The first day of spring and a teacher being late for class.

It's like a recipe for total madness.

My aunt Trudy calls it "double whammy."

That's what's happening right now in my potions class. Everyone has legit lost it—even me!

"Let's get some AIR in here!" I shout, thrusting open the windows and letting spring swirl into our classroom.

Ahhhhh.

The fresh breeze blows away months of dusty, closed-in winter air.

It also triggers some of the kids to shoot rubber bands and fly paper airplanes.

Snap! Swoosh! Doink!

Others hide behind chairs, laughing, dodging, and squealing.

Wow, it feels good to cut loose.

My friend Hunter McCann only adds to the wackiness. **He brought a prank sound machine to class.** He got it in a care package from his aunt.

He's pressing all the buttons, making one kooky sound after another. A blasting air horn, hideous laughter, squealing tires, shattering glass, and LOTS of really gross—*but funny*—bathroom noises.

We shriek with laughter.

Sophie Rodriguez laughs so hard, she falls off her chair.

Kabonk!

On the other side of the room, there are two kids hanging from the doorframe trying to see who can do more pull-ups.

As for my friends Isabelle and Melanie, they're crumpling up notebook paper and shooting them into our teacher Mrs. Kettledrum's wastebasket.

This is when Mrs. Kettledrum walks into the classroom.

Nobody even notices her, except for the boys doing pull-ups on the doorframe because they're blocking her way. Poor Mrs. Kettledrum does her best to get our attention.

"Class!

"Class!

"CLA-A-A-SS!"

Nobody hears her over the hubbub, though I'm vaguely aware of Mrs. K's dog, Momo, barking somewhere in a galaxy light-years away. Soon our teacher has to resort to stronger means to get our attention.

BONG! BONG! BONG! BONG!

OMGosh! What is that *deafening* sound? It's like we're inside a big bell.

We clap our hands over our ears. Then the room falls silent except for the tickity-tick of a pencil falling onto the floor.

"*Well, that's MUCH better!*" Mrs. Kettledrum exclaims, shaking her head. "My goodness! I've never *seen* such a dreadful case of spring fever!"

Momo hops onto Mrs. K's chair and barks sharply to echo our teacher's dismay.

We quickly take our seats without a word. By now the whole class has already moved on to something else. Something much more interesting than spring fever.

Mrs. Kettledrum has not only arrived late . . .

She's not alone.

There, standing beside our teacher, **is a new girl.**

I size her up in a millisecond.

She has straight chocolate-brown hair that falls halfway down her back and a thick curtain of bangs. Freckles smatter her perfectly upturned nose and cheeks.

Adorable.

Her eyes are a sparkling emerald green, outlined with dark feathery lashes. She's wearing a medium-wash denim skirt and a navy-and-oat-striped crocheted top.

My kind of outfit.

She's super-pretty *and* trendy—someone Melanie would **definitely** glom on to, which leads to my next question.

Who *IS* this girl?

What's she doing here?

Could she be Mrs. Kettledrum's niece? I doubt it. She's probably a visiting student.

Or maybe she's a new student starting today?

Why would Broomsfield Academy bring in a new student so close to the end of the year?

I look around the room to see what my classmates are thinking. They look like they're wondering the same thing as me.

"Okay, now that everyone has settled down," Mrs. Kettledrum begins, "I want to first remind you that Friday is our field trip to the American Natural History Museum."

We cheer our approval, though we hardly need reminding. We've been looking forward to this field trip for weeks.

What we *really* want to know is, **who is this mystery girl?**

But Mrs. K tells us more about the class trip.

"This field trip has such special meaning for me," she says, pressing one hand to her heart.

"Each year I take my first-year magical students to this museum. **It's so important to get out into the world and learn about a different kind of magic—the magic of science and the natural world. I know you're all going to love it!** We'll depart for the museum after lunch on Friday."

Then our favorite teacher clasps her hands together **and *finally* addresses the stranger standing beside her.**

"Our field trip is also perfect timing for our new student!"

My heart skips a beat when she says "new student." **Wow, this girl IS starting now. . . .**

Mrs. Kettledrum rests one hand gently on the new girl's shoulder.

"Attention, everyone!" our teacher says. "**I'm happy to introduce your new classmate, Jodi Thompson.**"

Jodi smiles and seems exceptionally comfortable with all of us staring at her. **It's like we're her adoring fans.**

One word: *confident.*

Mrs. Kettledrum tells us a little bit about the new girl.

"Jodi has moved here all the way from Canada," our teacher tells us. "I'm proud to share that

Jodi is also a *very* gifted witch, who was at the top of her magic classes at her former school. Please let's all give Jodi a warm welcome to Broomsfield Academy. . . ."

We clap courteously to make Jodi feel welcome.

I know this may sound weird, but the new girl already makes me feel a smidge uncomfortable. I'm pretty sure it's because Mrs. Kettledrum called her a *very* gifted witch.

It triggered a feeling of jealousy inside me.

How ridiculous is that?

I push those thoughts away.

The funny thing is, as soon as I *think* this, Jodi looks directly at me and smiles.

But it's not just any smile; it's a knowing smile.

I squirm in my chair.

Whoa, it's almost as if Jodi just read my mind!

Now, that really *IS* ridiculous. There's no way Jodi can read my thoughts.

Right when I think *that*, Jodi smiles at me again and raises her eyebrow.

Wait, *did* she actually hear what I was thinking?

I'm so caught off guard, I gasp loudly. The sound draws attention, so I cough to cover it up. But I must have coughed too loudly because Mrs. Kettledrum calls on me.

Eek!

"Is everything all right, Heidi?"

I quickly cover my mouth and pretend to clear my throat.

"Um, yes! I'm fine, Mrs. Kettledrum!" I say awkwardly. "Just had a little something caught in my throat."
I grab my neck and clear my throat again to make my cover-up seem more believable.

Mrs. Kettledrum seems to buy it, but not Jodi. **She just openly smirked at me!**

I turn around to see if Jodi could possibly be looking at somebody else, **but there's no mistaking it. She's definitely smirking at me.**

Okay, what is going on right now?!

Suddenly everything seems strangely out of control.

I tap Melanie, who's sitting next to me, on the arm. She looks at me like, *What?*

I give her a forceful look and nod slightly toward Jodi as if to say, *Do you notice anything weird about the new girl?*

Melanie shakes her head, totally clueless. She doesn't get what I'm trying to say, or what's going on, at all.

I huff.

Well, whatever *IS* going on, it's not good.

Something's definitely off. I can feel it.

Why would I be getting totally creepy vibes from this new girl? I don't even know her!

All I know is, she's a very gifted witch from Canada, who seems to be singling *me* out. What's the deal?

This is freaking me out.

Did she really just read my thoughts? Or was it my imagination?

One word: *chilling.*

USE YOUR NOODLE

Buzz of the new girl spreads across campus like wildfire. It's as if everyone wants to know her.

And I mean *everyone!*

It also appears that being *new* is the secret to popularity. All my classmates want to get to know Jodi, **but I don't.**

It's **not** because she's suddenly more popular than I am. I'm keeping a side-eye view on this whole new-girl situation.

I have yet to tell anyone about the weird vibes I've been getting from Jodi, but I won't be able to keep this to myself forever. At some point, I'll have to unload—or explode.

By dinnertime I'm starving. Feeling out of sorts has given me a whopper of an appetite, though it could be because I only had three red licorice sticks for lunch.

Oops!

I do have some good news! Jodi has *not* been assigned to my table.

Phew! At least I don't have to deal with her at mealtimes this week.

The other good news is that Hunter, Annabelle, and Sunny *are* at my table.

Yay!

But there's some bad news too. My crush, Nick, is at *Jodi's* table.

Argh!

She'd better not flirt with my crush.

Two words: *Paws off!*

Thankfully, Jodi momentarily slips my mind when I realize it's Pasta Night.

I *love* Pasta Night! It means we get to build our own pasta bowls.

Yum!

Melanie, Isabelle, Hunter, and I slide our trays in front of the pasta station.

"Look at all the **pasta-bilities!**" Hunter jokes.

Izzy shoves Hunter.

"*Oh, STOP it!*" she exclaims at his noodle pun.

We all burst out laughing, and Izzy keeps the fun going.

"Everyone, what type of noodle are you?" she asks.

Melanie narrows her eyebrows.

"What do you mean?" she questions.

Isabelle giggles.

"I mean, what's the pasta shape that best describes your personality?" she asks.

Suddenly we look at the pasta choices with new interest. *Hmmm, if I were pasta, what would I be?* I wonder.

It takes me all of two seconds to figure out my choice. I'm definitely spiral pasta because as usual, my life is spiraling out of control.

I decide to keep this to myself. Besides, Melanie goes first anyway.

"I'm *ANGEL-hair* pasta," she says dramatically. "That's because of my halo of blond hair." Then she flips her blond ponytail with the back of her hand.

"Is that so?" Izzy comments with a dash of snark-asm. "Does 'angelic' really describe your character?"

We all laugh—even Melanie because she may *look* like an angel, **but she doesn't always *act* like one.**

Melanie shrugs and turns to Hunter. "So, what type of noodle are you, Prince Charming?"

Hunter rolls his eyes at Melanie as he examines the dishes full of different kinds of pasta.

"Well, **my swag** is no secret," he jokes.

"That **must** mean I'm *bow-tie* pasta. Anyone who can wear a bow tie has to be fearless *and* confident, and, well, **that pretty much sums me up.**"

We roll our eyes and agree that bow-tie pasta definitely describes Hunter to a tee.

After that, Melanie takes it upon herself to dole out the rest of our noodle personalities—that's because she *loves* to be in charge.

No surprise there!

"Okay, if Isabelle and Hunter were a noodle *together,* then they'd have to be spaghetti because spaghetti is the *romantic* pasta," Melanie says.

Then she explains how in the movie *Lady and the Tramp* the two would eat opposite ends of the same piece of spaghetti **and wind up with** *locked* lips.

"**Wooooooo!**" Melanie and I croon at the same time.

Isabelle's cheeks turn pink, but Hunter just laughs it off.

Then Melanie moves on to me.

Oh no, here we go. . . .

"Heidi, you're the spiral pasta because you're kooky, fun, **and totally unpredictable.**"

I make a silly face because **she's right,** but I still keep the part about me being a spiraling, out-of-control noodlehead to myself.

Instead I decide to give Melanie **my take** on **her** noodle type.

"Well, Melanie, you may be angel-hair pasta, but you're also *ravioli* because you're so full of surprises!"

We all crack up, and that's when we notice that the kids behind us in line are getting annoyed and want us to hurry up.

We scoop some noodles into our bowls and top them with sauce and grated cheese before scurrying back to our assigned tables.

Yum!

When I get to my table, I plunk down beside Sunny and Annabelle. They're already halfway through their meals. Before I dig in, I sneak a glance at Jodi's table, which is the next one over from ours.

Melanie and Nick are both talking to Jodi a mile a minute.

Ugh.

I wish Nick wouldn't talk to Jodi.
It makes me feel so *blah!*

Sunny nudges me, and I snap out of my thoughts. "Heidi, have you met the new girl?" she asks innocently—**not knowing I've been stressing about the new girl *all* day.**

"Her name is Jodi and she's *sooo* nice," Sunny goes on. "She even offered to help me carry a bunch of sweatshirts to the lost and found in between classes. So sweet, right? She was also super-chatty and upbeat, too—our kind of person."

Annabelle nods in total agreement.

"Yeah, I bumped into Jodi at the bookstore," she adds, "and she complimented my outfit *and* my English accent. She even bought me some sour gummy worms—for absolutely no reason—when we were checking out. That was so BEYOND!"

My shoulders automatically slump because I feel like I'm caught in a raging storm of positivity, and this makes me feel like a total merg-a-saurus.

"What's the matter, Heidi?" Sunny asks, noticing my grumpy face and slouchy posture.

I stab a pasta spiral with my fork and sigh.

"Well, if I'm being totally honest, I didn't have the same happy experience with Jodi that you guys did."

Sunny and Annabelle look at each other like, *Whoa, what does she mean by THAT?*

"Well, how *did* she act around you, Heidi?" Annabelle asks. "She was in your potions class, *right*? Did Mrs. Kettledrum have to slow down so Jodi could catch up?"

I shake my head. "Nope, exactly the opposite."

Annabelle gives me another curious look, so I explain how the new girl is a *star witch*.

"Jodi had no problem keeping up in class," I go on. "It turns out she was at the top of her magic classes at her old school in Canada. I think she probably came here because she needed *more* of a challenge...."

Annabelle tilts her head and looks at me thoughtfully. "Wow, Heidi, she sounds a lot like *you*!"

Annabelle's comment makes me swallow wrong, and I start coughing. I cough so much that my eyes water. My friends look worried.

"Heidi, are you okay?" Sunny asks. "Try drinking something."

I sip some water and try to recover from my coughing fit.

"I'm fine," I say, still sputtering a little. "I *do* have something else on my mind." I motion for my friends to scootch closer. Their chairs clump across the floor as they huddle nearer to me.

"Okay, I'm not one hundred percent sure," I whisper to them. "But I think Jodi may have read my mind in class today."

Sunny and Annabelle lean back in surprise.

"Wow, that's SO cool!" Sunny exclaims.

Cool? I think. How could Sunny think this is cool? This is *NOT* cool.

ately, our stash of eggs now consisted only of carrots, mushrooms, and celery, which didn't really go with anything. Oh, and a single drumstick, which I gave to Dad.

It's *TERRIBLE.*

Sometimes Sunny is so positive, it can be annoying.

"What's cool about it?" I whisper angrily. "I find it totally unnerving and freaky."

Sunny and Annabelle both stare at me in disbelief. Clearly neither one of them has heard the terrifying news flash I just shared. Just the opposite!

Annabelle leans in closer. "Think about it, Heidi," she whispers. "You and Jodi could have *entire* conversations without having to say a single word out loud!" she says. "That sounds pretty cool, if you ask me."

I give her a major eye roll.

"But reading minds is *my gift*," I say defensively. "I don't want to share my gift with somebody else. *End of story.*"

As soon as the words leave my mouth, I know they sound selfish, and maybe even a tad babyish, but that's the way I feel.

"You're overreacting, Heidi," Sunny assures me. "You need to give Jodi more of a chance. To be honest, I'm more afraid that you'll become besties with *her*, and then you'll forget all about *us*!"

Annabelle nods.

Wow, all this friend love feels good, and who knows, maybe they *are* right. I could be overreacting a little. But one thing's for sure,

I'd never ditch Sunny and Annabelle for Jodi. *No way!*

"That would *never* happen!" I reassure my friends. Then Annabelle nudges me.

"Hey, look," she whispers, nodding toward Jodi's table. "Melanie has already become besties with Jodi, so I guess none of us has to worry."

I glance at the new girl's table. Melanie is still gabbing nonstop with Jodi. Nick is listening to both of them intently.

Ugh, I can't watch.

"Well, all I can say is that Jodi had better not move in on my crush!" I tell my friends.

Sunny and Annabelle laugh.

"Like *that* would ever happen!" Annabelle says pretty convincingly. "Nick **only** has eyes for *you*, Heidi, and I don't see that changing."

Sunny agrees 100 percent. Their vote of confidence helps **tame my loopy jealousy.**

My friends really are the best! I dig back into my pasta with more gusto.

Besides, why SHOULD I worry about Jodi being able to read minds? It could actually be fun to have someone to exchange thoughts with! For the first time since potions class, I feel more relaxed.

"Are you two excited about the field trip?" I ask, moving the subject off myself. "What are you looking forward to most?"

Annabelle slides her hand into her backpack, which is hanging from her chair. She pulls out a museum brochure and opens it, pointing to a kaleidoscope of butterflies. "Personally, I can't wait to see the butterfly vivarium!"

Annabelle hands me the brochure.

I heard there were butterflies at the museum, but I don't know much else about them.

"What exactly *is* a butterfly vivarium?" I ask.

Annabelle's face lights up.

"A vivarium is where they house the butterfly exhibit," she explains. "It's a warm, tropical enclosure, with trees, plants, water features, and tons of butterflies. You can walk around inside and look at all kinds of beautiful butterflies up close, and if you're lucky, sometimes the butterflies will even land on you!"

Hunter, who has tuned in to our conversation from across the table, starts cupping and flapping his arms like a butterfly, but truth be told, he looks more like a chicken.

What a goofball.

"Butterflies sound *okay*," Hunter says halfheartedly. "But the dinosaurs are the *best* exhibit."

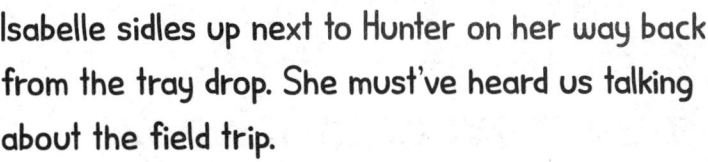

Isabelle sidles up next to Hunter on her way back from the tray drop. She must've heard us talking about the field trip.

"Everyone loves *dinosaurs*, Hunter!" she agrees enthusiastically. "You don't have to convince us!" Izzy is right. We all agree that dinosaurs are pretty cool.

"There's also a blue whale exhibit and a planetarium," Isabelle adds. "But Mrs. Kettledrum says we may not have time for everything."

"Dinosaurs and butterflies and blue whales, *oh my!*" I exclaim.

My friends laugh. It'll be great for us to get away from Broomsfield on a field trip together.

Unfortunately, these happy thoughts last all of about a minute—that's because out of nowhere, somebody barges into my thoughts without even knocking.

Don't worry. It's going to be fun, Heidi Heckelbeck! the intruder says.

At first I think the voice must be coming from Sunny, or at least I hope it is. I've always been able to hear Sunny's thoughts easily because we're such close friends.

But this voice sounds nothing like hers. Sunny would never refer to me by my first and last name.

Then a scary feeling washes over me.

Was it Jodi?

My eyes shift toward Jodi's table.

Yup! It's *her*, all right!

Jodi is staring *directly* at me, and not only that, she's also got a huge smile on her face.

My worst fears have just been confirmed.

Not only can Jodi READ my thoughts but she can SEND thoughts to me too!

What am I going to do NOW?

One word: *rattled.*

As we all get up to leave the cafeteria, I hear Jodi calling me.

"Hey, Heidi, wait up!" she says. I tell Sunny and Annabelle I'll catch up with them later, and I wait for Jodi.

"What's up, Jodi?" I ask.

"Heidi, what are you so worried about?" Jodi says. "Tomorrow is going to be super-fun. I can't wait to hang out with all your friends."

"Why?" I say. "Why all *my* friends? Why have you glommed on to me, Jodi?"

"Because you're the smartest, most popular girl in our grade, of course." Jodi pauses, and then she smiles. "That is, you **were** before I arrived. We'll see who's the favorite after tomorrow.

"See you later, Heidi."

And with a toss of her perfect, shiny brown hair, Jodi turns and walks away from me. I stare after her, slightly in shock.

If Jodi has a noodle type, it is most definitely *merg-o-lini.*

BRRROOOM! BRRROOOM!

I have to write a letter to Lucy.

I need to vent to my best friend.

And even though I can't tell her the witchy side of what's going on, at least I can spill my feelings. Maybe this will make me feel better.

Melanie is at her guitar lesson, so our room is quiet. I pull out a piece of lilac-bordered stationery and a lavender pen to match.

Now to spill my heart out.

HEIDI HELENA HECKELBECK

Hey, Lulu!

It's me, Heidi, your best-ever friend!

Hope things are well with you in good ol' Brewster. Can't wait to hear what's up.

You wanna know what's up with me? Hope so because all I can say is **my entire life has been turned upside down** in the space of one day.

Today we got a new girl in our class, named Jodi. She just moved here from Canada.

This probably doesn't sound like a big deal, but let me tell you,  IT IS!

My entire class treats her like she's a celebrity. It's kind of annoying if you ask me.

Here's the real problem. She just makes me really uncomfortable. I can't put my finger on it. All my friends think she's really nice, but that's not the vibe I get at all.

Tonight at dinner, she was sitting with Melanie and Nick.

What if Nick ends up liking her better than me? What if *everyone* likes her more than me?

Please write back as soon as possible, my wise and faithful friend. You always know the right things to say. Do you think things will get better? Am I overreacting?

Sorry to sound so pathetic!

Thanks for listening.
Love you tons!
Your totally freaked-out BFF,
Heidi Kins

I stuff Lucy's letter into a paisley-lined envelope. I address it and stamp it. I only use a stamp so it won't raise any eyebrows, if you know what I mean. Then I send the letter magically on its way to Lucy's mailbox. **Phew, it felt good to vent.**

✦ ✦ ✦

My regular classes are fine on Thursday—that's because **Jodi is only in one of them**, my social studies class.

But she *is* in my broomstick riding class with Mr. Craftwood.

The class starts out fine, even though it's hard to ignore Jodi. She's gotten into my head, even when she's not actually talking inside my head.

So far she's keeping to herself. I'm glad because we're doing something really special in class today. Mr. Craftwood is teaching us how to make our very own magical broomsticks!

We spent our last class walking around in the woods, collecting branches for our broom handles, as well as sticks and grasses for the end of the brooms.

Now we actually get to *make* our broomsticks. I focus intently on my teacher.

✦ 50 ✦

"Most of you know me as a wizard and a teacher," Mr. Craftwood begins. "But I'm also what's known as a 'broomsquire.' A broomsquire is someone who has been trained in the ancient art of making besoms. Does anyone know what the term 'besom' means?"

Jodi and I both raise our hands. But **of course** Mr. Craftwood calls on *Jodi* because she's popular **even with the teachers.**

Blah.

Jodi goes **out of her way** to wrinkle her nose at me before she answers.

"Most of you know me as a wizard and a teacher," Mr. Craftwood begins. "But I'm also what's known as a 'broomsquire.' A broomsquire is someone who has been trained in the ancient art of making besoms. Does anyone know what the term 'besom' means?"

Jodi and I both raise our hands. But **of course** Mr. Craftwood calls on *Jodi* because she's popular **even with the teachers.**

Blah.

Jodi goes **out of her way** to wrinkle her nose at me before she answers.

"'Besom' is an old English word for broom, and witches and wizards decided to use it as a term for a magical broomstick," she says in a **fake, overly sweet** tone of voice, **which is a total *act*,** in my opinion.

Mr. Craftwood nods approvingly. "Very good, Jodi."

Jodi looks my way and sends me a thought.

Ha! Beat you to it, Heidi. Gotta be quick when I'm around!

I glare back at Jodi because I want to show **her I'm tough stuff.** I don't *feel* like tough stuff at all. I feel totally uneasy, but I try not to act like it.

Oh, be quiet, Jodi! I just want to pay attention—okay?!

Then I brace myself for another snappy response.

But Jodi stays quiet. Maybe she decided to be quiet and listen for a change. I tune back into Mr. Craftwood.

"Today you're going to craft your besoms, and then we'll enchant them together," our teacher goes on.

"You'll assemble your broomsticks with the branches, twigs, and brush you collected during our last class. Jodi, in your case, earlier today. The instructions are provided in the handouts I gave everyone at the start of class. If you have any questions, I'll be here to answer them. Please begin."

I set my instructions in front of me and lay my broom handle on top of my desk. I chose a stick with just enough knots and crooks to give it some character. **The handle curls at the top, which gives it even more style.** Now to assemble the bristles and attach them to my broomstick.

I grab a handful of birchwood twigs and dried grasses from my bag. They will form my broom.

The next step says to glue and tie the bristles onto the broomstick. Not to brag, but most kids still have to use **glue guns** to attach their bristles, but Mrs. K taught me some glue magic.

Gluing with magic is way easier than a glue gun, and less messy too. I tailor my glue spell to suit my broomstick project.

A STICKY MIX OF WORDS DOTH BREW.
A PERFECT BLEND OF MAGIC GLUE.
GLUE THESE BRISTLES TO MAKE A BROOM.
FASHION THEM INTO A WITCH'S PLUME!

The sticks and dried-grass stalks dance magically as they attach themselves to my broom handle. As I watch the bristles move into place, I hear *you know who* calling me—inside my head.

Heidieee! Heidieee!

Paging Heidi Heckelbeck!

I'm still not used to someone randomly invading my thoughts. I also **blissfully** forgot Jodi while I was making my broomstick.

All I can say is, **this girl needs to give it a rest.**

But I can't exactly ignore her, so I reluctantly turn and look her way. She still has that annoyingly smug look on her face.

Heidi, why do you seem so surprised whenever I visit your thoughts? Did it ever occur to you that other witches can read minds besides YOU? It's not like you're the only one with this gift.

"**Merg!**" I say out loud, which causes some of my classmates to look up from their work.

They probably think I'm frustrated with my broom. That's not it, of course.

I'm a whirl of emotions.

Part of me is mad because Jodi is right about one thing. I *didn't* know other witches my age had the same gift as me.

I never thought about it before. I never would've believed another witch would use their gift of mind reading *against* me.

This is all-new territory.

And I don't like it one bit.

I also wonder how Jodi gets into my thoughts whenever she feels like it. The only other witch I've ever had mental conversation with is Mrs. Kettledrum. Jodi **somehow knew right away that she could have mental conversations with me.**

How come I can only do this with Jodi out of all the rest of the students at Broomsfield Academy? Why her?

I don't like Jodi hijacking my thoughts.

I'm going to tell her that *right now*. Knowing her, **she's probably been listening in on my thoughts the whole time.**

Grrrr.

Of course it shocks me when you burst into my head unannounced, Jodi! I tell her. *Why can't you talk to me like a NORMAL person instead of randomly popping into my head, like it's some public space? Would you please just STOP?!*

Jodi smiles devilishly. She watches me like I'm some form of entertainment. Luckily, she has to look away because Mr. Craftwood just stopped by her desk.

I go back to creating my broomstick, but I'm so upset, I can barely concentrate.

Focus, Heidi! I tell myself as I continue assembling my broomstick.

Okay, I need to secure the bristles to the broomstick by tying twine around them. I cut a long piece of twine and loop it around my broomstick, near the top of the bristles. I tug on the twine until it's tight around them. Then I wrap the twine around and around and tie it off in a knot.

The next step says to pound three nails through the twine and the sticks to make the broom secure. I grab my hammer and three short stubby nails.

Whack! Whack! Whack!

My besom is all assembled.

I hold it up to admire it. I glance at Jodi to see what her broomstick looks like.

I know I shouldn't compare, but I can't help it.

Jodi is holding her broom and admiring it too. Hers has a more dramatic curlicue at the top than mine.

Such a show-off!

Jodi sees me looking and immediately picks up the conversation where we left off.

The reason I can read your mind so easily, Heidi, is because that's one of the perks of two witches who have the same gift of mind reading. Kind of gives new meaning to the phrase "Great minds think alike!"

Jodi giggles out loud. How am I supposed to take this? It's sort of a backhanded compliment.

How dare she say we think alike? Our thoughts are nothing alike!

I wish Jodi had an off button so I could stop her from blabbing on in my head.

One word: *maddening.*

Jodi doesn't stop. She blabs on.

Heidi . . . you surprise me in two ways. (1) You didn't know witches with the same gift of mind reading have the power to read each other's thoughts, and (2) you didn't even know other witches could have the same gift as you! Jodi shakes her head in disbelief.

All the blood in my body rushes into my face.

I am officially FURIOUS.

First of all, **she's wrong.** I have had thought conversations with Mrs. Kettledrum, but I didn't expect this from another magical student.

Then I realize I'd better be careful what I think because Jodi's probably reading every single one of my thoughts.

Ugh, I need to stop this!

I remind myself to ask Mrs. Kettledrum how to stop Jodi from entering my thoughts, but for now I know I have to handle this on my own.

That's ENOUGH, Jodi Thompson, I think angrily. *I'm DONE with this conversation.*

Please see yourself OUT of my head. NOW.

Jodi's not even looking at me anymore. She's not listening, either. That's because Mr. Craftwood has begun to explain how to enchant our broomsticks.

Double ugh! I can't believe I let Jodi distract me from learning magic. **My favorite thing!**

I try to shake off **all this merg-i-ness** so I can hear what my teacher is saying.

"Has everyone completed a broomstick?" Mr. Craftwood asks. We all nod and look around to make sure everyone's done.

"Good!" our teacher goes on. "They're all so creative. Well done! Before we bring your broomsticks to life, I want you to give yours a name! Be sure to give it a name that reflects who you are because your broom is a reflection of you."

Everybody starts talking about names, but I already know what I'm going to name my broomstick.

High Jinks.

"High jinks" means "playful, fun, and mischievous," and that's what a magic broom should be. It also describes me pretty well.

Of course Jodi is listening in on my thoughts, and she's the first to know the name of my broom. I ball up my fists when I hear her voice in my head again.

"High Jinks" is a cute name, Heidi. You want to know what I named MY broomstick?

I look at this annoying new girl fiercely.

NO! I tell her firmly, but Jodi doesn't listen.

She acts like I didn't say anything at all!

I named my broomstick Nika. It means "victory" in Greek. Which means that together Nika and I will always win!

Why can't *I* get into *Jodi's* mind unannounced? This is another question for Mrs. Kettledrum.

Thankfully, Mr. Craftwood starts talking before I can respond to Jodi, which is probably a good thing. It's safer to listen to the teacher than to think about Jodi.

"Is everyone ready to enchant their broom?"

"YES!" the class cries, except me. I'm too mad to be gleeful, but don't get me wrong. I can't wait to enchant my broomstick.

Mr. Craftwood asks Jodi to pass out the broom enchantment spell, *of course*.

While Jodi hands out the spell, Mr. Craftwood pulls something out of an old leather satchel. It looks like a miniature flute. He holds it up for everyone to see.

"This is my magical fife. It's made of rosewood," he tells us. "A fife is a high-pitched woodwind instrument. I'll play the fife while you all chant the broom spell together. Please read the spell quietly to yourself before we begin."

The room falls silent—even Jodi is quiet—as we read the spell to ourselves. Mr. Craftwood waits for everyone to look up.

"Ready?" he asks.

"YES!" we say eagerly.

Mr. Craftwood rolls up his sleeves.

"Okay, everyone, please hold your broomsticks in one hand and hold your spell in the other. Heidi, will you please lead the class in casting the spell?"

I nod, secretly glad that I got a more important job than Jodi.

"Good," Mr. Craftwood affirms. "Heidi, please come to the front of the room with your broomstick and spell."

I get up and walk to the front of the room. Luckily, Jodi doesn't say a peep as I make my way to Mr. Craftwood's side. My teacher smiles at me.

"I want everyone to follow Heidi's lead. I'll begin to play a magical tune, and when I nod my head, that will be Heidi's cue, and yours, to begin chanting the spell. When the spell is complete, you may feel your broom shudder in your hand. This is no cause for alarm. It means your broom has come to life! And this is exactly what we want.

"Are you ready, Heidi?"

"Yes," I say, feeling very important.

"Class, are *you* ready?" Mr. Craftwood asks. My classmates nod in response.

Mr. Craftwood raises the fife to his lips and begins to play a magical tune. The sound is beautiful and bewitching. My teacher nods, and I begin to lead the class in chanting the spell.

STICKS AND TWIGS ALL WRAPPED IN TWINE,
MAKE THIS MAGIC BESOM MINE.
ENCHANT THESE BROOMS BY ROSEWOOD FIFE,
AND GIVE THESE STICKS THE GIFT OF LIFE!

Zing!

The magic takes hold instantly.

I can feel my broom vibrate in my hand. It's no longer just a branch, some twigs, and some twine.

It's *alive!*

"Welcome to the world, High Jinks!" I whisper to my broom.

Mr. Craftwood pats me on the back.

"Thank you, Heidi," he says. "You and your broom may return to your seat."

I walk back to my desk with my living broomstick, along with a new sense of responsibility, not to mention some awe. Wow, this is my very own broom, and I get to take care of it, love it, and train it from now on.

As I take my seat, I'm careful not to catch Jodi's eye. Thankfully, she's keeping quiet right now. Once I'm seated, Mr. Craftwood continues.

"It's time to get acquainted with your brooms," he says. "Say hello and make your broom feel welcome and comfortable in your presence. Be sure to tell your broom its name, too."

We engage with our brooms immediately. The sounds of greetings and happy chatter fill the room.

Think of it! Sixteen magical brooms have just entered the world. This is truly amazing.

"Hello, High Jinks," I whisper. "I'm Heidi, and I know we're going to get along famously." High Jinks swishes her bristles from side to side, like a dog wagging its tail.

Mr. Craftwood claps his hands to get our attention.

"Okay, I'm happy to hear you've all gotten acquainted with your brooms. We're going to learn how to *train* them. We must begin to train them right away so they form good habits."

A murmur of excitement echoes around the room.

This is so cool!

"Training a broom is a lot like training a dog," he tells us. "That's because magical brooms are naturally curious, and like a dog, they need to be taught how to behave.

"The good news is that your broom wants to please you. This makes it easy to teach the broom to do things through positive reinforcement. As you advance, you can also control your broom with magic, but that will come later. For today we're going to teach your broom how to come when it's called."

Mr. Craftwood steps in front of his desk, holding his own broom, Magnus. "Everybody, please stand beside your desk with your broom. I'm going to create more space in the classroom so you'll have room to train."

We all hop to our feet with our brooms.

With a wave of his hand, Mr. Craftwood makes our desks and chairs disappear. We gasp at his quick, one-handed magic.

Wow, I can't wait to do that someday!

With the furniture gone, there's tons of space in the classroom to train our brooms.

"Okay, here we go!" Mr. Craftwood begins. "Everybody, let go of your broom and back six steps away from it. Be sure to face your broom the whole time so it doesn't get scared. And remember this, *you're* in control of your broom. It's depending on you."

We slowly let go of our brooms. They hover in the air and don't go anywhere. Then we back away from them, counting six steps as we go.

Wow, this is incredibly cool!

"Good job," Mr. Craftwood says. "You're going to call your broom by its name and give it one command: *'Come!'* When your broom comes to you, I want you to reward it with praise. This lets your broom know it did a good job. Brooms love to be praised. Allow me to demonstrate."

Mr. Craftwood takes six steps away from his broom.

"Magnus, *come!*" he says in a firm but cheerful voice.

The broom goes straight to our teacher. Then he praises it. "Well done, Magnus!"

Mr. Craftwood releases his grip on his broom.

"Now, this is very important," he goes on. "You must always use the same command with your broom. 'Come!' You can't switch it up and say, 'Here, Magnus!' or, 'Here, Broomy Broomy!' **Always be consistent.** This is how you build trust. It's always important to use a cheerful voice when you call your broom too.

"Before we practice calling them, it's helpful to know that some brooms may learn more quickly than others. This is normal. **Just be patient. Never rush your broom.**

"Your broom will eventually get the hang of it. For more magically advanced witches and wizards, you will most likely have **no trouble** having it obey you. **Brooms are very sensitive to one's magical powers.**

"When your broom *does* learn to come when it's called, you may gradually increase the distance between you and your broom. Okay, I'll be here to help. You may begin calling your brooms."

I can't wait to try this!

"High Jinks, come!" I call as firmly and cheerfully as I can.

Whoosh! Without any hesitation High Jinks whizzes into my waiting hands.

Whoa! I didn't think it would be *that* easy. I look around the classroom. It's not as easy for some of my classmates. Most are struggling to get their brooms to come, except for Jodi. No surprise there.

Just ignore her, I tell myself.

So I do, and I get back to training. This time I take twelve steps away from my broom and try again.

"High Jinks, come!" I call.

Swooooosh! My broom is with me faster than you can say "sweep"!

Wow, this is so easy—and fun!

Things feel normal for about three minutes more until Jodi just can't help herself. She charges right back into my thoughts.

Watch this, Heidi! she says gleefully.

Uh-oh. This can't be good, I think.

And it isn't.

Suddenly Jodi's broom takes off by itself. It darts around the room—when Mr. Craftwood turns his back—and does a couple of loop the loops in the air. Some of our classmates see it and squeal.

Top that, Heidi Heckelbeck! Jodi says snootily.

This is getting totally out of hand.

*Come on, Jodi. Quit it! **You're going to get us both in trouble!*** I tell her.

Jodi makes a pouty face at me. *Has Heidi had enough?* she scoffs. *Come on, Heidi. Did you actually think you'd be the best witch in your class forever?*

Oh, and by the way, did I mention I'm also going to take advanced magic lessons with Mrs. Kettledrum? So much for you being the special one. . . . Well, I guess it was fun for you while it lasted.

I'm so mad right now, I could scream.

I hate to admit it, but I *have* always dreaded the idea of someone in my class being a better witch or wizard than me, but I never dreamed it would actually happen.

I stop my train of thought because I know Jodi is probably listening.

Yup, she is! I can tell by the look on her face. Jodi has me right where she wants me.

Let's not sugarcoat it, Heidi. I can't help it if I'm a better witch than you. . . . You MUST have heard I was legendary at my old school. . . .

Okay, that does it.

As soon as the words leave my lips, my broom takes off like a missile and goes after Jodi's broom. **Her broom panics and takes off.**

They chase each other around and around the room. The whole class is pointing and laughing. Two brooms playing tag does look pretty funny.

Mr. Craftwood is definitely *not* amused.

He points his fingers at our soaring brooms. "Terminate!" he shouts. The brooms freeze in place.

The whole classroom freezes too.

"At ease!" Mr. Craftwood commands. The brooms relax. "Return to your owners." High Jinks comes back to me, and Nika goes back to Jodi.

Mr. Craftwood walks back to his desk. He does *not* look happy.

"I want everyone to put their brooms into sleep mode. Please chant the following spell:

MAGIC BROOMS THAT SOAR AND SWEEP,
NOW IT'S TIME TO GO TO SLEEP.

"Once your broom is asleep, please place it in the broom closet. Then class will be dismissed, except for Heidi and Jodi. I'd like you two to please come see me."

I put my broom into sleep mode, and then I send a thought message to Jodi.

See what you did, Jodi?

We're in BIG trouble—and it's all because of YOU.

Jodi rolls her eyes. *You're the one who lost control, Heidi, not me!*

That's a laugh! I shoot back.

Then I turn away from Jodi.

I don't even want to look at her.

How can I shut her out of my thoughts? I have to figure this out.

Don't hurt yourself trying to shut me out, Heidi, Jodi mocks.

I ignore Jodi's jeers and focus on putting up walls in my thoughts. I'm way too proud of my gift and my magic to let this new girl make me feel bad about myself. Then I notice that my thoughts are quiet.

I did it!

Somehow I closed off my mind.

YES! I say victoriously. *I can't wait to tell Mrs. Kettledrum what I just did!*

I look at Jodi and mouth, *HA!* Jodi just shrugs, like she doesn't care.

The weird thing is, I feel bad about being mean to her. *But why?* I wonder. *She thinks nothing of being mean to me!*

I guess I feel bad because I'm not a mean person in general, so it feels kind of strange and uncomfortable.

But I *had* to defend myself.

This whole Jodi thing has become not only unsettling but scary. This is **infinitely worse** than when Melanie and I used to be enemies.

And now we have to go talk to Mr. Craftwood. **Jodi has only been here a couple of days, and she's ruining my life!**

Why do I feel like *I'm* the drama queen?!

HERE COMES TROUBLE!

After dinner I walk back to my room alone. **I don't feel like talking to anyone—not even my crush.**

I don't want Nick to think I'm a **mope-a-saurus**, even though I am. At least Mr. Craftwood didn't give Jodi and me detention for **totally disrupting his class.** He just gave us a good talking-to about being more mature with our advanced magic skills.

Fingers crossed that he doesn't mention the broom chase to Mrs. Kettledrum. The **last** thing I need is another detention. I've been doing **so** well at keeping out of trouble—that is, until Jodi arrived.

I sigh heavily before opening the door to my room.

Melanie is at her desk, decluttering her makeup bag.

"Hey, Heidi!" she sings. "How's it going? How did your broommaking class go today? We make ours next week. Did you name your broom?"

Melanie's singsong voice and good mood are both welcoming and annoying at the same time. It feels normal, which is nice, but it's annoying because I'm a wiped-out mess of emotions.

"Hey, Melanie," I say, trying to rally. "I named my broom High Jinks, and having your very own magical broomstick is the coolest."

Melanie turns around in her chair. "I know! I can't wait to have my own broom. I think I'm going to name mine Thomasina. I love that name. What were some of the other names?"

I think for a moment.

"You know, the typical names like Sabrina, Merlin, and Enchantra. One girl named her broom Miss Twiggy. Oh, and Hunter named his broom *Bruh*."

Melanie giggles, and it actually makes me laugh a teeny bit too.

"What did Jodi name *her* broom?"

That makes the smile march right off my face.

"She named hers Nika," I say coldly. *If you want my REAL opinion, she **should've** named her broom Cruella,* I think privately.

Melanie sticks out her bottom lip as she considers the name Nika.

"That's kind of cute," she says. "Sooooo I've been dying to ask you ... What do you think of Jodi anyway?"

Melanie wants to know what I think about Jodi? Wow, is that ever a loaded question. There's only one way to answer it.

"No comment," I tell her.

Melanie rolls her chair closer to me. She senses some juicy gossip, and she wants a front row seat.

Ugh, I feel so vulnerable.

I'm not sure I can keep my feelings about Jodi to myself any longer, but if I *do* tell Melanie, there's a good chance it'll get back to Jodi.

But Jodi already knows how I feel about her, so who cares?

I do, but not enough to hold back this dam of emotions.

As much as I don't want to think about Jodi, I could really use a girl-to-girl venting session right now.

"What do you mean by 'no comment'?" Melanie asks. "Did Jodi do something bad?"

Melanie knows how to get right to the point. I grab my chair and pull it in front of her.

"Well, let's put it this way, we've had a few run-ins since she arrived," I tell my broommate. "Jodi has been

getting into my head, **and I mean that *literally*.**

I stop and look up at Melanie. "I couldn't believe it at first, but Jodi has the same gift of mind reading that I do."

Melanie nods thoughtfully.

"Yeah, she actually mentioned that to me. She also told me she was taking **advanced private magic lessons** at her old school in Canada—just like you do with Mrs. Kettledrum."

I sigh heavily.

"Yup, and she'll be taking them with Mrs. Kettledrum *too*," I add.

Melanie crosses one arm around herself and rests her opposite elbow on it, letting her chin rest on top of her hand.

"Wow, sounds like you've got yourself some competition, Heidi!" she says.

I groan at the thought of it.

"You're not kidding," I say with heaviness. "Jodi is **super** competitive too, and I wouldn't call it *friendly* competition. It's like Jodi is **totally out to get me!**"

The very thought of it makes my eyes well up with tears.

Along with the tears, **everything that's happened between Jodi and me comes tumbling out. I tell Melanie *everything*,** like how Jodi just barges into my thoughts **unannounced.** I also tell her how she **brags** about how great a witch she is and how she was *legendary* at her old school.

"And she's **so** mean to me too," I add between sobs. "She thinks I'm a second-rate

witch and says she's **shocked** by what I don't know. **It's awful, Melanie. I'm scared nothing will ever be the same for me at Broomsfield again."** I wipe the corners of my eyes with my fingers. Melanie looks more serious than surprised.

"Sounds like Jodi's a bully," Melanie observes.

I scoff out loud. "Ya think?"

Melanie rolls her eyes at my sarcasm. "Don't you get it? I used to bully you in elementary school—remember?" she reminds me. "I tortured you for years! Then I found out you were pretty cool."

I crack a small smile at her compliment. I still find it hard to believe we're friends now. Melanie was my absolute archenemy at Brewster Elementary.

Melanie runs her fingers through her hair to get the wisps out of her eyes.

"Honestly, Heidi, I wrote the *book* on bullying," she goes on. "And I can help you with Jodi."

A speck of hope awakens inside me.

"How?" I ask, because I am **all ears.**

Melanie shrugs.

"You have to deal with her envy. **Envy is at the root of her behavior,"** she says matter-of-factly. "I'm sure of it. After all, I was jealous of you all those years ago on your first day at Brewster. I should know."

Well, I definitely didn't know that.

"Why would Jodi be envious of *me*? I hardly know her!"

Melanie smiles knowingly.

"That may be true, but I'm sure Jodi knows all about *you*. Like she knows you're an advanced witch with the same gift that she has.

She probably feels like she has to **prove herself** to you—**don't you see?"**

"I just wish she'd stop putting me down," I admit. "It's starting to really get to me."

Melanie pulls some lip balm from her pocket and smears it across her lips.

"She wants to intimidate you, so you'll be afraid of her. That way she'll feel like she has the upper hand."

I stare at Melanie, dumbfounded.

"Wow, not to sound totally clueless, but none of this makes any sense to me."

Melanie laughs. "You're not clueless, Heidi. Remember, *I'm* the expert," she says confidently. "Let me explain it another way.

"When you first came to Brewster Elementary in second grade, I was the most popular girl in the class. And you know what? I wasn't about to let you take my spot.

"But there you were—this cute, fun, outgoing, and smart new girl who walked in out of nowhere. It threatened my very existence!"

My eyes grow wide. I never heard Melanie spell it out like this before. I find it hard to believe.

Me—a threat? That would be like being afraid of a cute, fluffy bunny rabbit or something.

"Well, I just thought you were *mean*," I tell her.

Melanie nods, like, *Now you're getting it!*

"I *was* being mean. I was a mean girl with a capital *M.* I wanted to make sure you knew you couldn't mess with me **or my title as the most popular girl."**

Okay, this makes a little more sense to me—even though popularity was **the last thing** on my mind in second grade.

"What made you change?" I ask.

Melanie smiles.

"Two things, I guess. It turns out **it's more fun to be friends with you** than to be enemies. Plus, **I'm more confident in who I am now."**

I pull one foot onto my knee and smile at Melanie.

"It's **definitely** more fun being friends with you," I say, **and I mean it.** Melanie's friendship has been one of the best things about Broomsfield Academy.

Then I go back to my problem. "Speaking of friends, I'm pretty sure Jodi also wants to **steal** all my friends. Haven't you noticed she's, like, the **most popular girl in our class right now?**"

Melanie shrugs, like none of what I'm saying is a big deal.

"Trust me, Heidi, if there's one thing I've learned, **popularity is fleeting, especially with a new girl.** Don't worry. Her newfound status will wear off, and she'll just be another girl in our class."

I sigh because **I find this very hard to believe.** It feels like Jodi plans to be a thorn in my side **for the rest of middle school, then high school, and even beyond.** Melanie can tell she hasn't convinced me.

"The way I see it, you have a choice, Heidi. You can either win this girl over or you can sit around and feel your feels," she says. "I'm sure underneath it all, Jodi just wants to be friends with you."

I laugh, like, *Yeah, right.* Because that's about the most ridiculous thing I've ever heard.

Melanie hops up from her chair and grabs a bottle from her tray of perfumes—most of which are her own original scents. Potions is her gift as a witch.

"I've been working on some aromatherapy potions lately," she says, changing the subject. "This pillow potion not only guarantees to bring you a sense of well-being, but it'll also bring the sweetest sleep you've ever known.

"I made it with a dreamy lavender oil, sweet tangerine, chamomile, almond, and ylang-ylang, not to mention a few magical taps of my wand. You want to try it?"

I nod because this sounds like exactly what I need right now.

"A peaceful night's sleep before tomorrow's field trip **sounds really good**," I answer gratefully. "Let me wash up and put on my pj's." I get up and head to the bathroom.

When I come out, the room has a soft glow. Melanie has turned off the overhead lights and placed a few of her battery-operated tea lights on my nightstand. The only other lights are the glow-in-the-dark stars on my ceiling.

"Sweet dreams await you, Heidi," Melanie says soothingly. It feels like I'm at a fancy hotel, rather than in a dorm room.

I giggle as I tuck my slippers beside my bed. A shower and clean pj's have made me feel a whole lot better. Melanie spritzes my pillow with her magical potion. I crawl under my covers.

"Mmm, it smells amazing!" I say as I breathe in the enchanting scent.

Melanie smiles. "Doesn't it?" she says proudly. "Night night, and don't let the mean girls bite."

I give Melanie a look like, *Really?*

She winks back.

"Just joking," Melanie says. "Don't worry. You'll get past this whole Jodi thing. I promise."

I roll onto my side. "Well, thanks for being such a good friend, Melanie." That's the last thing I remember till morning.

Warm ribbons of light cross my quilt in the morning. It's a gorgeous day, and I feel well-rested.

Melanie's pillow potion has worked its magic, *literally*! I feel like *me* again, even though I haven't forgotten about Jodi.

At least I feel ready to face the day, and I can't wait for our field trip.

Three words: *Good vibes only!*

Melanie hops out of bed and pulls our curtains all the way back. The room lights up.

"Time to spring-ify our wardrobes!" she sings. "I'm going to wear a flirty flowered skirt and a lacy peasant top. I'll finish it all off with some sweet perfume.

"How about you, Heidi?"

I roll out of bed and head for my closet to consider my spring outfit options.

"Well, it may be time to break out **my lavender jeans**," I announce, pulling them from the top shelf, along with a white gauzy tee. I slide my jean jacket off the hanger and lay my outfit on my bed.

"Cuuuuuute!" Melanie approves.

We get dressed, give ourselves magical lavender manis, and head out the door. I decide to just have a cereal bar to hold me over till social studies class. We're making Danish pancakes in class today. **Yum!**

The rest of my morning **flew** by! I only have **one** more class to go before it's time for the field trip.

On the way to class, guess who I bump into?! Hint: it's **not** Jodi.

It's my crush, Nick.

Eeee!

"Hey, Heidi," Nick says, giving me a friendly nudge. "I've hardly seen you *all* week! How are you? I miss being at the same table." He makes a cute pouty face.

I sling my backpack over my shoulder, and we catch up a bit before, of course, he mentions Jodi.

Growl!

Nick thinks she's so *nice and friendly.*

Double growl.

As we chat, I suddenly hear Jodi's voice in my head again.

Hey, Heidi, is that your BOYFRIEND?

I whirl around and see Jodi and Isabelle walking down the path toward us.

Oh no! **Here comes trouble!**

What's Jodi doing with Isabelle? Isabelle is *MY* friend.

Oh no, I hope Jodi didn't hear that.

I wait for her reaction in my head, but I don't hear anything—probably because she's too busy running alongside Isabelle trying to catch up to us.

"Who's your *friend*, Heidi?" Jodi asks when they reach us, as if she didn't know. They sit at the same table, **for heaven's sake!** But I go along with her charade.

"This is Nick," I say with a dash of annoyance. "Nick, this is Jodi."

Nick smiles. "Hi, Jodi. We sit at the same table. Remember? Hope you're liking Broomsfield."

Jodi bats her eyes and smiles back at him. "I know you sit at my table," she says shyly. "I just wanted a formal intro. I love Broomsfield so far—thanks!"

Nick nods, says goodbye to us, and takes off for his class. That's when I remember that Jodi is in my social studies class.

Merg it all! My peaceful morning has just taken a dive.

Just rise above it, Heidi, I tell myself as we head for class. Isabelle and Jodi chitchat as we go. Jodi also talks to me in my head at the same time.

Isabelle has no idea this is going on, of course.

I can't believe you like Nick, Jodi says, like he's nothing special. **Why would you like him?**

He's not even in the School of Magic! He does have nice hair, though.

I don't dare look at Jodi because if I do, I might make a mean face. I have to defend Nick, so I send my thoughts on the matter right back at her.

How dare you insult my crush, Jodi! Nick is so super-nice, but that's something you obviously wouldn't understand. Being a good person **seems to be a stretch for you.**

And P.S. I would appreciate it if you would please keep your opinions to yourself.

Then I bar my mind from Jodi's thoughts again, and it works.

Yes! **I think I'm getting the hang of it!** But I'm also mad that Jodi would try to make me doubt my crush.

Jodi looks at me suspiciously. I know what she's thinking without even reading her thoughts. She can't believe I just locked her out of my head again.

Ha! Take that! I say privately.

When we get to social studies, I stay as far away from Jodi as possible. It's time to make aebleskiver, Danish pancakes, to close our unit on Denmark. **Jodi is not going to wreck this for me.**

Our teacher has set up five cooking stations. Each station has a mini-windmill and a Danish flag, which is a red flag with a white Nordic cross. There are also two cast-iron aebleskiver cooking pans on top of portable electric stovetop burners. These funky pans have seven little cup indentations, shaped like

a tennis ball cut in half. There are bowls with batter, along with smaller bowls with toppings: powdered sugar, jelly, syrup, and whipped cream. And of course, there are ten pairs of silicone gloves for us to wear when working with the cooking pans. Isabelle is at my station. Jodi is at Hunter's.

The first thing we have to do is melt some butter in each of the wells in the pan. When the butter is all melted, we pour the batter into the wells. Isabelle and I take turns. Then we wait for the aebleskiver to cook.

Dum-dee-dum-dum!

"They're puffing up!" Isabelle says, peeking under a pancake ball with some wooden tongs. "Ooo, it's golden brown!"

Isabelle and I turn the pancake balls over until they're lightly browned all over. Then we gently place them into a bowl.

We make another batch, **and then it's time to eat them.** We sprinkle powdered sugar on top of each of our aebleskiver.

Then we fill some dipping bowls with the jelly, maple syrup, and whipped cream.

Hunter waves us over to his table. While I was working with Isabelle, I forgot that Jodi is his partner today.

When Jodi sees me, she looks at me like, *Not* you *again.*

If anyone should be looking at someone like that, it should be **me** looking at **Jodi**.

She started all this hostility in the first place.

"These pancake puffs are SO good," Hunter exclaims, popping one covered in whipped cream into his mouth.

"*Sooo* good," Jodi emphasizes. "But Hunter might need some lessons on how to make them. A few landed on the floor. . . ." She giggles, and so do Hunter and Isabelle. Not me, of course, because *whatever*.

I dip a pancake ball into syrup and take a bite. *Wow, these ARE good!* They taste more like doughnuts than pancakes.

Yum! As I chew, I notice the blades on the windmill begin to turn, but there's no gust of wind in here.

Uh-oh. Is Jodi using magic again?

I look at her, and she pumps her eyebrows up and down. Oh my gosh, she IS making the windmill blades turn! The blades begin to spin faster and faster. Isabelle thinks it's me.

"Heidi," she whispers. "Stop using magic in a *non*-magical class. You'll get us all in trouble!

I nudge Isabelle with my knee.

"It's not *me*," I whisper back. "It's *Jodi.*"

I glare at Jodi. *Cut it out,* I think, hoping Jodi hears this one.

She winks and plays dumb to everyone else at the table.

Okay, that's it. I've had enough.

I pick up my plate from the table and turn to leave. Jodi is not going to get me in trouble for her pranks. Isabelle looks at me with surprise. "Where are you going, Heidi?"

I lean into Isabelle's ear.

"I'll explain later," I whisper, and without another word, I walk across the room and plant my plate on a table with non-magical kids. Jodi had better be smart enough not to do magic in front of *this* table. Mrs. Kettledrum would positively lose it if she found out.

I, for one, would love to see Jodi get in trouble. Maybe she'd learn to settle down.

The rest of the day through lunch is basically fine— other than me feeling grumpy. I hate to admit how much Jodi gets to me.

You know what's really maddening? After Jodi said all those mean things about Nick, she did nothing but flirt with him all through lunch.

One word: *rude!*

Well, at least we have the field trip to look forward to this afternoon. I'm still pretty excited about that.

The time has finally come!

Sunny, Annabelle, and I board Mrs. Kettledrum's bus together. Mr. Craftwood is on a second bus with the rest of the first-year students. As we walk down the aisle, I spy Jodi sitting with Melanie in the way back. They're laughing and talking and acting all buddy-buddy.

Jodi is **definitely** trying to become BFFs with Melanie.

No sooner do I think this than Jodi bursts into my thoughts again.

Of course I am trying to be Melanie's bestie! Jodi admits freely. *We have SO much in common! I've already got Isabelle on my side!*

Ugh, I think. *Jodi was listening to my thoughts. I have to learn to be more careful.* Meanwhile Jodi blathers on.

I plan to wiggle my way into your whole inner circle of friends, Heidi, she says. *When I'm done, you'll be a total outcast—not to mention the number-two witch in our class. You'll see!*

Jodi's words terrify me. Is there something seriously wrong with her? Who would even say something like this? It's so low!

Well, I have a few words for Jodi too.

*My friends will **never** turn on me, Jodi,* I tell her. *If you tell them lies about me, they'll **never** believe it because they know I'm a TRUE friend. Nothing you can say or do will hurt me!*

I want to believe what I'm saying so badly, but **I'm really scared Jodi may have the power to turn my friends against me.** I can't let her have the upper hand. Melanie warned me about this.

I look back at Jodi. She slits her eyes at me.

Well, you're right about one thing, Heidi. I DO have the upper hand, and it's already clear that I can outsmart you at anything.

Okay, that's enough bullying for me, I think, slamming the door shut on Jodi's insults. I can't listen to her mean comments anymore.

I wish I could tell Mrs. Kettledrum what's going on, but she's too busy managing all the students on our bus. Besides, if I tell, **that will make me a tattletale, and then Jodi would actually *have* something on me.**

Sunny, Annabelle, and I sit together, and once my back is turned on Jodi, it's much easier to ignore her. Sunny and Annabelle talk nonstop the whole way to the museum. After a while my smoldering anger gives way to giggles.

There's no way Jodi is going to steal my friends. Our bonds are too strong.
Jodi's words are nothing but empty threats, I tell myself.

Besides I'm a cool, fun person, and there's no way Jodi can take that or my friends away from me. I shove all the bad feelings into a closet way in the back of my brain.

We've arrived!

A humongous blue whale model greets us as we walk into one of the halls at the American Natural History Museum. The skeleton is one hundred feet long!

Wow, it's hard to believe creatures this gigantic actually live in the ocean!

Did you know that humans have only explored 5 percent of the ocean? That means there's a whole 95 percent that's totally unknown! I wonder what else waits to be discovered.

The whale is arranged in a diving position, like it's plunging after some food.

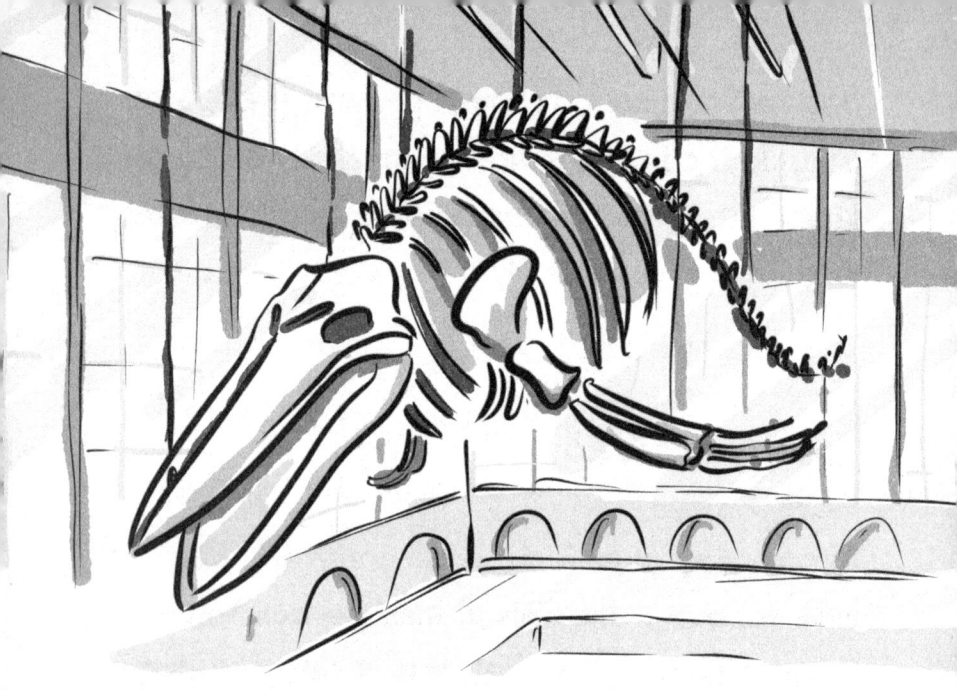

Mrs. Kettledrum just told us blue whales are the largest animal to have ever lived! She also said a blue whale's tongue weighs as much as a whole elephant.

One word: *hefty!*

Mrs. Kettledrum divides us into two groups. I'm in Mrs. K's group, along with Annabelle, Sunny, Hunter, Isabelle, and Melanie.

Jodi is in our group too.

Argh!

I wish Mrs. Kettledrum would clue in about the new girl. If she knew what was going on, she would've put Jodi in Mr. Craftwood's group. At least Jodi is still glued to Melanie. We gather around Mrs. Kettledrum.

"What would you like to see first—butterflies or dinosaurs?" our teacher asks.

"**Butterflies!**" most of us shout, except Hunter. He yells, *"Dinosaurs!"*

Butterflies win. We shuffle behind Mrs. Kettledrum, like a family of ducklings, all the way to the butterfly exhibit. Sunny leans against me, arm in arm, as we waddle along.

"I hope a butterfly lands on me," she whispers.

I lean back on her arm.

"I hope one lands on me, too!"

Annabelle leans on my other arm.

"I want a butterfly to land on me as well!"

We giggle.

I'm pretty sure we've just given new meaning to the term "social butterflies."

Ha!

BUTTERFLY MAGNET

Mrs. Kettledrum hands out disposable cameras so we can take pics in the museum—that's because at Broomsfield Academy we're not allowed to have our phones during the week. She also gives us a little talk before we go into the butterfly exhibit.

"The museum keeps the vivarium very warm and humid for the butterflies. If you would prefer to observe the butterflies from outside, then you may stay out here with me. Your choice!"

Everyone wants to go inside—that is, **until we walk in the door.**

"It must be a million degrees in here!" Sunny exclaims.

Annabelle points to a sign that says the temperature is 90 degrees with 100 percent humidity.

One word: *toasty!*

I tie my jean jacket around my waist.

"Frizzy hair, here we come!" I say, patting the top of my head.

Sunny laughs. "Mine's frizzing already!"

We giggle. I, for one, am going to do a de-frizzing spell as soon as we get back to school.

Soon the beauty of the butterflies takes our minds off the steamy air.

There are butterflies with tiger stripes, zigzags, curlicues, and polka dots, and **they come in all different colors:** pink, yellow, orange, turquoise, black, and white—**you name it.**

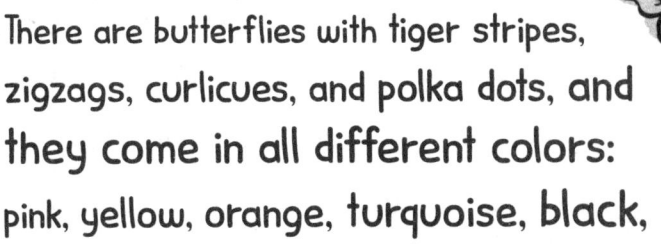

The butterflies flit and fly among the flowers, plants, and tropical trees in the vivarium. Isabelle stops to snap a pic of Hunter with a black-and-white butterfly on top of his head.

"That's a keeper!" she says, laughing.

Melanie, who is dressed like a flower garden, admires a butterfly that's landed on her fingertip.

The other thing that's still stuck on Melanie is Jodi. But I'd rather have Jodi focus on Melanie than on me. *That's for sure!*

Little do I know, these will soon become famous last words because suddenly my classmates are all **pointing at me and laughing.**

"What's so funny?" I ask Sunny and Annabelle. They're laughing too. "*Seriously,* what's going on?" I ask again.

My friends point at something above me. I look up to see a halo of butterflies circling my head.

At first I think the butterflies are attracted to the perfume Melanie gave me, but then more butterflies begin to land **all over my body.**

Before long I'm covered from head to toe in butterflies. I've become a **butterfly magnet!**

And they tickle!

I want to brush the butterflies off, but I don't want to hurt them. So I don't move!

Snap!

Click!

Snap!

Everyone is taking pictures of me!

"Heidi, how are you doing this?" Sunny asks, marveling at my butterfly bodysuit. "You look like some kind of cool butterfly statue!"

I shake my body in hopes that some of the butterflies will fall off.

"I am *not* doing this!" I cry.

Then I zoom in on Jodi. Her grin gives her away.

She's making this happen to me!

STOP IT, JODI! I mentally shout at her.

She laughs out loud.

Oh my gosh, Heidi! You look positively dazzling in that real live butterfly costume! This is so much fun, don't you think?!

I don't care what Jodi is saying right now. All these butterflies are making me feel claustrophobic.

I'm beginning to panic when Mrs. Kettledrum walks into the butterfly vivarium to see what's going on.

"What's all the fuss about?" she asks, looking around for answers.

Zing! Jodi calls off the butterflies. They go back to fluttering around as though nothing happened.

Of course, Mrs. Kettledrum doesn't suspect Jodi of anything. Mrs. K zeroes in on *me* instead. Well, that figures. **The one time I'm totally innocent!**

I probably look guilty because even though the butterflies are gone, I'm still totally freaked out.

Jodi walks up to our teacher.

"There's nothing going on, Mrs. Kettledrum," she says innocently. "The heat is just making us all a little goofy!"

Mrs. Kettledrum buys this **bald-faced lie.**

Don't believe her! I think loudly, hoping my thoughts are as clear as day on my face so that Mrs. K catches the hint!

But not today. She's too flustered by her students causing a scene in public. **Just my luck.**

Mrs. Kettledrum dabs her forehead with a handkerchief.

"You're right, Jodi. It is much too hot in here," our teacher says. "It's no wonder everyone's feeling a little loopy. Let's move on to the dinosaur exhibit!"

I race out the door because my anger has now turned to tears, and the *last* person I want to see me cry is Jodi. This will only make her think she won at her twisted game of Let's Torture Heidi.

Well, not if I can help it!

I wipe my eyes as Sunny and Annabelle jog toward me. I don't want *them* to see me cry either, so I try to pull myself together.

I quickly untie my jean jacket from around my waist and slip it back on. This helps me get ahold of myself a little by the time my friends catch up.

"Why'd you take off so fast, Heidi?" Sunny asks, studying my face. "Are you mad?"

I shrug casually.

"'Mad' would be an understatement," I say.

Sunny and Annabelle look at each other in surprise.

"Why?" Sunny questions. "Mrs. K didn't see anything, so you won't get in trouble for using magic outside school. Besides, it did look pretty amazing." Sunny and Annabelle both laugh.

I clench my fists. *Well, it didn't feel amazing,* I think. *Not one bit.*

"Listen!" I plead with my friends. "I had *nothing* to do with the butterflies swarming me! That was all *Jodi.*

"And for once I wish Mrs. Kettledrum *had* seen what really happened. Then Jodi would've gotten in trouble, and she would have totally deserved it!

"You have to believe me. That girl is **not** as nice as she appears."

Having to relive the anger I felt in the vivarium triggers more tears. My eyes are welling up again. I wipe the tears away as they roll down my face, but they keep coming.

My friends were not expecting tears.

"Okay, okay, Heidi," Sunny says gently. "Calm down. Everything's going to be okay."

I'm sniffling all over the place.

"It's *not* fair!" I complain. "Every time I get carried away with magic, I get caught.

"*EVERY TIME.*

"Jodi uses magic outside our magic classes all the time, and she *never* gets caught. And the worst part is, she uses her magic against *me*!"

My friends huddle around me to shield me from the rest of the class.

"You're right, Heidi," Sunny says. "You have paid a **hefty price** for your magical mess-ups."

Annabelle agrees with her.

"Here's the good news," Sunny goes on. "Nobody got in trouble this time, so let's just be thankful for that, *okay?*"

I know Sunny is right. If Jodi HAD gotten caught, Mrs. Kettledrum probably would've sent us all back to school.

"Come on, Heidi. Let's just enjoy the rest of our field trip," Annabelle encourages me. "This is supposed to be a fun day away from school. Let's not let anything ruin it."

I nod glumly.

Easy for her to say, I think.

I DO want to have fun, and I also really want to see the dinosaur exhibit.

"Okay," I say halfheartedly.

Annabelle and Sunny link their hands with mine, and we walk to the dinosaur exhibit.

Okay, I'll admit it, I feel a wee bit more loved right now, and this lifts my spirits.

But let's be clear, the day isn't over. . . .

6

MAGICAL MONKEY BUSINESS

The head of a Titanosaur curves out from inside the entrance to the dinosaur exhibit. It looks like it's peeking into the hallway to see what's going on. It's cool and creepy at the same time.

A sign on the wall beside the entrance says this is one of the largest dinosaur fossils ever to be discovered and is 122 feet long.

How's that for an epic doorkeeper!

My friends and I step into the dinosaur hall and gape at all the colossal dinosaur skeletons that surround us.

Our group assembles in front of a woman wearing a navy pantsuit and white blouse. Sunny, Annabelle, and I are the last ones to arrive.

Oops.

Mrs. Kettledrum nods to the woman in the pantsuit to let her know we're all here.

"Welcome to the hall of dinosaurs!" she says enthusiastically. "My name is Mrs. Martone, and I'll be here to answer any questions you may have during your visit. Does anyone have any before we get started?"

Sophie Rodriguez's hand goes up in a flash. Mrs. Martone calls on her. Sophie points to a skeleton hanging overhead.

"Is that a flying dinosaur?"

Everyone looks at the skeleton. It has a large pointy skull, a small torso, long skinny wings, and long birdlike legs.

"That's called a pterodactyl, and they did indeed fly!" Mrs. Martone confirms. "But the pterodactyl is not a dinosaur—**even though it may look like one.** This creature is a member of the order Pterosauria. As you walk around, you'll see their skeletons are very different from dinosaur skeletons. Are there any other questions?"

Nobody else raises their hand because all we want is to be unleashed to explore the exhibit. Mrs. Martone nods.

"Okay, feel free to roam the hall of dinosaurs for the next half hour, and remember, I'll be here to answer your questions."

Everybody takes off in different directions, except me. First I have to locate Jodi.

I need to know her whereabouts so I can be sure to avoid her.

Oh no! She caught me looking. Our eyes lock, and she shoots me another message.

Are you feeling better, Heidi? she asks sarcastically. *You sure acted like a baby in the butterfly exhibit. I was just having a little fun! Sheesh, I thought you were stronger than that. . . .*

I huff.

*Well, for your information, there's **nothing the matter**,* I tell her, doing my best to come off strong. *Just stay away from me and keep out of trouble. Okay?!*

Jodi smiles crookedly. How she finds any of this funny is beyond me. I used to think Melanie was mean, **but Jodi takes the prize.** I wish she would just shut up, but no such luck.

Why would you think I'D want to get in trouble, Heidi? Jodi questions. *I'm the new girl, and I just want to make a good impression. But if something WERE to go wrong, I could easily make it look like YOUR problem, like I did in the butterfly exhibit.*

Time to bar Jodi from my thoughts again.

Bam! I put up my mental walls.

Hmmm, I wonder what she meant when she said, *If something WERE to go wrong . . .*

✦ 163 ✦

The very idea of something else going wrong makes me shudder. As I'm thinking all these horrible thoughts, Melanie runs over to Jodi and tugs her by the arm.

"Come take my picture with the velociraptor!" she says. "I'll take yours, too!"

Before she leaves, Jodi gives me a high-and-mighty look and sends another dig.

Looks like your broommate chose ME over YOU, she says. *Guess I'll talk to you later. . . .*

Merg!

I must've let my mental guard down, I think as Jodi walks off with Melanie.

Look at those two! They act like they've been besties for years.

It's hard to see Melanie so chummy with Jodi.

I hope Melanie hasn't turned on me, **especially after I vented to her about Jodi.**

Will I be able to trust her anymore? Or has Melanie been sucked into Jodi's plan? I'd better be careful what I say to Melanie from now on.

I look around for Sunny and Annabelle. They're talking with Hunter and Isabelle. I step into their conversation. Hunter sees me first.

"Hey, Heidi! Isn't this place amazing?" he raves.

I must admit, Hunter's excitement is exactly what I need to snap me out of my misery.

Isabelle jerks her thumb at Hunter. "I told you this guy is all about dinosaurs!" she says. "Did you know Hunter had dinosaurs all over his bedroom when he was little?"

Hunter beams.

"And proud of it!" he affirms. "I had a dinosaur quilt, dinosaur pajamas, dinosaur posters, a herd of plastic dinosaurs—

not to mention a dinosaur sprinkler in the backyard."

Everyone laughs, except me. I'm not quite there yet.

"Hey, Heidi, is everything okay?" Isabelle asks with some concern in her voice. "You look a little pale."

Sunny and Annabelle shoot me a worried look too. Hunter is way too excited to notice any signs of drama.

I smile the most genuine smile I can muster.

"I'm fine," I reassure everyone. "I've just been stressing about something. No big deal. It's all good."

Hunter darts a finger at me to get my attention.

"Good because there's no stressing allowed on the field trip! Come on. Let's go check out the *Spinosaurus*! It's a dinosaur that can swim!"

Once again my friends—my *true friends*—lead me out of my funk.

We check out *Spinosaurus* and a bunch of other dinosaur skeletons mounted on platforms or in glass cases. Most of the dinosaurs seem to be in the stalking position.

One word: *monstrous*.

"Do you all know what some dinosaurs are related to?" Hunter asks as we study a brontosaurus.

We all take guesses because we've been reading about dinosaur descendants throughout the exhibit.

"Lizards?"

"Sharks?"

"Crocodiles?"

"Horseshoe crabs?"

Hunter nods.

"Yup, you're *all* right, but you missed one." He smiles slyly. *"Chickens!"*

We all look at each other and laugh.

Chickens? *Really?*

"It's true!" Hunter says. "Chickens are cousins of certain dinosaurs. Think about it! They both walk on two legs. They both have big heads, scaly feet, and sharp claws, and they both lay eggs. A chicken is basically a miniature *T. rex*!"

I, for one, will never look at a chicken the same way. *Brroock!*

Then we stop at an exhibit where we are allowed to touch a *real* fossil. The fossil is the footprint of a sauropod. One sauropod footprint is about three feet wide!

The sight of it makes me try to imagine dinosaurs tromping across the United States. I certainly can't picture dinosaurs walking around in my hometown, but wouldn't it be cool to *find* a dinosaur fossil?!

The next thing we observe are dinosaur egg fossils, which come in all shapes and sizes. After that we watch a mini movie about how dinosaurs became extinct.

Scientists say an asteroid the size of Mount Everest slammed into Earth about sixty-six million years ago. *KABOOOOOM!*

The asteroid struck Mexico, and the impact triggered wildfires, volcanic eruptions, and tsunamis all over the world. The fiery dust and debris blocked the sunlight and caused the temperature to drop drastically. If the asteroid and fires didn't destroy the dinosaurs, the change in climate probably finished them off.

One word: *mind-blowing.*

Next is the *Tyrannosaurus rex* exhibit. Hunter introduces us to Terry the *T. rex,* king of the tyrant lizards! The complete *T. rex* fossil stands twelve feet tall and forty feet

long, which is the same length as our school bus. Terry's teeth are the size of bananas, **except they're sharp, like daggers.**

I can't look at them for very long—too scary. *Eek!* As we gawk at the *T. rex*, Hunter arches his arms, like a monster.

"Did you know that Terry could eat all four of you and *still* be hungry!" Hunter tells us, followed by a monstrous roar.

We squeal at the thought of being dinosaur food.

"Thanks for the info, Hunter," Isabelle says, bumping her crush on the hip. "That's good to know."

Hunter roars again.

"Do you guys want to race a *T. rex*?" he asks.

Well, of course we want to race a *T. rex*!

We all follow Hunter to an interactive racetrack. Beside the racetrack is a superlong movie screen, where you can race against different kinds of dinosaurs.

Hunter wants to be the first one in our class to race the *T. rex*. He flings his jacket onto the floor and stands on track one's starting line, which is next to the movie screen. Isabelle stands on track two. We count down as numbers flash on the screen.

"TEN! NINE! EIGHT! SEVEN! SIX! FIVE! FOUR! THREE! TWO! ONE!"

Hunter and Isabelle take off and sprint alongside the virtual *T. rex*. The *T. rex*'s steps are *way* bigger than Hunter's and Isabelle's. The dinosaur looks like it's barely trying.

Hunter and Isabelle run as fast as they can. Hunter runs faster than Isabelle, but the *T. rex* is faster than both of them.

We cheer for our friends. Unfortunately, our cheers attract Melanie's and Jodi's attention.

Oh BOTHER! as Winnie-the-Pooh—*and my dad*—would say. Jodi watches us closely. She has this strange look on her face. I wonder why? Is she jealous that I'm having fun?

Melanie **did** say Jodi was probably jealous of me, which I still find hard to believe.

There is *one* thing I am sure of: I don't trust Jodi at all, and I'm going to keep

my eye on her while we're in the same hall.

What if she tries to pull something wacky again?

Well, at least Jodi seems to be acting fairly harmless right now. She's still clinging to Melanie, like a koala bear. The two of them are gabbing away, but every now and then I catch Jodi glancing at me. **It really makes me wonder what she's thinking.**

Maybe I should sneak into Jodi's thoughts and find out. It's *very* tempting. Jodi certainly thinks nothing of sneaking around in my brain, so why should I feel bad about sneaking around in hers?

I decide to give it a try. It's perfect because nobody's paying attention right now. Sunny and Annabelle are racing the *T. rex*, and Hunter and Isabelle are watching.

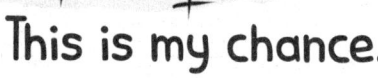

This is my chance.

I partially hide behind a column, but not so much that it looks like I'm hiding. Then I focus my mind on Jodi's thoughts. I don't hear anything at first, but then I become aware that I'm inside Jodi's head.

Oh my gosh!

I can hear what she's thinking!

Shhhh, keep quiet and listen, I tell myself. *The last thing you want is for Jodi to know you're in her thoughts.*

I keep my mind as still and as quiet as I possibly can, and I listen to what Jodi is thinking. . . .

Well, it looks like I've got my friendship with Melanie locked up! Now I can work on some of Heidi's other friends. It shouldn't be that hard to win them ALL over.

WHAT? I think, accidently logging out of Jodi's thoughts.

Jodi is a total FRIEND THIEF!

I don't get it. Why does she want to steal my friends? Why does she want to see me left out? What's her end goal? Does she plan to take over my class? And then the whole school?

I must find out more!

I take a deep breath and go back into her mind. Only, this time I catch her right in the middle of a much more disturbing thought. It's far more frightening than stealing my friends. I listen closely.

There's no way Heidi would ever know how to pull off a whopper of a stunt like this! But maybe I can.

Oh my gosh!

I can hear what she's thinking!

Shhhh, keep quiet and listen, I tell myself. *The last thing you want is for Jodi to know you're in her thoughts.*

I keep my mind as still and as quiet as I possibly can, and I listen to what Jodi is thinking. . . .

Well, it looks like I've got my friendship with Melanie locked up! Now I can work on some of Heidi's other friends. It shouldn't be that hard to win them ALL over.

WHAT? I think, accidently logging out of Jodi's thoughts.

Jodi is a total FRIEND THIEF!

I don't get it. Why does she want to steal my friends? Why does she want to see me left out? What's her end goal? Does she plan to take over my class? And then the whole school?

I must find out more!

I take a deep breath and go back into her mind. Only, this time I catch her right in the middle of a much more disturbing thought. It's far more frightening than stealing my friends. I listen closely.

There's no way Heidi would ever know how to pull off a whopper of a stunt like this! But maybe I can.

Then I can show Heidi, once and for all, that she's not ALL THAT.

That I'm not all WHAT?! I wonder, disconnecting from Jodi's thoughts again. *Since when have I ever acted like I was ALL THAT! How bizarre!*

This accusation is *nothing* compared to the other thing Jodi was thinking. *I wonder what she meant by pulling off a WHOPPER OF A STUNT. That doesn't sound good at all.*

What's she planning to do? And WHEN?! I'm officially a nervous wreck.

This sounds really serious. I have to find out more. I try to jump back into Jodi's thoughts, but this time she's onto me.

Heidi Heckelbeck, how long have you been listening to my thoughts? she asks suspiciously. I step out from behind the marble column and face my foe.

Long enough to know you're up to something, Jodi! **Whatever it is, you'd better stop it RIGHT NOW!** Remember, we're in a public place and you could get into serious trouble.

Jodi laughs, like this is the most ridiculous thing she's ever heard.

Don't worry about ME, Jodi replies. You should be more worried about YOU because maybe I DO have something big planned. . . . And you know what? There isn't a single thing you can do to stop me.

Then Jodi lifts her finger and magically slides a museum sign in front of me as if to block me. And you know what's funny? The sign's message is something Jodi should read! It says,

MUSEUM RULES
Please use indoor voices.
No running or horseplay.
Do not climb on the exhibits.

Well, all I can say is, **two can play at this game!**

Wow, cool trick, Jodi, I say haughtily. *Maybe you should READ the sign you just moved! I'm pretty sure "no horseplay" includes no magical monkey business too.*

I take a quick check around to see if anyone besides Jodi is looking. Nope. Then I magically slide the sign back to where it belongs.

Moving objects is pretty elementary magic, Jodi, I say coolly. *I could do that in fifth grade.*

Jodi raises an eyebrow, like she's glad I've engaged with her.

One word: *dangerous!*

You're right, Heidi—that was nothing. I merely wanted to get your attention so that you'll be ready for the MAIN event. Let's just say it will be IMPRESSIVE. . . .

Jodi hangs up from my thoughts, like someone ending a phone call.

Gulp.

WHAT will be impressive?! I wonder. *What's Jodi going to do? It had better not be something really bad!*

I try again to communicate with her through her mind, but it's no use. Jodi has locked me out of her thoughts.

Argh!

I wave to get her attention, but she's walking away. Where is she heading?

I'll bet she's plotting to put her evil plan in motion. I must do something! **But what?**

Should I go after her? Should I tell Mrs. Kettledrum? Oh, help?! It's like I'm in a scary dream, where you want to move but your body is frozen in place, and no matter how hard you try, you can't move.

I stand there helplessly watching Jodi, and all I can do is whisper one thing. . . .

"Help."

DANGEROUS THINGS AFOOT

A voice sounds from a microphone. Thankfully, it's not Jodi's voice! It's just Mrs. Martone, the museum lady.

Maybe *she* can stop Jodi from doing something, but I seriously doubt it.

"Broomsfield Academy students!" she calls. "I hope you've enjoyed spending time in the hall of dinosaurs!" She looks at her watch. "I'm going on a break right now, but you still have ten more minutes to explore the exhibit. Enjoy, and thank you for coming!" She switches off the microphone and heads out of the hall.

Sunny and Annabelle run to my side.

"Heidi, where have you been?" Sunny asks.

"Yeah, why didn't you race against the T. rex with us?" Annabelle asks. "It was SO much fun!"

Having fun is the farthest thing from my mind since Jodi disappeared. She completely snuck off when Mrs. Martone was talking.

Oh no! I can feel my hands tremble in a panic. Sunny gives me a weird look.

"Why are you acting so jittery, Heidi?" she asks.

I heard Sunny, but I'm also looking every which way for any sign of Jodi.

"Because I can't find her!" I blurt out. "Jodi is up to something really dangerous, and I don't know what it is because she shut me out of her thoughts!"

Annabelle's eyes widen. "Whoa, you mind readers can do that?"

I fold my arms tightly across my chest. "Annabelle, this is SERIOUS!" I shout.

Annabelle jerks her head back because I've never spoken so harshly to her before. Sunny rests her hand on my shoulder.

"Okay, Heidi, calm down," she urges. "Try not to let Jodi get to you."

Why is it that when something's really going wrong, your friends aren't helpful in any way? Sure, they understand I'm upset, but they have no clue what to do, so they try to distract me.

"Why don't we go see the rest of the *T. rex* exhibit?" Sunny suggests. "We didn't even get a chance to see the *T. rex* hatchlings yet. Or the tween *T. rex*."

I sigh loudly. This is so exasperating.

But I guess I might as well go with my friends because what else am I supposed to do? Jodi is nowhere to be seen, so maybe that's a good sign—even though every bone in my body says it's not.

"Okay, sure, let's go," I say reluctantly.

We walk back to the *T. rex* exhibit. It's just as crowded as when we arrived. Our whole class **is obsessed** with this dinosaur. Most of the kids are looking at the life-size *T. rex* skeleton because it's an actual fossil **of the real thing.**

My friends and I walk over to the two hatchlings. These baby *T. rex*es are only about the size of a turkey. There's also a four-year old *T. rex*, which is smaller than a full-grown *T. rex* but still pretty big.

There's another interactive movie screen with a *T. rex*. This curious *T. rex* comes over and checks us out.

Creepers! Then it trots away into some on-screen vegetation.

"Hey, look, you two!" Sunny says. "There's an opening in front of the *T. rex* skeleton. **Wanna take a selfie with it?**"

We hurry over to the massive skeleton and huddle together. Annabelle holds the disposable camera out, and we smile our cheesiest grins.

And you know what? **It feels pretty good to smile—even if it's a forced smile for the camera.**

But my smile vanishes when I spy Jodi out of the corner of my eye. My heart pounds like a jackhammer.

"Oh no!" I cry, pointing in Jodi's direction. "It's HER!"

My friends shove me playfully.

"Yup, there she is, Heidi," Sunny says with a hint of sarcasm. "Poor Jodi, standing all alone in the corner of the room. She probably feels awkward, being the new girl and all."

Annabelle nods. "I have to agree, Heidi. Jodi looks completely harmless."

I squint at Jodi suspiciously. "That's *exactly* what she *wants* you to think," I tell my friends, hoping they'll believe me.

"You're sounding a little paranoid," Sunny tells me.

I ignore Sunny and Annabelle because what's the point? They don't believe me anyway. Besides, I'm frazzled with worry. Jodi taps into my fearful thoughts.

Are you ready, Heidi? she asks. Her voice sounds so clear. It's as if she has spoken these words out loud. I honestly don't know if Jodi spoke the words or said them in my head.

I turn to my friends. "Did you hear that?" I ask.

Sunny and Annabelle stare at me blankly.

"Hear *what*?" Annabelle questions.

I groan because my friends are treating me like I have lost my mind.

"Jodi just sent me another thought message, but forget it. You wouldn't understand."

Annabelle clutches my arm. "Okay, okay, Heidi. If Jodi said something, at least tell us *what* she said."

Sunny actually wants to know what Jodi said too.

I tell my nonbelievers.

"Jodi just asked me if I was *READY*," I tell them as I look around madly for any sign of something unusual or impressive. "I *told* you she was up to something, but I just don't know *what*."

Now Sunny and Annabelle actually look a little nervous.

And they should be!

I've been warning them *all* day!

"Okay, that sounds a little weird and scary," Sunny says. "Maybe we should get Mrs. Kettledrum."

I grab Sunny by the arm, my desperation growing stronger by the second.

"Yes! *Please* get Mrs. Kettledrum!" I beg. "*Hurry!* There's no time to lose! Maybe I can keep Jodi occupied until Mrs. K gets here, and hopefully she can stop Jodi from whatever it is she's about to do!"

Sunny seems to believe me, and she takes off to get our teacher. Annabelle stays by my side. I sigh with some relief.

I need to talk to Jodi. Somehow I have to get her to stop whatever she's up to.

I knock on the door of her thoughts.

Jodi? Jodi, are you there? I call out. Jodi doesn't answer. She's eyeing the *T. rex* skeleton.

Oh no! She must've blocked me out again, but maybe not.

Jodi's gaze momentarily floats in my direction. Then it drifts back to the *T. rex*. No matter how hard I try, I can't get Jodi to listen to me.

"Jodi won't respond," I tell Annabelle. Annabelle is watching Jodi too.

"**Well, keep trying!**" Annabelle urges.

I focus with everything I've got. This time I get into Jodi's mind. As I listen in on her thoughts, I realize Jodi is chanting a spell.

Uh-oh! I'm too late!

T. REX STANDS SO HIGH AND MIGHTY. TIME TO SCARE OUR FRIEND HEIDI!

As soon as Jodi chants her spell, the *T. rex* skeleton begins to come to life.

This overgrown dinosaur fossil tugs its claws free from its mount.

SNAP! SNAP!

There's a massive intake of breath from everybody watching.

"OH NOOOOOOO!" I shout, cupping my hand over my mouth in total terror! Annabelle grabs hold of me.

"Heidi, I'm SCARED!" she shrieks.

Annabelle is not the only one. My classmates scream and scatter in every direction.

Jodi catches my eye. Her face beams with pride.

Yes, pride!

See, Heidi? I TOLD YOU I could do it!

This situation is WAY too serious—and dangerous—to send back a thought message. I opt for using my real voice—my *loudest* voice ever.

"*JODI!* What are you're trying to prove? Kids are going to get *HURT!*

"Stop it, Jodi! Stop that dinosaur right NOW!"

I get a smug mental retort in return.

Why should I stop it, Heidi? Don't tell me you're AFRAID of a bunch of T. rex bones?!

The *T. rex* stomps off its platform and lowers its head.

"ROOOOOOAAAAAARRRRRR!"

My classmates scream in terror. It's like we're in a horror movie, **only it's real!**

WHOMP! WHOMP! WHOMP!

The king of dinosaurs clomps across the hall of dinosaurs. Its skeletal tail rattles as it swishes from side to side. But this overgrown lizard is not coming to scare me, as Jodi instructed.

It's actually going toward JODI. *Yup!* The most ferocious predator

to have ever lived bends down and roars right in Jodi's face.

"ROOOOOOAAAAAARRRRRR!"

Jodi slams both hands over her ears and lets out a bloodcurdling scream.

"Okay, Heidi!" she shouts. "You WIN!!! YOU WIN!!!" Then Jodi sprints away from the *T. rex* and hides behind a giant marble pillar.

What exactly did I win? I wonder. *I wasn't even playing!*

This whole game of treachery was all Jodi's idea.

She brings a prehistoric, flesh-eating, top-of-the-food-chain, beady-eyed predator to life and then expects *ME* to fix it?

One word: *seriously?!*

What's *taking Sunny so long to get Mrs. Kettledrum? Where's our magical chaperone when we NEED her?!*

Hunter, Isabelle, and Melanie run to my side and glom on to me.

"Heidi! Are you trying to get us all *KILLED*?" Isabelle screams.

"YEAH!" Hunter shouts. "This is too much— *even for YOU!*"

Uh-oh, the *T. rex* is turning around and coming toward *us*. Still, I have to take the time to defend myself.

"This is *NOT* me!" I say defensively. "This is *all* JODI!"

But nobody cares about my issues with Jodi right now—that's because Terry the *T. rex* is stomping our way, and I'm pretty sure I see real saliva dripping from its jaws.

Every one of us is screaming, like we're on a roller coaster.

"Do something, Heidi!" Melanie begs. "*PLEASE!* Make the dinosaur *STOP!*"

If there was ever a time for an emergency spell, this would be it. It's hard to focus with everyone screaming and a *Tyrannosaurus rex* towering over us. But I give it my best shot and make up a spell on the spot.

> TERRY THE *T. REX*, TURN AROUND.
> NO MORE ROARING—NOT A SOUND.
> LISTEN NOW TO MY COMMAND.
> GO BACK TO YOUR DINOSAUR STAND!

My friends and I wait for my emergency spell to take hold. **But it doesn't!** Instead Terry the *T. rex* lowers her head until we're eye to eye, and then...

"ROOOOOAAAAAARRRRRR!"

Did the *T. rex* scare us? **You bet it did!**

We scream and scatter. We wind up in a heap, huddled in a corner—a corner that includes Jodi.

But whatever **because here comes Terry the *T. rex*!**

WHOMP! WHOMP! WHOMP!

I want to shut my eyes, but who wants to get eaten with their eyes closed?

Eeeeek!

We're goners, for sure!

FAREWELL! ADIOS! SAYONARA!

The *T. rex* lowers its skull and opens its jaws full of razor-sharp teeth, each one a spear unto itself.

"ROOOOOOAAAAAARRRRRR!"

We scream, and Jodi and Melanie grab hold of me. Yup! Jodi is holding on to *me* for comfort. But this **is Jurassic Museum, and we're about to be chomped to smithereens**, so I'll let it go.

As we brace for **whatever comes next,** Mrs. Martone returns from her break.

Her eyes go wide with horror when she sees the living *T. rex* skeleton. She reaches one hand out for something to hold herself up, but it's no use. Her **knees crumple and she faints to the floor.**

She was definitely not expecting to come back from break to a live *T. rex* in the hall.

But all hope is not lost!

Sunny and Mrs. Kettledrum rush into the hall of dinosaurs moments after Mrs. Martone passes out. Mrs. Kettledrum has the same look of shock on her face that Mrs. Martone did, but **thank heaven, she doesn't faint,** though she does look exceptionally pale.

Mrs. Kettledrum walks right up to Terry the *T. rex*, and she raises her hands in the air.

"TIME STOPS NOW!" she commands.

Just like that, **the dinosaur freezes in place.**

I sigh with relief, but my heart is still pounding out of control. I look around and notice that all my classmates are frozen too—**except two.**

Jodi and me.

I scramble to my feet and run to Mrs. Kettledrum. Sunny stands like a statue behind her. I look back at Jodi, who's struggling to crawl out from under the other kids. She finally frees herself, but she stays right where she is.

I'm so relieved to be free from the menacing *T. rex* that almost nothing else matters. Well, maybe one other thing. My favorite teacher just performed a momentous magical feat.

"*Whooooaaa*, Mrs. Kettledrum!" I say in utter amazement. "You can stop time, too?!"

Mrs. Kettledrum shakes her head gravely, making it clear that her magical feat is not what's important right now. **She is not pleased with Jodi or me.**

Mrs. K pulls a handkerchief from her pocket and dabs beads of sweat from her forehead **for the second time today.** Then she puts her hanky back into her pocket.

"I'm very surprised at you, Heidi," she begins. "I thought you had turned the corner and had learned something about magical self-control, but clearly I was wrong. Mr. Craftwood told me about your feud with Jodi. I have to assume this stunt has something to do with that."

Wait! I think. *Does Mrs. Kettledrum think this disaster is MY fault?* I keep quiet because my teacher has not finished talking.

"When will you understand that all witches and wizards must *earn* the privilege to use advanced magic spells. You simply cannot allow your emotions to dictate your magic! It will *never* end well. You are going to **have** to learn how to be more responsible with magic, and until you do, there will continue to be consequences. This time, Heidi, I'm afraid we'll have to have a discussion about **expulsion**."

Mrs. Kettledrum's disappointment in me and the word "expulsion," mixed with my *frustration* with Jodi, all come to a head at the same time.

BOOM! I blow my top.

"But, MRS. KETTLEDRUM!" I cry out. "This is *NOT* my fault! This is all JODI'S doing!

"Jodi's been bothering me since the moment she stepped onto campus! She barges into my head whenever she feels like it because she has the same mind-reading gift as me. All she ever says to me is not very nice things.

"Plus, she's been doing magic in the museum ALL DAY—even though she knows we're not supposed to!

"I PROMISE, this whole museum nightmare has *nothing* to do with me.

"This is one hundred percent Jodi.

"She's trying to ruin me!"

Mrs. Kettledrum lets out a long, seemingly endless sigh as she tries to comprehend what I've just said—not to mention having just seen a live *T. rex* skeleton—all on her favorite annual field trip. Mrs. Kettledrum turns toward Jodi.

"Jodi, would you please come here?" Mrs. Kettledrum says sharply.

I look over at Jodi. *HA!* I think. Finally Jodi is going to get what she deserves. But I'd better not gloat too much because this fiasco isn't over yet.

Jodi slowly walks over to us. She looks scared, and she *should* be!

All that fear on her face almost makes her seem vulnerable. I'm sure underneath it all she's also mad at me because I just told on her BIG-TIME. But that's *her* problem!

Mrs. Kettledrum looks over the rims of her glasses at Jodi—a look I know all too well.

"Jodi, I know you're new," Mrs. K begins. "I also know new students sometimes have a difficult time adjusting to a new school as well as fitting in with new peers. . . ."

I'll say . . . I think, and who cares if Jodi hears what I'm thinking? Still, I try to keep my thoughts quiet so I can listen to Mrs. Kettledrum.

"And I also know that *you know better* than to do magic in a public setting—or *anywhere* outside the classroom."

Jodi nods meekly. Mrs. Kettledrum pauses for a moment before she continues.

"Furthermore, young lady, if I *ever* hear that you're bullying a fellow student again, you will be suspended. There is *no* bullying at this school. Do you understand?" Mrs. Kettledrum waits for Jodi to respond.

Jodi nods and looks at her feet.

"Yes, Mrs. Kettledrum," she says meekly.

Mrs. K places her hands on her hips.

"And you will *never* pull another dangerous magical stunt like this ever again, or you will be the one facing expulsion. Are we clear?"

Jodi lifts her head. "We're clear," she answers.

Of course Jodi is saying all the right things, but I'm not sure I buy any of it. It's going to take a *very long* time for her to build any trust with me.

Mrs. Kettledrum gently nudges Jodi toward me. "I also want you to apologize to Heidi."

Jodi looks me in the eye for a tiny split second and then looks down again.

"Sorry, Heidi," she says. "I didn't mean for everything to get so out of hand."

It feels good to get an apology from Jodi.

"Apology accepted," I say, because even if I don't trust Jodi, I can still sympathize with how she's feeling. I know what it's like to get in trouble for doing magic I'm not supposed to, although I have never done something like what Jodi just did.

Mrs. Kettledrum tilts her head and looks up at Terry the *T. rex*, who is still bent over my classmates. She shakes her head again.

"Okay, girls, we'll talk *more* about this later," she assures us. "Right now we need to focus on the task at hand."

She looks at her watch. "I'm going to press rewind on all this to a few minutes *before* this whole **disaster occurred,** but the clock will stay the same in the museum.

"This will mean that only the *three* of us will remember what happened. Not even Mr. Craftwood will know what took place. We'll lose a few minutes of the trip, but that is all.

"And neither one of you will ever mention this incident to *anyone* EVER. Is this clear?"

Jodi and I nod earnestly—even though I'm thinking more about how Mrs. K is going to turn back time. This is something I want to learn how to do someday.

"You're going to turn back time in the museum only?" I ask curiously.

Jodi's face lights up, like mine.

"That's some top-tier magic, Mrs. K!" Jodi chimes in. Then we look at each other like, *How cool is THAT?*

But as soon as we remember we're not friends, we quickly look away.

"Yes, I can turn back time, freeze time, isolate time, and bend it in different ways," Mrs. K affirms. "Perhaps someday, with proper education and guidance, you two will be able to do the same. Now, are you ready to set things right?"

We both nod firmly.

"All right, then," Mrs. Kettledrum says. "Here we go!"

Our teacher raises her mighty and magical hand and recites a quick, powerful spell.

> To This MUSEUM
> caLMNESS BESTOW!
> SET BacK oUR DaY
> TO TEN MiNUTES aGO!

Poof!

Puffs of blue smoke fill the gallery, and everything starts moving back in time.

As soon as the fog clears, we hear talking and laughing and all the normal, echoey sounds in a museum.

There, standing firmly upon its mount, is Terry the *T. rex*, just like it's supposed to be.

I'm standing with Sunny and Annabelle right in the middle of a conversation that has already happened.

"Yup, there she is, Heidi," Sunny says with a hint of sarcasm. "Poor Jodi, standing all alone in the corner of the room. She probably feels awkward, being the new girl and all."

Annabelle nods. "I have to agree, Heidi. Jodi looks completely harmless."

I gulp hard. *Wow*, I marvel. *We really went back a few moments in time!*

Mrs. Kettledrum is amazing.

I look over at Jodi standing all by herself. The only difference is—*this* time she's not plotting a dangerous magical stunt. Instead she must deal with the consequences of her actions.

One word: *justice!*

I turn to my friends.

"You know what? You two are right about Jodi!" I say. "I'm sure she's just dealing with new-girl stuff. No more talk of her. Let's just enjoy the rest of our field trip."

My friends seem relieved that I've let all the Jodi stuff go.

If they only knew!

We head toward the *T. rex* skeleton. I'd prefer to keep my distance, **but I need to keep up appearances.**

As we walk, Mrs. Martone and Mrs. Kettledrum enter the room together, chatting happily—**very different from a few magical minutes ago.**

Eek!

"How's everyone doing?" Mrs. K calls to our group.

Annabelle points to the *T. rex* skeleton.

"We're admiring Terry the *T. rex*!" she pipes up. "Doesn't it look as if it could just jump right off this platform and pounce?"

Mrs. Kettledrum shoots a knowing glance at Jodi and then me.

"Well, let's hope Terry stays put *right* where it is!" Mrs. K declares.

I agree! I think. It's so strange that my friends have no idea what happened. I wish I could tell them, but there is no way.

I've gotten much better at keeping secrets, and Jodi and I promised Mrs. Kettledrum we wouldn't say a word about the incident.

Mrs. Martone turns on the microphone and hands it to Mrs. Kettledrum. Mrs. K taps the top of the mic with one finger.

"Attention, Broomsfield students!" she says. "It looks like time flew by and we're ten minutes behind schedule! We have twenty minutes before departure. Who would like to visit the gift store?"

Everyone cries, *"Yes!"*

The gift shop is always a huge draw at any museum. Normally I'd be into it too, but the last thing I want right now is a souvenir to remember this day.

One word: *roar!*

"Okay, everyone, follow me!" Mrs. Kettledrum says, hurrying along.

We follow our teacher, and on the way we pick up Mr. Craftwood's group.

I wonder if Mrs. Kettledrum really kept what happened a secret from Mr. Craftwood?

Wouldn't magic teachers want to confer on an event of this magnitude?

I catch Mr. Craftwood's eye, and he smiles at me, like he would on any other day. Hmmm, I guess Mrs. Kettledrum really *did* keep Jodi's monster mess-up to herself. Another reason why she's my favorite teacher.

The gift store has many dinosaur souvenirs, and I dodge all of them—even the plush ones. But the stuffed polar bears and blue whales are pretty cute. I wander off by myself and look at the polished rocks, gems, and meteorite specimens.

Then I move on to the jewelry section. Melanie is going wild over the jewelry and apparel. **No surprise there.**

I sneak off to the candy section and check out the chocolate dinosaurs. One package has a brontosaurus, a triceratops, and a stegosaurus all in one. They also have chocolate dinosaur eggs. **And dino GUMMIES.** I love gummies, plain or sour—I'll even eat the dinosaur-shaped ones. I slide a family-size pack from a hook and head for the checkout counter.

Somehow I must've lost track of time because I'm practically the last one in the store.

Eek!

Mrs. K waves to me urgently from the door. I make my purchase and sprint out of the museum to the bus. Sunny and Annabelle have saved me a seat because they're the best! They shake their shopping bags in my face. *Crinkle! Crinkle!*

"Look what I got!" Sunny exclaims as the bus pulls away from the curb. She reaches into her bag and pulls out a bright yellow tee with a cartoon image of a *T. rex* drinking a cup of tea. It says **TEA REX** at the top.

"I love it!" Annabelle gushes.

"It's adorable," I say.

Sunny shoves the T-shirt back into her bag. Then she fans some supercute butterfly stickers in front of us.

"Those will look great on absolutely everything!" Annabelle says. Then she flashes a snow globe in our faces and shakes it. Snow swirls around three mini dinosaurs inside.

"I have a weakness for snow globes," she says. "I collect them wherever I go! I also got a butterfly baseball cap." Annabelle jams the cap onto her head.

"What did *you* get, Heidi?" Annabelle asks.

I hold up my mouthwatering bag of dino gummies.

Annabelle laughs. "You're SO predictable."

I rip open the bag and hold up a dino gummy.

"Like they say, eat or be eaten!" Then I pop a gummy *T. rex* into my mouth. We all laugh, and I pass my bag around.

"You know what, Heidi?" Sunny says. "I'm glad you made it through the day without blowing up at Jodi."

My mind reels for a moment as the events of the day flash through my mind. **If she only knew what really went on.**

"Well, it wasn't easy," I tell her.

Annabelle seems to understand. "From what you've told us, it seems like Jodi sees you as a threat," she says. "And even if Jodi turns out to be a better witch than you, **then so what!**"

Annabelle's comment hits me hard. Doesn't she know that **this is the *LAST* thing I want to hear?**

✦ 238 ✦

This is my worst fear! It's even more terrifying than a *T. rex* staring down at you.

Sunny tries to make it better.

"And *you* may turn out to be a better witch than Jodi," Sunny reassures me. "Either way— so what?! Jodi will never be YOU.

"You're the *best* friend anyone could ever have!"

I blush because that's the nicest thing anyone has ever said to me. But it doesn't change the fact that I still want to be the best witch in my class. Believe me—I'm not afraid to put in the work.

I lean into my friends. "Thanks, you two."

We ride quietly for a little while. I'm sure glad Jodi and Melanie went home on the other bus. It makes the trip more peaceful and enjoyable.

Soon we turn off the highway and bump along the country roads toward school. Mrs. Kettledrum, who's sitting at the front of the bus, stands up to give an announcement.

"Listen up, everyone!" our teacher says. "Tomorrow we're going to have a *mandatory* spells and potions review class.

"The class will be held right after breakfast, and everyone must attend. Mr. Craftwood will tell the students on the other bus. This is *very* important!"

The news is met with moans and groans because who wants to go to a required class on a Saturday? *Not me.*

This is all Jodi's fault, of course.

Sunny looks to me for answers.

"Do you know what this is all about?" she asks. "I wonder if it has to do with what happened in the butterfly exhibit?"

I shrug, pretending like I have no idea.

"Beats me," I say, looking back out the window. The trees in the woods flicker by. I wish I could tell my besties the truth, but I promised not to say anything. Sigh. I hold out my bag of gummies again.

"Gummy dino, anyone?"

GiRL TALK

Guess what? We stopped for fast food on our way back to Broomsfield!

This never happens! I savored every delectable chicken nugget, fry, and sip of milkshake.

Best meal ever!

Don't get me wrong. I **love** *real* food too, but junk food is such a yummy treat once in a while.

When we get back on campus, I go to the mail room and find another surprise waiting for me. A letter from Lucy!

As I walk back to my dorm, I tear it open. The stationery has the cutest hedgehog blowing dandelion fluff.

Lucy Lancaster

To My Favorite Person of All Time!

Got your letter, and **no, you are *not* pathetic.**

You are wonderful.

Jodi sounds exactly like Melanie in elementary school. It's kind of eerie how similar they seem. Don't forget, Melanie was a BEAST too! And it was all because she was jealous of you. Now look how far you two have come! Well, the same will be true with Jodi.

I guarantee it will get better.

Here's my advice: stay above it no matter what. If Jodi sneers at, insults, or even threatens you—just remember, it has nothing to do with *you*. This is *Jodi's* problem. Not yours.

Don't make it your problem by taking her bait, no matter how tempting it might be. Eventually Jodi's meanness will backfire. I can promise you that.

Stay strong, and let's talk this weekend. Hopefully things will be better by then.

Love you bunches. Hang in there!

Your best friend on planet Earth,
　　Lulu Luzinski

P.S. When are you going to realize how ⋝AMAZING⋜ you are?

I love Lulu, I think as I tuck her letter back into the envelope. Her words confirm **everything** Melanie said too.

I hurry straight to my room and slip into my pajamas. Melanie buzzes about the field trip the whole time.

"Check this out, Heidi!" she cries, dumping her purchases from the gift shop onto her bed.

She lays each item out for me to see—all butterfly stuff. She got a dusty blue T-shirt

with two butterfly silhouettes, butterfly earrings, a butterfly charm for her backpack, a butterfly headband, a butterfly journal, a butterfly water bottle, butterfly sunglasses, and butterfly postcards.

Melanie prances around, **modeling *everything*** for me.

"I'm all aflutter!" she says, giggling and posing. "I even got doubles of all the postcards, so I can send some and keep the rest. They're so beautiful!"

I act excited for Melanie as I stretch out on my bed. Melanie smiles and trots into the bathroom to brush her teeth.

Wow, it feels so good to relax.

I'm almost asleep when Melanie shuffles back into the room. She kicks off her pink fuzzy slippers, hops onto her bed, and begins to brush her hair.

"I spent a lot of time with Jodi today," she tells me. Like, **no kidding.** "She's really nice once you get to know her. She also talked more about you. I mean like, A LOT."

This, **of course,** grabs my attention. I roll over. "Well, what did she say?"

Melanie stops brushing. "It's like I said the other day," Melanie begins, "Jodi is jealous of you, Heidi."

I hoist myself back up and lean against my headboard. I still can't believe Jodi would have any reason to be jealous of me. Lucy said the same thing. I need to know more.

"Why?" I ask.

Melanie brushes her hair a few more times.

"She just is," she says. "One thing she asked me was, 'What's the greatest magical thing Heidi has ever done?'"

Boy, am I ever listening now. "What did you tell her?"

Melanie stops midbrush. "I told her how you made Mrs. Kettledrum's dog, Momo, speak," she tells me.

"Jodi nearly fell over when she heard *that* one! *She* said, 'WOW! I've never made an animal TALK before!'"

Then it hits me. *That's why Jodi wanted to do something MORE impressive than me!*

Melanie gives me a weird look. "Why do you look so surprised, Heidi?" she questions. "It's not like you making Momo talk is a secret. Besides, Jodi was super-impressed."

I shake my head because that's not it at all. "It's nothing. *I just figured something out*—that's all. *Please*, tell me more!"

Melanie plunges back into her story. "I also **told her about how you made four identical Heidis!**"

My face flushes with embarrassment.

"Melanie, that is not something to brag about! I could've gotten expelled!"

Melanie laughs. "You would never get expelled, Heidi. You're a star at this school, and you *know* it. Besides, even though that spell bombed, everyone loved it."

I force out a laugh.

Little does Melanie know, Mrs. K actually mentioned expulsion earlier today. "It was such an epic fail, but I'm glad some people got joy out of it." I pause because I'm curious about something else. "What did Jodi think of it?"

Melanie shoots me a sly look. "Wouldn't *you* like to know?!"

I flop onto my pillow. "Tell me!" I beg.

Melanie laughs. "Okay, okay!" she says, giving in. "Jodi asked, 'Heidi is brave and smart?!'"

My eyeballs bug out. "She actually *said* that?"

Melanie nods emphatically. "Yup, her *exact* words." Melanie places the brush on her nightstand and crawls into bed.

"Mind if I turn out the light?" she asks, yawning. "I'm pooped."

I pull up my covers. "Sure, and thanks for filling me in on Jodi."

Melanie snaps on her pink silk eye mask. "Anytime!"

Our room falls quiet.

Wow, I think. *Underneath it all maybe Jodi* **DOES** *like me, but she sure has a strange way of showing it. . . .*

That is my last thought on what was the most frightening day of my life.

A TWO-HEADED MONSTER

Sunny and Annabelle **talk nonstop** about the field trip at breakfast the next morning.

I'm **so over it,** but I endure.

"What if *T. rexes* were still alive today?" Sunny asks. "Do you think we'd have to live in **shark cages** so we wouldn't get eaten?"

Annabelle laughs. "Yup, only they'd be called **dinosaur cages!**"

I'm barely listening because I can't stop thinking about what Melanie said last night.

Underneath all her meanness, does Jodi actually think I'm brave and smart? It's still hard to believe.

Well, maybe I should be nicer and more welcoming toward Jodi from now on. I *would've* been nicer on day one if she hadn't been so mean.

I glance over at Jodi's table, but for some reason she isn't there. That's funny. I wonder where she is. Isabelle catches me looking and knows exactly what I'm thinking.

"Are you looking for Jodi?" Izzy whispers. Isabelle is sitting with Hunter instead of at her own table—that's because assigned seating is more relaxed on Saturdays.

I nod, wondering, *Was I that obvious?* Isabelle leans in closer.

"I heard that Jodi had to meet with Mrs. Kettledrum before breakfast," Izzy whispers. "Somebody blabbed about the butterfly incident." Isabelle shakes her head, making her ponytail swish from side to side. "That new girl sure loves to push the limits!"

I frown. *She also likes to push my buttons,* I think as the old feelings simmer inside me.

"Well, she was bound to get caught," I add.

Isabelle nods, like, *No kidding.* Then Izzy nudges me and tilts her head toward the entrance of the cafeteria.

"Here she comes!"

Jodi and Mrs. Kettledrum enter the cafeteria together. Jodi's face is red, like she's been crying.

I actually feel bad for her.

Mrs. Kettledrum pats Jodi on the shoulder reassuringly, but Jodi doesn't even acknowledge the gesture. She walks straight toward the hot oatmeal station as Mrs. Kettledrum leaves the cafeteria.

As I watch Jodi sprinkle brown sugar and strawberries on top of her oatmeal, **I realize I'm having the same exact breakfast.**

Jodi and I have *something* in common.

Hey, it's *something!*

Melanie waves to Jodi.

"Sit here!" Melanie shouts.

Jodi beelines to the empty seat beside Melanie. But Jodi seems distracted.

Then I realize it's because Jodi is thinking about *me*. The reason I know this is because Jodi just scowled and sent another one of her unwelcome thought messages.

Oh no! Here we go again!

Heidi, why was I the only one to get pulled into Mrs. Kettledrum's office this morning? she snarls.

I sigh loudly. It hasn't even been twenty-four hours, and Jodi is already mad at me again! I thought the whole *T. rex* incident would've humbled her.

Guess not. I send a thought message back.

Hmmm, let's see, Jodi, I think with touchiness. *Maybe it's because YOU did some bad magic in the museum yesterday?!*

Jodi clamps her arms firmly across her chest and sends me another message.

Well, for your information, Mrs. Kettledrum gave ME a long lecture about not using magic in public places. She also lectured me about us talking to each other in our thoughts. Not to mention, I got a week of detention! You're such a tattletale!

The word "tattletale" stings.

It makes me feel like a bad person—not to mention a five-year-old.

Let's be honest. Jodi would've tattled on me if I had been the one mentally torturing *her*. I have no doubt.

And who even cares?

Somehow Jodi and I have to get past this. I send a positive thought message back.

Okay, how about we meet and talk about this for real—you know, **with our voices?**

Jodi shakes her head defiantly.

I guess **being positive** isn't her idea of a path to peace. She sends me **another** blistering thought message.

What's there to talk about, Heidi?! she shouts in my head. *This whole thing is NOT all my fault, and I'm gonna make sure YOU get punished too!*

I drop my spoon into my oatmeal. *Why should I be punished?* I wonder. *All I've done is defend myself against Jodi.*

And she's making me nervous.

Sunny, who's sitting next to me, notices I'm upset—*again.*

"Is everything okay, Heidi?" she asks.

I groan because I've *had* it. "It's Jodi," I whisper back. "She's mad because I told on her. She said she's going to make sure I get punished too!"

Sunny's eyes widen. .

"Wow, that sounds like a threat!" Sunny says with surprise.

I push my breakfast tray away from me.

"Yup, that's how Jodi operates," I say. "Guess we'll be best friends *NEVER.*"

Sunny looks at me thoughtfully.

"Well, I wouldn't take it *too* seriously," she says. "Jodi is really upset about getting in trouble. She won't stay mad forever. Besides, she'll soon realize it won't pay *not* to be your friend."

Sunny's words are comforting.

"Well, I hope you're right," I say with a sigh. "Middle school is hard enough without having someone in your class who hates you *and* who can read your thoughts."

One word: *harsh.*

After breakfast we go to Mrs. Kettledrum's mandatory review class, thanks to *you-know-who.* I'm not in the mood for this on any level.

Merg.

It's hard to stay mad when Momo greets me with yips of joy as I walk into the classroom. Her tail whips back and forth as I bend down and give her a quick love session.

As soon as I stand up, **I catch Jodi scowling at me.**

Give me a break! I think.

Jodi is probably jealous that I'm friends with Momo too.

I quickly take my seat next to Sunny and Annabelle.

Mrs. Kettledrum walks briskly into the classroom. She stands before us and links her fingers together, like a belt buckle.

"I know that most of you would rather not be in class on a Saturday," she begins. "But some magical mishaps have been brought to my attention, and I believe we need to revisit our magical rules and policies."

Mrs. Kettledrum holds up a finger.

"Number one, there will be absolutely *no* magic performed in public or anywhere outside the confines of the School of Magic. Understood?"

She waits for us to respond.

We nod and murmur, "*Ye-e-e-es.*" A few of us, including me, glance at Jodi. But Jodi keeps her eyes on Mrs. Kettledrum.

Mrs. K clears her throat to make sure we stay focused on her, not Jodi.

"These rules are for your safety *and* for the safety of our school community. If this rule is broken, there will be consequences. Is everyone clear?"

More nods and murmurs.

"Good," Mrs. K says firmly.

"Let's review the importance of getting magical spells *right*, so when the day comes, you'll be ready to practice magic safely and effectively *outside* the classroom."

Mrs. Kettledrum goes on to warn us about the usual stuff, like the importance of using the right words in a spell.

She also warns us of the dangers of using homonyms in spells—words that sound the same but have different meanings.

Then she tells stories about spells that went amuck. They're supposed to be horror stories, but some of them are pretty hilarious, like the one where a girl did a spell to perform a hat trick in a soccer game, but instead she produced a dancing top hat on the field.

Or the time this one boy did a spell to become a powerful ruler and turned himself into a measuring stick.

Mrs. K goes on to explain why *that* kind of spell is **wrong** and **forbidden on so many levels.**

Then, without naming any names, she shares the story of my forgetting spell that went topsy-turvy.

My face grows warm with embarrassment.

I botched this forgetting spell on Melanie because I wanted Melanie to forget that she had discovered that Isabelle is secretly a princess.

(Something no one knows to this day except me and Isabelle.)

I made Melanie forget Isabelle's secret, but I accidentally also made Melanie forget who I was altogether.

Oopsies.

Thankfully, nobody knows except for Mrs. K and me.

I'm glad my teacher doesn't mention any more of my magical mistakes.

I've had some doozies.

"Even a seemingly harmless spell for, say, **bottomless french fries** could turn into a problem of **epic** proportions," Mrs. Kettledrum warns us.

Everyone laughs.

After lecturing us, Mrs. Kettledrum quizzes us on magical rules.

Guess what happens?

Every time Mrs. K asks a question, Jodi raises her hand.

Zing! *Zing!* *Zing!*

It's like her hand is spring-loaded.

Nobody else gets a chance to answer a single question because Jodi's hand always goes up first.

One word: *annoying.*

It gets so out of hand that Mrs. Kettledrum has to shut Jodi down.

"You're a very bright girl, Jodi, but please give your classmates a chance to respond too," Mrs. K tells her after the fifth time.

Jodi smiles sweetly and lowers her hand. "Yes, Mrs. Kettledrum," she says politely.

Then Jodi turns around and gives me a triumphant grin, along with another thought message.

Mrs. Kettledrum may be a little mad about what happened yesterday, but watch me get back on her good side. Soon I'LL be her favorite student. You'll see!

I wrinkle my nose at Jodi. Why does she say things like this? Probably because she knows it'll get to me.

And it does.

Well, I'm just going to ignore Jodi.

So there.

This backfires, of course.

I know you're trying to ignore me, Heidi, Jodi taunts. *I also know I'm getting to you. It's so fun to bug you!* She laughs to herself.

I cover my ears because I can't stand listening to Jodi.

Nice try, Heidi! Covering your ears won't work. I'm in your head, remember? You can't shut me out!

I uncover my ears and stick out my tongue.

Then I try to block Jodi's thoughts, but for some reason it doesn't work this time!

Jodi cackles in my head, like some hideous storybook witch. *Looks like my magic is stronger than yours!*

Okay, *it's time for an emergency spell*, I think.

I can't stand Jodi's yapping anymore!

Right now Jodi is so caught up in herself, she's not even paying attention to what I'm thinking. I cast a spell on the spot.

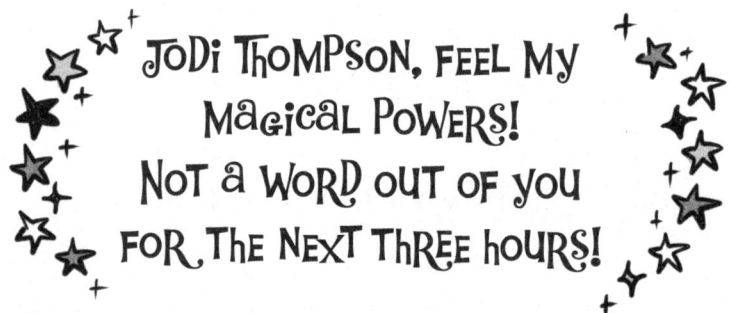

JODI THOMPSON, FEEL MY MAGICAL POWERS! NOT A WORD OUT OF YOU FOR THE NEXT THREE HOURS!

Zoop!

The spell takes hold.

But then I panic about the wording.

I said, *"Not a word,"* but what I meant to say was something more like, *No more thought messages.*

I bite my bottom lip.

Uh-oh. I hope I didn't mess up my spell.

Wouldn't that be classic?

Right when we're being reminded to be *careful* with our magical words?

I look at Mrs. Kettledrum to see if she noticed anything.

Nope. She asks the class another question.

"In your own words, how would *you* prevent a magical mishap?"

Jodi's hand goes back up. Mrs. Kettledrum calls on her since Jodi has kept her hand down for the last few questions.

The only problem is, when Jodi opens her mouth to speak, **nothing comes out.**

Not one word.

Jodi clutches her throat with her hands. Then she frantically points her finger at me.

Oh boy, I'm in BIG trouble!

It doesn't take Mrs. Kettledrum long to figure out what's going on.

"Heidi and Jodi, please meet me in the hall," she says crossly. "Everyone else, please read chapter nine of your textbook, *Magical Mishaps*, quietly at your desks."

Jodi and I get up and head for the door. The whole class watches with great interest.

Two words: *girl drama.*

Mrs. Kettledrum follows us into the hall and shuts the door behind her.

"Okay, girls, **what's going on *now*?**" she asks us.

Jodi points an accusing finger at me, which makes me go right on the defensive.

"This is not all my fault!" I say angrily. "Jodi keeps bothering me with her **never-ending stream of *mean* thought messages.**

"And **I tried to block them,** but it didn't work, so I cast a temporary **no-speaking spell** to make her *be quiet.*

"But I didn't mean to make her lose her voice—just her mean thoughts."

Mrs. Kettledrum raises her hands in exasperation.

"Heidi, this is *EXACTLY* what I've been talking about for the past hour! **When will you learn to slow down and use the *proper* words in a spell?**

"Furthermore, how could you be so bold as to cast a spell after all that's gone on? I just don't understand it!"

I hate upsetting my favorite teacher, but I need her to hear my side. "Believe me," I plead, "I know how bad this looks, but I was being bullied and had to act fast."

Mrs. Kettledrum looks disapprovingly at Jodi. She's not happy with either one of us.

One word: *fair.*

Mrs. K looks back at me. "How long will this spell last, Heidi?"

My eyes dart away from my teacher.

"Um, like, three hours," I confess.

Mrs. Kettledrum considers this for a long, painful moment.

"Well, that's too long to wait, and too long a time jump to fast forward."

Then our teacher opens the door to the classroom and pops her head inside. "Sunny, will you please join us?"

Sunny points to herself, like, *Who me?*

But she gets up obediently and walks over.

Mrs. Kettledrum seems to have a plan.

"Okay, girls, let's go," she directs. We follow our teacher outside and into the School of Magic's courtyard.

Jodi is still holding her throat, and Sunny's eyebrows are still furrowed in confusion.

"Heidi seems to have put a spell on Jodi's voice box," Mrs. Kettledrum begins to explain. "The only way to break the spell is with healing magic like yours."

Mrs. Kettledrum looks toward the sun. "With your gift and pendant—along with a well-thought-out spell—I think we can fix this."

Sunny touches the sun pendant around her neck. "I've never reversed one of Heidi's spells before, Mrs. Kettledrum," she says. "What if I can't do it?"

I reach out and grab Sunny's hand.

"Of course you can do it," I reassure my friend. "Remember when you healed my sprained ankle during orientation?"

Sunny nods, and I squeeze her hand.

"And that was *before* you took any magic classes!" I remind her. "You've got this!"

Mrs. Kettledrum expresses confidence in Sunny too.

"I'll guide you every step of the way," Mrs. K tells her. "I want you to begin by placing one hand on Jodi's neck. Is this okay with you, Jodi?"

Jodi nods.

"Okay, try to relax, Jodi," Mrs. Kettledrum encourages.

Jodi takes a couple of slow, deep breaths, and lets her hands fall to her sides. Sunny places one hand on Jodi's neck.

"Very good," Mrs. K says. "Sunny, with your free hand, I want you to turn your pendant toward the sun and repeat after me." Sunny tips her pendant toward the sun.

Mrs. Kettledrum chants a spell, and Sunny echoes each line.

> Radiant sun, blazing so bright,
> cast your beams of healing light.
> Free this voice,
> with rays unblock.
> Return Jodi Thompson's
> power to talk!

Whoosh!

The sun flashes off Sunny's pendant and onto Jodi's neck.

We watch in wonder at the radiant, glowing light.

Finally Mrs. Kettledrum says something. "Are you able to speak, Jodi?"

Jodi clears her throat, which seems like a good sign, and opens her mouth.

"Here goes!" she says.

When Jodi realizes she can talk again, she jumps up and down.

"It worked! It worked!"

Mrs. Kettledrum thanks Sunny and sends her back into the classroom. Jodi and I start to follow Sunny, but not for long.

"Hold up, you two!" Mrs. K demands. "I'm not done with either one of you!"

We stop in our tracks and turn around.

Mrs. Kettledrum looks over her glasses in that way that I dread.

"Okay, girls, we're going to handle this rivalry once and for all," she declares. "Jodi, you owe Heidi another deep, heartfelt apology. Not to mention that you've completely disobeyed me.

"Imagine if Heidi had come to your school in Canada and completely ambushed you and wouldn't stop saying mean things in *your* thoughts?"

Jodi's face turns bright red, and she wipes a tear from her face with the back of her hand.

She looks genuinely remorseful this time, and she gives me a **real apology.**

"I'm sorry, Heidi," she says, looking me in the eye. "I promise I'm not as mean as I seem.

"It's just that I've always been the star witch at my school, and I was really afraid of losing that when I heard about you.

"Everyone kept saying, 'Wait, till you meet Heidi Heckelbeck! She's SO amazing!' It made me feel like I had to prove myself to you.

"The only reason I was so mean was because I thought if I had the upper hand, I could be the star witch at this school. It got totally out of control, and I'm truly sorry. Will you ever be able to forgive me?"

I have to admit that this is a lot to process.

Melanie and Lucy told me the exact same thing, and now I can see they were right.

I'm pretty sure I would have felt the same way if I had been in Jodi's shoes. But I don't think I would've been SO mean. . . .

"I hear what you're saying, Jodi," I begin cautiously. "I feel for you being new and everything, but I **really** wasn't expecting to be put down and attacked, **especially by a *T. rex*.**"

As soon as I say this, Jodi hangs her head.

"That said," I continue, "I'm open to starting over, but if I'm going to trust you, **you have to stop being so mean to me. And you must stop coming into my thoughts uninvited.**"

Jodi nods humbly, and she quietly waits for me to finish talking.

"I'll admit, I was jealous of you at first too," I go on. "**When I heard you were a star witch at your old school, it scared me.**

"And when I found out we have the same magical gift, it scared me even more. To top it off, I was also mad at you because you were playing all these magical pranks and not getting in trouble. It seemed so unfair because I *always* get caught."

A playful smile sweeps across Jodi's face. "Like when I made the butterflies swarm you?"

I can't help it. I laugh.

"Yeah," I agree. "And when you made that *T. rex* come to life. . . . I mean, you've got more nerve than I do."

Jodi frowns. "Well, to be fair, I *did* get caught for that one."

Seeing Jodi's remorse reminds me of the many times I've taken magic too far. I know how she's feeling, so I offer a compliment. **"Well, it was pretty impressive."**

This makes Jodi's lip curl into a half smile, and I'm glad. No one wants to be kicked when they're already down.

Mrs. Kettledrum is not amused.

"Okay, girls, I'm glad to see you're getting along, but there's no need to bond over that **highly inappropriate incident**," she scolds.

"Besides, I don't know why you two ever **insisted** on being enemies. As two of the most powerful students in your grade—**possibly the entire school**—just imagine what you could accomplish if you took your powers **and worked *together*!**"

Jodi and I look at each other, wide-eyed. **Neither one of us ever considered pooling our talents and working together.**

Mrs. Kettledrum suggests I could start by helping Jodi learn how to meditate.

"You've come a long way from the days of your reckless spells, Heidi, and though you still have a long way to go, I think you could help Jodi learn to temper her emotions and impulses."

As I begin to mull this over, Mrs. Kettledrum turns her attention back to Jodi.

"Jodi, you must learn that **magic is not a sport**," she cautions. "A good witch doesn't **compete** at magic, but we do challenge each other to grow and bring out the best in each other—not the worst."

This makes me realize that Jodi actually **helped me over the last few days, even though it was under duress.**

"Mrs. K is right," I agree. "Jodi, you pushed me to learn **how to turn my gift of mind reading on and off. I didn't know that was even possible before I met you.**"

Jodi smiles sheepishly **because she knows I only learned it in self-defense.**

"Well, I guess it is silly for us to be jealous of each other's powers," Jodi agrees.

"I can learn a ton from you, and vice versa."

I feel a real smile form on my face, for what feels like the first time in three days.

If Jodi and I can be friends, then life at Broomsfield will get better again.

"*Agreed,*" I say with confidence. Then Jodi and I seal it with a handshake.

Mrs. Kettledrum looks at her watch.

"This is great progress, girls," she says. "However, there is one more thing I'd like you to do. I want you each to write a one-page essay on **kindness and moral courage.**

"You know what kindness is. And 'moral courage' means being brave enough to do the right thing **under *all* circumstances.** This will be due first thing Monday morning.

"Understood?"

We nod dutifully.

"Then you may both go because I'm about to dismiss class anyway." As Mrs. Kettledrum walks toward the building, Jodi turns to me.

"Magical partners?" she says.

I hold out my hand, and Jodi shakes it again.

"Magical partners!" I agree.

Mrs. Kettledrum glances at us over her shoulder before she steps through the door. Jodi and I can *both* hear exactly what our teacher is thinking.

Oh dear! What have I done? she wonders. **Have I created a *two-headed magical monster?***

Jodi and I cover our mouths and giggle.

"It's still going to take some time **to fully trust you, Jodi,** but everyone else seems to think you're really nice. And I have to admit that **you're a pretty cool witch.** I wouldn't mind being the other head to your magical monster. Like they say, **two heads are better than one!**" I tease.

Jodi and I both double over with laughter and growl. **"ROOOOOOAAAAAARRRRRR!"**

YOU DON'T NEED MAGIC TO FIND MORE BOOKS ABOUT HEIDI HECKELBECK AT BROOMSFIELD ACADEMY! LOOK FOR MORE

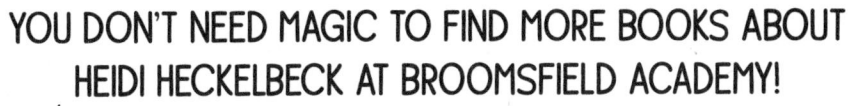

MIDDLE SCHOOL AND OTHER DISASTERS

BOOKS AT YOUR FAVORITE STORE.

HERE'S AN EXCERPT FROM

Worst Broommate Ever!

IT'S ALL ABOUT WHEN HEIDI FIRST STARTED CLASSES AT BROOMSFIELD AND FOUND OUT MELANIE WOULD BE HER BROOMMATE.

GOODBYE, BREWSTER!

Okay, here we go.

I, Heidi Heckelbeck, am officially freaking out, so I hurl myself onto my bed.

AAHHH!! Totally freaking out here!

Flump!

I bury my face in my pillow.

Please don't let boarding school be super, totally, and utterly horrible, I think.

Then I wonder: Why in the world did I agree to go anyway?

I mean, sure, I definitely want to become a better witch, and yes, I'll put on a brave face, but I'm not gonna lie, I'm terrified of living away from home.

This is a life-changing step.

I roll over and grab a framed picture of my two best friends, Lucy and Bruce.

There I am, standing in the middle, with one arm around each of them.

We look so happy by the pool!

This picture is definitely going with me— even though the sight of it tugs at my heart, and even though I hardly have any room left in my suitcases!

My door creaks open.

"Heidi?" Mom walks in with a stack of white towels. "Honey, what are you doing? We need to hit the road in *less* than an hour."

I push myself up to sitting and twist my hair into a messy bun.

"I'm having a *moment*."

Mom sets the towels on the bed beside me. "Well, it's totally natural to feel anxious before leaving for boarding school. To be honest, I was petrified."

It comforts me to know Mom was scared too.

I like all those subjects, but **wouldn't they be way more fun if they had a bit more magic in them?**

Like, what if I could enchant my books so the story would come to life in the classroom?

Or what if I could magically solve climate change in science class?

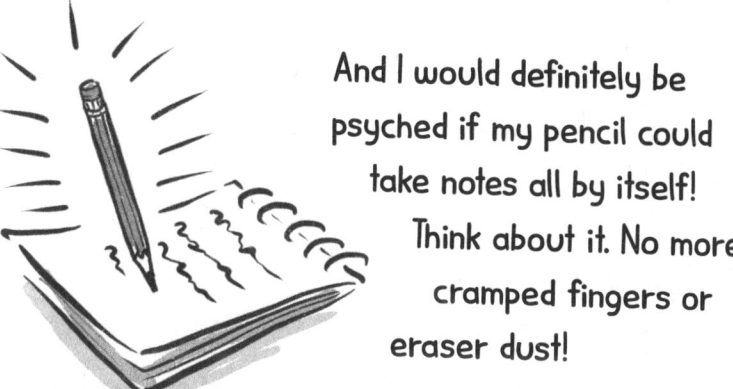

And I would definitely be psyched if my pencil could take notes all by itself! Think about it. No more cramped fingers or eraser dust!

Mom hands me a stack of sheets to pack with my towels, totally interrupting my thoughts.

She knows the way my mind works.

"It's just that I'm going to miss everyone SO much."

Mom rests her hand on my shoulder.

"Remember, your friends and family will *always* be here. And now you get to make *more* friends."

She gives me a smile before continuing.

"It'll be an adventure! The rest of us will be missing *you* more than you'll be missing us. And you'll love Broomsfield Academy—just like Aunt Trudy and I did. *I promise.*"

I press the picture of my friends against my chest. Mom points to my duffel bags. "Now, time to finish packing."

I drop to my knees beside my new comforter, neatly folded inside a see-through plastic case.

This comforter is totally *me*.

It has ribbons of patchwork, with spirals, paisley, polka dots, and itty-bitty flowers. The other side has navy-and-white stripes. Navy pom-poms dangle from the edges. It'll look SO good on my bed at school. This makes me feel a smidge better.

Mom nudges me again.

Okay, okay.

I grab the towels and begin to shove them into an empty duffel bag.

"Tell me more about Broomsfield Academy." Mom's already told me about it a bazillion times, but it helps to talk about it.

"Well, as you know, it's the only school in the country that has secret classes for magical students."

I sigh dreamily.

"I know! I wish I could take magic classes ALL day *every* day."

Mom laughs. "Well, you have to take *regular* like English, math, and science too."

"Slow down, Li'l Miss Witch," she says. "Remember that **ALL** Broomsfield witches and wizards are **sworn to secrecy**."

She puts a hand on my mine, and I turn to look at her. She locks eyes with me and continues.

"Heidi, absolutely none of the other students can find out about the School of Magic program. **That's the beauty of Broomsfield Academy.** The classes for magical students are hidden in what seems like a regular, run-of-the-mill boarding school. It's been this way for generations, and anyone who isn't a witch or wizard is none the wiser."

My mom *always* stresses this point.

It's like she thinks I'll be the ONE witch in the school's 150-year history to spill the beans!

Not a chance.

I LOVE secrets!

And I've never given away my own witch identity in all my life, so why would I start NOW?

Mom zips one of my suitcases. "And more important, you're not supposed to practice magic *outside* class," she adds as if I didn't know.

Blah, blah, blah, I say in my head, trying to block out this information.

But the truth is, **not practicing magic** when I feel like it will be **superhard** for me.

"It's just that I'm going to miss everyone SO much."

Mom rests her hand on my shoulder.

"Remember, your friends and family will *always* be here. And now you get to make *more* friends."

She gives me a smile before continuing.

"It'll be an adventure! The rest of us will be missing *you* more than you'll be missing us. And you'll love Broomsfield Academy—just like Aunt Trudy and I did. *I promise.*"

I press the picture of my friends against my chest. Mom points to my duffel bags. "Now, time to finish packing."

I drop to my knees beside my new comforter, neatly folded inside a see-through plastic case.

This comforter is totally *me*.

It has ribbons of patchwork, with spirals, paisley, polka dots, and itty-bitty flowers. The other side has navy-and-white stripes. Navy pom-poms dangle from the edges. It'll look SO good on my bed at school. This makes me feel a smidge better.

Mom nudges me again.

Okay, okay.

I grab the towels and begin to shove them into an empty duffel bag.

"Tell me more about Broomsfield Academy." Mom's already told me about it a bazillion times, but it helps to talk about it.

"Well, as you know, it's the only school in the country that has secret classes for magical students."

I sigh dreamily.

"I know! I wish I could take magic classes ALL day *every* day."

Mom laughs. "Well, you have to take *regular* classes like English, math, and science too."

I like all those subjects, but **wouldn't they be way more fun if they had a bit more magic in them?**

Like, what if I could enchant my books so the story would come to life in the classroom?

Or what if I could magically solve climate change in science class?

And I would definitely be psyched if my pencil could take notes all by itself! Think about it. No more cramped fingers or eraser dust!

Mom hands me a stack of sheets to pack with my towels, totally interrupting my thoughts.

She knows the way my mind works.

"Slow down, Li'l Miss Witch," she says. "Remember that ALL Broomsfield witches and wizards are **sworn to secrecy**."

She puts a hand on my mine, and I turn to look at her. She locks eyes with me and continues.

"Heidi, absolutely none of the other students can find out about the School of Magic program. **That's the beauty of Broomsfield Academy.** The classes for magical students are hidden in what seems like a regular, run-of-the-mill boarding school. It's been this way for generations, and anyone who isn't a witch or wizard is none the wiser."

My mom *always* stresses this point.

It's like she thinks I'll be the ONE witch in the school's 150-year history to spill the beans!

Not a chance.

I LOVE secrets!

And I've never given away my own witch identity in all my life, so why would I start NOW?

Mom zips one of my suitcases. "And more important, you're not supposed to practice magic *outside* class," she adds as if I didn't know.

Blah, blah, blah, I say in my head, trying to block out this information.

But the truth is, **not practicing magic** when I feel like it will be **superhard** for me.

I *love* to practice magic!

It comes in handy every day, and you can do so many cool things with magic, like clean your room without lifting a finger, make random stuff glow in the dark, or make a pencil bend like a wet noodle.

And how am I going to change my nail polish every morning, like I do now? And there's no way I can do my hair without magic.

I would never survive without my tangle-tamer and de-frizzing spells!

Okay, I'm seriously getting worked up about this no-magic rule.

Maybe I'll be able to sneak a little *everyday* magic in when nobody's looking—stuff nobody would suspect. . . .

I can be a very clever witch when I want to be. . . .

I look up and notice that Mom has a very stern look on her face. I'm pretty sure she

knows what I'm thinking, so I quickly change the subject.

"ANYWAY," I say a tad dramatically so I can move on to my next question. "What will I learn in my School of Magic classes?"

Mom wheels another suitcase into the hall and comes back to pack my bathroom stuff.

"Well, for one thing, you'll learn the history of magic."

Makes sense, but I want to learn new spells. I want to be able to make my scooter fly or travel to faraway places with a blink of my eyes.

"What else?" I ask.

Mom packs a green loofah and a pair of black-and-white-striped flip-flops for the shower.

"You'll learn how to brew potions and cast charms and spells, as well as learn the magical properties of plants and herbs," Mom goes on. "You'll also learn how to use a wand."

Now, that's what I'm talking about!

I squeal as I shove a neatly folded pillowcase into my bag.

I've never used a wand before.

"Hey, how come you never use a wand or practice magic at home?"

This is something I've always wondered about my mom.

"You know *very* well, Heidi. It's because I chose to be a *regular* mom. But that doesn't mean I don't use magic. I'm just discreet about it, and I learned *that* at school."

"But Dad makes more potions than *you* do, and he's not even a wizard!"

Mom frowns. "Yes, but *Dad's* potions don't have magical properties."

I shake my head. "Well, I disagree on that! Dad's soda recipes are magically FIZZ-i-licious!"

My dad's kind of famous. Everybody in Brewster knows he's the head of research and development at a soda company called the FIZZ.

"Okay, I see your point." Mom laughs. "But keep packing, kiddo, if you want to get to school before dinner."

I pull my flowery suitcase off the shelf in my closet. My favorite stuff will go in here.

First I wrap the picture of my friends and me, along with a picture of my family, in tissue. I tuck them into the bottom of my suitcase.

Next I lay down **my treasured *Book of Spells* and my Witches of Westwick medallion,** which are in their leather travel case. They're *really* old and belonged to my great-grandmother.

I cover them with my brand-new white jean jacket.

I can't wait to wear this!

I plop a clear zippered bag on top of it. The bag is stuffed with black-and-white-striped tights. **These have been my signature look since forever,** but who knows if I'll wear them at boarding school.

It may be time to go for a new style.

Right now I'm kind of into my striped sneakers. Next I plop two large bags of gummy bears into my suitcase for my secret stash. Then I place down a package of *compliment* pencils that Lucy gave me. One of the pencils says **YOU'RE MAGICAL**. I smile because Lucy still doesn't even know I'm a witch! And last but not least, I pack my new shaving kit because everyone knows girls shave their legs in middle school.

Duh.

Oh, I almost forgot my comics, word searches, and magazines! I drop them into my suitcase, zip it, and wheel it into the hall.

Then I stare at all my luggage.

Gulp! I'm actually totally packed and ready to go!

Butterflies flutter in my stomach.

Then **WHAM!** Henry's door slams shut.

I nearly jump out of my shoes.

My brother stands in the hall and looks at my bags and then at me.

"Well, I'm not sure what's weirder—having you around or NOT having you around."

My tongue rolls out like a party horn. It's an automatic reflex. Henry points both index fingers at me and makes a silly face.

"Just KIDDING!" he says. "I'm totally going to miss you! The only upside is, I'll have all the cereal to myself!"

I retract my tongue. Oh wow, I'll miss racing through boxes of cereal with Henry or fishing for all the yummiest pieces before he wakes up.

I wonder if they'll have cereal at boarding school?

I sure hope so!

"I'll miss you too, bub."

Henry and I each grab a suitcase and roll it downstairs.

Bonk,

bonk,

bonk!

Mom and Dad help with the other suitcases, duffel bags, comforter, fan, and desk lamp.

I race back into the house for one more thing.

It's something I've been working on my *entire* life.

I call it my Thingamajiggy and Whatnot Collection.

Inside this giant plastic storage tub **is every single prize I have ever gotten** from a gumball machine, trick-or-treating, or fast-food kid's meal— plus everything from all my birthday party goody bags.

Truth moment here.

I have never thrown even one of these little doodads away.

I have everything in here, from animal erasers and Mr. Potato Head parts, to Kool-Aid packets and miniature plastic foods—even leftover Halloween candy.

This miscellaneous stuff comes in handy for spells. You never know when you might need some weird trinket in a potion or mix.

It happens A LOT.

I plunk my tub full of treasures in the driveway with my other stuff, and Dad loads everything into the car. Henry and I hop into the back seat.

The butterflies in my stomach are really flapping now.

I take one long last look at our house. Home sweet home. I'm going to miss it so much.

"Farewell, house! I love you!"

I say this as Dad backs down the driveway.

We're not even to the end of the driveway when a car pulls up.

It's my absolute best friend in the whole world, LUCY!

She already threw me a going-away party with all our friends, but here she is to say one last goodbye! Dad stops the car, and I hop out.

Lucy and I run to each other and hug like koalas. She has a purple shopping bag in her hand.

What's in there? I wonder. Lucy pulls out a scrapbook.

"I finally finished it! It's a scrapbook filled with everything about *us* since second grade." She hands it to me. At the same time, my knees suddenly feel all wobbly, like Jell-O.

The thought of leaving Lucy hits me like a freight train.

Tears fill my eyes.

We grab hold of each other again.

"Thank you SO much," I manage to say. "I'm going to miss you more than all the Skittles in Skittlesville!"

Lucy pulls away so we can see each other face-to-face.

"Me too," she says. Her eyes also glisten with tears.

"What am I going to do without you?" I sniffle and laugh at the same time. "Maybe you and Melanie will become BFFs . . . !"

 Lucy laughs so hard, she snorts. "I seriously doubt it! You're so lucky to be rid of her!"

I can't help but start laughing too. "All good things must come to an end!"

Then we hug one more time.

"This isn't really goodbye," I say. "I'll come home on weekends sometimes. And there are phone calls and texting and letters."

Lucy nods. "I know. Love you forever."

"Me too."

Lucy runs back to her car.

I wave at Mrs. Lancaster.

Then I run back to our car and plop onto the back seat.

I glance at the scrapbook in my hands. The cover has a photo of me and Lucy. It was one of our first photos together, from when we were both about seven years old.

I can't look at it right now, or I'll go to pieces.

As our car rolls down our street, I watch the familiar scene disappear behind me.

"Goodbye, neighborhood!

"Goodbye, friends!

"Goodbye, life as I know it!"

Then Henry looks up from his tablet with one eyebrow raised.

"Adios, DRAMA QUEEN!"

I shove Henry. He shoves me right back. Then I roll down my window.

"Goodbye, Brewster!" I roll it back up. "And look out, magical new world! Because . . .

"HERE I COME!"

Then, with a tiny bit of magic, I make the leaves in our driveway swirl around and form the word

"goodbye." I don't even have to mix a spell to move things anymore. But *uh-oh*, Mom saw what I just did. *Oops.*

"HEIDI!" she says as she turns around and glares at me.

"Okay, okay!" I say, and I make the leaves swirl randomly again. Hey, can't a budding witch have a little fun?!

ABOUT THE AUTHOR

Wanda Coven has always loved magic. When she was little, she used to make secret potions from smooshed shells and acorns. Then she would pretend to transport herself and her friends to enchanted places. Now she visits other worlds through writing. Wanda lives with her husband and son in Colorado Springs, Colorado. They have three cats: Hilda, Agnes, and Claw-dia.

ABOUT THE ILLUSTRATOR

Anna Abramskaya was born in Sevastopol, Ukraine. She graduated from Kharkiv State Academy of Design and Arts in 2006. Then she moved to the United States, where she's currently living in the beautiful city of Jacksonville, Florida. Anna has loved art since she was little and has tried different materials and techniques. The process of creation and seeing beauty in the simple things around her always brings her joy and the wish to share that feeling with everyone. Anna wants to believe that art can help bring more love into people's hearts. Find out more at AnnaAbramskaya.com.

Would you like to read another book about **Heidi Heckelbeck**? You don't need magic to find one! Look for more

books at your favorite store!

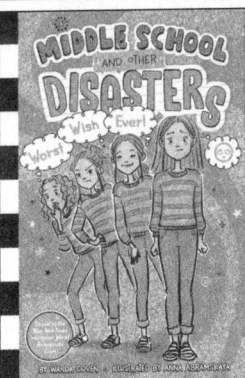

EBOOK EDITIONS ALSO AVAILABLE
PUBLISHED BY SIMON SPOTLIGHT
SIMONANDSCHUSTER.COM/KIDS

A SPOTLIGHT SPRINKLES BOOK

IYKYK

Middle school can be, like, so dramatic: knowing who to sit with at lunch, remembering your locker combination, figuring out the dynamics of your friend group, and, of course, dealing with boy drama. What's a middle schooler to do?!

Find out in the new tween rom-com series SPOTLIGHT SPRINKLES!

EBOOK EDITIONS ALSO AVAILABLE

Published by Simon Spotlight

simonandschuster.com/kids